In a snap of action, Seven locked her right arm around Admiral Jellico's throat.

She pulled him backward, off balance. Borg assimilation tubules extended from the steely implant still grafted to her left hand as she pressed her fingertips against his jugular. The tubules hovered above his skin but did not penetrate it—yet.

Around her and the admiral, the combat operations center became deathly quiet.

"If you do not escape beyond the Borg's reach, you will never be safe," she said, all but hissing the words into the trembling man's ear. "They know where you are, and they are now committed to your annihilation. Even if you collapse the subspace tunnels, they can still reach you by normal warp travel. It may take them decades. Perhaps even a century. But they *will* come. And when they do, your civilization will be eradicated. All that you have built, all that you have labored to preserve, will be erased from history. You cannot stop them, ever. As long as they exist, you will never be free."

She retracted her assimilation tubules and removed her arm from Jellico's throat. "I trust I made my point clearly, Admiral?"

"Get out of here before I have you shot," Jellico said, massaging his bruised windpipe.

She met Jellico's furious stare. "You are only postponing the inevitable," she said. "When the Borg have the Federation by the throat, they will not release it— they will destr

Jellico scow

"Precisely,"

STAR TREK®
DESTINY

BOOK II
MERE MORTALS

DAVID MACK

Based upon

STAR TREK and

STAR TREK: THE NEXT GENERATION®
created by Gene Roddenberry

STAR TREK: DEEP SPACE NINE®
created by Rick Berman & Michael Piller

STAR TREK: VOYAGER®
created by Rick Berman & Michael Piller & Jeri Taylor

STAR TREK®: ENTERPRISE™
created by Rick Berman & Brannon Braga

POCKET BOOKS
New York London Toronto Sydney New Erigol

Pocket Books
A Division of Simon & Schuster, Inc.
1230 Avenue of the Americas
New York, NY 10020

This book is a work of fiction. Names, characters, places, and incidents either are products of the author's imagination or are used fictitiously. Any resemblance to actual events or locales or persons, living or dead, is entirely coincidental.

First Pocket Books paperback edition November 2008

POCKET and colophon are registered trademarks of Simon & Schuster, Inc.

For information about special discounts for bulk purchases, please contact Simon & Schuster Special Sales at 1-800-456-6798 or business@simonandschuster.com

Designed by Alan Dingman, art by Stephan Martiniere.

Manufactured in the United States of America

10 9 8 7 6 5 4 3 2 1

ISBN-13: 978-1-4165-5172-0
ISBN-10:   1-4165-5172-7

For friends now gone but never forgotten

HISTORIAN'S NOTE

The main narrative of *Mere Mortals* takes place in February of 2381 (Old Calendar), approximately sixteen months after the events of the movie *Star Trek Nemesis*. The flashback portions begin in 1519 and continue through 2381.

Our torments also may in length of time
Become our elements, these piercing fires
As soft as now severe, our temper changed
Into their temper.

—John Milton, *Paradise Lost,* book 2

2381

1

—•—

Blue fire preceded a crimson flash, as one of the Borg cubes on the main viewer erupted into a cloud of blazing wreckage. The two that had followed it from the indigo fog of the Azure Nebula barreled through its spreading debris, accelerated, and opened fire on their lone adversary.

Pitched alarums of struggle surrounded Captain Jean-Luc Picard, who sat in the bridge's command chair, stone-faced and silent, watching and hearing the battle unfold around him.

Over the thunder of energy blasts hammering the shields of the *Enterprise,* Commander Worf bellowed, "Helm! Attack pattern Echo-One! Tactical, target the closer cube and fire at will!"

Picard tried to focus on the voices of his crew—Worf barking orders, second officer Miranda Kadohata relaying damage reports, security chief Jasminder Choudhury confirming her targets, and the low buzz of several junior officers manning backup stations and sensor consoles everywhere he looked—but they all were drowned out by the one voice that was many: the dehumanized roar of the Borg Collective.

Resistance is futile. You will be exterminated.

It had been more than fourteen years since the Borg's voice had first invaded the sanctum of his mind, when the Collective assimilated him. Transformed into Locutus of Borg, Picard had watched through a dark haze, a spectator to his own life, as the Borg used his knowledge and experience against Starfleet and against Earth. Even after he had been physically liberated from the Collective, he'd remained yoked to its voice, attuned to its soulless group mind.

His bond to the Collective had faded with the passage of years. He had expected to welcome its permanent absence from his thoughts, but then the Borg returned with an unprecedented ferocity marked by aggressive tactics and a disturbing new motivation. It had been several months since, in a desperate bid to understand the true nature of the new threat posed by the Borg, he had attempted to infiltrate the Collective by posing as Locutus. He'd thought he could outwit them, that experience and innovation would protect him as he dared to plumb their secrets. *What a fool I was,* he castigated himself.

A powerful concussion threw the bridge crew to starboard and strobed the lights. A port-side console exploded into smithereens. Glowing-hot bits of smoking debris landed in Picard's lap, and the momentary jolts of hot pain on his legs broke the spell that the Collective had held over his thoughts.

He swatted the blackened embers off his thighs as he stood and moved to stand beside Worf. The Klingon executive officer remained focused on directing the battle. "Helm," Worf shouted as Lieutenant Joanna

Faur scrambled back into her chair, "hard to port!" To Choudhury he added, "Ready aft torpedoes!" As Worf turned forward again, Kadohata switched the main screen to display the ship's retreating aft view. A Borg cube loomed dramatically into sight, dominating the screen. "Fire!"

Four radiant blue bolts flew from the *Enterprise*'s aft torpedo launcher and separated as they followed weaving, spiraling paths to the Borg ship. At the final moment they shot toward different faces of the cube. Two penetrated the Borg's shields and ripped through its hull. Within seconds, cerulean flames consumed the Borg vessel from within and broke it apart. A blinding flash reduced it to fading supercharged particles.

Two down, one to go, Picard mused as the main viewer image reverted to its normal, forward-facing perspective.

"Attack pattern Bravo-Eight," Worf ordered, and the bridge crew translated his words into action with speed and skill.

Picard heard the intentions of the Collective and saw the trap that Worf had just stumbled into. He snapped, "Belay that! Evasive maneuvers, starb—" The bone-jarring thunderclap of an explosion cut him off, and the deck felt as if it had dropped out from under him. He fell forward and landed on his forearms. A bank of large companels along the aft bulkhead blew apart and showered the bridge with a flurry of sparks and shrapnel.

Gray, acrid smoke lingered above the shaken bridge crew. "Continue evasive maneuvers," Worf said to Faur. He plucked a jagged bit of smoking debris from the rings of his metallic Klingon baldric as he stepped behind Kadohata, who was struggling to halt the erratic malfunctions that flickered across the ops console. "Damage report," Worf said.

"Hull breaches, Decks Twenty-two and Twenty-three," replied the lithe human woman of mixed Asian and European ancestry. Her Port Shangri-La accent was just similar enough to a Londoner's inflections that Picard had to remind himself again that she wasn't from Earth. "Direct hit on our targeting sensors," she continued. Then she swiveled her chair to face Worf and added with alarm, "Sir, we can't lock weapons."

Another shot from the Borg cube rocked the *Enterprise.* "Break off, Number One," Picard said.

"Full evasive," Worf said, "maximum warp. Engage!"

As Worf stepped quickly from station to station, gathering status reports, Picard moved forward and stood beside Kadohata's console. In a confidential tone, he said, "Casualty report."

Reciprocating his quiet discretion, she replied, "Four dead in engineering, several dozen wounded. Still waiting on official numbers from sickbay, sir."

"Understood," he said.

Worf finished his circuit of the bridge and returned to Picard's side. "Captain, the transphasic shields are starting to overload. Lieutenant Choudhury estimates—" Cacophonous booms resonated through the bulkheads. When the echoes had faded, Worf continued, "She estimates shield failure in nine minutes."

"Commander," Picard said to Kadohata, "we need

those targeting sensors. Devote all free resources to their repair. Mister Worf, help Lieutenant Choudhury find a way to target our torpedoes manually."

The XO nodded and said, "Aye, sir."

As Worf walked back to the tactical console, Kadohata confided to Picard, "Sir? The damage to the targeting system was major. I doubt it can be repaired in the next nine minutes. And manually targeting transphasic torpedoes is almost impossible. Without the targeting computer, we'll never adjust the phase harmonics quickly enough."

"What do you suggest, Commander?"

"With all respect, sir . . . a distress signal."

Picard frowned. "To whom? Our nearest allies are several hours away, at best."

Kadohata mustered a bittersweet grin and shrugged. "You have your desperate measures, I have mine."

He had to admire her ability to smile in the face of danger. "Make it so," he said. Then, dropping his voice again, he added with grim resignation, "And prepare the log buoy."

Captain Ezri Dax was seated and steady, with her hands relaxed on the ends of her command chair's armrests, but in her mind she was pacing like a caged beast, feverishly circling her anxiety.

"Time to intercept?" she asked.

Lieutenant Tharp answered over his shoulder, "Two minutes, Captain." The Bolian conn officer returned to his controls and faced the main viewer, whose image was dominated by the retreating mass of the Borg cube that was pursuing the *Enterprise*.

Her first officer, Commander Sam Bowers, returned from his hushed conference with Lieutenant Lonnoc Kedair, the Takaran chief of security for the *Aventine,* and stood beside Dax. "I feel like a dog chasing a shuttle," he said, watching the Borg ship. "Even if we catch it, what do we do then?"

"Sink our teeth in, Sam," Dax said. "As deep as we can."

Kedair looked up from the tactical console. "We've just been scanned by a Borg sensor beam," she said, her deep-green face darkened half a shade by concern.

"So much for a surprise attack," Bowers said.

"Lieutenant Mirren," Dax said to her senior operations officer, "signal *Enterprise*. We need to coordinate our attack."

Mirren nodded. "Aye, sir. Hailing them now."

"Sixty seconds to firing range," Tharp said from the conn.

The cube was large enough now on the main viewer that Dax could discern the layers of snaking machinery and the haphazard network of grids, plates, and crudely grafted pieces of alien machinery that this ship must have assimilated in its past. She couldn't tell by looking how long ago each component had been acquired, or even guess at how new or old the cube might be. Every Borg cube, from the raw to the battle-scarred, had the same weathered, dull look, the same drab utilitarian aesthetic.

"Incoming signal from the *Enterprise*," Mirren said.

"On-screen," Dax replied. A blizzard of visual noise and twisted images danced on the main viewer while banshee wails and the crackle-scratch of static muffled the words of Captain Picard, who Dax could recognize even through the storm of interference. "Mirren," she said, "can we clean that up?"

Mirren jabbed at her console and grimaced in frustration. "Trying, Captain. The Borg are jamming us."

Lieutenant Commander Gruhn Helkara, the ship's second officer and the head of its sciences division, called to Dax from one of the aft bridge stations. "Captain, I might have a way to bypass the jamming!" The wiry Zakdorn moved toward one of the starboard auxiliary consoles. "The Klingons use a super-low-frequency subspace channel to stay in contact with cloaked ships." He keyed commands into the auxiliary panel at furious speed. "I'll interlace an SLF signal on a subharmonic fre—"

"Less talk, Gruhn," Dax said. "Just make it work."

"Aye, sir," he said, and then he tapped in a few final details. "Channel ready. Try it now."

Dax waited while Mirren reestablished contact with the *Enterprise*. After several more seconds of garbled images and sounds, the visage of Captain Picard snapped into shaky but mostly clear focus. *"Captain Dax?"*

"At your service," Dax said.

"I thought your ship was in the Gamma Quadrant."

She was about to explain, then shook off the impulse. "Long story. We're coming up fast on the Borg. How can we help?"

"We need you to be our eyes," Picard said. He nodded to someone off-screen, then continued, *"We're sending you a set of targeting protocols. After we fire the transphasic torpedoes, you'll have to arm them and guide them to the target."*

"Data received," Mirren said. "Decrypting now."

At the auxiliary console, Helkara studied the incoming data, frowned, and then looked up at Dax. "I'll have to recalibrate the sensors."

"How long?" asked Dax.

"Four minutes," Kedair said.

Dax expected bad news as she looked back at Picard, and he didn't disappoint her. *"Our shields will fail in three."*

"Gruhn," Dax said to her second officer.

"I know, three minutes," Helkara said without looking up.

"Hang on, Captain," Dax said. "We're on our way. *Aventine* out." Walking back to her command chair, Dax said to Bowers, "Sam, let's give the Borg something new to think about for the next three minutes."

"Aye, sir," Bowers said. "Tactical, arm phaser cannons one and two, stand ready on quantum torpedoes. Helm, set attack pattern Alpha-Tango . . . and engage."

Dax settled into her chair and stared at the ominous mass of black metal that filled the bridge's main viewscreen like a spreading cancer. She wondered how close the Borg would let the *Aventine* come before the cube opened fire.

Then a searing flash of green light shot from the cube to the *Aventine,* and the *Vesta*-class explorer lurched forward like a ship at sea running momentarily aground over a sandbar. When the percussive din of impact finished resonating through the hull, Dax pushed herself fully back into her chair and said to her XO, "I think they're in range now, Sam."

"We'll only get one shot, Captain," Bowers replied. "I plan on making it count." He nodded to Kedair. "Fire at will."

Deep droning hums swelled rapidly in pitch and volume and ended in rushing thunderclaps of release as the *Aventine*'s experimental Mark XII phaser cannons fired their peculiar mix of supercharged high-energy particles at the Borg cube. The enemy vessel's shield bubble flared violet for a half second before it buckled. A series of blasts punched through the cube's hull and left fire and molten metal in their wake.

A volley of quantum torpedoes arced in alongside the phaser blasts, punching more holes in the Borg ship's dark exterior. Then the last two torpedoes impacted harmlessly against the Borg's resurgent defensive energy screen. Two more bursts from the phaser cannon were absorbed by the protective field.

"Hard to port," Bowers ordered, "full evasive!" The whine of the impulse engines grew louder as the *Aventine* veered away from the Borg ship. Bowers wore the slack expression of a man who knew all too well what would happen next. "Here's where the real fun begins," he said.

Then the Borg started shooting back.

Commander Geordi La Forge dodged through flames and smoke in the main engineering compartment of the *Enterprise,* trusting the enhanced-spectrum view provided by his cybernetic eyes to keep him a step ahead of the next catastrophe.

He grabbed the sleeve of a passing engineer and spun the dark-haired human woman back to face him. "Granados," he said, "shut down the starboard EPS tap, it's overheating!"

"The gauges read normal," the ensign protested.

"Maureen, they're wrong," La Forge shouted. He let go of her arm and pointed at the auxiliary control panel a few sections away, down the corridor. "Shut it down, now!"

She nodded. "Aye, sir." As she sprinted toward the control panel, La Forge continued on his original path and weaved around a running damage-control team in pressure suits.

The din of system-failure alarms, panicked voices, cries of pain and fear, and running footfalls all were drowned out by the overpowering percussive rumble of an energy strike against the ship's hull. A hurricane-force gust hurled La Forge several meters through the air for a few seconds, then it fell away and dropped him to the deck as emergency force fields and bulkheads engaged to isolate the breached compartment a few sections away.

A flash accompanied another ear-rending blast, this time from the already overtaxed electroplasma system energy tap, which routed power from the main reactor to the ship's internal power grid. Its magnetically sealed protective housing cracked and blew apart. The superheated plasma inside it jetted like lava from a volcano, engulfing a team of engineers who had been trying to prevent exactly that disaster. Even from a distance, the heat overpowered La Forge.

The lucky ones nearest the rupture were vaporized instantly, transformed into gases and trace atoms. The handful of technicians and mechanics who had been behind them were fighting to pull their maimed, burned bodies away from the fiery mess. Most of them had lost their legs in the first half-second of the explosion, as the falling tide of plasma cut their feet out from under them. One of them, a Benzite, had lost an arm.

Another hazard-suited damage-control team sprinted in from an adjacent compartment. La Forge pointed to the rupture. "Seal that breach, and raise the force fields!" His skin tingled with pain. *Great,* he brooded. *Now we'll all need anti-radiation shots.*

When he turned around, he saw a lot of young enlisted engineers and fresh-faced junior officers staring at the wounded and the dead, and only a few of his more experienced people minding their posts. He stepped between the young gawkers and the horrifying spectacle and started snapping orders.

"Gallivan, rebalance the power load on the starboard PTC. L'Sen, make sure the SIF is compensating for the hull breach. Newaur, stop chewing your claws and start patching that hole in our shields. The rest of you, back to your stations!"

The engineers had just resumed work when another hit by the Borg roared and echoed inside the *Enterprise.* La Forge moved at a quick step down the line of consoles, glancing past his people at their work and assembling the glimpses of data into a mental picture of the ship's condition.

As he neared the impulse system's power relays, he was intercepted by his assistant chief engineer, Lieutenant Taurik. The Vulcan's uniform was torn and smudged, and his face was obscured by dark gray carbon dust. "Commander," he said, "the targeting sensors have been almost completely destroyed. Rebuilding them will take up to a day."

La Forge cringed as a resounding boom shook the ship. He heard the crack of exploding consoles behind him a moment before he felt a blast of heat and the sting of shrapnel on his back. The impact knocked him facedown at Taurik's feet.

Within seconds, Taurik was lifting La Forge back to his feet. "Are you all right, sir?"

"No," La Forge said, gritting his teeth against the burning pain shooting through shallow wounds on either side of his spine. He turned and looked back at the damage. A quick scan in several different wavelengths revealed no other imminent overloads, but the body-heat readings of several downed engineers were alarmingly unstable. Pain and anger overpowered his sense of decorum. "Where are the medics, goddammit?"

"Sir," Taurik said, trying to lead La Forge away from the scene, "you need to get to sickbay."

La Forge threw off Taurik's helping hand. "What I need, Taurik, is two more minutes of shield power. Focus on that."

The Vulcan betrayed no hint of umbrage at La Forge's sharpness of tone. "Aye, sir," he replied, and he walked quickly toward the engineering control center for tactical systems.

La Forge limped in the other direction, one painful step at a time, back through the haze of toxic smoke and bitter dust, toward his fallen engineers. At long last, he saw a team of medics rounding the corner from the far corridor.

Another pounding blow resounded through the hull.

"Just keep it going a little longer, people," he said,

his mood grim and his voice strained by his fresh injuries. "One way or another, this'll be over in the next two minutes."

Helkara spun away from his console to report, "Sensors ready!"

"Signal *Enterprise*," Bowers said to Mirren.

The slender, blond ops officer tapped a ready key on her console. It flashed red twice before it turned green. Mirren replied, "*Enterprise* confirms. Torpedoes away in ten."

"Helm, all ahead," Dax ordered. "We need to get in close and arm the warheads before the Borg realize what we're doing."

Bowers threw a look at the captain that she recognized as one of apprehension. Putting the ship into easy firing range of the Borg was something her XO had wanted to avoid, but in this case it couldn't be helped. To his credit, she thought, he kept his objections to himself and resumed directing the attack as if nothing was amiss. "Tharp, show the Borg our port side. Kedair, reinforce the port shields for the flyby." He looked to the relief tactical officer, a Deltan woman named Talia Kandel. "Lieutenant, arm the *Enterprise*'s torpedoes as soon as they're away, and lock them onto the Borg cube as fast as you can."

"Incoming!" called Kedair. Then an erratic series of hard impacts scrambled monitors and companels around the bridge, which dipped deeper into shadow after each blow. The high-pitched whine of the engines began to fall. "Shields buckling," the security chief said.

"Six torpedoes away!" Mirren shouted over the clamor.

"Acquiring control," Kandel said as she worked.

On the main viewer, Dax saw energy pulses from the Borg cube slice past the *Aventine* into seemingly empty space. She was about to be grateful for the missed shot when she saw the flare of a distant detonation.

"We just lost two torpedoes," Mirren said. "The Borg are locking on again—"

Kandel cut in, "Torpedoes armed!" Her fingertips danced lightly across her controls as she added, "Target acquired!"

"Resume evasive maneuvers," Bowers ordered.

The remaining four missiles became incandescent, shining bright and blue against the blackness of space. They traced corkscrew paths through the Borg's defensive fusillade of energy blasts. A blinding pulse of light washed out the image on the main viewscreen, and a gut-wrenching sensation of collision lifted the bridge officers several centimeters into the air. Then the artificial gravity kicked back in and dropped everyone roughly on the deck.

"Stations," Dax said, the edge in her voice cutting through the daze and shock of the direct hit. "Mirren, get the viewer back on. Tharp, new evasive pattern. Kandel, report!"

It took a few seconds for the Deltan woman to coax her console back to full operation. "The Borg neutralized three of the torpedoes while we were down. Adjusting the last torpedo to compensate." The main viewer flickered back to life as she added, "It's through their shields—direct hit!"

Sapphire flames blazed from an erupting rent in the cube's patchwork hull, and fissures traveled with surprising speed and ferocity across all its surfaces as it began to tumble through space like a cast die. Explosions peppered its surface, ejecting chunks of its exterior in its wake.

Bowers turned and favored Kedair with a satisfied grin. "Feel free to have a little target practice, Lieutenant."

"With pleasure, sir." Seconds later Kedair opened fire with the *Aventine*'s phaser cannons and quantum torpedoes. Piece by piece, she vaporized the debris of the disintegrating Borg vessel, which now looked like a hollow shell; it had been all but consumed from within by the transphasic warhead's electric-blue fires. Staring at the gutted hexahedron, Kedair said, "Permission to finish the job, Captain?"

"Permission granted," Dax said, noting a subtle grin of agreement from Bowers. They both watched as a volley of ten quantum torpedoes plunged into the smoldering wreckage of the Borg ship and obliterated it. Watching the fire cloud disperse into the unforgiving vacuum of space, Dax noted the heavy odor of scorched metal and burnt optronics that permeated her bridge.

Mirren silenced a beeping alert on her console. "*Enterprise* is hailing us, Captain."

"On-screen," Dax said.

Captain Picard's visage filled the screen. "*Captain Dax,*" he said. "*My thanks and compliments for a fine rescue.*"

"The pleasure was all ours, Captain," Dax said. "We're still licking our wounds over here, but I have medics and damage-control teams standing by if you need them."

Picard sighed softly and nodded once. *"We're not too proud to say we're in need of assistance. Any help you can offer will be gratefully accepted."*

"Understood," Dax said. "Send us a list of any parts or equipment you might need. I'll have my chief engineer take care of the details."

Nodding, Picard replied, *"Very good. My second officer, Commander Kadohata, will apprise your crew of our needs. In the meantime, Captain, I'd like to invite you and your first officer to meet with me privately aboard the* Enterprise. *We came to the Azure Nebula on an urgent mission, and now that you're here, we need to ask for your help in completing it."*

"Of course, Captain," Dax said. "Commander Bowers and I will beam over as soon as you're ready to receive us."

"At 0230, then," Picard said. *"Enterprise out."*

The main viewer blinked back to the serene vista of deep space. Dax turned to Bowers. *"Enterprise* took some heavy damage in that fight, Sam. Make sure Mikaela knows to make their repairs a priority."

"Will do," Bowers said. Quietly, he added, "I guess it would be awkward to ask if they could loan us a few of those transphasic torpedoes, wouldn't it?"

"Not as awkward as it'll be for me seeing Worf again," Dax replied. "With all that's been going on for the last five weeks, I haven't had a chance to talk to him since my promotion. Last time I saw him, I was congratulating him for accepting the XO billet on the *Enterprise.* That was before I transferred here, when I was still a lieutenant commander. Now I outrank him."

Bowers shrugged. "Don't worry about it, Captain. Maybe he'll just be happy for you, as a friend."

"Maybe," Dax said. "But you know what they say: Rank is like sex—it changes everything."

Dr. Beverly Crusher moved quickly from one biobed to the next, supervising her staff of surgeons, nurses, and medical technicians as they tended to the scores of grievously wounded personnel being portered into sickbay by security officers, paramedics, and damage-control officers.

At one bed, Dr. Tropp, her Denobulan assistant chief medical officer, was already deep into a surgical procedure, trying to stabilize the vital functions of a Bajoran woman whose legs were gone, sheared away halfway between the waist and the knees, cauterized black and smooth by some hellish trauma.

Walking down the row of biobeds, Crusher saw only more of the same: the burnt and the broken, the amputated and the paralyzed. Her normally antiseptic-smelling sickbay was rich with the charnel perfume of scorched flesh and spilled blood. Pitiful moaning, wails of agony, the hoarse exhortations of the suffering and the dying dispelled the quiet ambience she had always taken for granted.

A woman's voice called out, "Doctor Crusher!" She turned and saw Dr. Rymond, a chestnut-haired female surgical intern, beckoning her into the triage center adjacent to sickbay. Crusher dodged past a pair of medical technicians carrying a wounded officer on a stretcher to the O.R., brushed a few sweat-soaked strands of her red hair from her face, and joined Rymond.

The patient, a youthful-looking man, lay on his side, facing away from Crusher. A jagged length of what looked like a fragment of a metal support beam skewered his torso. "Fill me in," Crusher said.

"Fell onto a broken railing segment," Rymond said. "The DC team cut him free and left us a few centimeters to grab on to, but it's stuck tight. He's in shock and fading fast. Pulse is one-forty and thready, BP fifty over thirty."

Crusher grabbed one end of the man's stretcher and nodded to Rymond to take the other. "Okay, front of the line, let's go." They carried him into sickbay, toward a biobed that had just been vacated. "Does our lucky friend have a name?"

"Lieutenant Konya," Rymond said as they set him down.

Hearing his name enabled Crusher to see past the blood and grime on the wounded man's face and recognize him. He was the ship's deputy chief of security. "Get a breathing mask on him. Try and bring up his pulse ox while we get a clearer picture of the damage. And watch his EEG, he's Betazoid." She called over her shoulder, "We need a surgical arch over here!"

She lifted her medical tricorder, which she kept holstered on her belt during crises like these, and began an exploratory imaging sequence of Konya's torso. "Damn," she muttered. "It's straight through the inferior vena cava." To the unconscious Betazoid she added, "You had to make it difficult, didn't you?"

A pair of technicians, one an Andorian *thaan* and the other a female Saurian, hurried over with a surgical arch for the biobed. They slipped past Rymond and Crusher, fitted the arch into place, then rushed away as Dr. Tropp called from across sickbay for a new pack of hyposprays.

Crusher powered up the arch, calibrated its settings for Betazoid male physiology, and downloaded Konya's medical history from the ship's computer, to serve as baseline data. "Activate the delta-wave generator and monitor his vitals for me," Crusher said. "I'm about to open the pericardium and put a circular constrictor field around the auricle of his right atrium."

Her touches on the arch's interface pad were delicate and precise. Its noninvasive surgical protocols were state-of-the-art medicine, but only if one knew how to use them. This seemed to Crusher like a good opportunity to pass on some of that skill to her fresh-faced intern. "Watch closely," she said to the younger woman. "We're going to constrict the auricle and create a virtual venous-return catheter from there to the IVC."

The procedure went exactly as Crusher hoped, with the surgical arch manipulating force fields and tissue regenerators in an intricately programmed sequence. "As soon as I detect resistance from the fragment, I want you to use the controls on your side to dematerialize it." She watched Rymond initialize the interface on the other side of the arch. "Ready?"

Rymond nodded and kept her eyes on her controls.

"Okay," Crusher said, watching the resistance gauges creep upward for the constrictor field, "now."

Rymond tapped in the micro-transporter sequence and removed all traces of the intruding metal fragment.

As soon as the transporter sequence ended, Crusher finished closing the constrictor field. "All right," she said. "The auricle's sealed, the catheter's functional, and we can start doing some repair work." She looked over at Rymond. "Feel up to finishing this one on your own?"

"Yes, Doctor." The young surgeon glanced at the display screens on the arch. "I'll need to transfuse him first." She turned her head and caught the eye of Nurse Mimouni, who was passing by. "Nurse, prep eight units of J-neg and two units of Betazoid plasma, stat." Mimouni nodded her acknowledgment without breaking stride.

"Let me know if you need a hand," Crusher said. Rymond nodded and continued repairing Konya's wounds as Crusher moved on, back through the chaotic hustle of bodies and equipment.

She paused in the open doorway to the triage center, which was packed almost to capacity. Patients lay on beds arranged in long parallel rows. Most of them were unconscious; a few stared blankly at the overhead. Multiple copies of the ship's female-personality EMH—Emergency Medical Hologram—moved from bed to bed, assessing the criticality of new patients as they arrived.

Closer to Crusher, the ship's senior counselor, a Bajoran man named Dr. Hegol Den, kneeled beside a wounded young medic and conversed in soothing whispers with the shaken Trill woman. Crusher admired Hegol's gentle bedside manner; for a moment she lamented that he lacked the surgical training to do more for the wounded, but then she noted the generally subdued mood in the triage facility, and she realized that much of it was likely the product of Hegol's calm attention.

From the main sickbay compartment, she heard Dr. Tropp's voice get louder and pitch upward with frustration. She turned back and watched a moment she had witnessed far too many times before: a surgeon fighting a losing battle against injuries so severe that nothing short of a miracle could fix them.

"Push one-twenty-five triox," Tropp snapped at his trio of assistants. "Cortical stims to two-eighty-five! Dammit, th'Shelas, that artery's bleeding again!"

"V-fib," said medical technician Zseizaz, through a vocoder that rendered the buzzes and clicks of his insectile Kaferian language into recognizable phonetics.

"Charge to three hundred," Tropp said.

"Belay that," Crusher cut in. "Your patient has total organ failure, and her EEG flatlined four minutes ago." She hated to pull rank, but Tropp could be obsessive in times like this, and she couldn't afford to let him fixate on one lost cause when there were a dozen other lives in need of his help.

Tropp stared back at her, wild-eyed, and his nurse, his technician, and his intern all watched him. Then his shoulders slumped and his head followed. When he lifted his head again, Crusher saw in his eyes that he knew what he had to do.

He shut off the surgical arch. "Time of death, 0227." Zseizaz and th'Shelas removed the surgical arch, and Tropp waved over a pair of medical assistants to remove the body. Then he nodded to Nurse Amavia and said, "Let's go see who's next."

Crusher watched the assistants transfer the body of the dead Bajoran engineer to an antigrav gurney. With decorum and gentility they stretched a clean blue sheet over the body from head to toe and guided it away from the living patients, into the recesses of sickbay, to the morgue, where it would be placed in stasis pending its final journey home to its next of kin.

Over in the triage center, Tropp and Amavia zeroed in on a patient and directed Zseizaz and th'Shelas to move the wounded Tellarite officer to a biobed in sickbay.

The fight goes on, Crusher told herself. Then she impelled herself into motion, and summoned medical technician Ellwood Neil to join her as she crossed the compartment to find a case of her own. "Look for criticals," she said to the sharp-eyed young man. "I'm in the mood to work miracles tonight."

"A subspace tunnel to the Gamma Quadrant," said Captain Picard, sounding intrigued by Captain Dax's account of how the *Aventine* had found itself in a position to charge to the *Enterprise*'s rescue. He reclined his chair from his ready room desk and continued, "That's a remarkable discovery, Captain."

Dax grinned. "I'll tell my science officer you said so."

Commander Bowers, who had accompanied Dax on this visit to the *Enterprise,* added, "It was Mister Helkara's suggestion to look for the subspace tunnel in the first place."

Picard nodded at Bowers and replied, "It sounds like you're blessed with an excellent crew."

"The best in the fleet," Bowers boasted. Worf, who was standing on Picard's right behind the desk, shot a fierce, challenging stare at Bowers, who quickly and nervously added, "Present company excluded, of course."

Worf signaled his acceptance of Bowers's capitulation with a muted growl from the back of his throat.

Captain Picard turned his chair away from Worf, stood, and walked around his desk to face Captain Dax. "I cannot dismiss as coincidence your discovery of a subspace tunnel and the recent entry of Borg ships into Federation space, both within the Azure Nebula," he said. "My instincts—not to mention common sense—tell me that these events are related."

"We're in complete agreement, Captain," Dax said, speaking with authority and serenity. Listening to her, Worf thought for a moment that he could hear and see echoes of Jadzia Dax in Ezri—the same confident timbre in her voice, the same poise and grace. Then the shadow of his slain wife faded and he was left with only the present.

"It's important we act quickly," Picard said. "Starfleet's defenses are faltering, and I can sense that the Borg are on the move. Another assault is imminent, unless we prevent it."

Bowers said, "We can have the *Aventine* ready for action by 0630." He cast a questioning look at Worf.

"Most of our systems will be functional by 0630," Worf said. "But Commander La Forge reports that repairs to the targeting sensors will take roughly twenty hours."

Picard nodded. "I see. Until we finish repairs, then, the *Aventine* will have to lead the investigation."

"Our pleasure, Captain," Dax said. "If I might make a suggestion . . . ?" Picard nodded for her to continue. "I think we should start our search at the coordinates where my ship emerged from the subspace tunnel. If there is another passage with a terminus inside the nebula, I think the best place to look for it is in proximity to one we already know about."

"Agreed," Picard said. "But before we begin the search, I want to reiterate our objective. If there is another subspace tunnel being used by the Borg, our mission is first to obstruct and then to destroy that phenomenon. It's imperative we deny the Borg access to Federation space, at all costs. Is that clear?"

"Absolutely, Captain," said Dax.

A look of resolution passed over Picard's face. "Very well. Let's get to work. We'll return to the nebula together at 0630."

Bowers and Dax nodded their assent and got up from their chairs. As the two visitors walked toward the door, Picard shook Dax's hand and then Bowers's. The portal sighed open ahead of them, briefly admitting the gentle humming and chirps of work being performed at numerous duty stations on the bridge. Then the door closed after the departed officers, leaving Worf and Picard alone in the captain's ready room.

Captain Picard walked to the replicator nook behind his desk and said to the computer, "Tea, Earl Grey, hot." His drink took shape inside a tiny, short-lived blizzard of atoms. He picked up the cup and saucer and eased himself into his chair.

Worf watched the captain take a sip and wince slightly at the sting of it on his lips. He wondered for a moment whether Picard was aware that he hadn't dismissed Worf. Then he wondered if his commanding officer was even cognizant of the fact that he was still there at all. Finally, Picard looked at Worf and said with a droll half smirk, "I understand your pride in the *Enterprise*'s crew, Number One, but do you think it was polite to intimidate Commander Bowers in front of his captain?"

Worf scowled. "He should choose his words with more care."

"Perhaps," Picard said. "Though I have to wonder . . . was your display really about what he said? Or did it have something to do with seeing your former colleague precede you as a captain?"

Worf looked away from the captain. "I do not resent Captain Dax's promotion," he said, and it was mostly true. However, he had to admit there was a certain dark irony to the situation.

During the Dominion War, Worf had decided, during a vital military operation, to save the life of his wife, Jadzia Dax, rather than complete his assignment. The ensuing fallout of that botched mission had resulted in a black mark on his service record, one which Captain Sisko had believed would prevent Worf from ever receiving his own command.

Years of distinguished service in Starfleet and the Federation Diplomatic Corps had mostly overcome the stigma of that old reprimand, but there were times when Worf still felt pangs of guilt for all the other lives that had been lost in the war because of his selfish choice. Despite all he had achieved since then, Worf still harbored serious doubts that Starfleet would ever place him in command of a ship of the line.

And now Ezri Dax—for whose previous host Worf had committed his professional *Hegh'bat*—was in command of a starship. He didn't begrudge Ezri her success, but he had to wonder how long the universe intended to mock him for his actions on Soukara.

"Do you wish me to apologize to Commander Bowers, sir?"

Picard's expression brightened. "Definitely not. Everyone knows the *Enterprise* has the best crew in Starfleet." He sipped his tea and smirked. "Dismissed, Mister Worf."

1519

2

———◆———

The future was the past, and the past was the present.

On Earth, Cortes was leading a Spanish expedition in Mexico and triggering the New World's first pandemic by introducing it to the influenza virus; Babur was conquering northern India, as a prelude to establishing the Mughal Empire; Magellan had begun his circumnavigation of the globe; and in Europe, Martin Luther was challenging the infallibility of papal decrees.

Adrift in the cold light and deep silence of interstellar space, however, time began to feel like an abstraction to Captain Erika Hernandez. During the months that she and her landing party from the *Columbia* NX-02 had spent on the planet Erigol as "compulsory guests" of the reclusive aliens known as the Caeliar, she had accustomed herself to the rhythm of natural days and nights. As much as she had shared her crew's desire to escape the aliens' custody and return home to Earth, she had on some level enjoyed being back in a natural environment.

Now that lush world was gone, annihilated by a supernova along with much of the Caeliar's civilization—and, as far as Hernandez knew, the *Columbia* itself.

Without the rising and setting of the sun, Hernandez had no sense of the passage of days or weeks or months. She slept when she was tired, ate when she was hungry, and filled the indeterminate spans of her waking hours with nostalgic remembrances of a life left behind. Her only indicator of time's passing was the length of her hair, which had barely reached her shoulder when she'd first come to Erigol; it now fell in dark, thick tangles a few inches below her shoulder blades.

Three other survivors from the *Columbia* had escaped the cataclysm of Erigol with her, as passengers inside the fleeing capital city of Axion: Commander Veronica Fletcher, the first officer; Dr. Johanna Metzger, the ship's chief medical officer; and Ensign Sidra Valerian, the communications officer. None of them had adapted to the formless, unstructured existence of the Caeliar with any more ease than she had.

Hernandez stood alone in the middle of an empty, granite-tiled plaza, surrounded by the majestic towers and spires of the Caeliar metropolis. Its delicate metal-and-crystal architecture captured the feeble illumination of starlight, which cast the city in stygian shadows, dull swaths of titanium white, and endless shades of gray.

The silence of the city pressed against her soul. It was so absolute, so unnatural. Despite the presence of millions of Caeliar denizens, the megalopolis appeared deserted. Its concert shells sat empty; shattered sculptures lay abandoned in the plazas and streets. Even the air was deathly still.

Footsteps, faint and distant, behind her. Drawing near by slow degrees. She felt no need to turn and look; she already knew that it was one of her officers. Only they ever walked in Axion. The Caeliar, with their bodies of catoms—sophisticated nanomachines—hovered and floated at will, and when the mood struck them, they could coalesce from glowing motes in the air.

A few minutes later the footfalls were crisp and close. Then they stopped, and in the perfect stillness of the city, Hernandez could hear the gentle tides of breathing behind her.

"Any idea what they're up to?" asked Fletcher, her New Zealand accent softened slightly by her years of service in the multinational Earth Starfleet.

The captain turned and regarded her blond, athletically toned XO with a dour look. "Considering I haven't even seen a Caeliar in . . ." She paused, momentarily at a loss for a unit of time she could be certain of. She gave up and continued, ". . . in God knows how long, I have no clue what they're doing."

"I don't suppose we could just ask Inyx," Fletcher said.

Hernandez shook her head. "I get the feeling he's not taking my calls right now. Can't say as I blame him."

"No, I guess not." Fletcher joined Hernandez in staring up at the stars. "It's not like we can send a fruit basket with a little card that says, 'So sorry our MACOs went haywire, blew up a city, and killed a million of your people.'"

"And then some," Hernandez said. "For all we know, by interrupting the Caeliar's work, Foyle and his men might have started a chain reaction that wiped out their planet."

An interval that felt to Hernandez like a long time and also like no time at all passed between the two of them while they watched the unchanging stars.

It was Fletcher who broke the silence. "So now what?"

"We wait," Hernandez said with placid resignation.

It didn't seem to be the answer Fletcher had hoped for. "That's it? We wait? For what?"

"Whatever comes," Hernandez replied. "We can't escape, Veronica. We don't have a ship, and even if we hitched a ride and somehow escaped the Caeliar, where would we go? Earth? We don't even know where we are, never mind which way to travel. And if, by some miracle, we actually got there, then what? It's the *sixteenth century*."

"Maybe we could catch a few Shakespeare plays."

"Sure, if you want to wait about seventy years."

Fletcher made exaggerated swivel-turns to her left and right, looked up at the deserted walkways and promenades, and then turned back and said to Hernandez, "I've got time."

The captain sighed. "We both do."

Another silence stretched out between them. At one point Fletcher started to shuffle her feet, creating a dry scraping sound that became too much for Hernandez to ignore. She glared at her XO, who put on a sheepish expression and stilled her fidgeting, restoring the city to eerie soundlessness.

After a time—how long, exactly, Hernandez couldn't say—a figure appeared on a distant walkway between two lofty towers. It moved at a languid pace, slowly crossing the yawning distance between its origin and the two women on the plaza.

When it was still more than a hundred meters away, it became clear to Hernandez that the figure was a Caeliar. She couldn't help but note the enormous, bulbous skull behind its long, distorted face. Its gangly arms swung awkwardly as the alien plodded on bony legs and broad, three-toed feet. There was a pronounced heaving of exertion in the ribbed air sacs that linked respiratory tubules on either side of its head to the anatomy inside its fragile-looking chest.

From the unique mottling of purple and green on his leathery gray hide, she recognized Inyx, the chief scientist of the Caeliar and her team's principal contact. Just a few months earlier, she had not been able to distinguish the majority of his people from one another, but now she was able to recognize the individual subtleties in the shapes of their ocular ridges and mandibular joints.

Inyx halted a few meters in front of Hernandez and Fletcher. "The Quorum wishes to speak to you, Erika."

"About what?"

"Many things," he said.

Fletcher scrutinized the alien, starting at his feet and ending at his drawn, always-frowning face. "Nice to see you walking on solid ground with us little people for a change."

"We're still weak from the wound to the gestalt," he said. "Our power is being conserved to repair the city while we seek out a new world on which to continue our Great Work."

Hernandez lifted one eyebrow in suspicion. "With all the power you folks had to spare on Erigol, I find it hard to believe you're this desperate now."

"We could marshal more," Inyx said. "However, it is imperative that we maintain a minimal energy profile, so as not to draw attention to ourselves. We must be extremely careful not to disrupt the course of this timeline now that we are here."

Hernandez was bursting with questions. "But why—"

He cut her off with a raised hand. "There will be time for your inquiries later. Now I must escort you to the Quorum."

She nodded toward her first officer. "Commander Fletcher is coming with me."

"As you wish," Inyx said. "Please follow me." He turned his back on the women and began his trudging return journey.

Hernandez fell into step behind him and motioned with a tilt of her head for Fletcher to follow her. "Come on."

Fletcher caught up to Hernandez in a few steps. "Why'd you have to drag me into this?"

"I'm sorry," Hernandez said with deadpan sarcasm, "did you have something else to do today?"

Narrowing her eyes in mock frustration, Fletcher replied, "Fine. But if they've changed their minds about executing us, I get to say 'I told you so.'"

Hernandez shrugged. "That's fair."

The walk through the city was long and slow.

Before its expulsion into the void, Axion had been filled with conveyances subtle and fleet. Moving sidewalks had hurtled pedestrians along the boulevards; floating disks of razor-thin, mirror-perfect silver had ferried groups large and small from one end of the city to another in minutes, and even between cities, back when there had been other cities to visit. Vertical shafts had once spiraled open on command and shuttled passengers, safe inside invisible shells, from the city's highest vantages to its deepest recesses.

Now there were ramps and stairs, and bridges too narrow for Hernandez's liking. And everything seemed so far away.

She and Fletcher followed Inyx as he loped forward, his long arms swinging in rhythmic opposition, like metronome bars forever parted by one beat.

Hernandez's gait grew heavier and clumsier with each step. Her knees hurt, and her feet had started to ache.

And that was *before* they reached the pyramid.

It rose ahead of the three travelers, a geometrically perfect peak of dark metal and smoky crystal, each face of it subdivided into triangular quarters, each of those quartered again, and so on, through hundreds of shrinking iterations.

At its base, a triangular portal several meters high slid open far in advance of their arrival, while they were still traversing the forlorn emptiness of the square promenade that surrounded the pyramid. Through the opening, Hernandez saw stairs. "Inyx, tell me we're not walking up."

"It is an unfortunate but necessary consequence of our power conservation," he said. "Do you need to rest before we begin the climb to the Quorum hall?"

She glanced at Fletcher, who nodded energetically. "Yes," Hernandez said. "Just for a few minutes."

"Take such time as you require," Inyx said.

When at last the trio reached the mountainous structure, Hernandez and Fletcher sat down and leaned against the base of the pyramid to rest. "I didn't remember it being this far," Fletcher said between heaving breaths.

"Neither did I," Hernandez said, huffing for air.

Inyx stood in the open portal while he waited for the recuperating women, as still as if he were a statue rooted into the gleaming black granite. His ever-present frown betrayed nothing. Hernandez wondered if she would ever be able to read the moods of the Caeliar. If there was some external cue to be parsed, it certainly wasn't to be found in the leathery slack of their inexpressive faces.

Fletcher sighed and slapped her palms against her thighs. "Ready to go see the happy brigade?"

"I can hardly wait," Hernandez said. Pushing off the pyramid, she forced her aching body back to a standing position and stretched to dispel the leaden stiffness of fatigue and the tension that had coiled into a crick between her shoulder blades. It released with a gentle *pop,* and she turned to face the steep grade of stairs that receded to a point far above them. She looked at Fletcher. "Ready?" The first officer nodded, and Hernandez said to their guide, "Okay, let's go."

The awkwardly built Caeliar ascended the stairs with ease. He walked with an unflagging stride, and after the first hundred steps had easily outpaced Hernandez and Fletcher, who labored to follow him. After the fourth time that he found himself forced to pause and wait for them to catch up, he relented and slowed his climb to accommodate them.

Hernandez felt as if she had scaled Everest by the

time the top of the staircase became visible. She could barely breathe, and the muscles in her legs and lower back had started tying themselves into a Celtic knot of pain.

At the apex of the climb, another triangular portal—this one only a few meters tall at its highest point—opened into the vast expanse of the Quorum hall, which occupied the uppermost level of the pyramid. Hernandez and Fletcher slumped against the edges of the doorway while they caught their breath.

The hall was a hollow pyramid, with towering walls of dark crystal over the lattices of metallic triangles. It had been quite some time—weeks, or maybe even months—since Hernandez and Fletcher had last been here, during the destruction of Erigol. From this room they'd witnessed Axion's desperate escape, through a subspace tunnel, to this remote corner of space and time.

Before the cataclysm, tiers of seating had been elevated above the main level of the hall; those had collapsed during the disaster. The wreckage was gone now, and the fissures that had marred the beauty of the fractal sunburst pattern adorning the polished marble floor had been repaired. The tiers, however, had not been repaired. Instead, the hundreds of Caeliar gathered in the hall milled about in clusters great and small on the main level, communicating by means of their atonal humming.

Then everything was silent, and the Caeliar turned to face the two women. Inyx turned toward them and said, "The Quorum is ready to receive you."

"Lucky us," Hernandez said.

"Follow me," Inyx said.

They walked with him toward the throng of
Caeliar, who spread out into a half circle around the
trio. At the center of the curved line was the crimson-
garbed de facto leader of the Quorum, Ordemo
Nordal. His own people called him the *tanwa-
seynorral,* which Inyx had explained to Hernandez
meant something akin to "first among equals." All
that she knew for certain was that, in this chamber,
Ordemo did most of the talking.

"Some members of this Quorum have suggested
we should hold you and your three remaining companions accountable for the tragedy of Erigol," Ordemo said. "There also has been debate over a
preemptive displacement of your homeworld and
your species, to prevent future disruptions of our
Great Work. However, I have agreed to postpone a
final referendum on these matters until after Inyx
presents his findings."

Inyx made a small bow from the waist toward Ordemo and then addressed the Quorum, in a voice that
sounded artificially amplified despite the apparent
absence of any means to do so. "I offer you the sum of
my research," he said, spreading his arms wide. "The
gestalt will attest to its veracity." A mellifluous drone
coursed through the assemblage. "The humans' interference with the apparatus had no effect on the Great
Work." A discordant buzzing undercut the group's
melodious tones as Inyx continued. "Even as they in-
terfered with the apparatus's locus in Mantilis, the
other loci compensated for its loss. There was no disruption in, or corruption of, our transmission to the
shrouded galaxy."

Ordemo lifted one arm, and the dissonant noise of the Quorum faded away. "How, then, do you account for the hostility of the response we received?"

"It was intentional," Inyx said. "The damage it inflicted upon the apparatus, and throughout our energy matrix, was quite precise and crafted with expert knowledge of our technology. It was intended to annihilate us, and to do so with such alacrity that we couldn't hope to respond in time. The most interesting fact, however, is that it also was made expressly to prevent us from purging the humans' time-travel formulae from the apparatus. This, as well as several unique characteristics of the signal pulse itself, leave no doubt as to the identity of the civilization that committed this barbarous act."

Hernandez heard the ire in Ordemo's voice as he demanded, "Who, Inyx? Who did this to us?"

Inyx faced the *tanwa-seynorral*. "We did."

Ordemo sounded stunned. "Why?"

"Two more of our cities escaped through time-shifted subspace tunnels, just as Axion has. One of them I have been unable to locate, but the other had a chroniton signature so profound that I couldn't help but see it. If my calculations are correct, it traveled back nearly to the dawn of time. Our own people, or perhaps their heirs, built a new civilization in the nascent universe, and then they waited nearly fourteen billion years to smite us—in order to create themselves."

"A predestination paradox," Ordemo said in a shocked hush.

"Technically, this would be considered a self-consistent causal loop," Inyx said. "Regardless, it absolves our human guests of ultimate culpability for the Cataclysm. And as we have already established that Captain Hernandez and her fellow survivors were as much victims of their renegade compatriots as we were, it would be unjust to treat them as accomplices."

The susurrus of debate charged the air in the Quorum hall for several seconds. Then the cavernous chamber fell silent again, and Ordemo stepped forward from the line. "Very well. The Quorum has consensus. Captain Hernandez and her companions will remain as our guests." To the captain herself he added, "I am certain you will understand, however, if we choose to exercise a heightened degree of caution in our future dealings with you."

"Of course," Hernandez said.

Ordemo brought his arms together and intertwined his tendril-like fingers. "This convocation is concluded. If you'll excuse us, Captain, we have much work to do."

Without awaiting her response, the *tanwa-seynorral* walked past her and merged into a line of Caeliar walking toward one of the four exits from the chamber.

Inyx lingered for a moment beside Hernandez and Fletcher. "Are you and your companions well? Do you need anything?"

"Physically, we're fine," Hernandez said. "But we could use something to keep our minds occupied."

With a flourish of raised arms, Inyx replied, "You could always take up art."

Hernandez couldn't help but smirk.

"I might just do that," she said.

2381

3

———◆———

"Welcome to New Erigol," said the woman who Commander Tuvok had identified as Erika Hernandez.

Commander Christine Vale's first, unspoken reaction was to wonder what the hell had happened to Old Erigol.

Her next thought was that Hernandez looked amazing for someone who had been missing for more than two centuries. The woman's enormous mane of dark, unruly hair spilled over her shoulders and framed her youthful face, and her physique—loosely garbed in drapes of gauzy fabric that were barely equal to the demands of modesty—was equally trim and toned. If Vale hadn't known better, she'd have assumed Hernandez was barely out of her teens.

Even though Vale was the away team commander, Counselor Troi took the lead in speaking for the group. "I'm Commander Deanna Troi, senior diplomatic officer of the *Starship Titan*," she said. Gesturing back at the other *Titan* personnel behind her, she continued, "These are my shipmates and friends. Commander Christine Vale, first officer; Commander Tuvok, second officer; Dr. Shenti Yisec Eres Ree, chief medical officer; Lieutenant Ranul Keru, chief of security; Ensign Torvig Bu-kar-nguv, engineer; and Lieutenant Gian Sortollo and Chief Petty Officer Dennisar of our security division."

Hernandez nodded to the away team. "Hello," she said. Looking to the being on her right, she said, "This is Edrin, our chief architect." Turning to her other companion, she continued, "And this is Inyx, our chief scientist."

Inyx made a subtle bow toward Troi. "Welcome to the city of Axion, Commander Troi," he said, his voice a rich baritone.

Vale stepped forward and stood shoulder-to-shoulder with Troi. To their hosts she said, "Hi, nice to meet you. It seems you know quite a bit about us, no doubt thanks to Captain Hernandez. But I'm afraid you have us at a disadvantage."

Behind her, Tuvok quipped, "In more ways than one."

"Of course," Hernandez said, her voice strangely subdued in its inflections. "Inyx and Edrin are members of a species known as Caeliar."

"For simplicity's sake," Inyx interrupted, "you may use Caeliar as a singular or plural noun, or as an adjective." Vale thought she caught a fleeting look of mischief between the alien scientist and Hernandez.

"Good to know," said Troi. "Captain Hernandez? Forgive me for prying, but finding you alive raises many questions."

"Yes," Hernandez said, her face betraying no emotion. She looked at Inyx, who returned her gaze in silence, and then she looked back at Troi. "What do you wish to know?"

Troi lifted a hand and gestured at the magnificent city of platinum and crystal that towered behind them. "For starters, how you came to be here, so far from Earth."

"And why you're still alive two hundred years after your ship disappeared," Vale added.

Their questions provoked a sly grin of amusement from Hernandez. "As the saying goes, it's a long story."

The two Caeliar turned and looked at each other. Then they looked at Hernandez, who shifted her downcast gaze back and forth between the aliens before she looked up at Vale and Troi.

"Forgive me," Hernandez said. "I was sent here to deliver a message, and I should do as I was instructed before I digress."

A chill of foreboding washed through Vale. "What kind of message?"

Hernandez's manner became cold and aloof. "At this time, your shipmates on *Titan* are being informed of what I have to tell you now. Although no violent measures will be used against you or your vessel, the Caeliar will not permit you to leave this place, nor will you be allowed to have any further external communications. Those of you who have come to the planet's surface must remain here. *Titan* will be expected to remain in orbit, though any of your compatriots who wish to join you here in Axion will be free to petition the Caeliar for entry."

With sour sarcasm, Vale replied, "How generous of them."

"The power has been drained from your weapons," Hernandez continued. "If the Caeliar detect any effort on your part to recharge them, they will disintegrate them. You may retain your scanning devices, provided you don't use them against the Caeliar or to jeopardize the safety of the city." She paused while gauging the away team's reaction. "It is important that you understand the Caeliar do not see you as prisoners."

Tuvok inquired in reply, "How, then, are we to perceive our incarcerated status?"

"Like me," Hernandez said, "you are all considered to be guests . . . with restrictions." Another glimmer of silent interaction passed between Hernandez and Inyx.

With acidic sarcasm, Vale said, "You've been away a couple hundred years, so maybe you don't know this, but English has a word for that now: It's called a *prisoner.*"

"I understand this will be a difficult transition for many of you," Hernandez said. "Some of you may find it impossible. But it's my hope, and that of the Caeliar, that you'll learn to accept this new paradigm." She nodded to the second Caeliar. "Edrin will escort you to your accommodations. If you need anything, just say it aloud. The Caeliar will do the rest."

Edrin extended his arm and waggled his tendril-like digits. Tiny droplets of quicksilver formed like dew on blades of grass, rose into the air, and fused into a sliver-thin disk of mirror-perfect metal four meters in diameter. The disk hovered a few centimeters above the ground. The Caeliar stepped onto it and gestured to the away team. "Please join me," he said in a melodic tenor. "It's quite safe."

Vale nodded to the rest of the away team. Keru was the first to climb atop the disk, which remained as stable as bedrock. The bearish, bearded Trill man nodded to his security officers, who shepherded Dr. Ree and Ensign Torvig onto the levitated platform. The reptilian physician alighted onto the disk, the talons of his nimble feet clicking against the metal. Torvig—who Vale thought resembled a wingless ostrich with a sheep's head, cybernetic arms, and a bionic hand grafted onto his prehensile tail—bounded lightly onto the disk beside Ree. Keru waved Dennisar aboard, and the Orion security guard complied. Lieutenant Sortollo followed him.

As Vale turned to walk to the disk, Troi asked Inyx, "Will we be allowed to contact *Titan*?"

"No," he said. "I'm sorry, but our past experience has made it clear that any contact you have with your ship would likely be used to collude in your escape. We don't wish to separate you from your friends and colleagues, but we can't risk allowing you to plan coordinated action that might be to our detriment."

The half-Betazoid counselor nodded, but her expression was forlorn. "I understand," she said. Then she followed Vale and Tuvok to the disk. As soon as the three of them joined the rest of the away team on the circular platform, it ascended several meters with no sensation of motion that Vale could detect.

Hernandez looked up at them with a longing gaze. "I'll come to see you once you're settled. And I'll tell you my story."

"I can hardly wait," Vale said, already stewing in her own anger. She made a flippant gesture at the two Caeliar. "Bring your friends. They're a hoot."

Troi, however, was gentler in tone and word. "I'll look forward to seeing you," she said.

Then the disk was hurtling forward in silence, through the gleaming canyons of the city, soaring over the plazas and under the causeways of the sprawling metropolis. Vale fought to take it all in as it blurred past, trying to remember the shapes of the city and the grid of its streets.

Because it was never too early to start planning an escape.

Captain William Riker was irate. "That's all they said?"

"Yes, sir," said Lieutenant Sariel Rager, *Titan*'s senior operations officer. She held one hand a few centimeters above the touchscreen interface of her console. "Do you want to hear it again?"

"That won't be necessary," Riker said. He stalked back to his chair and fumed at the arrogance implicit in the audio-only message *Titan* had just received from the Caeliar. In effect, the aliens had just declared the away team and *Titan* itself to be their prisoners. There had been no warning, no opportunity to discuss terms—just a standing invitation for those on the ship to change the setting of their incarceration.

Adding to his anger was the fact that this new crisis had deprived him of most of his senior officers, including his wife, Deanna Troi. His concern for her, especially in light of her fragile medical condition, was only slightly offset by the knowledge that Dr. Ree was with her.

He stood behind his chair and rested his hands on top of it. On the main viewer, the world the Caeliar called New Erigol was concealed inside a spherical shell of dark metal. A similar hollow globe encased its star, rendering this system all but invisible to most detection protocols.

Lieutenant Commander Fo Hachesa, a Kobliad man who served as *Titan*'s gamma-shift officer of the watch, occupied the first officer's seat. He tracked the crew's ongoing efforts to repair the damage to the ship's sensors that had been inflicted a day earlier by one of the Caeliar's long-range scans.

Commander Xin Ra-Havreii, *Titan*'s chief engineer, handed off control of his engineering station console to a junior officer and joined Riker behind the command chair. The slender Efrosian man pensively stroked his long, flowing white mustache and stared at the forward viewscreen. "It's quite a feat of engineering," he said. "Whatever it's made of, I can't get a clear sensor reading from it."

From the tactical console, Lieutenant Rriarr called out, "Captain? The passageway through the shell that the shuttlecraft *Mance* used to reach the surface has closed."

Riker nodded to the Caitian, who was filling in for Keru. "Keep an eye open for any other changes."

"Aye, sir."

Ra-Havreii asked Riker discreetly, "Do you want me to look for a way to punch a hole in it? Maybe take a shot at beaming the away team back?"

Shaking his head, Riker said, "No. I doubt we'd even scratch it. And with the level of technology the Caeliar must possess, I'd rather not provoke them into a fight."

"Sensible," said Ra-Havreii, who then nodded past Riker, to Lieutenant Commander Melora Pazlar, the head of the ship's sciences division, who had just joined them.

The thirtyish blond Elaysian woman looked strangely incomplete to Riker's eyes, because he had become accustomed to seeing her limbs and torso surrounded by a powered exoskeletal armature. The mechanical suit—which Pazlar often jokingly referred to as "the armor"—had been necessary because she was a native of a world with a microgravity environment; in the Earth-normal gravity of most Federation starships, starbases, and worlds, her bones would snap under her own weight.

Now she stood beside him, at ease and unencumbered by her armature, thanks to the latest innovation of Commander Ra-Havreii: holographic telepresence. The figure next to Riker was not the flesh-and-blood Pazlar but her holographic avatar, which could go anywhere aboard the ship by means of a network of holographic sensors and emitters. Meanwhile, the real Pazlar was safely ensconced in the microgravity environment of the ship's stellar cartography lab, interacting with perfect holographic simulacra of her shipmates in a real-time re-creation of the bridge.

"I presume we're not simply giving up," she said to Riker.

He felt his jaw tighten even as he replied, "Never."

Hachesa looked up from his work and joined the conversation. "If we cannot fight the Caeliar," he said, "and we do not wish to surrender to them, how shall we proceed?"

"As I see it," Riker said, "we have two paths left to us: diplomacy and deceit. Our best diplomat is already on the surface, so I'd recommend we leave any negotiations to her."

Pazlar folded her arms. "What kind of deception do you have in mind, Captain?"

"I don't know yet," he said. "What I want is for you and Ra-Havreii to go over everything we know so far about this system, this planet, and this species. Look for anything we can exploit, either tactically or politically. I don't want to use violence while our away team is down there, so focus on making contact with our people and gathering intel any way we can."

Ra-Havreii's snowy eyebrows twitched upward. "I should advise you, Captain, that this is a task whose progress will likely be measured not over the course of hours but of days, even under the best of circumstances."

"Then the sooner you get to work, the better," Riker said, in a tone that brooked no debate. "Don't you agree, Commander?"

Pazlar's avatar tugged at Ra-Havreii's shirtsleeve. "Come on, Xin. I have an idea where to start. We can work on it in your office."

"An excellent suggestion," Ra-Havreii said. "Fewer distractions down there." He followed the holographic Pazlar into the turbolift. Before the doors closed, Riker was certain that he caught sight of a smug grin on the lean, angular face of the Efrosian, whose reputation as a ladies' man was well earned.

Riker sighed. "Commander Hachesa, I'll be in my ready room. You have the bridge."

"Aye, sir," Hachesa said, and he returned to administrating the minutiae of the ship's business as Riker walked aft and withdrew to the privacy of his ready room.

After the door had hissed shut behind him, Riker collapsed heavily onto the sofa, tilted his head back, and stared blankly at the overhead. It had been a long couple of days for him and *Titan*'s crew. Weighing most ponderously in his thoughts was the emotional turmoil that had been wrought in his and Deanna's marriage by her miscarriage of their first successful pregnancy several months earlier, and the recent news, delivered by Dr. Ree only a few days earlier, that their second attempt had become not only nonviable but also a risk to Deanna's health and life. Talking about it with his first officer had proved explosive, and Deanna's refusal to heed Ree's medical advice had only made an already tumultuous situation even more volatile.

The tension and grief that filled every silence between himself and Deanna had made it almost impossible for them to communicate these past few days. All the same, he wished she were here now, even if only as his diplomatic officer and not as his wife, so that he wouldn't feel so adrift. At times such as this, he relied on sage advice from Deanna, Christine Vale, and Tuvok. Drawing on their experience and insight, he had come to think of command as a process of synthesis rather than one of genesis.

He closed his eyes and tried to focus on the tides of his breathing, because for the first time since he'd taken the reins of *Titan,* he felt the true loneliness of being in command.

Night had been falling on New Erigol's northern lati-
tudes for weeks without quite arriving. Arctic twilight
suffused the sky with a dusky haze along the horizon,
and outside Axion's protective shield, fierce winds
howled and whipped spindrifts across a dark and ice-
choked sea.

Erika Hernandez stood next to Inyx on a circular
platform at the end of a narrow walkway, which extended several dozen meters beyond the city's periphery. She sensed his influence on the invisible cloud of
catoms that surrounded them, as he used them to extend and shape Axion's protective field around their
just-created and temporary widow's walk.

She stared into the half-light and let the vista im-
print on her consciousness. Its qualities of color and
shadow changed by slow degrees. "Please ask the
Quorum to take the city south," she said as mournful
winds caterwauled between nearby glaciers.

"I thought you admired the austerity of the arctic,"
Inyx said, passively resisting her request.

"It's very pretty," Hernandez said. "But it's going to
get darker soon, and I'm concerned about the effect
that a prolonged night might have on the humans
from *Titan.*"

Inyx sounded almost contrite. "Yes, I should've
considered that. I'll pass your request to the Quorum
now." She felt a low crackle of energy surround him
as he communed with the gestalt. For a moment she
was tempted to eavesdrop, but she decided that it
would be too risky. Instead, she waited for his response, which she knew was imminent when the tingle of psychic communion faded from the air between
them. "The city will be under way very soon," he

said. "We'll complete the transition while our guests are asleep, and we will try to match our longitudinal position with the proper phase in their endogenous diurnal cycle."

"Thank you," Hernandez said. "It should ease their adjustment to life in the city. And if I'm to be completely honest, I was starting to miss our sunrises."

"As was I," Inyx said. "Though if some in the Quorum have their way, we may not have many more to share." She felt a slight chill as he expelled all the free nanoscopic catoms from their immediate vicinity and configured those closest to them into a spherical scattering field to grant them privacy. "It has been proposed that if *Titan*'s crew accepts our invitation of sanctuary, our new guests should be exiled to remote settlements on the surface, and segregated by gender to reduce the risk of infesting the planet with a new civilization."

Hernandez remained calm as she replied, "I object to the use of the term 'infesting.'"

"As you should," Inyx replied. "However, I think the more important issue is to oppose this crude and repressive measure."

She was surprised to hear him speak out on behalf of *Titan*'s personnel. "I presume you have a different solution?"

"Absolutely," he said. "Though it would take greater effort, I think that more harmonious and sociologically balanced communities could be created if we segregate the visitors not by gender but rather by genetic incompatibility."

"Genetic incompatibility?" she repeated. She understood its meaning; she simply couldn't believe that Inyx had suggested it.

As usual, he rambled on, oblivious of her objection. "It's my hypothesis that a mix of male and female personalities, regardless of species, will help curb aggression in these new communities. By combining only those individuals who are not genetically compatible, however, we can achieve the desired state of negative population growth."

"In other words, they can pass their days pursuing futile labors until they die," Hernandez said with disdain. "Just like everyone else in the universe." She sighed and looked at the purple silhouettes of mountain peaks in the distance. "Why do your people always resort to such draconian measures? Why can't you try anything new?"

Inyx's tone became stern. "You've lived among us long enough to understand our ways and our reasons."

"Long enough to understand they're misguided," she said.

Undeterred, he continued, "I empathize with your desire to permit *Titan* into orbit, and even to let its emissaries come to the surface. But after what happened with your people on Erigol, we cannot risk such vulnerability again."

"Then why did you let them come here?"

"Because their civilization is too large to be displaced without drawing unwanted attention to ourselves. If we shifted the worlds and peoples of the Federation into another galaxy or quantum universe, we would be obliged to do the same for all the many

powers that neighbor it. Likewise, all the astropoliti-
cal entities across the galaxy that know of the Federation would have to be displaced, as well. Ultimately,
it seems to be a more prudent use of our resources to
restrain and impound one starship and its crew than
it would be to disrupt a significant fraction of all
known galactic civilizations."

Hernandez considered Inyx's argument and realized that, in the centuries since the *Columbia*'s disap-
pearance, Earth and its allies—its Federation—had
become a formidable power in local space. When she
and her crew had first come to Erigol, the Caeliar had
not hesitated to level a threat against Earth if the *Columbia*'s personnel breached the Caeliar's precious
secrecy. Now, however, they seemed reluctant to
make such threats. It was the first sign of weakness
they'd shown in all the time that she had known
them—but she didn't believe it would be enough to
make a difference.

After more than 860 years in Axion, Hernandez
had learned to accept defeat as a given. The sooner
Titan's officers embraced that essential truth, the
sooner they would be able to let go of the past and
find a new modus vivendi here among the Caeliar.

With a thought, she directed the ever-attentive
catoms in the air to disassemble the widow's walk.
Inyx found himself standing on air, high above the
churning sea. Hernandez strode away from him, followed by the vanishing edge of the walkway, and
said, "Call me when there's a sunrise."

4

———◆———

Five hours had been barely enough time to make jury-rigged repairs on the *Enterprise* and render the ship strong enough to brave the volatile embrace of the Azure Nebula. The supernova remnant looked to Commander Miranda Kadohata like a bruise without a body as it grew larger on the main viewscreen. Then it swallowed the stars as the *Aventine* and the *Enterprise* moved inside it, less than a minute's flight from the coordinates at which the *Aventine* had exited a subspace corridor from the Gamma Quadrant.

Kadohata was finding the task of coordinating the effort complicated by her body's urgent desire for sleep. It took almost all of her concentration to stay awake as she tried to enter one more bit of data and assign one more damage-control task.

"La Forge to ops," said the chief engineer over the comm.

Her eyes snapped open. "Go ahead, Geordi."

"Miranda, we need some more bandwidth freed up on the subspace interlink."

She scrambled to reorganize her interface to call up an inventory of available and committed computer resources. "How much more do you need?"

"At least four megaquads," La Forge said. *"Five if you can spare it. The* Aventine's *data-burst capacity is incredible."*

Even though La Forge couldn't see her, she shook her head in dismay. "Even if I dump the nontactical systems from the primary network, the most I can give you is three-point-six megaquads. Is there any way you can trim their signal?"

"Not without reprogramming their main computer," La Forge said. There was a pause as he conferred with someone else, whose voice Kadohata couldn't hear clearly. Then La Forge continued, *"Lieutenant Leishman suggests we take all but our navigational sensors offline while we make repairs, since we'll be relying on the* Aventine's *sensors inside the nebula, anyway."*

"I see," Kadohata said. "Does the *Aventine's* chief engineer have any suggestions for how I should monitor our damage-control efforts without an internal sensor network?"

La Forge stammered, *"I, uh, I'm not sure I—"*

"Because if she's that interested in doing my job for me, I can knock off early, and maybe tell Ensign Rosado she can sleep in, too, since *Lieutenant* Leishman has the *Enterprise's* operations-management needs well in hand."

She could almost hear him rolling his eyes. *"Getting a little defensive, aren't you? There's plenty of starship to go around, you know."*

Calling up some additional options on her console,

she replied to La Forge, "This isn't about territoriality, Geordi. It's about balancing conflicting needs." She authorized some changes to the *Enterprise*'s status and added, "Speaking of which, I just isolated the internal sensors and comms on the emergency backup system, changed our protocol for incoming subspace radio traffic, and launched a subspace relay buoy to act as a signal buffer. That just bought you another point-six megaquads of bandwidth."

"Thanks, Miranda," Geordi said, sounding grateful. *"You're the best. We're starting the relay from the* Aventine *now."* Adding a teasing quality to his voice, he added, *"I'll let* you *decide what to do with the data."*

"Don't test me, La Forge," she said through a tense smirk. "Routing it to aft stations one through four."

The row of consoles along the bridge's aft bulkhead came alive with mad flurries of data and imagery piped in from the *Aventine*'s sensors. Lieutenant Dina Elfiki, the *Enterprise*'s strikingly attractive, Egyptian-born senior science officer, took half a step back from the display, her dark brown eyes wide. "Wow," she said. "That's amazing." She turned toward Kadohata and flashed a smile. "Commander, you have to see this. The level of detail is incredible."

Kadohata got up from her chair and nodded to one of the relief officers to take over for her at the ops console. The young Saurian looked excited to finally be getting his webbed fingers on some real work as he slipped into her chair.

At the aft duty stations, Elfiki and two more lieutenants from the ship's sciences division—theoretical physicist Corinne Clipet and subspace-particle physicist James Talenda—watched in awe as a flood of raw information poured in from the *Vesta*-class starship that was leading the *Enterprise* into the nebula.

"Dina," said Kadohata, ever so gently, "is all that data going to analyze itself?"

The question snapped Elfiki back into motion. "Talenda, start looking for high-energy triquantum wave by-products. If there's another subspace conduit out here, that's how we'll find it." She turned toward the slender Frenchwoman. "Clipet, help Talenda filter out false positives by screening triquantum wave artifacts from any Borg ships still operating in this sector."

Kadohata watched the three scientists' hands fly across the consoles in a desperate and probably futile effort to keep up with the rapid crush of sensor input from the *Aventine*.

Clipet's hands kept moving as she reported, "The *Aventine* crew is already running a triquantum filter on the stream."

"Confirmed," Talenda said. "I'm finishing a sweep around the *Aventine*'s subspace tunnel terminus. If there's anything else like it within a hundred thousand kilometers of those coordinates, we should know in . . . a . . ." His voice tapered off as he finished, ". . . few minutes." He let his hands fall by his sides, and he stared slack-jawed at the complex schematic the computer had just rendered on the large display in front of him.

Kadohata waited for Elfiki to follow up, and then the second officer noticed that all three science officers had the same stunned expressions on their faces. "Ahem," she said with a loud and unnecessary clearing of her throat. Elfiki turned at the sound, prompting Kadohata to add, "What's going on?"

Elfiki nervously fiddled with a lock from her stylish coif of mahogany-brown hair. "I know we're looking for a different subspace tunnel than the one the *Aventine* used," she said.

"Yes," Kadohata said, "that's correct."

"Um . . ." Elfiki crossed her arms and leaned back a bit from the wall of consoles and screens. "Would you happen to know *which one,* exactly?"

I don't like the sound of that, Kadohata mused. "Dare I ask how many there are?"

The senior science officer stalled. "About . . . roughly . . ."

"Twenty-seven," Clipet declared.

Kadohata closed her eyes and wished that she were already asleep, so that this could be just a banal anxiety dream. Already braced for more bad news, she asked, "I don't suppose there's any way to tell which one the Borg have been using?"

"No, sir," Talenda said. "For all we know, they might be using more than one."

"Splendid," she said, rubbing her eyes gingerly.

The chrono on the console showed ship's time to be 0750. Her shift was scheduled to end in ten minutes, but sleep was going to have to wait, and there was no telling for how long, because the entire nature of their mission had just changed.

She tapped her combadge. "Captain Picard and Commander Worf, please report to the bridge."

Dax appreciated Captain Picard's courtesy in coming aboard the *Aventine* to meet with her in her own ready room, but his gesture wasn't making her any more receptive to his plan. The fact that she'd only been able to steal two hours of sleep since their last meeting wasn't improving her mood, either.

"I think you're making a mistake, Captain," she said. "It's like using a phaser to swat a fly."

Her metaphor seemed to fray the edges of Picard's already careworn patience. "I would hardly call the threat of a massive, genocidal Borg invasion 'a fly,' Captain Dax." He paced like a tiger not yet resigned to life inside its cage. "Whether we're talking about one hole in the Federation's defenses or several, our mission remains the same—close the gap."

"We will," Dax said, pulling back hard on the reins of her own temper. "But that's a short-term goal. We also have to consider long-term objectives." It was important to keep this discussion civil. Though they were both captains, Starfleet protocols clearly recognized his many years of command seniority and afforded him considerable privileges under circumstances such as these.

He narrowed his eyes. "I'd consider the survival of the Federation both a short- and a long-term mission priority."

"So is exploration," Dax replied. "Think of where some of those subspace tunnels might lead. What if some of them are passages to other galaxies? Or short-cuts across our own? Their value to science is immeasurable."

"As is the threat they represent to our survival," Picard shot back. "If there was some way to tell if the Borg had access to only one, and if we knew which it was, I might consider a surgical strike. But both our science departments concur: there's no way to be certain. For all we know, the Borg are exploiting several of these tunnels through subspace. And as far as I'm concerned, even one is too many. They *must* be destroyed."

Shaking her head, Dax ruminated aloud, "We could open them up, go through, and scout ahead. If we could save even a few safe passages—"

"We don't have that luxury, Captain," Picard said. "Your science officer wrote in his report that it could take hours to calculate the frequency for opening the aperture of one tunnel, and that they all resonate to different harmonics. It could take days to scout all these passages—and I have reason to suspect the Borg won't be giving us that much time. Collapsing the passageways is the swiftest means of ending this Borg invasion, and it lets us do so without further conflict or loss of life."

Dax turned away for a moment and looked out the window behind her desk, at the swirling violet and blue fog of the Azure Nebula. Like most officers in Starfleet, she had heard the rumors of Picard's bizarre mental link with the Borg Collective, and the advantages that it had given him in combat against them. He seemed convinced of the imminence of the Borg threat, and that was enough to persuade her. She swiveled her chair back to face him and folded her hands atop her desk.

"All right," she said. "I see your point. All the research opportunities in the galaxy don't mean much if we're not here to enjoy them. Do you have a plan for how to proceed?"

Picard stopped pacing and leaned on one of the chairs in front of Dax's desk. "I'd like our science, engineering, and operations teams to keep working together," he said. "This is a new phenomenon, and we need to comprehend it before we can find a way to dismantle it."

"Tall order," Dax said. "Learning how to take it apart might take as much time as scouting each passage. Or more."

"Perhaps," Picard said. "Certainly, it will take time to complete our analysis. Reinforcements are en route, but we should take aggressive precautions."

"Aggressive precautions," she repeated with a smirk. "Is that one of those phrases I'm supposed to learn as a captain, or did you just make that up?"

"I have been known to coin a phrase once in a while," he said, with his own disarming grin. "As for securing these passageways, we can take advantage of the fact that all the apertures surround a central position. If we mine that zone heavily enough, we can prevent further incursions while we complete our research."

Something about his suggestion didn't sound right to Dax. "A minefield? Inside a nebula full of sirillium gas?"

"Exactly," Picard said. "We'll make the environment work for us, use it to amplify the potential impact of the mines."

Dax tried to remain calm as she considered the consequences of Picard's strategy, but anxiety set her index finger to tapping on her desktop. "At this range, the blast effects of a full-scale detonation would probably cripple both our ships."

Nodding and adopting a grave countenance, Picard said, "I've already made it clear to my officers and crew that the *Enterprise* is to be considered expendable if that's what it takes to seal this breach in the Federation's defenses. I need to know that you and your crew share this commitment."

I must have missed the memo about this being a suicide mission, she brooded, and she wondered for a moment what pointed words her symbiont's former host Curzon might have hurled at Picard in a moment such as this. Going along with Picard's plan to wipe out an invaluable scientific discovery in the name of security had already rankled her; now he was asking her to pledge her ship's destruction and her crew's collective demise to accomplish it. *If he's wrong, this'll be a disaster,* she told herself. *But if he's right . . .*

"During the Dominion War," she said, "Deep Space 9 used self-replicating cloaked mines to prevent Dominion reinforcements in the Gamma Quadrant from traveling through the Bajoran wormhole. I'm not sure the cloaking technology will work here inside the nebula, but if we make the minefield self-replicating, it'll be able to sustain and rebuild itself even if our ships are destroyed or forced to retreat."

"An excellent suggestion, Captain," Picard said. "How soon can it be done?"

"We're still fabricating parts for your repairs," she said, thinking out loud, "but after that's finished, we can build the first dozen mines in a few hours. Then we can release them and let them do the rest of the work, replicating themselves to build a defensive cluster between the subspace tunnels. The entire zone could be filled in about four hours."

Picard stood tall and gave her a curt nod. "Make it so."

"It's a right awful shame, if you ask me," said Miranda Kadohata, keeping her eyes and her hands on her console at ops. "One of the most amazing things we've ever discovered, and the captain wants us to destroy it."

Worf had no wish to debate Kadohata regarding the wisdom of their assignment, and not just because she was right. The simple fact was that the Federation had once again found itself in a state of war with the Borg Collective. Discipline and morale were more important at times like this than at any other.

"I concur," he said. "It is an interesting phenomenon, and it is regrettable that we will not be able to study it. But the captain's orders stand."

From a few meters behind him, Worf heard contact specialist Lieutenant T'Ryssa Chen mutter to another junior officer, "If we really wanted to know what makes these things tick, we'd have found a way to avoid blowing them up."

Muscles in the Klingon's jaw rippled with tension as he bit down on the rebuke he felt Chen so richly deserved. He stalked toward her, his unblinking gaze locked with Chen's as her young confidant prudently slipped away to work at a different station on the other side of the bridge.

He loomed over the youthful woman of mixed Vulcan-human ancestry, and his voice became quiet even as it sharpened to a fine edge. "Do you have something to share, Lieutenant Chen?"

She swallowed once while staring up from beneath eyebrows lifted to steep peaks of anxiety. "No, sir," she said. "I'm just, you know, compiling sensor logs and collating data. Sir."

"I see," Worf said. A menacing smirk tugged at his mouth and put a malicious gleam in his stare. "Carry on, and keep Commander Kadohata informed of your progress," he said. As he stepped away, he added, "The captains want regular updates."

"They always do," Chen mumbled under her breath, and Worf felt frustration force his hand to clench by reflex into a fist. With effort he had opened his hand by the time he reached the security console, where Lieutenant Jasminder Choudhury, the chief of security, was plotting the minefield's distribution pattern. She had been laboring at the task for some time—longer, in fact, than Worf had expected it to require. He watched the serene-faced woman work at it, her agile hands rearranging patterns and data on her console. A subtle knitting of her brow was the only evidence of her mounting frustration.

He asked, "Is there a problem, Lieutenant?"

Choudhury stopped working. "There are some challenges." Her face was emotionless, her voice low and controlled—all hallmarks of a bad mood for her. "The fluid dynamics of the nebula are making it very difficult to keep the minefield's position stable relative to the subspace tunnels. And I'm still waiting for an updated analysis from stellar cartography about the behavior of the apertures themselves, so I can correct for any distortions."

"We can request help from the *Aventine*'s crew," Worf said. He noted the dubious stare of his security chief—with whom he had also recently become more closely acquainted—and concluded that she wasn't embracing his suggestion. "Or I could let you take more time with it."

Her lips pursed into a frown, and she shook her head in small, slow motions. "I'm sorry, sir, I can do this—really. I just don't know that I agree with it."

"Why not?" It wasn't like Choudhury to question orders, and Worf began to suspect that Kadohata might not be the only member of the *Enterprise*'s senior staff who was balking at Captain Picard's tactical directive. Noticing Choudhury's reluctance to answer, he added, "Speak freely, Lieutenant."

"Commander Kadohata's right," she said. "Aside from their scientific value, the subspace tunnels would be a major tactical resource for the Federation if we could secure them."

"And if we cannot, they are a vulnerability," Worf said. "One of these passages is being exploited by the Borg. We have no way of knowing what threats lie beyond the others."

Choudhury's face flushed slightly. "For all we know, most of the passages might not need any defending at all. Why don't we explore them, figure out which ones the Borg have compromised, and conduct surgical strikes to collapse just those passageways? Then we'd still have the others for exploration."

"I agree . . . in principle," Worf said. "But that approach would take a great deal of time—which we do not have."

"But if we did," Choudhury said, "and we could target only the Borg's subspace tunnels—"

"It would make no difference," Worf cut in. "If the Borg found one passage, they can find others. And now that they know what to look for, they will not stop until they find it." He hardened his countenance to drive home his point. "The safest choice is to collapse *all* the tunnels."

The security chief sighed. "You're right." She closed her eyes, took a deep breath, then set herself back to work. "I'll let you know when I've stabilized the deployment pattern," she said, and then she let herself become consumed in her task.

As Worf returned to his chair, an ensign handed him a padd. The XO sat down, skimmed the padd's contents, and was pleased to see that the *Aventine*'s damage-control teams working on the *Enterprise* were beginning to get ahead of schedule. If all continued to go well, the *Aventine*'s engineering division would be able to repurpose its industrial replicators for mine production shortly before midday.

On a less encouraging note, he reviewed the casualty statistics from sickbay and imagined it must have seemed like an abbatoir in the immediate aftermath of the battle. Before he could dwell too long on that morbid thought, Kadohata called back from ops, "Commander? Can I show you something?"

Worf put down the padd on his chair as he got up, and he walked at a quick step back to Kadohata's side. "Report."

"The *Aventine* just sent over its telemetry from its trip through the subspace tunnel," Kadohata said. "Watch what the aperture does when it opens." She played a computer-simulated animation that graphed the phenomenon's behavior, and pointed out details of the tunnel's interaction with normal space-time. "Something tells me Choudhury won't like that."

"No, she will not," Worf agreed. Eyeing the display

with a more critical eye, he asked, "Will this interfere with our plan to destroy the tunnels?"

"If by interfere you mean scuttle, then yes." Kadohata pointed at a string of data. "Maybe I'm off the mark, but I think these readings mean that collapsing those passages is far more dangerous than we thought." She swiveled her chair toward Worf. "Sir, I'd like to get a second opinion on this data from Commander La Forge and my counterpart on the *Aventine*."

Her request prompted a subtle double take from Worf. "I have never heard you ask Geordi for a second opinion before."

With quiet humility, Kadohata replied, "That's because I've never been on the verge of making a galactically catastrophic mistake before."

Jean-Luc Picard was always grateful for those rare days when everything went according to plan. Alas, this would not be one of those days.

He entered the Deck 1 observation lounge of the *Enterprise* to find Worf standing beside his chair near one end of the table. Next to Worf were La Forge and Elfiki.

On the other side of the table stood Captain Dax, Commander Bowers, and the *Aventine*'s science officer, Lieutenant Helkara. The normally warm-colored, indirect lighting of the conference room was overwhelmed by the violet illumination from the nebula outside its broad, sloped windows.

Picard walked in brisk steps to his chair at the head of the table, and as he sat down he said, "Please, be seated." Everyone settled in at the table and leaned forward. He looked at Dax and asked, "Why has production halted on the minefield?"

"Because it won't work," Dax said. She nodded to her science officer. "Mister Helkara, the details, please?"

The svelte Zakdorn used the touchscreen on the table surface in front of his seat to activate a brief presentation on the wall monitor opposite the windows. "Our sensor telemetry of the subspace tunnels reveals a curious feature of its apertures," he said, narrating as the computer-generated animation on the screen continued. "When they open, they cause a localized disruption of the space-time curvature, to a range of approximately a hundred thousand kilometers. The effect is subtle enough that a starship's navigational system can compensate with little difficulty. Position-stabilized mines, on the other hand . . ."

He triggered a new animation sequence of an aperture opening into a region occupied by the minefield cluster. In a brief blur, the area was swept clean. "The space-time distortion is powerful enough within one thousand kilometers to disperse any minefield we install. Most of the mines will collide with one another and detonate. Any that are left will be brushed aside and ejected from the nebula, into deep space."

"It's possible that a few might remain intact after the aperture closes," Bowers added, "but not enough to stop a Borg ship, or to regenerate the minefield."

"Plus," Helkara said, "the mines that get tossed from the nebula will become hazards to interstellar shipping and travel."

Captain Picard presented a calm and professional demeanor as he looked to his science officer. "Lieutenant Elfiki? Have you had a chance to review this data?"

"Yes, sir," she said. "Our own sims confirmed it. The subspace tunnels' apertures will violently disperse the minefield. Mister Helkara and I think it might be a deliberate safety feature of the passageways."

Worf asked La Forge, "Could the mines be altered to compensate for the distortion?"

The chief engineer shook his head. "No, they just don't have that kind of maneuverability."

"Could we build it in?" Picard asked.

"I doubt it," La Forge said. "We can remove the replication systems, but there still won't be enough room for the hardware and computing power these things'll need to make those kinds of adjustments on the fly. Even if there were, without the self-replication feature, each mine would have to be produced and deployed by us or by the *Aventine*. And once triggered, the field would be unable to regenerate."

Picard scowled, exposing his ire at seeing a perfect plan thwarted by incontrovertible facts. "Very well," he said. "We'll simply have to proceed without a safety net. Reinforcements will arrive within fifty-one hours. Until then, we'll have to hold the line while we work on collapsing the subspace passages."

Elfiki, who rarely spoke up in meetings, seemed cowed as she said to Picard, "Um, Captain?"

"Yes, Lieutenant?"

Her eyes darted nervously from Picard to Helkara and then back again. "There's just one problem with that plan. We should stop trying to collapse the tunnels."

The captain lowered his voice to mask his irritation, but in the hushed conference room, he still sounded upset. "Why?"

She took a deep breath and seemed calmer as she replied. "All the passages resonate at different subharmonics of one interphasic frequency, so any pulse that collapses one of them safely will cause a domino effect that'll collapse the others. But the uncontrolled implosions will have amplified effects that could resonate throughout galactic space-time."

Worf swiveled his chair toward her. "Such as . . . ?"

"Stars could explode," she said. "Whole systems could vanish. Spiral arms could be dispersed into the void."

Helkara added, "Pluck the wrong string on this instrument, sir, and you could wipe out a quadrant in one note."

Certain that he felt a headache forming inside his skull, Picard muttered, "*Merde.*" For a moment he let his mind go quiet, to see if he could hear the voice of the Borg Collective. He sensed no contact, but he felt as if the silence held its own menace. The Borg were out there, lying in ambush, waiting for him, awaiting some final call to action. He was certain of it.

It was Worf's voice that drew him back into the moment.

"What are your orders, Captain?"

Picard sighed. "Captain Dax, suspend production of the minefield—but I want both our crews to continue looking for ways to safely collapse the subspace tunnels."

"Aye, sir," Dax said.

Nodding to the group, Picard added, "I'll take all your recommendations under advisement and review them in my ready room. Captain Dax, I'll contact you as soon as I've reached a decision." He stood, and the others followed suit. "Dismissed."

Captain Dax stood as the door to her ready room opened and Captain Picard strode in. She smiled. "Two visits in one day," she said. "I feel special."

He seemed less enthused about this visit. "I had considered delivering my decision over the comm," he said as he stopped in front of her desk. "However, given the tenor of our last meeting, a follow-up visit seemed warranted."

"I appreciate that," Dax said. She motioned to a chair. "Have a seat, I'll get you something from the replicator."

Picard waved away the offer. "No, thank you." He sat and gestured for her to join him. "I've apprised Admiral Nechayev of our tactical options, and the unacceptable risks of trying to implode the subspace tunnels at this time."

Dax made a small nod. "And what did she say?"

"Teams at Starfleet Research and Development, the Daystrom Institute, and the Vulcan Science Academy are all working to find a safe means of destroying the subspace passages," Picard said. "But until one is found, Admiral Nechayev agrees we should shift the front line of this war away from Federation space."

"A counterattack," Dax said.

"Precisely. Admiral Akaar is petitioning President

Bacco to rally our allies and assemble an expeditionary force to take this fight to the Borg."

Her brow creased with concern. "We can't possibly conquer all of Borg space," Dax said. "So what's the strategy here?"

"A holding action," Picard said. "We advance the front line to the other side of whichever aperture the Borg have been using to reach our space, and there we establish a stronghold. Our task then becomes to hold the line there until we have the means to collapse the passageways. Then we fall back and implode the subspace tunnels behind us."

She frowned as she imagined spending the next several months engaged in a brutal, nerve-wracking battle of attrition. "I'm going to make an educated guess here," she said. "Since we'll need to know which aperture the Borg are using before we can launch a counteroffensive, Admiral Nechayev wants us to start scouting ahead through the passageways until we find it."

"Correct," said Picard.

"Calculating the frequency for opening each aperture takes time," she said. "And it takes processing power. We'll need to suspend our own research into imploding the tunnels if we want to start making scouting runs before our reinforcements arrive."

"My second officer said as much before I beamed over," Picard said, nodding. "So be it. We need to start scouting ahead for the expeditionary force as soon as possible. The *Enterprise* is still fourteen hours away from completing its repairs. How soon can the *Aventine* be ready to proceed?"

Dax activated her desktop monitor and checked

the latest readiness report from Commander Bowers. "We'll be done assisting your engineering teams in about five hours, but it might take longer than that to pick the lock on one of the passageways."

"Then we'd best get started," Picard said as he got up. "We have a long road ahead—but heaven help us all if the Borg strike the next blow before we do."

5

———•———

"Why does Captain Picard hate me? What did I ever do to him?"

"I have no idea, ma'am."

President Nanietta Bacco reclined her chair while her chief of staff, Esperanza Piñiero, stood facing her, barely inside the pool of amber light from the antique lamp on Bacco's desk. Bacco shook her head as she continued to work through her denial. "An expeditionary force? Is he out of his mind?"

"Shostakova doesn't think so," Piñiero said, invoking the name of the secretary of defense. "It's the first time Picard's called for reinforcements since the Klingon civil war."

The office comm made a soft double tone, which was followed by the voice of Bacco's executive assistant, Sivak. *"Madam President,"* the elderly Vulcan man said. *"Secretary Safranski is here."*

"Send him in," Bacco said.

To her right, across the curved room, one of the office's two doors to the reception area was unlocked by her senior protection agent, Steven Wexler, a trim and wiry ex-Starfleet officer who was shorter than average for a human male. What he lacked in height, however, he made up for with speed, security experience, and martial-arts expertise. As the door slid open, a broad slash of bright light poured in. Wexler stepped inside and moved to his left to admit the secretary of the exterior.

Safranski crossed the room in long strides as Wexler stepped out and shut the door behind him, once again steeping the sprawling executive space in deep shadows. Seconds later, as the Rigellian secretary breached the penumbra that surrounded Bacco's desk, he nodded in salutation. "Madam President. We're almost ready."

Piñiero pounced, sparing Bacco the trouble. "How much longer till we get started?"

"Two minutes," he said. "Five at most. I have my undersecretaries wrangling diplomats."

Bacco arched one graying eyebrow in accusation. "And why didn't you wrangle with them?"

"Oh, but I did, Madam President," Safranski said. "I personally rousted Ambassador Zogozin from the Gorn Embassy in Berlin and escorted him back here, to the Roth Dining Room."

The president showed him a forgiving smile. "Criticism withdrawn. Who are we waiting for?"

"Tezrene," Safranski said with weary resignation.

"As always," added Piñiero, who rolled her dark brown eyes. "So much for the stereotype of Tholian punctuality."

Rising from her desk, Bacco replied, "There's a difference between being late out of negligence and being late on purpose. I get the feeling this is a case of the latter."

"Almost certainly," Safranski said.

"What about Ambassador Emra?" asked Piñiero.

The secretary shook his head. "He won't be joining us. The Tzenkethi recalled their entire embassy staff four days ago."

"And when were they going to tell *us*?" Bacco replied.

"When we asked," Safranski said. "Which was roughly fifteen minutes ago." A low buzzing emanated from his torso. He grimaced with embarrassment, reached inside his jacket, and retrieved a personal communicator. "Excuse me, Madam President," he said, accepting the incoming call with a press of his thumb. Into the device, he said, "Safranski. Go." He listened, nodded, and replied, "Good. We're on our way." He thumbed the device into standby, tucked it back under his jacket, and said, "Tezrene just reached the table."

Piñiero looked anxious. "Time to go to work."

"Let's get to it, then," Bacco said, motioning with a sideways nod for Piñiero to follow her. As they walked past Safranski, she said to him, "Thanks for the wrangling."

"My pleasure, Madam President."

The door to the reception area opened a few seconds before Bacco reached it, and as she passed through into the lobby, she squinted against the sudden change in brightness. Agent Wexler fell into stride a few steps ahead of her, on her right. Piñiero remained on her left, matching her relaxed stride and purposeful expression, but the frown dimples in Piñiero's cheeks betrayed her concern about the imminent summit.

They followed Wexler into a turbolift, which he set in motion with a whispered command through his implanted, subaural communicator.

The lift began its brief descent to the thirteenth floor of the Palais de la Concorde. "Esperanza," Bacco said. "The sound of gears turning inside your head is getting deafening. Out with it, before we reach the dining room."

Piñiero said, "Out of nine ambassadors, I can only think of two we can really count on."

Bacco smirked. "That many?" Noting her chief of staff's aggrieved frown, she continued, "K'mtok and who else?"

"I figured Kalavak kind of owes us, after last year."

"Don't be so sure," Bacco said. "Romulans aren't known for their deep sense of gratitude. And if Martok hadn't already ordered his fleets to our border, I'd tell you not to put your chips on K'mtok, either."

The turbolift slowed.

"Shostakova says we can't repel another full-scale attack without at least four of these states as allies."

Bacco harrumphed. "She's being optimistic. We need at least six of them on our side, or this war's already over."

Piñiero asked, "What are the odds of making that happen?"

"No idea. And if you find out, please don't tell me."

The turbolift doors opened, and Piñiero remained behind as Bacco and Wexler proceeded toward a towering scarlet curtain that concealed the lift from the rest of the dining room. Once she was through the artfully concealed gap in the curtains, it was only a few meters' walk to the raised dais on which stood the president's round table. It boasted fourteen seats around its polished, lacquered surface, which was composed of recycled wood recovered from sunken sailing vessels of ancient Earth. As Bacco had expected, the beauty of the table stood in stark contrast to the ire on the faces of those who surrounded it—nine ambassadors, all but one openly seething at having been summoned by Bacco on absurdly short notice.

Ambassador K'mtok was tall, broad, and brutish, even by Klingon standards. It had been Bacco's experience that he loved using his height and prominently sharp incisors to intimidate other humanoids. Kalavak, his counterpart from the Romulan Star Empire, on the other hand, relied on his cold and unyielding stare to unnerve his political opponents. The two diplomats regarded each other with profound suspicion.

The one person at the summit whom Kalavak was pointedly ignoring was Ambassador Jovis, of the Imperial Romulan State. The former warbird commander had been appointed by Empress Donatra several weeks earlier, after the recognition of her government by the Klingon Empire had left the Federation little choice but to demonstrate solidarity with its ally by doing the same. Though Bacco had been careful to keep her government neutral in the internecine Romulan conflict, her decision to establish diplomatic relations with the nascent state had led to unavoidable resentment from Praetor Tal'Aura and, by extension, her diplomatic representative.

On the far side of the table from Bacco were the two ambassadors whose moods and reactions she had the most trouble understanding. Zogozin of the Gorn Hegemony frequently eschewed the use of the universal translator he had been offered, preferring instead to express himself with a series of hisses and growls. The archosaur's facial expression seemed frozen, locked in a perpetual mask of predatory intensity. Because of her years of experience as the governor of Cestus III, Bacco knew that the emotional states of the Gorn were often expressed in thermal changes in the olive-scaled reptilians' faces. Without the ability to see in the infrared spectrum, however, that knowledge did her little good at that moment.

Equally inscrutable to Bacco was the ever-tardy Tholian diplomat, Ambassador Tezrene. Hidden inside a shimmering suit of loose, golden Tholian silk whose interior was filled with searing-hot, high-pressure gases, Tezrene's metallic shriek of a voice was translated by a vocoder that invariably rendered her speech into an ominous monotone.

Derro, the Ferengi Alliance's ambassador to the Federation, was quiet for a change—but only because he found himself caught between the imposing presences of Breen Ambassador Gren and Talarian Ambassador Endar, both renowned as ruthless soldiers.

Then there was the one diplomat at the table who favored Bacco with a polite smile, and he was the one who she found most unnerving of them all—the eloquent and alarmingly intelligent ambassador from the Cardassian Union: Elim Garak.

He lifted his voice and silenced the room. "Everyone! Order, please! Our esteemed host has arrived." He nodded to Bacco. "Madam President. I yield the floor."

"Thank you, Ambassador Garak," Bacco said, uneasy with the realization that he had already positioned himself as having done her a favor, thereby elevating his status in the room. *He's a crafty one,* she reminded herself. *Don't give him an inch.* "And my thanks to all of you for joining me here this evening."

Endar, ever the epitome of boldness, declared, "This is about the Borg invasion of your space."

Bacco made eye contact with the Talarian. "Yes, it is. The situation has escalated, and it now threatens all of us."

Derisive sounds filled the air—a rasping hiss from Zogozin, a crackling squawk from Gren's vocoder, and a shrill scrape of noise from Tezrene. "Do not drag us into your war," said the Tholian ambassador. "Your conflict with the Borg is an internal matter, and of no concern to us."

Tezrene's comments seemed to fuel K'mtok's anger, and it left both the Romulan representatives silent and guarded, watching with caution to see what happened next.

"Nothing could be further from the truth," Bacco replied. "In the past day, the Borg have launched an attack against the Klingon world of Khitomer, and they have a history of striking worlds inside Romulan space. Given the scope of their latest actions, it would be foolish to think their campaign would be limited to Federation planets."

Derro cowered and nodded, as usual aligning himself with the most recent strong opinion spoken aloud. Then he flinched as Gren spoke; the Breen's voice was harsh and mechanical through his helmet's snout-shaped speaker. "The Federation and its Kling-

on allies have a history of provoking the Borg," the
Breen said. "And the Romulans' expansion in the
Beta Quadrant may have done the same. But no Breen
vessel or citizen has ever been a foe of the Borg."

"Of course not," said K'mtok, his gravelly voice
like a cutting saw. "You've been too busy hiding."

Zogozin growled, and then he said through a razor-
sharp smile of gleaming-white fangs, "Why does
Qo'noS still send an ambassador here? Didn't the Federation annex your empire?"

K'mtok reached for his *d'k tahg* and found only its
empty sheath on his belt. "Count yourself lucky," he
said to the Gorn. "If our hosts hadn't disarmed us—"

"Enough!" snapped Garak. "This posturing is use-
less."

Kalavak narrowed his eyes at Garak. "Curious," he
said, the cultured inflection of his voice rife with im-
plied mockery. "I should not have expected the infa-
mous Elim Garak to be such an ardent friend of the
Federation."

Garak's stare bordered on maniacal, and he spoke
with such soft courtesy that his words cut like knives.
"My dear ambassador, I am an ardent friend only of
self-preservation, common sense, and the general wel-
fare of the Cardassian Union. We all share the same
charge—to advocate and negotiate on behalf of our
peoples. Petty bickering does not become us."

"Indeed, it does not," agreed Jovis, who met
Kalavak's glare with his own cool gaze. "The Imperial
Romulan State is willing to put aside past enmities
and seek new alliances."

Unable to contain his contempt for Jovis, Kalavak
asked, "And is Empress Donatra prepared to offer

reparations to the Romulan Empire? Will she release the worlds she took hostage?"

Before Jovis could answer, K'mtok shouldered his way between them and jabbed at Kalavak with his index finger. "If any reparations are to be made, they will be made by your Praetor Tal'Aura for the attack on Klorgat IV!"

"Ah, yes," Kalavak said. "Because the Klingon Empire made itself the guardian of all Remans. What was Martok thinking when he did that? Was he running short of *jeghpu'wI'*?"

Bacco cast a summoning glance at Agent Wexler as K'mtok stalked toward Kalavak.

"At least when Remans go to war, they fight their own battles," the Klingon said, clenching his fists.

As the two ambassadors squared off, Jovis and the others moved back. K'mtok cocked his fist and threw a punch at Kalavak, who deflected the attack, grabbed the Klingon's wrist, and twisted it as he reached for K'mtok's throat.

Then came a blur of movement and the rapid patter of falling blows, and both ambassadors were on the floor, meters apart, still conscious but dazed. Agent Wexler stood between them, his hands empty and his dark suit as pristine as ever.

Bacco's eyes hadn't been fast enough to note the details of Wexler's thrashing of the two men, but she was determined to take advantage of the precious seconds of shocked silence that followed it. "I didn't summon you people here to argue among yourselves," she said. "I called you here to make you understand your role in what's about to become our mutual fight for survival."

She began circling around the table, staring down each ambassador, one by one, as she continued. "The Borg invasion isn't an internal Federation problem, and it's not a localized threat. If the Federation falls, there will be nothing standing between the Borg Collective and all of you. The Borg have no allies. They don't make nonaggression pacts. They honor no truces, no cease-fires. They don't consider the enemy of their enemy to be anything except another target. The Borg conquer, assimilate, and destroy."

As she passed by Kalavak, she saw Wexler help the ambassador back to his feet. K'mtok, in a rare display of humility, permitted Jovis to lend him a hand. Stopping between the two bruised diplomats, she finished, "I'm not asking you to sign any permanent treaties. All I want you to do is be smart enough to know when we ought to unite for our common survival. This isn't politics, goddammit—this is life and death. Take up arms and fight, or lie down and die." She looked around the table and still found it impossible to gauge the nonhumans' reactions by visual cues, but she had no choice but to continue. "It's time to put this to a vote. Show of hands: Who's ready to stand with us? Who's ready to join the fight for survival?"

Bacco lifted her own hand high over her head. It came as no great shock to see K'mtok lift his hand, as well. Then, as she looked around the table, she saw Jovis's hand raised, as well as Endar's. To her surprise, despite his earlier displays of courtesy and support, Garak's hands remained at his sides.

She lowered her hand, and K'mtok, Jovis, and Endar did the same. "All right," she said. "Who votes no?" As she'd expected, Tezrene, Gren, Zogozin, and

Kalavak each lifted a hand or its equivalent to vote nay. To her disappointment, Garak also lifted his hand. That brought Bacco's roving stare to the Ferengi ambassador, Derro, who cowered behind the Breen diplomat.

"Ambassador Derro," Bacco said. "How does the Ferengi Alliance vote?"

"We'd like to abstain, Madam President."

"And I'd like to be able to take a peaceful, month-long vacation on Risa, but we don't always get what we want, do we? This is a binary question, Your Excellency. You're either in, or you're out. Will the Ferengi Alliance stand with the Federation and its allies, or would it prefer to stand alone when the Borg come?"

Eyes darting from the Breen to the Gorn to the Tholian, Derro was like a bag of nervous flinches disguised as a pudgy, big-eared Ferengi. Finally, he stammered, "I, I mean we, I mean—the Ferengi Alliance votes yes."

"Yes to *what*, Ambassador Derro?" prodded Bacco.

"We're in," he said, suddenly firming his resolve against the hostile glares directed at him by Zogozin and the others. "The Ferengi Alliance stands with the Federation."

Bacco grinned. "Welcome aboard, Ambassador." She nodded to the motion's *yea* votes. "Ambassadors K'mtok, Jovis, and Endar. Thank you for your support. I'd like to ask each of you now to take your leave from these proceedings so that you can make arrangements with your governments to deploy ships and personnel to join our expeditionary force against the Borg."

Endar made a small bow in Bacco's direction. "Right away, Madam President. And might I add, it's a pleasure to hear a Federation leader who speaks a language Talarians understand."

"Her knowledge of *thlIngan Hol* is equally impressive," added K'mtok. He nodded to Bacco and followed Endar away from the table. Derro hurried out, close behind them.

Jovis paused long enough to offer his hand to Bacco, who accepted it. "Humans and Romulans have a long and troubled history, Madam President. But it's the hope of Empress Donatra that today we can begin a new era of amity between our peoples."

"You may tell Empress Donatra that the desire is mutual," Bacco said. Jovis bowed his head, released her hand, and slipped away, off the dais and out a side door.

Then, with her allies gone, Bacco turned back toward the table and faced the emissaries of her rivals and foes. "I suggest you all take a seat and get comfortable," she said. "The easy part is over. Now we get down to business."

"We've already made our decisions," Kalavak said, with naked malice. "This summit is over." He moved to step off the dais and found his path blocked by Agent Wexler.

The goateed human agent said, "Sit down, Your Excellency."

Angry chatter buzzed between Gren and Tezrene, and a steady growl resonated from Zogozin. As before, only Garak maintained an untroubled veneer of civility as Kalavak demanded in a heated tone of voice, "Madam President, what is the meaning of this?"

"The meaning, Mister Ambassador, is that we're going to continue discussing this matter until I'm satisfied that all diplomatic possibilities have been exhausted."

A wail of staticky noise spewed from Gren's vocoder, but it was Zogozin who growled with rage and bellowed, "How dare you hold us hostage!"

In her smoothest and most annoyingly diplomatic timbre, Bacco replied, "Don't be so melodramatic, Mister Ambassador. You're not hostages. For the time being, let's just call you 'compulsory guests,' shall we?"

The Gorn roared with indignation, adding his fury to the cacophonous protests of Gren and Tezrene. Kalavak, for his part, fumed in menacing silence.

None of their reactions troubled Bacco. The only one who worried her was Garak.

Because he was utterly serene . . . and smirking.

Admiral Edward Jellico couldn't remember the last time he'd slept. A mixture of adrenaline and desperation fueled his continuing struggle to keep his eyes open.

Sequestered inside his office on the top floor of Starfleet Command Headquarters in San Francisco, he was surrounded by a panorama of holographic displays, all of them crowded with information that had long since begun to bleed together in his vision.

Fleet deployments. Casualty figures. Probable targets. Projected losses. And an ever-growing queue of communiqués to which he had lost the will to respond.

He turned away from his desk and plodded to the replicator on the rear wall. "Coffee, hot, double-strong, cream and sugar," he said, planting one hand against the wall and leaning forward with fatigue. He closed his eyes and for a moment almost drifted into a reverie while listening to the musical drone of his latest caffeine fix swirling into existence. Then, with great effort, he opened his leaden eyelids, picked up his coffee, and shambled back to his desk.

Sagging back into his chair, he knew that he had no one to blame for his circumstances but himself. *You always wanted to be top dog,* he chided himself. *Should've been more careful what you wished for.* He sipped his coffee. The sweet liquid warmth felt good in his scratchy throat—he wondered if he was coming down with a cold—but it did nothing to sharpen his dulled senses.

His door chime sounded.

He winced, groaned, and said, "Come in."

The door slid open, and Admiral Alynna Nechayev stepped inside. She recoiled as soon as she got a good look at him. "Sir, have you been here since last night?"

"I liked you better when you called me Ed."

Nechayev moved farther into his office, and the door closed behind her. "You sound terrible, sir. Let me call a medic."

"No," he said, his voice roughened by the pain in his throat. He planted his stubbled face in his hands and sighed. "They'll just tell me I need to sleep."

"Might be sound advice, sir."

"Dammit," he said, looking up. "Stop calling me that."

She put on a mocking air of affront. "Well, excuse me, but you *are* the appointed C-in-C, aren't you?"

"Yes, and I'm giving you a direct order: When we're alone, *call me Ed*." He tried to scowl and ended up grinning instead.

"Aye-aye, Ed," said Nechayev, smiling back at him. "Permission to speak freely, Ed?"

He was too tired to argue, even in jest. "Oh, go ahead."

"You're hanging on too tightly," she said. "Loosen up. Take a few hours' downtime—you need it."

His head lolled backward against the headrest of his chair. "Not yet," he said. "There's too much to do."

"And you're surrounded by thousands of highly trained officers who are ready to get the job done," she replied. "You need to delegate, Ed. You can't fight this war by yourself, no matter how much you might want to." She circled behind his desk and eyed the wraparound wall of holographic data. Pointing at one screen after another, she said, "Let Nakamura handle deployment orders. T'Lara can cut through the red tape with the Council. I'll take over on strategic planning."

"Hang on, now," Jellico said. "I haven't authorized—"

"Ed," she cut in, "how long has it been since you took off your boots?" She paused while Jellico looked down at his own feet, and then she continued, "By my best estimates, you've been awake and cooped up inside this office for almost sixty-one hours. Have you taken off your shoes even once?"

He tried to make sense of her question and failed. "What are you driving at?"

"Take off your boots and tell me what condition your feet are in," she said. "I'll wait." The blond woman folded her arms and stared at him, her expression stern and unyielding.

Ignoring the pain in his back, he bent forward, reached down, and struggled to pull off his left boot. "This is the dumbest thing I've ev—" The smell hit his nostrils and silenced him. Then he noticed the itching, burning sensation that spread like a brush fire from his toes across the top of his foot.

"One to go," Nechayev quipped.

"No thanks," Jellico said.

His longtime friend and colleague shook her head. "Ed, you're so tired, you couldn't remember to air out your boots once a day, and you gave yourself a case of what used to be called trench foot. Now get serious— if you couldn't see *that* coming, how ready do you think you are to plan a major, multinational counteroffensive against the Borg?"

Jellico's head drooped as he felt the inevitability of his surrender close in on him. He really had lost count of the hours as the Borg's invasion had escalated, and it was time for him to admit he'd gone not only to the limits of his effectiveness but far beyond. And he was simply so very, very tired.

"I wish I'd never been promoted," he said grimly.

Nechayev nodded sympathetically. "I understand," she said. "Everything seemed so much easier when all we had to worry about was the ship under our feet."

"Yeah, that too," Jellico said. "But mostly I meant that if I hadn't leapfrogged over you in the chain of command, you could be the one sitting here with trench foot instead of me."

All traces of mirth and charity left her face as she departed his office. "Go home and get some sleep."

Seven of Nine was alone in a room filled with strangers.

She knew their names and their titles, but that was all. In the ways of knowing that mattered, they were mysteries to her.

"We need to see what's worked so far and figure out what'll work next," said Raisa Shostakova, the secretary of defense. The highest-ranking person in the Palais de la Concorde conference room, she was human by ancestry but Pangean by birth, and her high-gravity upbringing showed in her short, squat physique. "The crew of the *Ranger* innovated a phase-shifted attack at Khitomer—"

"To which the Borg have already adapted," Seven cut in.

Jas Abrik, the senior security adviser to President Bacco, and Seven's direct superior in the governmental chain of command, replied in a tense whisper, "Let her finish first."

Shostakova continued, "And, as noted, a subsequent attempt by the *Excalibur* to repeat the tactic failed. Captain Calhoun and his crew compensated by creating a salvo of variably phased quantum torpedoes, but we have evidence the Collective has already learned to counter this, too."

"Undoubtedly," muttered Seven, who noted Abrik's glare and added in a confidential tone, "I am reasonably certain she was finished." Abrik rolled his eyes and looked away.

Seven held her tongue as the meeting dragged on, rehashing one failed weapon after another. Every time she opened her mouth to offer advice, Abrik silenced her with a look and a wave of his hand. It perplexed her to wonder why these seemingly intelligent individuals were so convinced that the formula for success must lie hidden in the legacy of their myriad failures.

She longed for her days aboard *Voyager* in the Delta Quadrant. Despite the awkwardness and loneliness that had come with her separation from the Collective, she had been able to rely on Kathryn Janeway to show her the way back to a human life. It had been as if Janeway had adopted her, instinctively replacing the mother who had been taken from Seven by the Borg.

Then, after all the travails Janeway had endured to lead her crew home, she herself had been ripped away from Seven by the Borg, and turned into the enemy she had so despised and against which she had struggled so ferociously.

That loss had left Seven with no comfort except her aunt, Irene Hansen, who now was being stolen from her, day by day, by an incurable, progressive neurological disease. Watching her aunt's persona disintegrate was like witnessing a slow-motion assimilation. *Soon, I will have no one left,* Seven realized.

An irritating voice disrupted her lonely reflections.

Participating in the meeting via one of the conference room's wall-mounted viewscreens, Admiral Elizabeth Shelby pursed her lips into a narrow frown. *"What about regenerative phasers?"*

The president's Starfleet Intelligence liaison, Captain Holly Hostetler Richman, shook her head. "Sorry, Admiral. Those failed in the Battle of Acamar."

Shelby huffed angrily. *"But the transphasic torpe-does still work, don't they? Why are we being so stingy with them?"*

"Admiral Nechayev's orders," Shostakova replied. "She thinks if we use them too much, the Borg might develop a resistance, like bacteria to antibiotics."

The fair-haired admiral folded her arms. *"Oh, give me a break,"* she said, her mouth hinting at a sneer. *"How do you develop immunity to something that kills in one shot?"*

Galled by Shelby's ignorance, Seven replied, "Even death is a learning experience for the Borg. Every time your new weapon destroys another cube, the Collective learns more about it. It is only a matter of time before they adapt a defense."

"You almost sound like you admire them, Miss Hansen," said Shelby, whose narrowed stare conveyed utter contempt for Seven.

It wasn't Shelby's glare that stoked Seven's ire. "I prefer to be addressed as Seven," the former Borg drone said, the coldness of her warning leaving no room for debate. The use of her former name was a privilege Seven reserved for her aunt.

Shostakova picked up a padd from the conference table and used it to call up a tactical display on a secondary viewscreen. "Let's move on, please, everyone," she said. "I suggest we leave tactics and weapons development to the experts. For now, I'd like to stay focused on big-picture strategy. Any ideas?"

Seven folded her hands on the table as she spoke up. "Yes, in fact. Redeploy all your forces to the Azure Nebula."

Abrik, seated next to her, coughed as he aspirated a small mouthful of his coffee. Wiping the splatter from his chin and the front of his shirt, he replied, *"All of them?"*

"If you are committed to exploiting the transphasic torpedo to its fullest extent, you will have to land a decisive blow as quickly as possible," Seven said.

Shelby looked horrified by the suggestion. *"Your plan would leave our core systems completely undefended."*

"They are all but undefended now," Seven said. "If you wish to prevail against the Borg, you should do exactly as Captain Picard has suggested—go on the attack. Once the Borg enter your space, the momentum of the battle will turn against you."

Hostetler Richman threw a dubious look Seven's way. "If we do send a force through one of those anomalies and find a Borg invasion fleet, how many ships are we likely to face?"

"That depends," Seven said.

"On . . . ?" prodded Shostakova.

Turning to the secretary, Seven replied, "On whether the Borg intend merely to destroy Earth, or to destroy every world in the Federation and those of all its allies."

"Could they really do that?" asked Hostetler Richman.

Seven met the woman's fearful stare. "Yes. They can."

"Then we ought to seek every advantage," interjected Captain Miltakka, the president's liaison to Starfleet Research and Development. The Rigellian amphiboid got up from his chair, picked up a padd, and changed the tactical display on the secondary screen. He pointed out details as he spoke. "Though our ships' phasers are not compatible with transphasic modulation, their shield emitters can be. I have compiled some upgrade plans that should be compatible with the defensive systems of most of the vessels currently active in Starfleet." As he sat down, Seven mused that the mottled skin on the back of his head reminded her of a Borg's complexion.

"That is a good first step," Seven began. "However, it will not be enough. To halt the Borg invasion on your own terms, you will have to resort to more drastic measures."

Suspicious stares fell upon Seven from every direction. It was Abrik who dared to ask, "Such as . . . ?"

"You will need to replicate the thalaron weapon that the Remans made for Shinzon," Seven said.

Abrik shot back, "Are you out of your mind?"

She was barraged by overlapping rebukes from all sides. "It'd violate our treaty with the Romulans," said Shostakova. Shelby protested, *Do you have any idea what will happen if the Borg capture it?* Hostetler Richman said, "Never mind the risk of it being copied by the Tholians," and Miltakka added, "It'd defeat the whole pcint of destroying it in the first place!"

"It is your only chance," Seven said, her voice sharp enough to cut through the opposition.

"It's illegal," Shostakova replied. "It's *immoral*."

"That is irrelevant," Seven said. "Without it, you do not possess the firepower to stop a full Borg attack fleet."

Her insistence was met by denial in the form of shaking heads and closed eyes. *They do not trust me,* she brooded. *None of them wants to be the first to agree with me.*

"When you find the Borg's staging area, you will have only one chance to destroy it," Seven said. "The only weapon you possess that is powerful enough to do so in a single shot, and to which the Borg have not yet adapted, is the thalaron array."

Shostakova slammed her palms flat on the tabletop. "I don't care, Seven," she said. "Thalaron weapons are an abomination, which is why we signed a treaty outlawing them. The Federation won't endorse the use of genocidal tactics."

"Then I cannot help you," Seven said, "because the Borg have no such reservations—and they will exterminate you."

1519

6

———

There were no hours or days in Axion, only what felt to Erika Hernandez like interminable years of night as the metropolis made its slow transit of the void.

Hernandez and her fellow survivors from the *Columbia* basked in the honeyed glow of artificial sunlight. An array of solar lamps had been installed above the courtyard that lay between their respective living quarters. In the long drag of time since they had become stranded in the past, Inyx had arranged new, more spacious accommodations for them at "ground level" in the city, to remove the need for the Caeliar's energy-intensive version of a turbolift.

The last piece of advice that Inyx had given to Hernandez and Fletcher was that they should pass the time by taking up art. Hernandez had yet to find a creative outlet that suited her, but Fletcher had submerged herself in her new hobby: writing. Using an ultrathin polymer tablet and a feather-light stylus, she had lately spent most of her waking hours scribbling and revising a novel that she refused to let anyone else read until it was finished. Remembering the often muddled state of Fletcher's mission reports, Hernandez had decided to keep her expectations low for Fletcher's prose.

"What's another word for 'oozing'?" Fletcher asked, and Hernandez's hope of reading one more great novel in her lifetime diminished by another degree. Before anyone could answer, Fletcher looked to Valerian, who sat in an arched window portal, staring out at a cityscape surrounded by a star-speckled dome of deep space. "Sidra, you must know a good synonym for 'oozing.'"

Valerian said nothing. Her face was blank, and she didn't give any sign of acknowledging Fletcher. The young Scotswoman sat with her knees against her chest, arms wrapped tightly around her legs, face half hidden from view. It had been a long time since she had said anything to anyone. She often had to be coaxed and half-pulled from her residence by Dr. Metzger for regular sessions of solar therapy, which all four women needed in order to stave off the onset of seasonal affective disorder and make at least a passing attempt at preserving some of their bodies' natural diurnal rhythms.

Metzger, who was meditating in a lotus position an arm's reach from the younger woman, opened one eye and glared with mild annoyance. She extended her arm and poked Valerian. "Sidra," she said. "Veronica asked you a question."

The mentally fragile redhead recoiled from Metzger's touch. Trembling, she cast fearful looks at her shipmates, and then she bolted from the window and jogged across the courtyard and out an open door, disappearing around a corner into the city beyond.

Fletcher looked mortified. "Should I go after her?"

"I'll do it," Metzger said, standing slowly.

"Be careful," Hernandez said. "If she seems like she might be out of control, ask the Caeliar for help."

Metzger's mood darkened. "I don't need their help," she said, and then she was out the door, in slow pursuit of the runaway communications officer who didn't talk anymore.

Silence descended once more on the courtyard.

Hernandez sat on a bench and watched Fletcher tapping at a virtual keyboard on her tablet, committing words to the device's memory, losing herself in a world of her own making. It was hard for Hernandez not to envy her friend. Whatever aesthetic value her writing might possess or lack, it had one undeniable virtue: it offered Fletcher a means of escape, however temporary or illusory, from the monotony of their imprisonment.

Lucky her, mused Hernandez.

At one end of the courtyard sat a mutilated block of granite and a set of diamond-edged chisels that Hernandez had found too unwieldy for comfort. She had chipped and chopped and hammered at the dark slab, at first without even an image in her mind of what she meant it to become. Choosing a shape—in this case, a spiral—hadn't helped, even after Fletcher had offered her teasing, inexpert advice, "Just chip away everything that doesn't look like a spiral."

Music hadn't come naturally to Hernandez, either. Inyx had crafted her a Caeliar instrument that seemed reminiscent of an old Earth device known as a theremin, but the only sounds she had been able to elicit from it had sounded like the crystal-shattering whines of feedback or chaotic, bloodcurdling wails.

She had told herself she would keep trying to master the instrument despite her difficulties—and then she'd produced two unnerving pulses of sound in quick succession. The first had been a high-frequency screech that sent torturous vibrations through her teeth; the second was an almost inaudible low-frequency drone that had shaken her from the inside out and made it imperative that she wash her uniform jumpsuit a few days sooner than she'd planned.

Other artistic talents whose total absence Hernandez had confirmed included painting, drawing, and singing.

The fact that Caeliar society had abandoned the theatrical arts more than a thousand years earlier had tempted her to focus on acting. Even if she turned out to be the worst actress in Axion, as the *only* actress in the city she would also, by default, be its best. As her comrades had pointed out, however, they would likely be her only audience, and they had no desire to suffer through whatever one-woman dramatic atrocity she might be tempted to inflict upon them.

So she passed her days as stagnant as the windless city.

She thought of Fletcher writing, Metzger meditating, and Valerian going mad by leaps and bounds. The future, which she constantly reminded herself was a replay of the past, promised more of the same. Routine without purpose. Night without end.

"I'm taking a walk," she said.

Fletcher didn't look up from her tablet as she waved. "Have a nice time. See you at dinner."

Leaving the blonde to her unfolding fiction, Hernandez left the courtyard through the same door by which Valerian had fled. She walked away into the ashen sprawl of the silent metropolis.

A new understanding came to her as she walked. She'd failed at art not for lack of talent or effort, but because she had a greater need for something else. Not a hobby—a job. She didn't want to just pass the time anymore; she wanted to contribute. To do something that mattered.

Ordemo Nordal would likely object. So would the Quorum. That left her only one option.

She had to persuade Inyx.

"I fail to see what meaningful contribution you might make to our efforts," Inyx said, his ungainly stride swaying his body side to side like a sailing vessel at sea. "You lack the knowledge and technical expertise to assist us."

"Only because I haven't been taught," said Hernandez, who followed him through a glowing, hexagonal tunnel.

The Caeliar scientist made a derisive-sounding bleat of air from the tubules on either side of his bulbous cranium. "Perhaps, if your species was longer-lived, we could impart the fundamentals of our Great Work, but it would be for naught."

"Why?"

"Our tools," he said. "They are not operated with buttons and levers and dials, as on your vessel. We direct them with infinitely more subtle measures, by means of the gestalt."

Unfazed, she insisted, "So? Teach me to do that."

Near the end of the corridor he paused and looked

back at her. "I doubt that your mind would survive the experience."

He led her out of the passage and into a vast chamber deep inside the city's foundation. Like the corridor they had traversed, the room was hexagonal in shape, resembling a single cell from a honeycomb laid flat. The walls, ceiling, and floor shimmered with stars. For a moment, Hernandez wondered if the room even had a floor; for all she knew, this was a vantage point on the reaches of space beneath Axion. As she stepped forward, however, her perception of stars passing underfoot was too swift for normal parallax with very distant objects, and she concluded that it was a starmap.

Several clusters of Caeliar huddled in ostensibly arbitrary locations throughout the chamber. Inyx walked toward one trio, who stood in a tight group several dozen meters away.

"Is this where the Great Work gets done?" she asked.

"Its current phase, yes," Inyx said. "Though a separate inquiry of equal importance is also in progress."

His choice of terms intrigued her. "Equal importance? What ranked high enough to horn in on the Great Work?"

"I prioritized an investigation into the temporal effects of Erigol's destruction. One of our other cities traveled to the distant past, and its descendants triggered our cataclysm. Another city might have made a similar though less drastic journey, as we did. If our analysis indicates that the past has been altered, then we might need to risk taking steps to prevent the catastrophe, regardless of the paradoxes it might create."

Stepping over an asymmetrical red nebula, Hernandez said, "How would you be able to tell? If the past changed, wouldn't we have changed with it?"

"Not necessarily," Inyx said. "All our cities have long been temporally shielded to guard against potential changes in the timeline. Our data archive contains detailed records of this era's chroniton signature. By comparing the universe's current chroniton dispersal pattern to the one we have on record for this period, we can identify any variances that would suggest the timeline has been changed by the passage of our cities into the past. If significant changes are detected, the Quorum might consider initiating corrective measures."

"Sounds important," Hernandez said.

"Very much so."

Looking around at the murmuring groups of Caeliar standing far apart in the massive chamber, she remarked, "Too bad the others don't seem to share your sense of urgency."

"By our standards, this is a frantic burst of activity."

They were a few meters from the trio, which turned to face them in unison, like birds changing direction in flight. The three Caeliar bowed to Inyx, who reciprocated. Then all four of the aliens began making noises that were part groan, part hum. The tonal pitch of the chorus oscillated, and the intensity of the vibrato rose and fell. As quickly as it had started, it stopped, and Inyx said to the others, "Are you certain?"

"Yes," said the shortest and bulkiest of them.

The tallest, who was nearly three meters in height,

added, "I verified the results several times. We await your permission to apprise the gestalt."

"Proceed," said Inyx, who turned away from the trio and resumed walking.

Hernandez hurried after him. "What'd they say?"

"They have already concluded the temporal analysis," he said. "There is no variance in the chroniton signature."

She didn't know whether his reluctance to elaborate was evidence of boredom with her questions or a misguided display of faith in her ability to know what the hell he was talking about. "Okay, no variance," she said. "What does that mean?"

"It means that all is as it was, and is as it should be." This time he seemed to sense her unspoken desire for clarification. "Because the passage of our cities and the others into the past has resulted in no detectable change of the timeline, we have deduced that these events must have occurred in the timeline that we consider standard. Consequently, the destruction of Erigol and our own exile in the past appear to be part of the natural flow of events. Therefore, no steps will be taken to alter the outcome we have witnessed. Instead, we will move forward with the Great Work from this new vantage point."

He was still a few steps ahead of her, so she knew he couldn't see her jaw hanging open in disbelief. "How can you do nothing? You know that a few hundred years from now your world and millions of your people will be destroyed, and you're just gonna let it happen *again*? Why?"

"Because that is the shape into which time has unfolded," Inyx said, as if he was explaining the matter to a child. "Once time has chosen its form, it is not our place to change it."

"So, you're saying you won't save your people because it's their destiny to get blown up?"

He stopped and turned back to face her. "That is a crude reduction of a complex issue, but in essence . . . yes."

She shook her head. "Sorry, but I'll take free will over fatalism any day."

"As would we," Inyx said. "Free will exists in the present moment. But the present is always in flux, slipping on one side into the past while pulling from another on the leading edge of the future. We only accept as predestined the events that we know will transpire between this moment and the last moment before we entered the past. When we return to that moment in our subjective future, we will once again treat time's shape as a revelation in progress. Until then, our work continues."

Inyx walked away, and Hernandez stayed close behind him. He stopped in the middle of a broad swath of what seemed to be empty space in the middle of the starmap. When he squatted to study an image on the floor more closely, his long, bony legs folded up on either side of his narrow torso; he reminded Hernandez of a grasshopper perched on a lawn. She watched with great curiosity as he tapped at several points of light on the floor. Ghostly symbols twisted upward from each mote, as if written in curling smoke. They snaked between his tendril-like fingers and were absorbed into his mottled gray-blue skin.

"What are you looking for?" she asked.

He rested his long arms across his knees and gazed

at the map of the sky inscribed under his feet. "A new world to call home," he said. "A system where we can finish the Great Work."

"Well, there must be plenty to choose from," she said. "Hell, if the Drake Equation is right, there are millions of Minshara-class planets you can colonize."

The Caeliar scientist straightened and shuffled his huge, three-toed feet. "It is not so simple," he said. "We have many criteria for a world on which to settle. Its star must be the right age, neither too young nor too old. Its planets cannot be too recently formed to sustain life, nor must they be past the ability to do so; they cannot be geothermally inert, nor overly volatile. A viable star system will need to be rich in many rare elements and compounds. Most important of all, no part of the star system can be populated by sentient life, indigenous or otherwise, in any form—including cosmozoans."

"I'm sorry, hang on," Hernandez said. "Cosmo-what?"

After making a few clicking sounds, Inyx said, "My apologies, I'd forgotten your species hasn't encountered their kind yet. The galaxy is home to a great variety of spaceborne life-forms, many of which are sentient. They tend to thrive near stellar clusters, so we are focusing our search on star systems that are relatively remote in nature, in order to avoid them."

Hernandez quipped, "Glad to see you're not being picky."

"If we are selective, it is not without reason," Inyx said. "At this point, our discretion is as much for our privacy as for the safety of the galaxy at large. We must remain unknown."

"Good thing you're not doing anything conspicuous, then," she said. "You know, like moving an entire city through space."

Inyx regarded her with his pupil-free eyes. "Do you think that because I am physically incapable of what you call laughter, I don't understand humor? Or sarcasm?"

"I hadn't given it that much thought," Hernandez said. "Mostly, I just like ribbing you."

"I see," he said. "If I agree to teach you the methods of our search for a new homeworld, and include you in the process, I would appreciate fewer gibes at my expense."

She nodded. "Sounds fair. When do we start?"

Gesturing at the vast, star-flecked chamber that surrounded them, he said, "We already have."

Dinner was finished, and Fletcher, Hernandez, and Metzger sat together at a round table in their courtyard. As usual, Valerian had refused invitations to come out and eat, preferring instead to sequester herself and mumble the story of her-life-that-was at the walls inside her bedroom.

"Your turn," the captain said to Fletcher, who picked at the remains of yet another bland and texturally unsettling Caeliar interpretation of vegetable lasagna.

Setting down her fork, Fletcher thought for a moment and said, "Meat, to be honest. Tonight, it's meat."

The game was called *What do you miss most tonight?*

DAVID MACK

Fletcher forced another bite of the slightly soupy casserole into her mouth, swallowed, and looked at Metzger. "You're up, Jo," she said.

The doctor, who had already cleared her plate, was sitting with her arms folded behind her head. She leaned back in her chair and stared at the stars that were always overhead. "Constellations I recognize," she said. "Back to you, Erika."

Fletcher had lost track of when they had all started calling one another by their first names. It had begun not long after they had surrendered to the proposition that the four of them would spend the rest of their lives here, in this alien city roaming deep space, lost in the gray mists of history.

"Wine," Hernandez said, closing her eyes. "Red or white. Merlot, Chianti, Rioja, Cabernet, Zinfandel, Riesling, Malbec, Pinotage, Chardonnay, Sauvignon Blanc. All of them. I'd do anything for one glass of good Burgundy right now." She tilted her head back, closed her eyes, and sighed. "Go, Ronnie."

Certain subjects had always felt too awkward to broach, given their circumstances, but the truth was straining to be free of Fletcher's conscience. "I'm sorry, I have to say it. I bloody miss men. The way they look, the way they sound, the way they *feel*. I'd trade you ten cases of wine for one strappin' lad willin' to give his ferret a run, know what I mean?" She felt a bit guilty when Metzger and Hernandez glared at her, but the damage was done. "I know, I know. We're not supposed to bring it up. I said I was sorry."

"And then you brought it up anyway," Metzger said.

Hernandez held up a hand and cut in, "It's fine. We had to talk about it eventually. We can't ignore it forever."

"I can," Metzger said, rising from the table. "If you two want to negotiate some kind of deviant relationship, that's your business, but count me out." The gray-haired physician walked away to go check on Valerian, at whose side Metzger had spent most of her waking hours since the younger woman's breakdown.

Fletcher rolled her eyes. "Back to the river in Egypt."

"What's wrong with you?" Hernandez said. "Couldn't you just lie and say you missed Vegemite? Or margaritas? Or jazz?"

"I do miss margaritas and jazz, but you can keep the Vegemite," Fletcher replied. "Look, this is daft. We're all going crazy in this place without any lads"— she cast a look in the direction of the departed doctor—"those of us who don't hate them, anyway, and I think it's mad we can't say it." She kicked away her chair as she stood and hollered to the silent heavens, "I want a hard shag, and I don't care who knows it!"

With droll calm, Hernandez said, "Keep your voice down. You'll scare the natives." She motioned for Fletcher to sit. As the XO pulled her chair back to the table, the captain continued, "If you're really this hard up, I'm sure we can work something out."

"No offense, Erika," Fletcher said, "you're flash and all, but I just don't see us that—"

"Not with me," Hernandez chided her. "Remember what you told me about the Caeliar—a long time back, before the disaster? How they shape-change and mimic us? Maybe one of them can stand in for one of the MACOs." She put on a teasing smile. "I know I saw you checking out Yacavino a few times."

Horrified, Fletcher stared aghast at Hernandez. "Are you mad? You think I'd let myself get rogered by one of *them*?"

"Funny, I thought some of the MACOs were rather dashing."

"Not the MACOs!" She lifted her chin and looked away to indicate she was talking about the Caeliar. "*Them.* The enemy."

Hernandez rolled her eyes. "Don't you think you're being a little bit melodramatic?"

"Oh, I see. They give you a job, and suddenly you forget they're holding us prisoner, hundreds of years and thousands of light-years from home." She regretted it as soon as she'd said it. *Apparently, it's my night for putting my foot in my mouth.*

"I haven't forgotten anything, Ronnie," Hernandez said. "Earth, my ship, my crew . . . Jonathan. Do you really think I could forget him? The way he used to touch me? Or the sound of him whispering in my ear when I was half asleep?" A bitter mood replaced her previous joviality. "We're all stir-crazy here, Ronnie, but torturing ourselves over it doesn't make it any better. Ranting about how badly you want to get laid doesn't make the days go by any faster, either. If you want to let off steam, go running. Do a thousand pull-ups. Find a place with a nice echo and take up primal screaming. Or shut your door and just be your own best friend, like the rest of us do."

Contrite, Fletcher sank back into her seat. She draped her limbs over the seat as if she were a rag doll. "Sorry. Guess I was a bit 'round the bend there."

"Forget it. We're all bound to snap sooner or later. You just got it out of the way early."

Fletcher chuckled softly through an abashed smile. When it faded, she felt a crushing sense of loneliness pressing in on her from all sides. "Erika? Tell me the truth. . . . We're really never going home, are we?"

Hernandez's smile was sympathetic and bitter-sweet.

"Never say never."

2381

7

———

Worf was surprised by the sharpness of Captain Picard's voice as the captain dropped the padd on his ready room desk and said, "These numbers are completely unacceptable, Mister La Forge."

The chief engineer shrugged and lifted his palms in a gesture of surrender. "They're the best we have, Captain. All engineering teams are working around the clock, even the walking wounded. We're at the limit."

"Then go past the limit, Geordi," Picard said. "Suspend any other operations that use computer power and focus everything on the task at hand." He picked up the padd again and waved it as an object of contempt. "If we have to spend six hours trying to open each of these passages—"

La Forge interrupted, "It may take longer than that, sir. On this side, we have the *Aventine* to help us. Once we split up, whichever ship goes through the tunnel will have to calculate the return frequency on its own. If we're lucky—"

Picard held up his hand. "Split up?"

The chief engineer looked to Worf, who explained, "Until reinforcements arrive, either we or the *Aven-*

tine will have to remain here, as a sentinel against the Borg."

The captain nodded. "I see."

"In any case," La Forge said, "processing power is only half the problem. After we analyzed the logs from the runabout that opened the passageway the *Aventine* used, we found out that the creature who'd hijacked the runabout altered its deflector output somehow. He stabilized the subspace aperture by emitting a triquantum wave—something we're not set up to do."

Folding his hands together, Picard asked, "How do we plan to remedy this?"

"I'm working with the *Aventine*'s chief engineer to design and install some upgrades to our sensor grids. We should be ready to start opening tunnels in less than three hours."

"Very well," Picard said. He turned to Worf. "How soon will the *Enterprise* be battle ready, Number One?"

With grim regret, Worf replied, "It will require at least another eight hours."

"Why so long?" Picard asked.

Worf traded a knowing look with La Forge before he answered, "Personnel and resources are currently . . . limited, sir."

La Forge added, "What he's too polite to say is that I've commandeered all the engineers and damage-control teams to make the modifications to the sensor grid. When those are done, we'll move the tactical system repairs to the front of the line."

"See that you do, Mister La Forge. If we're to stay behind as sentries, I'd prefer not to do so unarmed."

The chief engineer nodded. "I understand, sir."

"Dismissed, Mister La Forge. Mister Worf, stay a moment."

Worf clasped his hands behind his back as La Forge left the captain's ready room. When the door closed, Picard said to Worf, "I want your honest opinion, Worf. Is this crew really ready to face the Borg?"

"They have already done so several times," Worf said, perplexed by the captain's question.

Shaking his head, Picard said, "I'm not talking about starship combat, Number One. I'm referring to close-quarters combat. There's no telling what we'll find when we uncover the tunnel that leads to the Borg's invasion staging area. Starships might not be enough to win the day—we may find ourselves tasked with infiltrating and destroying anything from a unimatrix complex to a transwarp hub. So, if it comes to that, I need to know: In your professional opinion, are Lieutenant Choudhury's security personnel equal to the task?"

"Some are," Worf said. "Some are not. But until they are tested in battle, there is no way to know who will falter."

Picard seemed dubious. "Simulations—"

"—are unreliable," Worf said. "Some trainees will not commit themselves, masking their true abilities. Others will indulge in bravado, inflating their egos while learning nothing. The only true measure of a warrior is combat."

"Very well," Picard said. "Putting aside the readiness of the individuals, how would you rate the department as a whole?"

"Exceptional, sir."

The captain leaned forward. "Splendid. Tell Lieutenant Choudhury to start scheduling drills for her most experienced combat personnel. I want multiple small units capable of independent action. See to it that they're briefed on all our latest intelligence about the absorptive properties of Borg cubes—just in case. And, at the risk of fueling their bravado, have them conduct intensive training simulations as soon as we get the holodecks functional."

"For what objective should they be trained, sir?"

Picard's aquiline visage tensed, and his frown lines deepened as he said, "To seek and destroy the Borg Queen."

The door sighed open ahead of Bowers, and he walked into the *Aventine*'s gymnasium to find Captain Dax laboring to swing a *bat'leth* through a simple series of parries and strikes. She wore an off-white gi, and her feet were bare. As the pixyish Trill woman pivoted through a turning slash, she saw Bowers and lowered the crescent-shaped Klingon blade.

"Sam," she said, sounding exhausted and annoyed.

"Captain." He nodded at the *bat'leth*. "Looks a bit on the heavy side for you, don't you think?"

"It was a gift," she said. "One of these years, I'll get the hang of it, the way Jadzia did."

He decided not to mention that, from all accounts he had heard, Jadzia had been several inches taller than Ezri and had begun her martial-arts training at a much younger age. "I just wanted to let you know we're less than two hours away from our first scouting run. Helkara says we'll have the ingress frequency for the nearest tunnel by 2100 at the latest, and Leish-man's team is almost done modifying the sensor grid."

Dax plodded to a bench along the side of the com-partment, rested the *bat'leth* against it at an angle, and picked up a towel to dab the perspiration from her forehead and the nape of her neck. "How long until the *Enterprise* is ready?"

"Not till 0200, but they have to hang back to watch for the Borg, anyway," Bowers said, partly distracted by the exquisite workmanship of the engraving on the side of the *bat'leth* and the fine temper of its edge. "We're on our own for the first run."

She noticed his attention to the blade, and she smirked. "Want to spar?" she asked, toweling sweat from her short, dark hair. "We can replicate one for you, go a few rounds. . . ."

"No, I don't think so," he said with a self-deprecating grin and a wave of his hand. "Not really my weapon of choice."

The captain shrugged. "What's your preference? I'm flexible."

Bowers wondered if he was just imagining a note of manic desperation in Dax's manner. Then he saw the anxiety in her wide-eyed gaze, and he knew that some-thing wasn't right. "Are you feeling okay, Captain?"

"We have the gym to ourselves, Sam, you can drop the rank."

Her attempts at familiarity felt like more deflection, but if it helped her open up, he'd take advantage of her offer. "It just seems a bit weird, this sudden need to spar. Have you tried using the holodeck?"

"What's the point of sparring in the holodeck? There's no satisfaction in it." She tossed her towel on the bench, picked up the *bat'leth,* and lugged it back to the middle of the gym.

He watched her arms quake with the effort of heaving the blade level with her shoulders and holding it steady. "Why can't you get satisfaction sparring on the holodeck?" he asked. When she made no attempt to answer, he speculated, "Is it because a holodeck character can't hang out in the lounge and tell the crew he got his ass kicked by the captain?"

She closed her eyes as her concentration broke, and the sword dragged her buckled arms halfway to the deck. "Goddammit, Sam," she exclaimed. "I'm just trying . . . I just want to get my focus back so I can feel like I'm in control." Dax turned away, and then she dropped the *bat'leth.* She planted one hand on her hip and used the other to cover her eyes. "Maybe you won't understand this, but I feel like I'm faking my way through every minute of the day, and that everyone around me knows it." Her hand dropped from her face, which was pale except for the circles under her eyes. "Five weeks ago, I was the second officer on this ship. Third in the chain of command. Then one direct hit by the Borg, and it was like I was watching Tiris Jast die on the *Defiant* all over again."

Bowers recalled the death of *Defiant's* female Bolian commander, during an attack by rogue Jem'Hadar ships several years earlier. That incident had been a key moment for Ezri, then still a counselor. She'd tapped into the Dax symbiont's past lifetimes of experience, taken charge of the *Defiant,* and proved adept at rising to the challenges of command.

"If your moment on this ship was anything like the one you had on *Defiant,* you deserve to be in the center seat," he told her, because it seemed to be what she needed to hear.

Dax shook her head. "It wasn't just that incident. It feels like my whole career's been like that. Just one lucky coincidence after another. What if they'd found another host for the Dax symbiont on the *Destiny*? Then I'd just be Ezri Tigan now, counselor un-extraordinaire. If Jast hadn't been killed in that attack on Deep Space 9, I might still be wearing medical-division blue. Or what if Captain Dexar or Commander Tovak had survived the Battle of Acamar?"

Bowers rolled his eyes and sighed. "Bullshit." Her head snapped toward him, and the fiery anger in her eyes confirmed that he had her attention. He continued, "Who cares how or why you ended up in those situations? What matters is what you *chose* to do each time you faced a challenge." He stepped toward her. "You could've refused to host the Dax symbiont, but you didn't. You could've let someone else call the shots on *Defiant* when Jast fell, but you took command and saved the ship. During that crisis with the alternate universe, and the fallout that came after it, *you* were the one who stepped up when it mattered the most. And from what I've read in this ship's logs, you did *exactly* what you were supposed to do at Acamar."

He stopped in front of her, kneeled, and picked up the *bat'leth* from the deck. It was a perfectly balanced weapon, and it rested in his hand with a reassuring heft.

Then he straightened, rotated the blade with both hands, and offered it grip-first to Dax. "You're in command because you're a natural leader. When others shrink, you rise. And you've got the advantage of *eight lifetimes* of experience—that's seven and a half more than most captains."

She looked up at him with grateful eyes and hesitantly accepted the *bat'leth*. As she took hold of it, he added, "You're a hell of a good CO, Ezri. And I bet the man who gave you that sword would tell you the same thing—if you let him."

Geordi La Forge braced himself inside the steep, nearly vertical crawl space that led to the *Aventine*'s sensor control nexus and reached down toward the ship's chief engineer, Lieutenant Mikaela Leishman. "Gravitic calipers," he said.

The slender, thirtyish woman passed the tool up to him. "How's it going up there?"

"Almost done," he said. "I have to say, I almost envy you. This is quite a ship you've got here."

She grinned. "Yeah, she's a beauty. I still feel like I'm getting to know her, though. I only came aboard a few weeks ago, with the other replacements." She chuckled. "There are systems on this ship I still haven't read the manuals for."

"That's confidence-inspiring," quipped Lieutenant Oliana Mirren, the *Aventine*'s senior operations officer, who stepped up behind Leishman and peered up the crawl space at La Forge.

Leishman cast a sour frown at the pale-complexioned blonde. "Shouldn't you be on the bridge?"

"Finished my double shift a few hours ago," she said. "Now I'm checking up on the damage-control teams." Looking up, she called to La Forge, "Hope our prototype systems aren't giving you too much trouble, sir."

"Not at all," La Forge replied, even as he wondered what had led to so much tension between the two women.

Folding her arms, Leishman said to Mirren, "Geordi has everything under control, so you can go find someone else to hassle." La Forge wondered when he and Leishman had come to be on a first-name basis, but since he wanted to stay clear of her cross fire with Mirren, he let that go for the moment.

"I'm sure Mister La Forge is an excellent engineer," Mirren said, "but we're equipped with a lot of test-bed systems. It would be a good idea to monitor his work a bit more closely."

Leishman replied defensively, "He doesn't need me to show him around a sensor grid, Oliana."

"Actually," La Forge cut in, pointing at a series of linked components, "I have no idea what those are. A heads-up before I disconnect something that ought to stay online might not be such a bad idea."

Mirren's smug smirk at Leishman said, *I told you so.*

The *Aventine*'s chief engineer flashed an insincere smile in return, and then she clambered swiftly up the crawl space toward La Forge. He tried to wave her back. "Whoa, hang on! Space is a little tight up here right—" The last word of his sentence caught in his throat as Leishman pulled herself up beside him in the narrow tube and let her body press firmly against his.

She reached past him, which pushed their torsos together even more than before. A subtle, floral scent of shampoo in her hair teased his nostrils. "That," she said, pointing at one bundle of optronic cables, "is a multidimensional wave-function analysis module."

Using her outstretched hand to grab a support, she extended her other arm over his opposite shoulder. "That bulky thing over there is an experimental sympathetic fermion transceiver, whose counterpart is currently being installed in a secure facility somewhere ultra top secret." She pulled herself a bit higher than La Forge, placing her bosom in front of his face as she pointed at a complicated apparatus. "And this marvel of modern science is a chroniton integrator, which in theory will let us take sensor readings from several seconds in the future when our slipstream drive is engaged."

"Very impressive," La Forge said, only half certain that he was talking about the ship.

Leishman smiled. "Believe it or not, there are actually a few more things up here that are so secret that if I told you what they were—" She lost her grip suddenly on her handhold and whooped in surprise as she fell. Without thinking, La Forge caught her, and she held on to him, her arms around his neck, her legs wrapped around his waist. "Nice catch," she said.

"All part of the service," La Forge said, a grin tugging at his own features.

From below the two chief engineers came an exasperated huff. La Forge and Leishman looked down and were met by the censorious glare of Lieutenant Mirren. "Heaven defend us from engineers in love," she groused. "Let me know when you're done."

The operations officer walked away, leaving the engineers to their strangely intimate clutch in the crawl space. After a few seconds, Leishman cast a wide-eyed look of amusement at La Forge and broke out laughing. "She's so easy to tweak!"

"I take it this is a running gag for you?"

The sylphlike brunette shrugged. "It's getting to be." As if she'd suddenly become self-conscious now that no one was looking, she averted her eyes from La Forge's and said, "We'd probably better get back to work."

"Yeah, I guess so," La Forge said as he helped Leishman disentangle herself from him. "Besides, it usually takes me three or four dates before I go this far." Flashing a grin, he added, "I might be a cheap date, but I'm not easy."

She climbed back down to the corridor and grinned up at him. "Well, then, we might have a problem. Because I'm easy—but I'm not cheap." She reached into her roll-up bag of specialty engineering tools, pulled out a flux coupler, and passed it up to him. "Take this," she said. "You'll need it to balance the plasma flow to the triquantum coil."

Taking the tool, he didn't know what to make of Leishman. Was she just goofing around to annoy Mirren, or had she actually been flirting with him? The question nagged at him from the back of his thoughts while he finished his adjustments to the new systems in the *Aventine*'s sensor grid. "That ought to do it," he said as he deactivated the flux coupler. "Thanks for letting me go hands-on with this. It'll make refitting the *Enterprise*'s grid a lot easier while you guys are off on your scouting run."

"My pleasure," Leishman said as La Forge climbed down and out of the Jefferies tube. He handed the coupler back to her. She turned to tuck it back into its pocket in her equipment roll-up, but then she turned back toward La Forge with a deeply thoughtful expression. "I just want to say, in case there was, you know, any confusion or anything about that whole business with us in the tube . . ."

"It's okay," La Forge said. "I understand. You were just kidding around."

"No, I was totally hitting on you." She turned away, jammed the flux capacitor into her bag, rolled it shut in a blur of motion, and fastened its magnetic strap. When she turned back, La Forge was still at a loss for words. "But I get it, sir. You're just not that into me. It's no big deal." She picked up her bag and walked past La Forge, away down the corridor.

He called after her, "Can I buy you a drink sometime?"

She stopped and turned back. With a smirk and a raised eyebrow, she asked, "Just a drink?"

He spread his arms in dismay. "Dinner?"

Her eyes narrowed in mock suspicion. "Appetizers?"

"Of course."

Planting a hand on her hip, she asked with exaggerated doubt, "*And* dessert?"

"Naturally," La Forge said, liking her style.

"And I'll expect flowers or something pretty," she said.

"Pushing your luck, aren't you?"

"Easy but not cheap," Leishman said. "Take it or leave it."

He laughed and said, "Sold."

"All right," she replied. "As soon as this war's over, you've got yourself a date." Patting a bulkhead, she added, "You've got my number." Then she turned and walked away around a bend in the corridor, leaving

Geordi La Forge to wonder why this sort of thing didn't happen to him more often.

His elation was short-lived as he considered the obstacle that lay in front of him. *All I have to do to get a date with Mikaela is end the Borg invasion. If that's her idea of being easy, I don't even want to know what "not cheap" really means.*

Dax followed the instructions of the *Enterprise*'s computer as she moved through the ship looking for Worf. Her visit to the 1701-E was unannounced, and she wanted it to stay that way, but it was making it hard to find her old Deep Space 9 comrade.

When she'd first beamed aboard, the computer had dutifully informed her that he was in the forward sensor control center. By the time she'd walked there, however, he'd long since gone. Another query of the computer had led her to the auxiliary phaser control compartment, where she was told by a helpful young Bolian chief petty officer that she'd just missed the XO.

Now she was riding in a turbolift down to the main engineering compartment, in the hope of catching up with him at last. The doors hushed open, and she stepped out into the frenetic activity of a massive repair effort. The sharp smell of scorched metal was heavy in the air, and the clangor of voices, plasma welders, and echoing announcements over the ship-wide comm fused into a gray din of noise.

A team of engineers moved past her, escorting a convoy of antigravs loaded with newly fabricated replacement parts and stacks of optronic cable. Everywhere she looked, there were panels open on the bulk-heads, revealing the ship's inner machinery. She dodged clear of a hazard-suited duo of damage-control mechanics laden with tools.

"Excuse me," she said to a passing ensign. "Have you seen Commander Worf down here?"

The frazzled-looking young Tellarite pointed back the way he'd come. "By the main reactor with Lieutenant Taurik." Noticing the four rank pips on Captain Dax's collar, he added belatedly, "Sir."

"Thank you, Ensign," Dax said, and continued on her way.

She found Worf exactly where the Tellarite had said, and the Klingon was still conversing with the *Enterprise*'s Vulcan assistant chief engineer. Not wanting to intrude or interrupt, she lingered several paces shy of being able to eavesdrop on them—not that she could have heard much in the clamorous bustle of the all-hands repair effort.

Taurik nodded and stepped away, and Worf turned to head toward the turbolift. His eyes widened as he saw Dax watching him, but he didn't break stride as he passed her. "Are you returning my chief engineer?"

"He'll be back any minute," she said, falling into step beside him. "But I'm actually here to talk to you."

His dark brows furrowed as he glanced sideways at her. "Is there something you need, Captain?"

She followed him into a waiting turbolift. "Can we drop the ranks and just go back to being friends for a minute?"

The doors closed, and Worf's shoulders relaxed by only the slightest measure. He lifted his chin and softened his voice to a less authoritarian baritone.

"Computer, hold turbolift." A feedback tone from the overhead comm confirmed his order, and he looked at Dax. "I apologize," he said. "Tracking the repairs is time-consuming. . . . Are you all right?"

"I'm fine," she said with a grin, touched as ever by his terse but genuine concern for her well-being. "It's just that you and I haven't talked since before I trans-ferred to the *Aventine,* and suddenly I'm a captain. Must be weird for you."

"How so?"

Dax didn't know how to answer. In two words, he'd worked a dexterous bit of conversational judo and left her speechless. Reflecting on her feelings, she saw that she'd been wrong in her assumptions, and she decided to be honest with herself and with Worf. "Let me start over," she said. "The truth is, I have no idea how you feel about my promotion. I was project-ing my feelings about it onto you, and I shouldn't have. I'm sorry."

"You do not need to apologize," he said.

She held up her palms, as if to deflect his gracious words. "No, I do, Worf. I should've given you more credit, but I was afraid you'd resent me for making captain ahead of you."

He nodded. "Because of the reprimand I received after saving Jadzia on Soukara," he said.

"Yes," Dax said, relieved to have the matter in the open.

His sharp inhalation and heavy exhalation gave Dax ample notice that he was on the verge of saying something important. "I regret nothing that I did for Jadzia," he said. "I accepted the consequences then, and now." His stern features brightened. "You earned command by leading in battle. Jadzia would be proud of you—as I am. Your success honors her, and vindicates my decision to save her."

The decorum of command was the only thing keeping Dax from becoming completely overwrought at Worf's rare expression of his feelings for her, and for Jadzia. "Thank you, Worf. It means a lot to me to hear you say that. And for what it's worth, I've never seen you look more relaxed and contented than you do right now." A moment of self-doubt prompted her to ask, "I'm not just imagining that, am I? Are you happy with your life?"

He looked away for a moment, his demeanor pensive. Then he looked back and said, "The *Enterprise* is where I belong, and I consider it a great honor to be Captain Picard's first officer."

She reached out and rubbed his shoulder. "I'm glad." Flashing a broad smile, she added, "Don't get too settled in, though. I bet you'll prove Captain Sisko wrong and have a ship of your own before long."

"I am in no hurry."

"Of course not," Dax said. "You always did take your time."

A low grunt rumbled in his chest before he said, "Computer, Deck Five," and the turbolift hummed into motion.

Dax folded her hands behind her back as the lift made its rapid ascent. "It's funny, isn't it? Just at the point you and I are finally living up to our potential, the Borg are trying to exterminate us. What would you call that? Irony? Or tragedy?"

Worf smirked. "Bad timing."

8

———

"Strike team ready," reported Lieutenant Pava Ek'Noor sh'Aqabaa, the tall, sinewy, and breathtaking Andorian *shen* who was filling in for the absent Ranul Keru at *Titan*'s security console.

Captain Riker wanted to be on his feet, moving from station to station, but he knew his role called for him to stay in the command chair and project certainty to his crew. His acting XO, Commander Fo Hachesa, double-checked the readouts on sh'Aqabaa's console and nodded his confirmation to Riker.

At the aft science stations, chief engineer Ra-Havreii and the holographic avatar of science officer Pazlar were racing through their final adjustments. Ra-Havreii pivoted away from the console and declared, "Ready, Captain!"

"Engage!" Riker ordered.

Lieutenant Rager keyed in commands on the ops console. "Charging the inverters now," she said.

"Power levels steady," Pazlar said, watching the gauges on her station's monitor. "Initializing subspatial trajector."

"Calibrating targeting beam," Ra-Havreii said, his

own hands moving with speed and grace across his console's controls.

Riker crossed his fingers. This was a plan that had a lot of ways to go wrong. Distilled to its essential elements, *Titan* would use a folded-space transporter—a technology with proven deleterious effects on organic tissue—to bypass the protective shell of black metal around the Caeliar's hidden planet and sneak a strike team inside.

Because they had no way to scan the planet's surface, Pazlar had estimated the likely size of the planet and the approximate thickness of the hollow sphere that surrounded it. The strike team, outfitted with orbital skydiving gear, would be shifted past the sphere into the planet's atmosphere and free-fall to the surface. Once on the ground, they would don isolation suits to cloak themselves from the Caeliar, seek out the away team, and then, once they found them, trigger a transdimensional recall beacon.

Listening to the rapid volleys of technical information from one bridge officer to the next, Riker fixed his mien into a mask of calm resolve.

"Trajector at full power," Pazlar said.

"Sensor module buffers holding," Rager added.

Ra-Havreii chimed in, "No lock for the targeting beam." He poked at the console controls. "There's a multiphasic scrambling field inside the sphere," he said.

Riker asked, "Can you break through it?"

"I'll need more power," Ra-Havreii said. "Increasing to five-eighty . . . five-ninety . . . six hundred."

A droning whine began vibrating the deck. It made the bulkheads ring like a struck tuning fork.

"Feedback pulse," Pazlar said, raising her voice over the rising hum. "We need to reduce power!"

"Negative," Ra-Havreii said. "Increase to six-twenty-five, we're almost through!"

Rager interjected, "Buffer overload!"

"It's a transition rebound effect," Ra-Havreii shouted back. "Negate it with a canceling frequency, quickly!"

A port-side engineering station erupted in a storm of shattered black polymer shrapnel and jetting sparks. The blast knocked Ra-Havreii off his feet and peppered his drooping white mustache and flowing white hair with smoldering motes, which he frantically finger-combed away before brushing clean his shoulders and chest.

Overhead, the lights flickered, and several consoles stuttered under the hands of people trying to keep them working. Pazlar reported with rising frustration, "Cascade failures in the sensor module! We're losing the trajector's targeting system!"

Hachesa stood close to Riker and bent low to offer in confidence, "I recommend we abort the mission, sir."

Riker frowned at the Kobliad, even though he knew the acting XO was right. Then he nodded and said in a voice that cut through the din, "Abort mission. Rager, shut down the inverters. Lieutenant sh'Aqabaa, tell the strike team to stand down. Secure from Yellow Alert." He saw Hachesa help Ra-Havreii stand up, and he said to the chief engineer, "Commander, deploy damage-control teams to the sensor module."

"Aye, sir," Ra-Havreii said, shaking off Hachesa's hand and walking stiffly toward a functioning duty station.

All around *Titan*'s bridge, Riker saw dejected expressions, faces reflecting failure and disappointment. Looking over his shoulder, he saw Pazlar switch off a mission-command screen as she grumbled, "I guess that's it, then."

The bad morale had a toxic quality, one that Riker was determined not to grant a foothold on his ship. He stood and stepped forward to the center of the bridge. "Rager," he said, "put me on a shipwide channel."

The ops officer keyed in the command, turned her head back in his direction, and replied, "Channel open, sir."

"Attention, all decks," Riker said. "This is the captain. By now you're very likely all aware that our latest rescue mission has not gone as planned.

"Though we've only been at this a short time, I'm sure some of you are beginning to harbor doubts about our chances for saving the away team—and ourselves. Given the obstacles that the Caeliar have left in our path, I can certainly understand why you might feel that way.

"But we aren't going to give in to doubt or frustration or fear. I know that each time another plan fails, it seems like we're running out of options. But I assure you, we're not.

"Every step of the way we're learning. Every failure teaches us something new. And if there's one thing I know about Starfleet—and especially about this ship, and this crew—it's that we've got a million tricks up our sleeves. If none of them work, we'll pull out a million more. And a million after that.

"As long as our away team continues to be held prisoner on the surface, we will keep looking for a way to free them, and ourselves. We will use every means at our disposal, every technology we possess, to free ourselves.

"We will never relent, and we will never yield, no matter how long it takes—and we'll *all* go home, together."

He signaled Rager with a small slashing gesture beside his thoat to cut the channel, and then he returned to his chair. Pazlar and Ra-Havreii stood next to it. The science officer's holographic avatar flickered and wavered a moment. "So," Riker said to the pair, "what's your next plan?"

"The way you were talking, I figured you already had one," Ra-Havreii said, pinching another charred granule of companel composite from his singed mustache.

Riker smirked. "Not yet," he said. "But give me time, Commander. Give me time."

Ranul Keru tried to keep an open mind as he wandered with Ensign Torvig through the deserted avenues of Axion, but there was something about the city that put him perpetually on edge. The morning was bright and beautiful, its air temperate, sweet, and mild in humidity. Sunlight glinted off surfaces in every direction. It was as pristine an urban environment as Keru had ever seen, yet everything about it sent a chill through him.

Torvig, on the other hand, gamboled from one discovery to the next, his curiosity insatiable. His sleek, ovine head bobbed and swiveled as he trotted along several meters ahead of Keru, with a tricorder clutched in one cybernetic hand. He pivoted back toward Keru just long enough to report, "I'm reading a new energy wave ahead." Then he was off again, loping along through the gleaming canyon of bright metal and smoky crystal.

"Slow down, Vig," Keru called ahead to his friend. "It's a recon, not a race."

The Choblik engineer didn't seem to be listening to him. It was several minutes before Torvig halted long enough for Keru to catch up to him, and only then because he was engrossed in his study of a peculiar Caeliar construct by the side of the road. The three-meter-tall object was composed entirely of perfectly polished obsidian. Its base had a distinctly organic shape, but from a height level with Torvig's shoulder—and Keru's midriff—it became an asymmetrical fusion of hard angles and irregular polyhedrons. Some of its surfaces seemed to have been arbitrarily inscribed with symbols or characters of the Caeliar language.

Keru waited until he caught Vig sneaking a look back at him with one eye, and he asked the engineer, "Any clue what it is?"

"I have hypotheses," Torvig said. He circled the object and kept his head only centimeters from its surface as he continued. "The shapes might be directional indicators. The inscriptions may denote the names of locations in the city, or perhaps distances to known places from this point."

Narrowing his eyes at Torvig's knack for complicating the simplest of answers, he replied, "You mean it's a road sign."

"Maybe," Torvig said. "That's only one possibility." He stopped on the far side of the object from Keru, reached forward, and removed a loose piece, which was formed from the same ultrasmooth black stone. Shaped like a spike, it caught the sunlight and gave off indigo flashes as Torvig turned it in his left bionic hand while scanning it with the tricorder held in his right. His small mechanical appendages handled the object with tremendous dexterity and gentleness. "There is another piece like this one," he said. "Identical in every way. Thirty-one centimeters in length. Weight, one hundred forty-one-point-seven grams. Variable diameter, from two-point-one centimeters along the majority of its length, tapering to zero-point-four centimeters before widening again at the end, before a final tapering. Most interesting."

Circling around to stand beside the ensign, Keru said, "Vig, can I see those a minute?"

Torvig handed Keru the first slender object, and then he grabbed the other and passed it to the burly Trill security chief. Keru held the two stone sticks at their broader ends and felt the weight of them. He paid particular attention to the narrowing of each rod, and the slightly bulbous barrel tip that bulged at the end of that taper. Then he grinned.

"I know what these are," Keru said. "Step back a little."

Keru took a moment to examine the tall object for flat surfaces. He imagined which angles of attack would feel most natural. Cautiously, he reached out and used one of the spikes to tap on an inscribed panel of the obelisk.

A rich, gonglike tone pealed from inside the black object and resonated in the towering buildings all around him. It sounded as if he'd struck a colossal xylophone with the hammer of the gods, yet all he'd done was tap the thing. He didn't listen to the instrument's phenomenally sustained note so much as he felt it vibrating through his flesh and bones.

When he looked back, Torvig cocked his head to one side. "Perhaps you should strike it again, sir. Someplace different."

Choosing another spot, Keru gave it a gingerly tap with one of the stone sticks, and a brighter note rebounded off the cityscape. Feeling bolder as the sound overwhelmed him, he began a slow exploration of the device, and he was astounded to find that, no matter how randomly or arbitrarily he percussed the black statue, he couldn't sound a discordant note. As he continued, his pace accelerated to a frenzy, and he was all but dancing around the object like a wild shaman, seeking out some new note to play, some new melody to coax into existence.

It was difficult for him to stop, but he knew that he had to. The instrument's sounds felt addictive to him. With great effort and more than a touch of remorse, he stopped playing, took a deep breath, and put the obsidian sticks back into their storage slots on the side of the instrument as the last note echoed and faded to silence. He stroked his beard pensively.

"Why did you stop?" asked Torvig.

"I felt like I was losing myself in it," Keru said. "I can't really explain it. I was taught at the Academy that the effect of sound on the humanoid brain is minimal. Certain infrasonic frequencies can produce anxiety and physical effects, like blurred vision or shortness of breath, but this wasn't like that. It was . . . something else."

Torvig sounded concerned. "Are you all right, Ranul?"

"I'm okay, Vig, thanks. I just want to get away from this thing as soon as we can."

"Of course," the engineer said. He pointed himself toward a boulevard that led to the city's outskirts. "There is an energy surge in this direction." Before Keru could protest, the Choblik was trotting away, eyes glued to his tricorder screen.

A few kilometers and minor detours later, Keru caught up to his diminutive friend once again. Torvig was perched on the edge of an overpass, supporting himself with his spindly bionic arms while he leaned over to stare at something of interest below.

Keru lowered himself to the ground and crawled over beside Torvig to peer into the space beneath the footbridge. Several dozen meters below, a Caeliar hovered above a dark, oval pool of liquid. Globes of the black fluid rose from the pool's surface without making a ripple of disturbance. In the air, a few meters away from the Caeliar, the dark spheres semisolidified, fused, and were reshaped into something new, which rotated slowly and on more than one axis as more matter accreted on its surface. Although the Caeliar made no motions or sound, and there was no visible connection between it and the object taking shape, Keru was certain that the alien was driving the process, directing its outcome.

His friend whispered to him, "Isn't it interesting how they manipulate forms? Their methods are economical and precise."

"Just like machines," Keru said, straining to keep his own voice a whisper.

"Not quite," Torvig said. "It's true that claytronic atoms enable them to mold their bodies and environment, but it would be a mistake to equate the Caeliar with cybernetic organisms such as myself." After a tense pause, he added, "Or the Borg."

Far below, the Caeliar transformed into a shimmering golden mist that fused with the black sculpture and vanished inside of it. The bizarre creation began changing shapes, shifting into ever more unusual configurations while the two Starfleet officers observed its mutations.

Torvig continued, "The Caeliar and their city are far beyond even our most advanced understandings of cybernetics. They represent a nearly perfect organic-synthetic harmony."

The Choblik paused as the golden mist flowed out of the abstract shape below. The Caeliar had turned the piece into something that reminded Keru of a ball of energy with countless ribbons of current dancing across its surface.

Finishing his thought, Torvig added, "The Caeliar have achieved everything to which my people aspire."

Keru grimaced. "Really? Do the Choblik daydream about taking innocent people hostage?"

That gave the engineer a moment of overtly self-conscious pause. "Perhaps the Caeliar are less than *ideal* role models. . . ."

"Vig, that's like saying the Gorn are less than ideal vegetarians. Or that Chalnoth make less than ideal nannies." He pushed himself back from the edge and stood. "Come on, let's keep moving. We need to finish this recon and get back."

x

Torvig sprang back from the edge of the bridge and fell into step beside Keru. "With proper dietary supplements, a Gorn *could* subsist on a vegetable-based diet, Ranul."

"So not the point, Vig. So not the point."

Melora Pazlar hadn't meant to fall asleep. She'd wrapped herself in a wispy sleep-cocoon, intending only to relax while listening to the musical emanations of the crystal sculptures that adorned the high walls of her vertically oriented quarters. She felt safe and comfortable in the microgravity environment, which simulated that of her native Gemworld, but days of overwork and sleep deprivation had finally caught up with her, and she'd found herself chasing multicolored giant insects over a lush dreamscape of ruggedly beautiful lapidary spires.

She awoke with a shudder and looked down to see someone gazing up and watching her. "Computer! Lights!"

The glow strips set into the walls gradually brightened, adding fire to her sculptures' facets while giving her eyes time to adjust to the increasing brightness. When the illumination had increased to roughly fifty percent of full, she recognized her unannounced visitor as Counselor Huilan Sen'kara.

On a ship packed with a staggering variety of lifeforms, the S'ti'ach was one whom Pazlar found especially memorable. His four short arms, two squat legs, and stubby thick tail, coupled with his large-eyed, broad-eared visage, bright blue fur, and sub-meter height, reminded her of a child's plush animal toy.

The illusion was belied, however, by the row of sharp spines on his back—and by his fangs.

"Sorry to wake you," he said, sounding insincere.

She unfastened the safety loop of her cocoon and rolled free of it. Falling slowly, she asked sharply, "What are you doing in my quarters?"

"I think we need to have a talk," Huilan said.

"Do you?" Spreading her arms as if to catch the air, she kept her angry gaze directed squarely at him as she neared the deck. "I don't recall making an appointment, Counselor. I also don't remember inviting you in."

Her toes touched the carpeted floor, and she let her calf muscles tense just enough to spring her back into the air, where she hovered over Huilan.

He flattened his spines against his back and pivoted awkwardly, apparently preferring to keep his feet planted on the deck. After surveying the narrow room, he looked back up at Pazlar. "I would invite you to sit down with me, but you don't seem to have any place to sit."

"My people don't have much use for chairs or anything like them," she said. "We find floating more comfortable." With a small push off a protrusion from one of the bulkheads, she sent herself a few meters higher. "Feel free to come up to my level if you want to keep talking."

The S'ti'ach made a sound that was part growl, part purr. "Not my first choice, Commander," he said. "My species evolved in a high-gravity setting. Neither floating nor flying comes naturally to us."

"Fascinating," Pazlar said. She reached the overhead and halted herself by pressing her fingertips against it and resisting ever so gently, bending at the elbows to absorb her momentum. The artificially generated pull of a few centigees of gravity slowly reeled her back toward the deck. She glared at Huilan. "You came to talk. So talk."

The spines on his back bristled back to full attention, betraying his reaction to her brusque tone. "Several of your shipmates have noticed that you spend an inordinate amount of time inside the stellar cartography lab," he said. "Since the introduction of your holographic avatar, none of your colleagues have seen you in the flesh."

"So? That was kind of the whole point."

As she touched down in front of him, he asked, "What was?"

"Being able to go anywhere, anytime, holographically," she said. "That's why Xin built it for me—so I could experience life on the ship just like everyone else does."

Huilan's sigh was tainted with mockery. "Well, that's a relief. And here I thought you were using it to shut yourself off from contact with other people. Silly me."

"That's ridiculous," Pazlar retorted. "Now that I'm free to move around the ship, I've had more face time with the rest of the crew than ever before."

"At a comfortable remove, no less," Huilan shot back. "It must be nice. Safe."

She backed up half a step from the counselor and launched herself up and away once more. "It is nice," she said, more defensively than she had meant to. "It's a great invention. Why do you have to go and make it into something dysfunctional?"

"That's not my intention, I assure you." Huilan watched her with keen attention as she continued to ascend. "And in principle, I don't disagree. I am happy to see you freed from your constraints. But too much of a good thing can be a cause for concern, Melora."

The metal of the overhead was cold against her fingertips as she pushed off it and began another descent. "What're you trying to say? That I need to spend less time using the holopresence system? Why? I spend most of my time working in stellar cartography, anyway. And clunking through the ship in my armor is hardly my idea of a good time, Doc."

"I sympathize," Huilan said. "But I think you need to stay in practice, so to speak, at living and working in the higher-gravity parts of the ship. If you don't use those skills, they'll atrophy—and you know it."

She landed a bit more firmly than she had intended, and she let the momentum carry her forward a few steps, toward Huilan. "I've heard the spiel before," she said. "Use it or lose it—blah, blah, blah. But it's not like I'm barricaded inside my quarters with the gravity off. I get around just fine."

"Is that a fact?" The small, blue S'ti'ach gazed at her with an almost feral intensity, as if accusing her with a look.

She taunted him with a shake of her head and thrust her empty palms upward in frustration. "What?"

"Where do you store your gravity-assist armature?"

She pointed toward the custom-built frame on the bulkhead. "Right over—" Her armature wasn't there. "What the . . . ?"

"Computer," Huilan said. "Deactivate holopresence module." As soon as he'd said it, Pazlar's quarters vanished, and she found herself standing on the observation platform inside stellar cartography. The walls of the spherical chamber were dark, dull, and blank. Her armature and cane rested against one railing of the catwalk that linked the platform to the entrance portal. "I'm glad you don't think you've blurred the line between illusion and reality," Huilan continued. "But you've been in here for thirty-nine consecutive hours."

He turned and shuffled a few paces toward the exit before he stopped, turned back, and added, "If you'd like to talk about this a little more, you know where my office is. But if you come by, do us both a favor— come in person."

"Here they come," Tuvok said, activating his tricorder. As he ducked behind a low wall for cover, Vale crouched beside him.

She peeked over the wall's edge. Several dozen meters away, a trio of Caeliar were crossing an open courtyard surrounded by flowering trees. Their long, bony limbs moved with more grace than Vale had expected. They walked directly toward a solid wall of dark crystal in a frame of immaculate, polished metal.

"Watch for a device or a trigger," Vale whispered.

Her brown-skinned Vulcan colleague arched one eyebrow into a dubious peak, but he said nothing. Instead, he did as she'd asked and kept his attention on the Caeliar.

As the three aliens made contact with the wall, it seemed to offer no resistance to their passage. "They walked through it like it was a hologram," she said.

Tuvok lifted his tricorder and checked its readings. "Negative, Commander. No sign of holographic projection. But I did pick up a momentary, localized surge in baryonic particles."

"And that means . . . ?"

His expression was exquisitely neutral, but Vale was certain she saw a hint of irritation in Tuvok's eye. "That something powered by dark energy affected either the particles in the wall, those in the Caeliar, or both."

"So that wasn't just an illusion," she said. "They really did just walk through a wall."

He turned off his tricorder. "In essence, yes."

From far behind them came the swift patter of footsteps. Vale looked back and saw the away team's two security officers, Lieutenant Sortollo and Chief Dennisar, jogging toward her and Tuvok. Their footfalls echoed off the dizzying vertical faces of the Caeliar's majestic towers. Vale looked askance at Tuvok and remarked, "The acoustics out here would make it damn hard to sneak up on someone."

"Indeed," Tuvok said. "I heard them several minutes ago."

She considered chiding him for boasting, but she knew he would say that he was only making a statement of fact. Then he would insinuate that her accusation was rooted in insecurity. *You know you've meshed with your people when you can have the entire argument without saying a word,* Vale mused.

The two security officers slowed as they drew near to Vale and Tuvok. "Commanders," said Sortollo. "We finished our recon. What do you want first, the good news or the bad news?"

"Life is short," Vale said. "Give me the good news.".

Sortollo nodded. "The shuttle's still on the platform, about a hundred meters from the city's edge," he said. "So, at least the Caeliar didn't ditch it at sea."

That was something, at least. "And the bad news?"

An anxious glance passed between Sortollo and Dennisar. The lieutenant replied, "We haven't found a single door anywhere in the city. Not at ground level, at least. The Caeliar seem to levitate from place to place, or just appear out of nowhere."

"And they're watching us," said Dennisar. "And listening to everything we say. All the time."

Doubt creased Vale's brow. She asked the Orion, "Are you sure you're not just being a little paranoid?"

"I'm sure," Dennisar said. Looking up and away, he raised his voice and said, "Who's observing us right now?"

To Vale's surprise, a gentle breeze moved past her, warm and pleasant on her skin, and then a slow, gentle swirl of luminescent pinpoints formed behind the two security officers. The glowing motes spread and cohered into the shape of a Caeliar. Within seconds the figure solidified, and then it spoke with a pleasing, feminine voice. "I am Avelos," she said.

Tuvok inquired, "Have you been observing us?"

"Yes," said Avelos. "For a time."

"She isn't the one we met," Sortollo said. "His name was Bednar." He added, to Avelos, "Are there others watching us?"

"There are many of us," Avelos said. "We share the responsibility. Bednar followed two of you here, but once the four of you were together, there was no need for two monitors. So I volunteered to stay and released Bednar."

Thinking aloud, Vale said, "There are monitors with all our people, right?"

"Correct," said Avelos. "Our intent is not malicious, merely vigilant. The Quorum feels that precautions are prudent, given the outcome of our last dealings with your kind."

"Do you refer to the crew of the *Columbia*?" Tuvok asked.

The Caeliar turned toward him. "Yes. Members of its crew, whom we'd welcomed as guests here in Axion, resorted to violence in their bid for escape. Their methods caused the deaths of millions of Caeliar, and the loss of one of our cities."

Vale cut in, "There are other cities?"

Avelos's reply was heavy with resentment. "Not anymore." She calmed herself before she continued. "The gestalt has made its adjustment to the new paradigm, and your predecessors' actions, though tragic, ultimately proved necessary in the larger scope of the timeline. However, we have only this city now to defend, and we cannot allow you or your shipmates on *Titan* to put us at risk. We wish you no harm, but we have learned from experience not to assume the reverse is true."

"Most logical," Tuvok said.

His reply seemed to satisfy Avelos. She said, "Do you have any other questions you would like to ask me?"

"How do you walk through walls?" Vale asked.

"Programmable matter," Avelos said. "We and the city are composed of the same kind of malleable subatomic machines, and powered by a shared energy field. . . . I'm afraid I'm not permitted to share any information more detailed than that."

Sortollo visibly tensed. "Hang on a second—you and your people . . . are all *machines*?"

"We prefer to think of ourselves as synthetic lifeforms. Our catoms mimic much of our original biology, in both form and function. Though your scanners probably don't see us as organic beings, from our perspective, life looks and feels as it ever did. We are as we were . . . and as we shall remain."

The four Starfleet personnel stood in silence and absorbed Avelos's information. Finally, Vale looked at her and said, "Thanks. You can go back to being a breeze or whatever it is you do. We'd like the illusion of a little bit of privacy."

"As you wish," Avelos replied. She became semitransparent, and then she grew blurry and faded away in a balmy rush of air.

Vale looked at Tuvok. "Time for Plan B."

"I was not aware that we *had* a Plan B."

"We don't," she said. "But we'd better get one. Fast."

Deanna Troi leaned against the balcony wall, her weight on both her hands. From her lofty vantage point she gazed beyond the spires of Axion into the distance, out across fog-draped tropical forests and low clouds dragging dark rain shadows.

She heard the air displaced behind her as much as she felt it against her back, and she wasn't surprised to hear Erika Hernandez's voice. "The Quorum will meet with you soon," she said. "I should warn you now not to expect much. The Caeliar tend to resist change—and suggestions."

Troi didn't turn around. Instead, she swiveled her head just enough to catch sight of Hernandez over her shoulder. "We just want to talk to them," Troi said.

Behind her unannounced visitor, Dr. Ree sauntered out of the corridor that led to the away team's respective private quarters. The therapodian physician flicked his forked tongue at Hernandez, no doubt tasting the woman's scent on the air. "I heard voices," he said. "I didn't mean to interrupt."

Hernandez tilted her head in a birdlike manner as she stared at Ree. "May I ask what your species is called?"

"Pahkwa-thanh," Ree said.

The youthful brunette nodded. "Humanity hadn't met any life-forms like yours when I was a starship captain. If it's not too forward of me, I think yours is a very handsome species."

"Well, we've always thought so," Ree replied, sauntering closer to the two women. "But it's nice of you to say." He stopped at a large, rough-textured boulder, which sat beneath a square light fixture that bathed it in a warm, white radiance. In a graceful hop, he was atop the beige-hued rock, and he stretched out to sun himself. "Don't mind me," he said.

"The Caeliar certainly saw to our comfort," Troi said, in a derogatory tone.

Hernandez didn't take the bait. She joined Troi on the balcony and stood forward against the low wall, her fingertips resting lightly on its ledge. "They try to be good hosts."

A fleeting stab of pain swirled inside Troi's abdomen. She masked her profound discomfort with an intensity of anger she didn't really feel. "Don't you mean 'jailers'?"

"My landing party and I felt much the same way when we first came here. Some of us got over it. Some didn't."

The pain faded slightly, and Troi regained more of her emotional control. She didn't want to give Hernandez or the Caeliar any more information than she had to about her condition, but she was even more intent on concealing her symptoms from Dr. Ree and Commander Vale until the mission was done. The last thing she wanted was to be relieved of duty and treated like a casualty. "You've been living with the Caeliar for quite some time," she said. "Do they trust you?"

"To a point," Hernandez replied. "I have more liberties than you do, but I'm still subject to many restrictions."

Troi's half-Betazoid empathic skills sensed the veracity of Hernandez's words. It was a relief to Troi that whatever change had imbued Hernandez with nigheternal youth and rendered her biology unrecognizable to the tricorders had not hampered Troi's ability to detect her emotions. She asked Hernandez, "Have you ever tried to defy them?"

A smirk tugged at the corner of Hernandez's mouth. "Many times," she said. "More than I could count."

"And how did the Caeliar respond?"

Hernandez cast a sly look at Troi. "Gauging your own risk before you challenge them?"

"I just want a sense of what kind of civilization they've created. Their values, their beliefs . . . their point of view."

Now it was Hernandez's turn to stare out across the mist-dappled tropical mountain slopes as Axion roamed the skies. Troi watched the sunset paint the sky amber and scarlet along the horizon for a few minutes while Hernandez pondered her query. The sweet, refreshing scent of rain and earthy perfumes from the jungle below reached Troi in a soft, humid upswell.

"The Caeliar," Hernandez said at last, "are very often just what they seem to be: reclusive xenophobes with a frightening amount of raw power. They can be distrustful and stubborn."

Everything she'd said had the ring of truth, as far as Troi's empathy could tell. "How do they punish disobedience?"

"They don't," Hernandez said. "All they ever do is stop the action that bothers them and then lecture you about why it's in your best interest to do as they say."

"And they don't resort to threats or punitive measures?"

Hernandez shook her head. "Not on a personal level. They're pacifists—they won't kill, and they hate violence. Besides, even if they weren't, they'd hardly need to use force to get their way. You've barely seen a fraction of what they can *really* do." In a more ominous timbre, she added, "Trust me, it's a waste of time butting heads with them. You won't win. Ever."

There wasn't a single trace of deception or exaggeration that Troi could sense behind Hernandez's words—just a deep and profound despair, tinged with bitterness. Troi decided to try and coax something more substantial from her hostess. "You say they're nonviolent. But are they fair?"

"They can be." A sullen mood took hold of Hernandez, and Troi felt the other woman's resentment being stoked by her reminiscences. "Though I have to admit . . . in recent centuries, their decisions haven't always been as reasonable as they'd like to think. Some of their decrees have seemed, well . . . arbitrary."

Pushing a bit more, Troi asked, "Did they seem malicious?"

"No, just selfish."

"I see." Another pang of sickly discomfort made Troi wince. Hernandez didn't seem to notice, and a glance back at the boulder confirmed that Ree's eyes were still closed while he basked in his artificial sunlight. To Hernandez, Troi continued, "I'll just have to hope I catch the Quorum in a good mood."

"Don't count on it," Hernandez said. "Visitors always make them edgy." She turned as if to leave, then she stopped. "I'll be back to escort you to the Quorum hall when they're ready for you. In the meantime, can I ask you a favor?"

Fighting to suppress the sick feeling in her stomach and keep her poker face steady, Troi replied, "It depends."

"Would it bother you if I stopped pretending not to have abilities that you've already seen me use?" She looked back across the residence's open great room. "I could use the pod lift to come and go if it makes you feel better, but . . ."

Troi flashed a crooked grin. "Be my guest."

"Thanks," Hernandez said. She walked to the railing, rolled her hips over the low barrier with a gymnast's grace, and pushed away from the edge into open air. Troi peeked over the wall and watched Hernandez make her slow descent, arms wide, her diaphanous raiment and sable hair billowing in an updraft.

Watching her float to the ground, Troi envied Hernandez's freedom . . . until she remembered that, for all her powers and privileges, Hernandez was as much a prisoner as she was.

1525–1573

9

The years had flowed like water, one into the next, until Erika Hernandez no longer knew where one ended and another began.

Axion was a mountain moving through an ocean of night. Its slow passage of the void between stars was motivated in part by the Caeliar's obsessive need to conceal their presence from the galaxy at large, which necessitated a reduced energy signature. Hernandez's work with Inyx had also given her reason to suspect another cause for their languor: they had no idea where to go.

She stood half a meter behind Inyx in the center of the vast hexagon that she had nicknamed the Star Chamber. The alien scientist's bony limbs were doubled over on themselves as he squatted above a holographic representation of a star system on the black, nonreflective floor. He teased it with his tendril-fingers. Smoky symbols curled up and away from the tiny, orange sun-sphere. "Stable," Inyx declared. "Energy output . . . adequate."

"What about the planets?" asked Hernandez, who

waited to enter notations on a sleek, paper-thin polymer tablet.

Inyx enlarged the system as he pushed it high above their heads. Six worlds formed. "Four iron-cored inner planets, two gas giants," Inyx said. "One planet in the habitable zone. Mark this one for further investigation. System D-599."

"I'm naming it Xibalba," Hernandez said.

"You may name it anything you wish, provided you log it in the catalog under the heading System D-599." The simulated star system overhead dissolved and vanished. Inyx strolled toward some other speck of light, several meters away.

Hernandez followed him as she jotted the system's bland catalog designation on the tablet and added her more colorful appellation as a footnote. "That's the second possibility you've found this month," she said. "You're on a roll." Her estimate of time's passage was approximate at best. There were no days in Axion, no changing of seasons, no moon to wax and wane like a celestial timepiece. Just the enduring darkness.

"This latest discovery was most unexpected," Inyx said. "Unfortunately, it's also quite distant. It will be some time before we can reach that sector."

Carefully excising all eagerness from her voice, Hernandez said, "You could build a scout vessel and send a small team to survey the system."

Without deigning to look back, Inyx replied, "I presume you would volunteer for that survey? And that your three companions would be ideal assistants?"

"It is the sort of mission we were trained for."

As she caught up to Inyx and walked beside him on his left, he asked, "What do you think are the odds that the Quorum will give you its permission for such an endeavor?"

"Zero," she said as they passed over the image of a bright stellar cluster on the floor. "Because you won't even present it to them as an option."

"Correct," he said. "I'm glad you've learned that much."

She smirked. "I told you: I'm a quick study."

"Yes, you have absorbed a great deal of information more quickly than I'd expected," Inyx said. "Though I still have much to teach you, I must admit I've enjoyed your enthusiasm . . . and your stories. You've led a colorful life for one so young."

"Kind of you to say," she said, smiling at his flattery.

He slowed, stopped, reached up, and pulled down a yellow marble of fire from high overhead. "I hope you can sustain your zeal," he said. "It would make the next several decades far more pleasant for all of us."

It took her a few seconds to let herself hear what he said, and even then she was still somewhat in denial. "Decades?"

"Yes," Inyx said. "Many of these candidate systems are quite distant from one another. Given the limitations on our power output, and the need to avoid detection in regions where contact with starfaring races would be a risk, it will take some time for us to complete all our surveys."

Hernandez felt stunned. She had been mentally prepared to spend a few years, or even several years, aiding the Caeliar in their search for a new homeworld. Decades were another matter.

Inyx extracted more smoke-symbols from the burning dot that hovered between his undulating tendrils. After the vaporlike sigils vanished into his mottled skin, he released the tiny orb, which drifted upward, back toward the ceiling. "Not enough essential elements," he said. "It also had only one terrestrial planet, which was too close to the star to be habitable." He moved on, oblivious of Hernandez's state of shock.

"I have a question," she said.

He halted and turned toward her. "Ask."

"If we found a habitable world, but in a star system that didn't suit your more exotic needs, would the Quorum consider letting me and my companions settle there, in exile?"

The tubelike air sacs that ran from Inyx's neck to his chest swelled and then sagged, a Caeliar equivalent to a heavy sigh. "I suspect they would refuse such a request," he said. "There would always be the risk, once you left our custody, that another starfaring species might rescue you, or find you when it came to colonize. Even the discovery of your remains, long after your demise, might raise unfortunate questions. And then our security would be in peril."

"Well, what about displacing us?" she said. "Your Quorum threatened to do it before—fling us to an Earth-like planet in some distant galaxy. Why not do that now?"

He seemed caught off guard. "We'd have to expend a great deal of energy to move you so far. Because we are presently unshielded, doing so would attract significant attention to us. Someone would almost certainly investigate."

"All right," she said, unwilling to surrender. "Then leave us here and move yourselves to another galaxy, one with no one else in it. Then you can have all the privacy you want."

"Why do you have this sudden need to get out of Axion?"

The rusty wire that held the cork on her bottled-up anger finally broke. "There's nothing sudden about it, Inyx! I've wanted out of this place since the moment I got here! I brought my crew here to get help, not become inmates." She paced away from him, then pivoted back. "Human beings aren't meant to live their whole lives in space," she said. "We need a break once in a while. Some fresh air, a walk on the grass, a swim in the ocean. And now you tell me I can look forward to several more decades of night in this wandering ghost town? I'm not sure I can take that, Inyx. I'm not sure my friends can take it."

He sounded genuinely contrite. "I'm sorry. I didn't realize how hostile this environment must seem to you." He looked around at the Star Chamber as he continued, "Holographic simulation is a fairly simple art. Perhaps our chief architect, Edrin, could construct some therapeutic artificial environments for you."

"Holograms?" she replied, unconvinced. "I know they say a picture's worth a thousand words, but I doubt a trick of the light can stand in for a night on the beach in Cancún or a day spent rock-climbing in Clark Canyon."

"You may be surprised," was Inyx's last word on the subject. And despite his permanent frown and unreadable body language, Hernandez was certain that something in Inyx's tone rang unmistakably of mischief in the making.

Johanna Metzger sat slumped in her chair, with her head tilted over the back so she could stare straight upward. "Is it my imagination," she asked, "or are there a lot less stars than there used to be?"

Veronica Fletcher stopped poking at what felt like her millionth plate of bland Caeliar vegetable gruel and looked up at the sky above their courtyard. "That's been happening for a while now," she said. "According to Erika, it's 'cause the Caeliar moved the city a few thousand light-years above the galactic plane. Most of what we're seeing from here are close globular clusters and other galaxies."

"They never do anything the easy way, do they?"

Pushing her plate aside, Fletcher replied, "Why would they, when they have all the time in the universe?" She reached up and released her golden hair from the French knot that kept it from getting in her way. It fell the entire length of her back, to her waist. Metzger had refused to indulge in such extravagances and had kept her hair shorn to a utilitarian crew cut.

The doctor stiffened as Erika Hernandez walked through the open archway into the courtyard and quipped, "I'm home."

Metzger got up and avoided contact with Hernandez, as usual. "I have to go check on Sidra," she said. "Find out if she felt like eating any of her dinner tonight."

Hernandez eyed Metzger's exit with a weary stare, but she said nothing. In the long, dark blur of indistinguishable days and nights, the reasons behind grudges and resentments had long since been lost. The four women, in Fletcher's opinion, were all stuck in a loop, going over the same ground from moment to moment and year to year. Sidra had taken refuge in her psychological meltdown; Metzger had made a fortress of her anger and resentment; Hernandez had submerged into work, as always; and Fletcher sat on the sidelines, trying and failing to think of a way to quit this pointless game.

She watched Hernandez sit down across from her and stir the vegetable paste in the ceramic pot that sat on the table between them. "Another failed attempt at soup?" the captain asked. "Why don't they ever listen to us and put in more water?"

"Because we're just humans," Fletcher griped. "What the hell could we possibly know about cooking our own meals?" She tilted her head back and gazed at the sparse starfield. "Find any good planets today?"

Hernandez shook her head. "We thought we did, but when we looked closer we picked up radio signals."

"Off-limits, then," Fletcher replied.

"Exactly. Another day, another system off the list." She picked up a clean bowl and spooned some greenish vegetable goop into it. "How was your day? Do anything interesting?"

Fletcher grinned. "I finished my novel."

"As in, you finished a first draft? Or as in, it's done?"

"Well," Fletcher replied with a shrug, "great works of art are never finished, only abandoned."

"I see," Hernandez said, lifting a spoonful of accidentally condensed soup. "Glad you're so modest about it." As soon as she had the spoon in her mouth, she winced. Then, with effort, she swallowed. "So," she continued, twisting her tongue in disgust, "what is this great work of art?"

Trembling with excitement, Fletcher picked up her writing tablet, which also doubled as the storage and retrieval device for her manuscript. She was about to proffer it to Hernandez, but she hesitated and hugged it to her chest instead. "Do you want to read it?"

"Do I really have a choice? I mean, come on—it's what, the early sixteenth century? You've just written the first modern novel by a human being. I'd say that makes it required reading, from a historical perspective if not a literary one."

"Thanks for the vote of confidence," Fletcher said, thrusting the writing tablet across the table to Hernandez, who took it and stared at its title page with raised eyebrows.

"*Revenge of Chaotica: A Captain Proton Adventure?*" Disbelief or disapproval creased Hernandez's brow. "The first work of long-form modern human prose is an unauthorized space-fantasy *sequel*? Please tell me you're kidding."

"Well, since you've already decided that you hate it . . ." She reached across the table to take back the tablet.

Hernandez leaned back and pulled the tablet beyond Fletcher's grasp. "Hang on," she said, holding up her free hand. "You're right, I should read it before I judge it. And I'm honored that you're letting me be the first to see it."

"Well, you're the second, actually," Fletcher said, feeling sheepish. "I had Johanna proofread it. You know, just for style and spelling and all that." A slack-jawed look from Hernandez made it clear to Fletcher that she'd hit another nerve.

The captain protested, "English isn't even her first language! Unless you penned your magnum opus in German, I can't imagine why you'd let her see it before I did."

"Because I wanted it to be bloody great when you saw it," Fletcher said sharply. Then, more modestly, she added, "I wanted it to be perfect."

Then it was Hernandez's turn to hang her head in shame. "That's sweet of you," she said. "I'm sorry if I got all high and mighty on you there."

"No worries," Fletcher said, shrugging it off.

"I'll start reading it tonight," Hernandez said. She looked at her bowl of vegetable food product and grimaced. "I get the feeling I won't be sleeping too well, anyway." She set down the tablet and resumed poking at her dinner. "What are you doing tomorrow night after dinner?"

"Let me check my calendar," Fletcher deadpanned. "Why?"

"I have something to show you," Hernandez said. "And Johanna and Sidra, too. I think you're all gonna love it."

"What is it?"

Hernandez smirked. "A surprise."

Fletcher felt a surge of curiosity and dread. "I don't like surprises."

"You'll like this one."

She looked up at the empty spaces of the void. "We'll see."

"Keep your eyes shut," Hernandez said as she led her friends through the sublevel passage toward the threshold. "No peeking."

Fletcher and Metzger walked on either side of Valerian, each of them cupping one hand over the younger woman's eyes. Metzger whispered to the nervous young redhead, "Relax, Sidra. It's going to be all right. Breathe."

Inyx and Edrin stood on either side of the broad portal, awaiting the foursome's arrival. As they had agreed beforehand with Hernandez, they said nothing as she led the other three women to the edge of the world that lived beneath the city.

"Stop here," Hernandez said, and the women halted. "Take a deep breath. Hold it. . . . And on the count of three, let it go and step forward. One. Two. Three." She backpedaled ahead of them as they passed through the wide, oval doorway. Radiant warmth, a roar of white noise, the cawing of circling birds, and the scent of salt air swept over them as she said, "Open your eyes."

Metzger and Fletcher did as she'd asked, and they removed their hands from Valerian's eyes. In contrast to Hernandez's excited smile of expectation, Fletcher and Metzger reacted with wide-eyed stares of shock. Valerian, on the other hand, shrieked with joy and sprinted forward, across the white-sand beach, toward the frothing breakers that surged in on a high tide.

"Sidra, wait!" cried Metzger, who stumbled forward in belated pursuit, arms futilely outstretched.

Hernandez caught Metzger's sleeve. "It's all right, Johanna, she's safe." She turned and watched Valerian, who doffed her clothes and waded through the crashing waves before diving headfirst through a churning white breaker.

Fletcher pivoted in a slow circle, taking in the scene. High, white cliffs rose behind them, and wind-sculpted towers of limestone ascended majestically from the teal sea, bleached fingers poking up from the deep, some as close as a few dozen meters from shore. Farther out, almost halfway to the horizon, stood jagged islands of gray rock dotted with gnarled, anorexic trees.

"Where are we?" Fletcher asked, sounding wary.

"In a special chamber beneath the city," Hernandez said. "Inyx and Edrin built it for us."

Valerian had shed the last of her clothing, some of which floated behind her as she propelled herself away from shore with a choppy crawl stroke that had once been well practiced.

Shaking her head, Metzger said, "I don't understand."

"When they told me we might be in deep space for several more decades, I told them I couldn't take that—and I didn't think any of you could, either," Hernandez said. "They thought we only needed artificial sunlight, because it's all we ever asked for. Once I explained that we need a planetary—"

"No," Metzger interrupted, "I don't understand how they built us an ocean."

Before Hernandez could explain, Fletcher cut in, "It's some kind of high-tech simulation, isn't it?"

"Yes," Hernandez said. "Holographic, I think. I don't really get all the technical details, but it has something to do with force fields and optical illusions."

Twenty meters from shore, Valerian switched to a backstroke as she crested a rising swell of blue-green water, and she paddled easily into the trough behind it.

On the beach, Fletcher looked back at the white stone cliffs and asked, "Where's the bloody exit?"

Stunned, Hernandez replied, "What? You're *leaving*?"

"Tell the Caeliar they can keep this, whatever it is," Fletcher said. She started running her hands over the chalky cliff face. "What do I have to do, say 'open sesame'?"

A moment later, Metzger joined Fletcher's search.

"Johanna!" Hernandez protested. "You, too?"

Metzger looked back at her and scowled. "This is a trick, Erika. And you're falling for it."

She began to suspect her friends were crazy. "What're you talking about? Exactly how is this a trick?"

Fletcher gave up probing the cliff and turned back toward Hernandez. "Don't be so thick, Erika. I know a gilded cage when I see one." Metzger abandoned her own search and stood by Fletcher in solidarity as the XO continued, "It might look like home, but it's not."

"No one ever said it was," Hernandez said, frustrated with Fletcher's accusatory manner. "So it's a gilded cage. So what? Endless night was turning us all into basket cases, Ronnie, and you know it. We *need* this."

"I don't," Fletcher said, folding her arms.

Holding out her arms, Hernandez replied, "Don't you? Smell that air, Ronnie. Feel the sand under your feet. Listen to the wind and the water. Who cares if it isn't real? What difference does it make that we're still prisoners? Would you really rather be an inmate in that dark, gray box we've been living in? Or would you rather serve your time in the tropics?"

Fletcher laughed, but it was a mean-spirited chortle. "You just don't get it," she said. "It's not about whether it's real. It's about them wanting us to be happy as prisoners."

"You're right," Hernandez said. "I don't get it. What the hell are you talking about?"

"I'm talking about surrender, Erika. That's what accepting gifts from them would be. A bunk to sleep on, basic nutrition, clean water, sanitation—those are basics any prisoner ought to expect. I can take those and feel like I'm not letting them do me any favors. The solar therapy was pushing it, but Johanna made it a doctor's order, so that's that." She kneeled and picked up a handful of sand that spilled between her fingers. "But this? This is a gift, from *them,* with a big shiny bow on top. Living in here would be a lot easier; I know that. But it would also be the same as telling them, 'I give up.' And if I give them that last ounce of my pride, I'll have nothing left." She opened her hand and turned it to let the last grains of sand fall back onto the illusory beach. "I won't give them that, Erika. Not now. Not ever." She squinted into the bright blue dome of the sky. "Not even for this."

A ball of fire, red as an ember, lay in Hernandez's wrinkled palm. Gray ghosts condensed above it. In their serpentine motions and changes, Hernandez read the star system's life story.

"One-point-three billion years old," she said while

Inyx stood behind her and listened. "Rich in actinides, very rare for a system this old." A long and especially complex symbol split and snaked in a double helix around her index finger. "All the building blocks for unbihexium-310." A short parade of simple glyphs traveled up the side of her left hand. "No terrestrial planets, only gas giants. Forty-eight natural satellites, including one rich in lead-208. All but one exhibit profound geological instability. The only stable one is a cold hunk of silicon and carbon at the edge of the system."

Inyx asked with the quiet satisfaction of a proud teacher, "What about life-forms?"

"None," she said, studying the slow unspooling of smoky sigils. "Not even cosmozoans. I'm guessing the heavier elements made this system a bit rich for their tastes."

"Recommendation?"

A turn of her index finger set the crimson sphere spinning in her cupped hand as she gave it a push back into the virtual heavens of the Star Chamber. "Unsuitable for colonization, but it's rich in the elements you've been looking for. You should exploit this system for resources while colonizing another." She pointed up at a brilliant yellow-orange dot near the red orb she'd just released. "Have we looked at that one?"

"It's on the short list, as you would say." Inyx reached up and summoned the bright spot down to Hernandez's waiting hands. "I thought I might let you do the honors."

She placed her hands on either side of the warm-hued star's miniaturized doppelganger and puffed a small breath across it. A misty stream of data curled upward from it like smoke from a snuffed taper. Her eyes widened at the tale it told. "K2V main sequence star, mean temperature 4,890 degrees Kelvin. Seven planets, four terrestrial, two in the habitable zone, one at optimal distance. No sign of cosmozoan activity."

"Hardly surprising," Inyx said. "It's rather far from the nearest OB cluster. In fact, I'd daresay it's remote from most everything in this sector." He passed his undulating tendrils over the glowing orb in her hands and changed the image to a blue-green world streaked with white. It turned slowly before her. "Tell me about its third planet," he said.

"Minshara-class," she replied, reading more gray-ish-white Caeliar runes as they formed above the tiny globe. "Nitrogen-oxygen atmosphere. Gravity is ninety-eight percent of Erigol-normal. No artificial satellites, no radio emissions. No sign of industrial pollutants in the oceans or atmosphere. No evidence of synthetic electrical power generation on the surface. Geothermal activity is minimal, but it still has a molten iron core." She was almost giddy as she looked up at Inyx. "It's perfect."

"Perhaps," Inyx said. "We'll still need to survey the surface to make certain there are no sentient life-forms there. If there are, we mustn't interfere with their habitat."

"Of course," Hernandez said. "You know, I have to admit: On the one hand, it makes me happy to find out so many Minshara-class worlds are populated by sentient species. But I have to wonder why so many of the races we've found have been humanoid. Even some of the more exotic ones we've seen have been bipedal and demonstrated bilateral symmetry."

"The result of an ancient bit of genetic interference," Inyx said. "I'll tell you about it someday, after Axion is settled and secure." Before she could pester him for details, he looked away. When he turned back, he said, "I've petitioned the Quorum for a survey of that world. Efforts are under way."

She released the planet, which floated languidly back into the darkness above. "I want to join the survey," she said.

"It's not a literal visit to the world's surface," Inyx said. "We'll use a number of subspace apertures to make undetected inspections of the planet, from its core to its oceans to its highest elevations. Noninvasive scans will be made of any life-forms we encounter."

"And how long will that take?"

"Not long," Inyx said. "No more than two of your years."

Once upon a time, she might have laughed at the Caeliar's conception of human time scales. Now she just swallowed her sarcastic remarks and moved on. "I presume we'll keep looking for new candidate systems while the survey is conducted?"

"Yes," Inyx said. "though we can stop for today, if you're feeling fatigued."

Her eyes itched as though they'd been rubbed with sand, but she lied, "I'm fine. What's next?"

He reached up, and a bluish-white fireball the size of a grape answered his call and floated down to Hernandez. It came to a gradual stop in front of her, and she interpreted its fleeting dance of wispy pictograms. When she'd finished and released it, Inyx remarked, "I have been meaning to commend you for the way you've mastered our written language."

"All it took was time," she said. "And I had plenty of it."

He gestured for her to follow him as he moved toward the nearest exit from the Star Chamber, and she walked beside him. "I don't think you appreciate how special your achievement is," he said. "You are the first non-Caeliar to learn our language in more than eighty thousand years."

She responded with a rueful smirk. "Did you ever give anyone else the chance?"

"Well . . . no, not as such," Inyx said.

"Then I can't feel that impressed with myself."

He turned his bulbous head just enough to glance down at her. "You seem to be learning some of our other abilities, as well," he said.

Unable to discern what he was talking about, she furrowed her brow in confusion. "What other abilities?"

"Transmogrification," he said. "Your changes in form."

"Okay, you've lost me."

He waved his arm in a slow arc, and a metallic pinpoint formed in the air ahead of them. They stopped and watched as it grew, flattened, and expanded into an immaculate silver mirror that hovered before them. Gesturing at their reflections, Inyx said, "Your change has been quite gradual, but it's no less impressive for its subtlety."

It was the same face she saw in her own mirror every morning now. Her face was wrinkled and marked by dark brown age spots, and her once mostly black hair had long since turned a leaden gray. Her cheeks sagged beside her chin, under which drooped a small waddle of loose flesh. A stroke of genetic good fortune had preserved her eyesight all these decades, and though her eyes now were sunken within age-darkened sockets, they were the only part of her that still resembled the woman she had been when she had come to Axion a lifetime ago.

"Inyx, are you talking about the changes I've gone through since I came to Axion? The deterioration of my skin, the fading of my hair, the compression of my spine?"

"Of course," Inyx said.

She sighed because she was too tired to actually get angry anymore. "It's not a conscious shape-change," she explained. "It's just cellular breakdown. Or, as my people like to say, it's called getting old."

"I know," Inyx said. "I was just trying to make a joke."

Hernandez detoured around the mirror and continued toward the exit. Inyx loped along and caught up to her. She scowled at him. "If you need a hobby, stick to sculpture," she said. "'Cause you're *definitely* not cut out for comedy."

Johanna Metzger held Sidra Valerian's hand and walked with her onto the beach that wasn't really a beach but was real enough for the younger woman's daily escape from reality. A long time ago, it had been Valerian who'd needed the reassurance of contact, the steady guidance from the bleak confines of their quarters to this blinding, sunlit lie.

Age had taken its toll on them both since then. Valerian's fiery red hair had faded to a dull rusty hue flecked with gray, and Metzger's own gray crew cut had turned bone-white and now spilled far beneath her shoulder blades. It was Valerian, the silent athlete, the mute woman-child, who supported Metzger now. Frail and doddering, the elderly Swiss doctor could barely see. To her, the world had become little more than soft-edged shapes and blurs of color, washes of light and darkness, elusive shades and specters. She relied on Valerian to escort her through the labyrinth of Axion's streets each day, to and from this refuge.

They crossed the threshold, and the false sun warmed her skin and reduced her world to a red glare through her closed eyelids. With wordless tenderness, Valerian touched Metzger's face, then released her hand. Beyond the wall of white noise, Metzger heard her surrogate daughter's soft steps in the sand, then the splash as Valerian plunged headlong into the crashing surf for another day of aquatic reverie.

Swimming was all Valerian did anymore; it was all she had done for as long as Metzger could remember. Once, the Scotswoman had been young and beautiful. Now she was age-worn, like Fletcher and Hernandez, and the extra time that Valerian spent in the glow of the Caeliar's artificial tropical sun had blemished her once-milky skin with a million brown freckles and several dark spots that Metzger was certain would eventually become malignant melanomas. And she never spoke. She had been silent for so long that Metzger no longer remembered her voice.

Metzger added that to the ever-growing list of things she no longer recalled.

Routine and repetition were all that Metzger had

left, and all that Valerian had left. In the mornings, they walked to the beach. Sometimes, Metzger had stayed the entire day, until the sun set and Valerian took her arm and guided her home again, to the court-yard.

Before Metzger's vision had deteriorated, however, she had often left Valerian to enjoy the ersatz paradise alone, excusing herself to take refuge on the top level of a nearby tower, one of the highest vantage points in Axion. Elevated above the spires of the metropolis, Metzger had lost herself against the vast canvas of space and stars.

"The outer darkness," she had called it, in the days before darkness had become her norm.

She breathed in the salty air and tried to make her-self believe that it was real, but she couldn't. There was no cure for knowing it was a lie—a hoax, just like the sand and the surf and the sun. There was nothing here worth believing in.

Except for Sidra.

Turning around was a labor of small steps, uncer-tain pauses, calculated risks. It felt as if it took forever before she was facing the cliff wall that concealed the exit. Metzger could have sworn that the angle of her shadow was moving faster than she was. Then she nudged herself forward through an act of sheer will, and said to the Caeliar's machine, "Let me out."

The exit appeared. The oval aperture was wide, and its bottom was perfectly flush with both the beach and the corridor floor on the other side. Metzger was grateful to be spared the need to step over anything; she left the simulation with weak, shuffled steps. She doubted that Valerian would even note her absence until dusk. Maybe not even then.

I've held on for so much longer than I thought I would, Metzger thought, shambling along. *I must be a crone by now.*

Minutes passed, or maybe hours, while Metzger forged ahead in quaking steps, her weight supported by a simple cane. As much as she had disdained the Caeliar's moving walkways and pod lifts in the past, she depended on them now. Once she'd reached the city's pedestrian network, it whisked her along in ease and comfort, straight into the main level of her favorite tower.

Calling down a pod lift was effortless; she stood in the empty, illuminated ring, and a pod formed around her. "To the top," she croaked, her voice brittle and breathy. Without delay, the transparent cocoon surrounded her. She was hurtled upward, past the blur of one level after another, until she found herself on the tower's top floor. The pod dissolved, and she stepped forward, through an arched portal onto a balcony surrounded by black sky and stars.

A blank slate, she thought, peering into the endless night. *I stared into it so long that I became it. I gazed into the abyss and erased myself.*

Her past was gone, fled from her, and had been for a long time. *I can't remember the faces of my children,* she lamented. *My sweet, lovely Franka . . . why can't I see you when I dream? Jörn, my little man . . . you looked so much like your father, but I've lost you both.* Tears ran from her half-blind eyes, down her slack and fissured cheeks. She couldn't even remember her own past—the images of herself as a child and as a young woman were faded and out of reach. Her life was a gray memory, dim and lost.

Metzger had tried to be strong and defiant like Fletcher, but Fletcher had never had a family. At first, Metzger had thought that the hope of returning to her kin might be a source of strength. Then months had turned into years, and years had become a lifetime . . . and hope had become despair.

There's nothing left to hope for, Metzger told herself. She'd held on longer than she'd wanted to, and she knew that it was because of Valerian. She had found some measure of meaning in her life by caring for the emotionally fractured younger woman, but it no longer felt like enough. *I can't live for someone else,* Metzger admitted to herself.

She had told herself the same thing every day for what felt like months now, during her daily retreats to this perch above the city. Her intentions had been clear from the beginning, but one thing or another had held her back. A lifetime of losses, grudges, and mistakes had burdened her and rooted her in place.

One by one, she had made her peace with them all. Day after day she had come to the top of this tower, stared into the void, and shed her emotional ballast.

Fear was the first burden she'd cast off into the night. Guilt was the second. Then all that remained had been a legion of regrets: words left unspoken, wounds left unmended, debts left unpaid. The last was one that could not be helped—there was no way she could explain herself to Valerian.

She won't understand. But that's not my fault.

Looking up, she let the fathomless darkness consume her final lamentations, the end of her hope, and the vestiges of her memory, until nothing remained. There was no more cause for joy or weeping, no more grieving for the life she had lost or the one she had lived in exile.

There was only blessed emptiness.

Metzger leaned forward, over the balcony railing. Her stiff, arthritic back protested as she forced herself to double over. *The pain is an illusion,* she reminded herself. *It's just the last hurdle. Up and over.* Tucking her chin toward her chest, she felt her toes come away from the balcony deck. Then gravity took hold, tugged the rest of her body over the railing, and pulled her in its steady, loving embrace toward the ground—toward release. For a moment, she felt weightless.

Then she was free.

Hernandez looked down into Valerian's glassy blue eyes and saw no spark of life left in them. The mute woman's chest expanded and contracted with slow, shallow breaths, and her heartbeat was barely palpable when Hernandez pressed her palm on Valerian's sternum. "It's been almost three days," she said. "She can't last like this, not for much longer. She'll dehydrate."

"I just can't believe it," Fletcher said, standing on the other side of the bed. "I wasn't even sure she heard what we were saying when we told her about Johanna."

Stroking a wild tangle of Valerian's unkempt hair from her forehead, Hernandez was struck by the prospect of losing two of her only three friends in less than a week. After Inyx had broken the news of Metz-

ger's suicide, it had fallen to Hernandez to go to the
simulated beach and collect Valerian.

The change in the daily routine had immediately
made Valerian edgy. Neither Hernandez nor Fletcher
had meant to confront the fragile younger woman
with the tragedy right away, but the empty seat at
their shared dinner table, and their own grave moods,
had made the subject unavoidable. The consequences
had proved worse than they'd feared; the revelation
that Metzger had taken her own life and was gone forever had pushed Valerian into a denial so profound
that she sank into catatonia.

Inyx stood at the foot of the bed and waited on Hernandez. "What do you wish to do?" he asked.

"I haven't decided yet," Hernandez said, torn between what she felt she could live with and what she
thought was merciful.

Fletcher took Valerian's left hand in hers and
squeezed it. She looked at Inyx. "What could you do
for her?"

"I'm not entirely certain," Inyx said. "Our examina-
tions of her through the years have always suggested
that her malady is purely psychological in nature. As
such, we would advise against any pharmaceutical in-
terventions."

Bitterly, Fletcher replied, "In other words, with all
this power and all these gadgets, there's nothing you
can do."

"On the contrary," Inyx said, "there is a great deal
that we can do. I only doubt that the great majority of
it would be of any therapeutic benefit to her affliction.
In the end, I suspect that anything short of our most

invasive efforts would serve only to prolong her current, isolated existence." He directed his next words to Hernandez. "But if that is your wish, Erika, we will do as you ask."

She reached down and clasped Valerian's other hand. "I don't know what to do, Ronnie. I want to save her. . . ."

"Why?" Fletcher's grief was as raw as Hernandez's own, but her defiant spirit was as strong as it ever had been. "What would be the point, Erika? She'd be alive, but that's not the same as living, and you know it."

"I don't know anything of the sort," Hernandez said. "Inyx, she has brain wave activity, doesn't she?"

He made a slight, concessionary bow, arms apart. "Of a very limited kind," he said.

"So, who knows what kind of life she's living inside her head? Maybe it's paradise in there."

"And maybe it's limbo," Fletcher said. "Or purgatory. Or hell, or just plain, simple oblivion." Sorrow moistened her eyes as she looked down at their stricken friend. "Face the truth, Erika. She's gone, and you know it. We have to let her go."

Hernandez shook her head. Valerian's hand was still warm to the touch, and even if the light had gone from her eyes, there was still blood coursing in her veins and breath moving in her lungs. Her heart was beating, and her synapses were firing—even if it was only a lonely few of them holding the fort until true consciousness returned. It didn't matter to Hernandez that Sidra Valerian was old—she was alive and worth fighting for.

"Inyx," she asked, "can you do more than just keep

Sidra's body alive? Is there anything you can do to help her heal her psychological injuries?"

The question made the lanky alien think for several moments before he answered. "It's difficult to predict," he said. "Our methods would involve making significant alterations to her biology and linking her mind to our communal gestalt."

Fletcher was horrified. "You'd turn her into one of you?"

"Not truly one of us," Inyx said. "But she would become integrated into our community. If we can achieve a balanced communion with her consciousness, we might be able to quell her emotional turmoil and restore her to a greater semblance of her former self." His enthusiasm waned as he added, "The process would, however, entail a significant risk. We've never tried to fuse our catoms with non-Caeliar life-forms before."

That earned a contemptuous snort from Fletcher. "I take it back. You wouldn't be turning her into one of you. You'd be turning her into a bloody guinea pig." She glared at Hernandez. "Don't let them do it, Erika. She's not a piece of meat to be experimented on. Let her die with some dignity."

It was tempting to think of Valerian being restored to the woman she'd been fifty years ago—at least, in terms of her personality. And it was the very sense of temptation that told Hernandez she had to resist. There was something wrong about it, something unnatural. And maybe Fletcher was right—perhaps it was also, in some distinctly human-specific way, undignified.

Still pondering her options, she asked Inyx, "What about sedating her into a gradual cardiac arrest?"

"The word you're avoiding," Inyx said with sharp sarcasm, "is 'euthanasia,' and its practice is forbidden here. We will not engage in it, nor will we tolerate its use in Axion."

"But suicide seems to get the stamp of approval," Fletcher sniped. Hernandez threw a silencing glare at her old friend.

Inyx continued, "We can apply pain-blocking medications and protocols as a precaution, in case the patient's mind is still conscious on some level and cognizant of the body's suffering or discomfort. However, this prevention of pain is accomplished without the risk of aggravating the patient's condition."

"Sounds reasonable," Hernandez said, short-circuiting any further dissent from Fletcher. Pointedly, she asked the other woman, "Any problem with that?"

Fletcher sighed and averted her eyes, back toward Valerian. "No," she said. "No problem."

Inyx folded his tendril hands in front of him. "Of course, to impose a medical procedure on someone without proper consent would be an act of violence. Because Sidra is not competent to make an informed decision, and you're her commanding officer, we consider you to be her guardian, Erika—and we will engage no medical efforts without your permission."

Hernandez looked at Valerian, and then she looked up at Fletcher, who said simply, "It's your call, Erika."

She looked to Inyx. "You promise she won't suffer?"

"We will do all that we can to prevent it."

She palmed tears from her puffy, wrinkled cheeks and nodded in the face of the inevitable. "Let's get on with it, then."

The waiting was the worst part. Encamped at Valerian's bedside with Fletcher, all that Hernandez could do was sit and be numb as she watched Valerian deteriorate. Only a week earlier, despite being in her seventies, Valerian had been vital, able at least to savor her moments in the Caeliar's ersatz sea.

Now her cheeks were gaunt, her eyes sunken. Her skin had become sallow and flaky. "Maybe we should give her water," Hernandez said, second-guessing all her decisions.

"It'll only prolong her decline," Fletcher said. "Ketosis is a good way to go if you let it take its course. If she is conscious of anything, there's a good chance she's semi-euphoric from all the fat her body's burning."

It had been six days since Hernandez had made her decision to let Valerian fade away. Since then, either she or Fletcher had been at Valerian's side, and usually it was both of them. They'd taken turns eating, napping, and using the lavatory so that, in case Valerian regained consciousness, there would be someone there to halt the process. That moment hadn't come.

Valerian had gone all these days without food or water. Hernandez knew that renal failure must be imminent for Valerian, if it hadn't already occurred. Once Valerian's kidneys failed, the end would come within a day or two as toxins in her blood disrupted her heart.

Time had crawled during Hernandez's decades in Axion, and it also had flown. Trudging through the monotony of routines and rituals had felt like slow time, a life sealed in amber sap, barely moving, trapped in stasis. But then, one day, she'd looked up to find forty years had passed. Now nearly fifty.

Most of my life went by before I knew what happened, she realized. *Measured against that, a few days should be nothing. But this feels like forever.*

There were no clocks to watch, no calendar pages to turn. In the cosmic scale of the Caeliar's search for a new world to claim as their own, nothing marked the lost hours and seconds. Valerian's irregular gasps for breath made it clear that these insignificant increments of time were all that were left to her; she'd see no more days, no more years.

An upwelling of panic impelled Hernandez to her feet. Trembling in her steps, she shuffled away from the bed at a pace only the elderly would consider hurried. Her hands shook as she reached out for something to steady herself.

From behind her, Fletcher asked, "Where are you going?"

"To call for Inyx," she said.

Fletcher's tone was sharp. "Why?"

"I've changed my mind." She reached the doorway and was gathering her strength to cross its threshold when Fletcher stopped her with the piercing anger in her voice.

"Stop, Erika," Fletcher commanded. "Don't do this, not like this. It's almost over, and she's not in any pain."

Hernandez shut her eyes and leaned against the doorway. "I can't just let her die, Ronnie. We can't know what Sidra really wants. What if she wants to live? What if she's in there, wishing she could wake up?"

"No, Erika, stop." She heard Fletcher get up from her chair and walk toward her in slow steps. "If Sidra wanted to be here, she would be. But she's been running away for a long time, ever since Erigol was destroyed. This is just the last step for her. Let her take it in peace."

She opened her eyes to find Fletcher beside her. "What if the Caeliar can help her, Ronnie?"

"They can't do anything without changing her," Fletcher said. "What they're proposing would make her something not quite human anymore. It'd be invasive and would violate the very core of what Sidra is. Is saving her life worth taking away her humanity, Erika? Is death that frightening?"

Turning away, Hernandez looked to the stars and said, "Inyx, are you listening? I need you. Please."

Fletcher grabbed Hernandez's shoulders. "Think about what you're doing! Sidra's ready to go—don't force this on her!"

Specks of airborne dust seemed to catch the starlight for a moment, and then they coalesced into glowing motes. In seconds the flurry of tiny lights swirled together and fused into a white radiance that faded to reveal Inyx on their doorstep. He gave a small, courteous bow and said, "How can I help, Erika?"

Guilt made her look to Fletcher for forgiveness, but she found only seething resentment and disappointment in the other woman's gaze. To Inyx she said, "I've reconsidered your offer. I want you to help Sidra, any way you can."

Inyx looked past her, toward Valerian. "Her condition has worsened. The process would be challenging for her, under the best of circumstances. She's very fragile. Are you sure you want to change course now?"

"Is there any chance that you could save her? That she could talk to us again?"

The tall, gangly Caeliar scientist crossed the room to Valerian's bedside, reached out, and let the tendrils of his right arm caress the dying woman's face and throat. Then he looked back at Fletcher and Hernandez. "There is a chance."

"Then do it," Hernandez said. "Hurry."

He pushed his arms under Valerian's emaciated body and lifted her from the bed. Fletcher was sullen as Inyx carried Valerian into the courtyard, where he summoned one of the Caeliar's signature silver travel disks. He stepped onto the disk and said, "Erika, you'll need to come with me. Veronica, you may attend the procedure if you wish."

"No thanks," Fletcher said, and she walked away.

Hernandez joined Inyx on the silver disk. She gently took Valerian's hand as the platform ascended from the courtyard, hovered above their residence, and accelerated into the heart of the city. Traveling above dark boulevards in a city of perpetual night, and seeing Valerian cradled in Inyx's skeletal arms, gave Hernandez the troubling sensation of being a passenger on the ferry of Charon, crossing a black river into the underworld.

"Hang on," she whispered to Valerian. "It'll be all right." She knew what Fletcher would call this, and she didn't care.

Forced to choose between letting Valerian die or

letting her be transformed by the healing gifts of the Caeliar, death no longer seemed like a victory, and she no longer thought of surrender as a defeat.

It was simply the price of survival.

Despite having spent most of her life in Axion, Hernandez had never before seen the chamber into which she followed Inyx.

It was long, narrow, and high-ceilinged. Bizarre, semi-organic-looking alien machines were crowded into the tight space. Silvery cables drooped on long diagonals high overhead, and at the top of the laboratory was a broad, clamshell-shaped skylight through which she saw the black sky dotted with stars.

Inyx carried Valerian to a long, flat metallic table that Hernandez grimly thought of as a slab. Its surface was dark gray, several centimeters thick, and unadorned. As he set the dying woman on the table, a sepulchral droning began to fill the echoing silence. Looking around, Hernandez saw several of the machines in the room begin to pulse with a violet light.

"Please watch from behind that barrier," Inyx said, pointing to a transparent wall that curved around a large, odd-looking console. "You will be safer there."

She did as he asked and walked behind the protective shield. Motion from overhead caught her eye. It was an ungainly contraption, long and asymmetrical and covered with alarming protuberances. It glowed with the same purple radiance as the other machines in the lab, and it glided through the air without any obvious means of support or locomotion. She tensed as it settled into position directly above Valerian.

Watching the device move into place, she noticed more subtle movements, much higher up along the far wall. There she saw a row of wide observation windows, in front of which more than a score of Caeliar had gathered. That was when she understood that this wasn't simply a lab—it was an operating theater, and Valerian was to be that night's main attraction.

On the other side of the barrier, Inyx levitated himself a few meters off the floor and made some minuscule manual adjustments to the large machine. Apparently satisfied with his modifications, he floated back to the floor and joined Hernandez behind the see-through wall. "We're almost ready," he said. "I just need to make some detailed scans of her brainwave pattern to be certain the catoms are set to the correct frequency."

"What's going to happen to her?"

Manipulating the console's controls with his tendrils, Inyx replied, "I'm going to infuse her body with the same sort of catoms that now constitute Caeliar bodies. In Sidra's case, the concentration will be infinitesimal, but it should be enough to let us repair any damage to her vital organs. Once that's done, we'll bring her back to consciousness and let her mind make contact with the gestalt."

"What if she doesn't understand what's happening?"

"The gestalt has gentle ways of making itself understood," Inyx assured her. "Whether she will be able to understand the message will depend greatly on her frame of mind." He turned and eyed a wall of liquid-textured panels that were strobing with information faster than Hernandez could decipher. "Excuse me a moment," he said, moving toward the rippling screens. "I have a few more details to check before we begin."

While he worked, she busied herself with studying the master control panel. Unable to discern most of its operational components, she looked up again at their Caeliar audience and saw a familiar figure lurking behind one of them. It was Fletcher, who Hernandez deduced must have changed her mind about boycotting the procedure. *One of the other Caeliar must have brought her here,* she figured.

"It's ready," Inyx said. "This is your last chance to change your mind, Erika. Once the procedure begins—"

"Do it," Hernandez said.

His tendrils moved over the console and never seemed to make contact, yet toggles changed positions and functions were triggered. Ominous churning noises filled the operating room, though Hernandez had no idea what was causing the sounds, which were followed by deep, rhythmic percussions that shook the floor. The incandescent core of the machine above Valerian turned a blinding shade of magenta.

Valerian was bathed in rose-colored light.

Her physical transformation was subtle—her skin regained its healthy color, and her eyes suddenly seemed less sunken.

"Now we rouse her," Inyx said. "This will take a few seconds." He made more fine adjustments to a delicate crystal console in front of him and Hernandez. Then he looked up and waited to see what would happen, his own sense of nervous anticipation as tangible to Hernandez as her own.

Valerian's blue eyes fluttered open.

And she screamed.

Her piercing wail, pure terror as sound, filled the lab.

Then she began thrashing, pounding her fists on the metal slab, kicking wildly—all as she kept on screeching.

"Turn it off!" Hernandez cried. "Make it stop!"

"It's too late," Inyx said. "We—"

Panicked, Hernandez bolted from the console, tried to run to Valerian, hoping to pull her off the table. Before she could round the safety wall, Inyx snared her in his grip, which was stronger than she had ever imagined it would be. "Don't, Erika. It's not safe."

"Let me go!" she pleaded. "I can't just let her—"

Then the screaming stopped, and Valerian curled in upon herself, hands pressed over her face like a mask, her eyes wide with horror and shock. Hernandez froze in place, and Inyx let go of her and returned in a flurry of motion to the console.

"Synaptic failure," he said, his dismay and surprise evident. "Something in her mind rejected contact with the gestalt." His hands began to work faster.

"What's going on?"

Growing more concerned, he replied, "Her disharmony with the gestalt is causing the other catoms in her body to fall out of sync with the city's quantum field."

Frustrated by the opacity of his reply, she angrily prompted, "Meaning . . . ?"

"Her body's rejecting the infusion," Inyx said. "The catoms are becoming chaotic." He turned, stepped between Hernandez and her view of Valerian, and tried to lead her away from the console. "You should step out, Erika, quickly."

She shook off his guidance. "Don't tell me what to—"

Words caught in her throat as Valerian started screaming again. Shrieks of agony, primal and inchoate, erupted from her . . . and then her body began to dissolve. Her skin sagged and her torso caved in. She clawed at her face with skeletal hands as her eyes sank into her skull. Then her cries of pain and fear rattled into silence, and what was left of her collapsed into a boiling froth that turned to black dust.

Hernandez stood paralyzed, in anguished silence, and stared at the carbonized stain that was the only evidence of Valerian's gruesome demise. Beside her, Inyx shut down the machines, which returned to their dormant state with a long, dwindling groan.

He looked up at the Caeliar spectators. Then he turned away from them in what Hernandez could only imagine was shame. "The Quorum demands my presence," he said in a subdued voice. "I'll send someone to escort you back to your residence."

Like a pile of leaves blowing away in an autumn wind, Inyx disincorporated in a rush of warm air. Reduced to a flowing stream of golden motes, he rose like smoke and vanished into the dense machinery that lined the high walls.

The other Caeliar who had gathered along the observation deck's windows departed, leaving only Fletcher, who stared down with cold anger at Hernandez.

Tears of guilt and rage streamed down Hernandez's face. *My God, what have I done? Sidra was at peace. All I had to do was let her go. Why couldn't I just let her go?*

She looked up at Fletcher and said, "I'm sorry."

Fletcher turned her back and walked away.

Alone in the darkened lab, Hernandez stood in silence. Failed and friendless, overwhelmed by sorrow and shame, she felt that she finally understood what it meant to be in exile.

The tree was long dead, its branches bare and brittle after decades in the dark. It sat on a mound of dusty earth that once had been a miniature island at the end of a long, rectangular pool of dark water. The pool was gone now. In its place was a dry stone cavity some two meters deep.

Hernandez stood beneath the expired tree and remembered it as it used to be, before Axion's panicked flight into the past. She and her landing party had met in the shade of its leafy boughs to weigh their chances of escape. Its shelter, however illusory, had been a comfort to her and to the others. Now its exposed, gnarled roots and fissured bark served to remind her only of life's fragility—and its brevity.

Something unseen stirred the air. She inhaled, caught a faint hint of ozone, and felt a warming tingle on the back of her neck. They were familiar sensations to her now. An illumination from behind her brightened the tree trunk, but she didn't need to turn around to know that Inyx had joined her.

"I thought I might find you here," he said.

She drew a line with her bare left foot in the coarse sand. "It's not like I have anywhere else to go."

He stepped forward to stand beside her. "I came to say that I'm sorry. For my failure, and for your loss."

"Thank you," she said. "But it wasn't your fault. It was just an accident."

"I still feel responsible," he said.

She sighed. "Don't. The decision was mine. You only did as I asked. If anyone's to blame, it's me." They stood together for a short time, saying nothing. Her mood took a melancholy turn. "I wonder sometimes if every decision I've made since the day the Romulans ambushed my ship has been wrong."

Inyx sounded perplexed. "Why would you think so?"

"Why wouldn't I?" she replied. "I risked traveling at relativistic speeds to seek a safe haven instead of waiting for a rescue. I took my ship to an unknown world instead of setting course for home. I led my people into captivity here." She paused as the wrenching impact of her recent tragedies hit her in full force. Her voice caught in her throat as she continued, "I missed or ignored all the warning signs that Johanna was planning on committing suicide. And instead of letting Sidra die with peace and dignity, I made her final moments agonizing and humiliating . . . because I was too scared to just let her go."

Inyx asked, "Did your decisions seem rational at the time?"

She shrugged. "I suppose."

"In that case, unless you've secretly possessed the power of precognition all this time, I would posit that you made the right decision in at least some of those moments. Even if you feel the outcomes were negative, it could be argued that some of the alternatives might have been far worse."

"In my mind, I know you're right. But part of me can't shake the fear that all I've been doing since the ambush is failing the people who depended on me, who trusted me. Maybe it's not rational to think so, but it's how I feel."

He made a strange grunt of acknowledgment. "I understand, Erika. After your shipmates' interference helped spark the destruction of Erigol, I grieved for millions of my brothers and sisters—including Sedín, my friend of several millennia. She'd castigated me for persuading the Quorum to grant you and your crew sanctuary on Erigol. In her eyes, I had defiled our home. At the time, I was certain I had made the right and merciful decision, but after Erigol was lost, I . . . I wasn't sure anymore. I felt that I'd failed my people and jeopardized the Great Work."

The profound pathos of his confession moved Hernandez. She turned toward him and let herself look at him, in an effort to see past his stern, alien visage. His grim countenance remained inscrutable, but she could hear the changes in his voice and his breathing, and she saw the vulnerability and openness of his body language. It was the first time that she felt as if she could understand the nonverbal cues of his species.

He continued, "Even when the Quorum exonerated me, I didn't believe I deserved to continue as Axion's chief scientist. Not after my lapses in judgment."

"But you went on," she said. "You found a reason."

"He looked at her. "Yes, I did. It was you."

She was caught off guard. "Me? I don't understand."

"Because you sought me out, in the Star Chamber," he said, calling Axion's observatory by the name she had given it in jest. "You came and asked to help us, and to be taught. I knew that you were burdened by losses, as I was. But you coped with your suffering by seeking to aid others. You reminded me that sometimes the way to heal oneself is to tend to others first."

"Wow," she said with a grin. "And I thought I was just trying to make the days go by a little faster. I had no idea I was such an inspiration." Flexing the stiffness from her fingers, she winced at the brittle dryness of her skin, a reminder of time's ravages and her advancing years. She masked her anxiety with glib humor. "What'll you do when I'm gone?"

"Do you intend to leave the city?" he asked with genuine surprise. She wasn't sure if he was joking, sincere, or just especially obtuse as a consequence of denial.

"In a manner of speaking, yes," she said. "I probably don't have much time left, Inyx."

A somberness settled upon him. "You mean you're dying."

"I don't know that I'd put it quite like that," she said. "I'm not saying I'm at death's door, for heaven's sake. My body's just starting to wear out, is all. It's part of life, Inyx. Everything that lives has to die eventually."

"Yes," he said. "Eventually. But some die sooner than others, and many before they should or need to."

Hernandez nodded. "On Earth, we call that Fate." She reached out and rested her hand on his bony, grayish arm. "I'm sorry. I didn't mean to upset you by bringing up dying."

His voice sounded smaller, softer than usual. "I'd prefer that you didn't."

"Talk about it?"

"No," he said. "Die."

His earnestness almost made her laugh.. "No offense to you and your supertoys, but I don't think it's your call to make."

"You're absolutely right," he said. "It's yours."

It had been several weeks, or possibly even months, since the twilight had descended on Fletcher's friendship with Erika. Though they continued to live in residences off the same courtyard, Fletcher had taken pains to avoid contact with her captain since Sidra's grotesque desecration by the Caeliar's untested technology and Erika's clouded judgment.

Whenever Fletcher saw Erika dining alone in the courtyard, she made a point of sequestering herself in her residence until after Erika had left, no doubt for another turn of collaboration with the Caeliar scientist in his observatory. Once, a few weeks earlier, Fletcher had emerged after Erika's departure to find that one of the white pawns on the chess board she'd carved had been moved from its starting position at c2 to c4.

So, Fletcher had mused. *She wants to play.*

Unwilling to indulge Erika's feeble attempt at contact, Fletcher had picked up the board and pieces and taken them back into her suite of rooms and tucked them inside a drawer.

The thought of the chess set inside the dresser had nagged at her ever since, to the point that she had begun having recurring dreams about chess. In one she played against a hooded opponent. The outcome of that game, she knew, had been preordained. Playing it to its end was merely a formality. She'd tried to take the inevitable loss in stride.

In another nightmare, she was a piece on the board, trying to exert her queenly power by dashing diagonally across the ranks to strike down a haughty bishop, only to stumble and fall over her own feet. When a cavalier reached down from his steed to help her back up, he'd laughed. "What were you thinking?" he said. "You know pawns can't move diagonally except to attack, and there's no one here within your reach."

There were as many variants on her nightly reveries as there were strategies for chess. She'd look down to find all her pieces missing except her king, who stood completely exposed. Or her king would betray his own army and cut them down, one by one. Or she would pick up a piece to move it, only to discover that all her pieces were carved of sand, which would crumble between her fingers and be carried away in a whisper of wind.

Her pieces burned and turned to ashes. They'd rebel and cut her fingertips. The entire board would turn black and become a portal into the void, and all the pieces, white and black alike, would fall through it and vanish into the emptiness of nothing.

That day Fletcher had awakened, opened her eyes, and gritted her teeth against the cramps and pains that had become as familiar to her as old friends whose company was obnoxious but was tolerated for lack of an alternative. Seeing no sign of Erika in the courtyard and no lights on in the other woman's residence, Fletcher retrieved the chess set from her drawer, carried it out to the table in the middle of the court, and set it up, with the white pieces facing herself.

Then she waited.

Lost in her thoughts, she had no regard now for time's passage. It slipped past as it always had: seeming to move impossibly slow in the present, the future always so far at bay, until the day when one looked back on uncounted expired moments and realized how few must then remain.

Fletcher had played both sides of an entire game of chess in her thoughts by the time Erika stepped through the entryway into the courtyard. The captain hesitated, as if fearful of intruding on Fletcher's privacy. For a moment, Fletcher considered picking up the chess pieces and retreating again into her private spaces. Instead, she made eye contact with Erika and allowed the moment to linger. Then she reached forward and moved the king's knight to f3—a clear invitation to play.

Erika's manner was cautious as she approached the table and, with some effort and apparent mild discomfort, eased herself into a seat across from Fletcher. She gave a shallow sigh, studied the board, and advanced her queen's pawn to d5.

Moving a pawn to g3 beside her knight, Fletcher said nothing and waited for Erika's reaction.

The captain lifted one eyebrow. "The Réti Opening?" she said. "With the King's Indian attack? Really?"

Exhaustion made it easy for Fletcher to betray no reaction to Erika's brazen inquiry. She spent those moments picturing the likely next sequence of moves, the captures of pawns, the development of pieces for the middlegame. If Erika remained as predictable as always, in five moves Fletcher would be ready to flanchetto the king's bishop to g2, assert command of the center, and set the stage for a kingside castling.

A sharp pang in Fletcher's side made her wince as she reached forward to advance another pawn.

Although Erika's eyes never seemed to leave the board, she asked, "Are you all right?"

"Just a cramp," Fletcher said.

The game continued in silence for several minutes, until Erika perplexed Fletcher by making a number of irregular moves. Suddenly, Fletcher's plan to control the board's center from its wings with her bishops and knights began to seem unworkable. With equal measures of amusement and irritation, she said, "Don't tell me—Tayvok's Gambit?"

It was Erika's turn to give away nothing. She folded her hands and continued eyeing the ranks and files of the board.

"I finished another novel," Fletcher said. "The sequel to *Lightning Shy*."

Erika steepled her fingers in front of her chin as she said, "Finally. I've been waiting for you to resolve that story for ages." She looked up. "What's the new book called?"

"*Flashpoint Sinister*."

The answer provoked a half smirk from Erika. She moved her queen's bishop to a6 and asked, "What does the title mean?"

"Read it and find out."

Before she could take any satisfaction in prolonging Erika's suspense, Fletcher looked again at the board and saw that she'd been lulled into a careless blunder two moves earlier—a mistake that had become apparent only as more of the pieces were developed by both sides. Within three moves she would either have to risk losing significant pieces or watch her pawn structure collapse under a skewer attack that Erika had developed with remarkable subtlety.

While Fletcher pondered some strategic adjustments that might let her recover her tempo, Erika remarked casually, "I learned today that a star system I singled out for investigation has been selected as the site of New Erigol. Inyx tells me we'll reach its Minshara-class planet in less than a year."

"That's great," Fletcher said, swallowing her anger. It rankled her every day to know that Erika was helping the Caeliar in their search for a new homeworld. As far as Fletcher was concerned, as long as the Caeliar remained her captors, they were the enemy, not to be aided or abetted in any way. But the fact remained that Erika was the captain, and it was up to her to follow the dictates of her own conscience.

Fletcher let her queen's knight brave the center as a lure for Erika's queen. If the bait was taken, Fletcher could capture black's queen with her bishop; if Erika responded in a more conservative fashion, it would become possible to weaken her kingside pawn structure as a prelude to a check scenario.

"Once we reach the planet, Inyx says the Caeliar will let us leave the city and live on the surface if we want." Erika's tone seemed to be imploring forgiveness from Fletcher. "We could have grass under our feet again, Ronnie. Breathe fresh air." Getting no reaction from Fletcher, she continued more earnestly.

DAVID MACK

"We could wade in the ocean—a real ocean, not a Caeliar simulation. It wouldn't be a gift. It'd be more like a well-earned parole." She had the cautious expression of someone expecting a harangue. "Would that be okay?"

Fletcher shrugged. "I suppose."

Erika shifted her queen to a position from which she could better defend her center, but Fletcher knew that she'd developed her own knights and rooks in ideal positions to pick off Erika's queen if it tried to interfere with her knight's burning-and-salting march through Erika's rear ranks.

Looking up from her move, Erika said, "The Caeliar would also be willing to build us a house on the surface. Is that an act of charity you could live with, or would you rather build a lean-to and sleep on the ground out of principle?"

Before answering, Fletcher captured Erika's king's bishop with her knight, exposing an important weakness on that flank of Erika's formation. At the same time, Erika's previous move, combined with this latest attack, now presented Erika with another imminent threat, this time to her king's rook. If she moved it to spare it from this discovered attack by Fletcher's queen, she would lose her queen's knight and see her king placed in check on the next turn. Or she could let the rook be captured, move the king to delay the inevitable, and—in the most favorable scenario for black—fight on to a stalemate.

"Sure, build a house," Fletcher said, as Erika assessed her tactical vulnerabilities. "I'm sure you'll be very happy in it."

Angrily, Erika asked, "What does that mean? You'll

sit here in your 'cell' and rot rather than share a real house with me?"

Fletcher frowned and looked at Erika with tired eyes. "No," she said, choking down the sickening sensations that swelled upward from her gut. "It means I think I'm dying."

2381

10

———

Ezri Dax's eyes had just adapted to the rings of bluish-white light flashing by on the *Aventine*'s main viewer when the pulses vanished and released the ship back into normal space with a nerve-wracking shudder.

"Confirm position," Dax said.

Lieutenant Ofelia Mavroidis tapped at the conn and replied, "Delta Quadrant, between the Perseus and Carina arms."

Bowers leaned forward in his chair and asked, "Distance from the Azure Nebula?"

The Ullian woman checked the conn display and replied, "Sixty-four thousand, five hundred ninety-two light-years."

Unable to stay seated, Dax got up and moved toward the science station, where Helkara worked with quiet, singular focus. "Gruhn," Dax said. "What's the word on the subspace tunnel? Do both ends open to the same frequency?"

"No, Captain," Helkara said. "It seems to need a unique frequency pulse for each aperture, just like the passage that brought us from the Gamma Quadrant to the nebula. It's likely this'll be true of all the tunnels."

Turning his chair toward the tactical console, Bowers asked, "Any sign of the Borg out here?"

Ensign Padraic Rhys, the gamma-shift tactical officer, replied, "Negative. But we're picking up a massive debris field bearing three-three-one mark one-five." The fair-haired, broad-shouldered young Welshman made rapid adjustments on his panel as he continued, "Lots of refined metals—duranium, rodinium, terminium, and semirigid polyduranide."

Dax asked Rhys, "Enough mass to suggest a starship?"

"More like a hundred thousand ships, sir," Rhys said. "It's pockets of pulverized metal orbiting the nearest star system."

Curiosity nagged at Dax. "Range?"

"Just under a light-year," Rhys said.

Mavroidis swiveled her chair around from the conn. "At top speed, we could reach the debris ring in about an hour."

"I don't think we can afford the distraction," Bowers said, rising from his chair. He walked over to join Dax. "We should hold station while Gruhn works out the aperture frequency for our return trip."

The lithe Zakdorn science officer looked up and flashed a crooked grin that lifted his facial ridges. "Don't hang around on my account. This'll take a few hours, at least."

"Ofelia," Dax said, "set a course for the debris field. I want to check it out."

Leaning in close, Bowers said in a quiet voice,

"Captain, if something did destroy hundreds of thousands of ships, we could be heading into a trap."

"Or maybe we just found an archaeological treasure," Dax said. She noted the grim frown that was deepening the creases on Bowers's face, and she relented a bit in her enthusiasm. "A little caution never hurts, though. Mister Rhys, scan the region for subspace radio activity and any other artificial signals."

"Aye, Captain," said Rhys.

While the tactical officer executed his sensor sweep, Mavroidis reported, "Course plotted and laid in, Captain."

Rhys finished his scans and said, "No short-range signal activity, Captain. Minimal subspace radio traffic at long range. No sign of transwarp signatures or other vessels."

"Glad to hear it," Dax said. "Helm, maximum warp. Engage."

The *Aventine* resonated with the rising hum of its warp engines accelerating to their limits, and the stars on the main viewer became snap-flashes of light coursing past the ship. "Warp nine-point-nine-seven," Mavroidis said, reading from her gauges. "Warp nine-point-nine-eight. Warp nine-point-nine-nine and holding steady, Captain."

Dax walked back to her chair, and Bowers followed her. As she sat down, she said to him, "Don't look so glum, Sam. We might actually learn something while we're stuck out here."

"It's not the learning that worries me," Bowers said as he settled into his own seat beside hers. "I just have to wonder if any of that debris is from ships whose captains also got a little bit curious."

She teased him with a smirk. "Y'know, Sam, for someone who likes to think of himself as 'a man of action,' you sure don't—"

"Long-range contacts," interrupted Rhys. "Multiple bogeys leaving the debris-ringed system."

Bowers called back, "Speed and heading?"

"Warp two," Rhys said. "Intercept course. At that speed, they'll reach the debris field around the same time we will."

The first officer narrowed his eyes as he looked back at Dax. "I suppose this'll go in your log as a coincidence."

"Maybe," Dax said, conceding nothing to her XO's anxiety.

Ensign Svetlana Gredenko—a woman whose mixed human and Rigellian ancestry was betrayed only by her eyes' disturbing, crimson-hued irises—swiveled around from the ops console and asked Dax, "Captain, should we consider breaking off our investigation of the debris field?"

"No," Dax said. "Whatever's on its way out to meet us knows we're here. If it's friendly, I want to make contact."

The XO kinked one eyebrow. "And if it's not . . . ?"

"Then we'll have to hope we can outsmart it, outrun it, or outgun it, in that order. Steady as she goes." As the rest of the bridge crew returned to work at their posts, Dax leaned toward Bowers and added in a low whisper, "However, it might not be a bad idea to take the ship to Yellow Alert."

He triggered the intraship klaxon, which whooped

once and left golden warning-status lights activated on bulkheads around the bridge. "I thought you'd never ask," he said.

Beverly Crusher heard someone limp into the *Enterprise*'s sickbay and grunt with pain. She looked up from the padd in her hand to steal a glance out her office door.

It was Commander Worf. He was garbed in a loose, off-white exercise garment, similar to the gi he usually donned during martial-arts training. This one was scuffed and torn in places. His nose and upper lip were bleeding, and his right arm dangled limply beneath his drooped shoulder.

"Worf!" she said, bolting from her chair and jogging to him. "What happened?"

"I was exercising." He tried to turn his head to the right, stopped, and winced. "I fell."

She picked up a medical tricorder from an equipment cart and made a fast scan of his injuries. "Looks like you fell several times," she said with a teasing gleam. "In addition to your broken clavicle, you've got four cracked ribs and multiple deep bruises all over your body."

"It was a very good workout," he said.

"I'm sure it was," Crusher said. She nodded to the closest biobed. "Have a seat. I'll get the osteofuser." Worf eased himself onto the bed as Beverly rooted through the lower drawers of the equipment cart.

"Once we fix the break, I'll take the swelling down on those bruises," she said. With the surgical implement in hand, she stepped in front of the seated Klingon and asked, "Do you want any anesthetic before I reset the bone?"

He shook his head once. "No."

"Suit yourself." She placed the surgical device on the bed. Then she put her left hand behind his right shoulder and tensed her right hand in front of his broken clavicle. "This'll hurt. A lot. You need to promise not to hit me."

His glare betrayed his fraying sense of humor. "I will try not to. Please proceed."

She slammed her palm into his jutting clavicle and hammered it back into place with one strike.

His bellow of agony and fury was deafening. Crusher recoiled from his roar and covered her ears. Averting her eyes from his, she saw that his hands were clenched white-knuckle tight on the edges of the biobed.

Then he was silent and gasping for breath to relax himself. "Thank you," he said.

"You're welcome," she replied.

He sat with his eyes closed while she used the osteofuser to mend his clavicle. "I haven't seen you do this to yourself in a while," she remarked. "Are the holoprograms getting tougher, or are you getting a bit careless?"

Her observation opened his eyes, and he pondered her words for a moment before he replied, "I felt it was time for a greater challenge." She finished fixing the bone and adjusted the fuser. He rotated his arm forward once and twice in reverse, and he grinned. "Much better."

"Good. Open your jacket and let me fix your ribs."

As he untied his black belt and opened his jacket, Worf said, "I did not expect to find you here so late."

"I wasn't *planning* on being here," she said, starting work on his left side, which was purpled with bruises. "But we didn't stabilize the critical cases from last night's battle until after 0800, and it was almost 1300 by the time I scrubbed out of surgery." Switching her efforts to the cracked ribs on his right side, she continued, "I didn't get to sleep until almost 1400, and I woke up a few hours ago. Now my sleep cycle's completely turned around. I'll probably be up all night."

Satisfied that his ribs were healed, she switched off the fuser and traded it for a tissue regenerator. "You know, Worf, as your doctor, I really have to suggest you ease up on your calisthenics programs. You're not getting any younger, and—"

She was interrupted by the opening of the sickbay door. The ship's security chief, Lieutenant Jasminder Choudhury, stumbled in looking haggard and disheveled. Her long, wavy black hair was a wild mess, and the left side of her face was an indigo bruise. Rips, bloodstains, and streaks of dirt marred her flowing, orange athletic garment.

Crusher rushed to Choudhury's side and helped her to the biobed next to Worf's. "And what's your story?" she asked.

"I fell," Choudhury said. "In the holodeck."

The lieutenant's choice of words made Crusher throw a curious look at Worf. Then she said to Choudhury, "Let me guess: a 'calisthenics' program?"

"Rock-climbing simulation," Choudhury replied.

Reaching for her tricorder, Crusher mumbled, "I'll bet." She scanned the security chief and was not surprised by what she found. "Seven cracked ribs, a hairline fracture of your skull, and a mild concussion. Plus, more bruises than I can count." Closing the tricorder, she added, "Ever heard of safety protocols, Lieutenant?" Choudhury seemed content not to respond to that query. "Mister Worf, I'm afraid you'll have to live with your bruises for a few minutes while I see to the lieutenant."

"I can wait," Worf said.

Crusher retrieved the osteofuser and set herself to work on closing up the microfissures in Choudhury's ribs and skull.

Worf and Choudhury's situation seemed so transparent that Crusher couldn't help but grin. Odd as it seemed at first, she understood it. In the face of so much death and horror, it was natural to want to affirm life in the most potent ways possible. Seeing the two of them together, she appreciated for the first time that, for all of their superficial differences, the XO and the security chief had a great deal in common. It made sense to her that they would be drawn to each other.

A few minutes later, as Crusher treated Choudhury's concussion, she chided her, "When it comes to using holodecks without safeties, I expect that kind of thing from Worf. But I thought security personnel were smart enough to know better."

"I admit, I was careless," Choudhury said. "Maybe I just got a bit overconfident."

"That's possible." She switched off the subdural probe and looked at Worf. "What's your excuse?"

"An error," he said. "I misjudged the skill level of my . . . new holoprogram."

Crusher grinned. "I have a simpler explanation," she said. "I think you two beat each other up."

Worf shot an intense look at Choudhury, who remained as serene as ever. The security chief's cool discipline over her passions went a long way toward explaining why she won so many more hands than Worf did at the senior staff's poker games.

"Relax," Crusher said to Worf. "I won't tell anyone. But if you two keep *this* up, I won't have to."

Cooling his glare to a frown, Worf said, "Thank you. For your discretion."

"Please," Crusher said, with raised eyebrows, a wide grin, and a weary chortle. "I'm married to the *captain*. Discretion's my middle name."

The closer the *Aventine* got to one of the vast pockets of dark, metallic debris, the more anxious Sam Bowers became.

"Two minutes until the alien craft enters optimal sensor range," reported Ensign Gredenko.

Bowers looked to his right and caught the attention of Ensign Rhys at tactical. "I want a detailed threat assessment as soon as possible."

"Aye, sir," Rhys replied.

Captain Dax stood in the middle of the bridge and watched blackened wreckage tumble on the main viewer. Her gaze was focused, and Bowers could see by the expression on Dax's face that she was troubled by the image on the screen. "Sam," she said as he stepped beside her, "do you notice anything unusual about all the wreckage in that cluster?"

He looked at it with as much intensity of focus as he could muster, but if there was some insight to be found, it eluded him. "No," he admitted. "It all looks the same to me."

"That's exactly what I mean," she said. "The color, the composition, the forms—it's obviously a starship graveyard, but I've never seen one this uniform, have you?"

Inspecting the spaceborne flotsam and jetsam, he realized that Dax was right. There was no variation in the debris field's contents. He asked Gredenko, "Are there more pockets like this?"

"They're *all* like this, sir," the operations manager replied. Her red eyes widened as she added, "Exactly like this."

He turned to Dax. "Could it all be from the same ship?"

"My guess is that it came from thousands of *identical* ships," she said. The anxious peaking of her eyebrows conveyed her meaning to him with perfect clarity.

"Gredenko," Bowers said. "Run an icospectrogram on the debris and tell us if it came from the Borg."

"Aye, sir," Gredenko answered as she started the scan.

From tactical, Rhys interjected, "Sixty seconds until the alien vessel enters optimal sensor distance."

Dax folded her arms and confided to Bowers, "I'm beginning to think this might've been a bad idea."

"Do I get to say 'I told you so'?"

"Only if you want to get court-martialed."

Gredenko swiveled halfway around from the ops console and said to Bowers and Dax, "All of the debris shows subatomic decay consistent with exposure to tetryons and high-energy chroniton exposure—just like the hulls of Borg ships."

"Good work," Bowers said to the ensign. To his captain he added, "Looks like we're definitely in Borg territory."

"Maybe," Dax said. "Maybe not. The Borg may have made it here, but judging by the number of ships they must've lost, I don't think they've set foot in that star system."

Bowers was cobbling together a response when he saw Mavroidis stand up slowly from her post at the conn. The Ullian woman made an awkward turn to face the rest of the bridge crew. She regarded them with a blank, wide stare. Her voice sounded deeper and oddly resonant as she declared, "You are not Borg."

Everything about the young conn officer's body language and enunciation gave Bowers the impression that the woman was being used as a puppet. *Probably by something that tapped into her native telepathic abilities,* he reasoned.

"To whom am I speaking?" inquired Dax.

"The children of the storm," something said via Mavroidis.

Rhys beckoned subtly to Bowers, who slipped away to the tactical station as Dax continued to converse with the entity that was using their flight controller as a medium.

"I'm Captain Ezri Dax of the—"

"You are trespassers," the voice said. "But you are not Borg, so you may live—if you depart now."

On the tactical console, Bowers saw the deep-resolution scan of the entity that had intercepted them. As far as he could tell, it wasn't any kind of vessel, nor was it a creature native to the vacuum of space. What the sensors revealed was an energy shell without any apparent power source or means of being projected. Inside that spherical force field was an atmosphere of incredibly dense, superhot, semifluid liquid-metal hydrogen laced with trace metals. Suspended within that volatile, hostile soup of radioactive atmosphere were hundreds of individual energy signatures that had the cohesion of life signs.

He whispered to Rhys, "Patch in an exobiologist, *now*."

While Rhys covertly signaled the ship's sciences division for an expert consultation, Dax said to the entity that was speaking through Mavroidis, "We only wish to establish peaceful contact and communication, on behalf—"

"Contact is not desired," the entity insisted. "It has taken many centuries to purge these systems of Borg. We will not permit them to be defiled again. Reverse your course, and make no attempt to violate our possessions."

Rhys handed Bowers an in-ear subaural transceiver, and then placed one in his own ear. Bowers did likewise, and Rhys opened a muted channel to one of the science labs as Dax continued her futile back-and-forth with the entity.

"Could we return at a specified future time and—"

"We do not wish you to return. Ever."

Lieutenant Lucy D'Odorico, one of the *Aventine*'s exobiology researchers, appeared on a small inset screen on the tactical console. Bowers and Rhys heard her through their transceivers. *"Based on the compo-*

sition and pressure inside their enclosure, I'd posit this species evolved in the middle atmospheric region of a gas giant," she said. *"Also, their brainwave patterns are consistent with species that demonstrate high-level telekinesis and other psionic talents—and it looks like you've detected the same frequencies in their energy field. I think this species might have mastered space travel and warp flight through the power of thought alone."*

Dax sighed in resignation, apparently having lost hope of making any meaningful contact with this potent but xenophobic entity. "Very well," she said. "We'll reverse course and leave—as soon as you release your hold on our conn officer."

"It is done," said the child of the storm. Mavroidis's eyes closed and fluttered for a moment. She swayed, as if afflicted with vertigo. Dax lunged forward and caught the young Ullian, who had begun to lose her balance. Mavroidis shook off the side effects of having been manipulated like a marionette and nodded to Dax. "I'm all right, Captain."

"Resume your post, Lieutenant," Dax said. "Then reverse course, back to the subspace aperture, maximum warp."

Mavroidis sat down and entered the commands into the conn. On the main viewer, the starfield swept past in a blur as she pivoted the ship 180 degrees from its previous heading. "Course laid in, sir," she confirmed.

"Engage," Dax said, and the ship jumped to warp speed.

At the tactical station, Rhys examined the sensor logs of the aliens' force-sphere, and he looked perplexed. "I don't see anything that looks like a weapon," he said. "And according to my readings, one good shot from a phaser should have been enough to burst their bubble. So how did they ever fight off that many Borg ships?"

"Rhys," said Bowers, "I think this is one of those times we should just be glad we didn't find out the hard way."

11

"According to the Breen domo," said Esperanza Piñiero, "our compulsory summit is an insult to his people's sovereignty, and the Tholian Ruling Conclave is calling it a war crime."

President Bacco faced away from her chief of staff, reclined her chair, and regarded the dreary, gray morning outside her office window. Thick fog and a misting rain had settled upon Paris. "What did the Gorn Imperator say?"

"Only part of it translated," Piñiero said. "The gist was that Zogozin might try to eat you, or a member of the cabinet."

"Let's hope I get to choose," Bacco replied, turning her chair away from the urban vista of spray and sprawl.

The door to her office opened. An aide entered to collect from a side table the tray on which Bacco's breakfast of French toast, strawberries, and coffee had been served. As he gathered the linens and cutlery and glasses, under the watchful eye of protection agent Alan Kistler, Bacco continued her conversation with Piñiero. "Zogozin makes a fuss in front of the others, but I think I made some progress with him last night. If we can get him to talk in private, we might sway him."

"Sounds like a long shot," Piñiero said.

"So is a counteroffensive against the Borg."

Tray in hand, the aide exited Bacco's office through the north door. Agent Kistler secured the portal behind the man.

Piñiero checked her data padd. "If you've got such a warm-fuzzy for Zogozin, why is your first one-to-one with Garak?"

"Because he's the one I least want to talk to," Bacco confessed. "Plus, if I can win over the Cardassians, we'll have a better chance with the Gorn—and it'll cow the Tholians and the Breen, so we won't have to watch our backs so much."

A doubtful expression sent Piñiero's eyebrows climbing toward her hairline. "On the other hand, if Garak leaves us high and dry, there's a good chance the Breen and the Tholians will be annexing our border systems by dinnertime."

"Thanks for the pep talk," Bacco said with a dour grimace. "I knew I could count on you to bolster my confidence." She pressed the intercom switch to her executive assistant. "Sivak, we're ready for Ambassador Garak."

The droll old Vulcan replied, *"So soon, Madam President? His Excellency has been waiting less than an hour."*

Bacco's fists curled shut. "Now, Sivak."

"The ambassador is on his way in, Madam President."

In the anticipation-filled moment before one of the doors opened again, Bacco straightened her posture and pulled her chair up closer to her desk. She folded her hands in front of her as loosely as she could, in an effort to appear calm and statesmanlike. Images and impressions were critical in politics, and she expected to call upon all her years of experience in order not to be outmaneuvered by the wiles of Elim Garak.

The south door opened, and Garak was ushered in by another of Bacco's protection agents, a tall Andorian *chan* whose face looked as if it had been chiseled by wind from a slab of blue ice. As the lean, smiling Cardassian diplomat crossed the room, he was closely shadowed by Agent Kistler.

"Good morning, Madam President," Garak said.

Bacco got up and stepped out from behind her desk to meet him. "Good morning, Your Excellency. Thank you for coming."

"The pleasure is entirely mine."

She gestured to the chairs in front of her desk. "Please, Mister Ambassador. Have a seat."

He eased himself with grace and impeccable balance into the closest chair, while Bacco returned to her high-backed, padded pseudo-throne behind her desk.

Once they were both settled, she forced herself to establish and maintain eye contact with Garak. The intensity of his stare made Bacco want to avert her eyes. She cheated by staring at the intersection of cranial ridges above his nose. "Would you mind if we dispensed with the usual obfuscations and denials and skip ahead to the real reason I asked you here?"

Garak leaned forward and grinned mischievously. "I'd be delighted," he said.

"After all the strides we've made since the end of the Dominion War, why did you vote against joining our counterstrike against the Borg? And spare me the flimflam about politics, because we both know you aren't earning any favors from the Tholians or the Breen just for turning your back on us. So what's the real reason, Garak?"

He seemed to be highly amused by her question. "My," he said. "You're every bit as direct as I'd been told. It's an unexpected quality in a political leader, I must say—and a refreshing one, at that."

"You won't distract me with compliments, Ambassador," said Bacco. "So drop the flattery and answer my question."

The glimmer in his eye lost its humor and became one of cold, ruthless calculation. "You say you want the truth?" At her nod, he continued, "It's simply this, Madam President. We aren't joining your war because we can't afford to."

"If your castellan is worried about reprisals by the Breen or the Tholians, we—"

"I wasn't speaking figuratively, Madam President," Garak cut in. "My meaning was quite literal. Even now, Cardassia has yet to recover from the Dominion War. As dire as your conflict with the Borg certainly is, my people face more imminent crises. Housing, for one; starvation, for another. Without foreign aid, we can't even secure our borders or enforce the law inside them. The Romulans withdrew their forces months ago when their empire fractured, and now your forces and those of the Klingon Empire have deserted us in order to prosecute your war with the Borg."

Bacco leaned forward. "I think you might be exaggerating a bit, Mister Ambassador," she said. "Cardassia is more than capable of maintaining order in its core systems, and allied security patrols were always limited to your border sectors. I also happen to know you have a full battle group deployed on a training exercise to the Betreka Nebula. They could reach the Azure Nebula and join the expeditionary force in sixty hours."

Garak conceded the point with a slow, single nod. "I can suggest that to the castellan," he said. "You might find the crews of those ships woefully inexperienced, however. They are on a *training* exercise for a reason, after all."

"True," Bacco said. "But we all have to learn sometime."

He weaved his fingers together in front of him and relaxed back into his chair. "It seems prudent to caution you, Madam President, that the castellan will likely refuse your request. Unlike her predecessor, she has little interest in foreign affairs unless they translate into immediate gains for the well-being and survival of the Cardassian people."

Nodding, Bacco replied, "And you say that, right now, the Cardassian people are most in need of . . . ?"

"Land and food," Garak said. "The Dominion's retaliation for our rebellion at the war's end left several of our worlds radioactive and wiped out key agricultural resources. It will take decades to find, colonize, and cultivate new worlds."

"Unless we give them to you," Bacco said.

Her apparently offhand comment seemed to catch Garak off guard. "Excuse me, Madam President?"

She nodded to Piñiero, who had been standing a respectful few meters behind Garak. As the chief of staff approached the desk, Bacco said to Garak, "I'm quite serious, Ambassador Garak. We're well aware of the Cardassian Union's troubles, and of your new castellan's political inclinations." She paused as Piñiero reached over Garak's shoulder to hand him a padd, which he scrutinized as Bacco continued. "Your people face grave times and have serious needs. The same is true of my people. Events are in motion, Your Excellency, so permit me to be blunt. If your castellan will order Gul Erem's battle group to join our forces at the Azure Nebula, the Federation will transfer three star systems to Cardassian authority."

Piñiero chimed in, "Specifically, Argaya, Lyshan, and Solarion—all on the Cardassian-Federation border, with stable Class-M planets and numerous exploitable natural resources."

Bacco added, "That would go a long way toward easing some of Cardassia's difficulties, wouldn't it, Mister Ambassador?"

"Indubitably," Garak said. "Though considering the role that Cardassia played in destroying your previous colony on Solarion IV, your generosity seems rather difficult to believe."

"The offer is genuine," Bacco said. "The question now becomes, do you think it's good enough to recommend to your castellan? And is risking one battle group of starships an acceptable price to pay for three new worlds?"

Garak's eyes widened, along with his smile. "Perhaps. Though a commitment to also provide us with new ships for our internal defense would be an even more magnanimous gesture."

"Yes, it would," Bacco said. "But I doubt the Federation Security Council would approve." With a tilt of her head she added, "If security's your concern, we could petition the Bajoran Militia to step in and patrol your trouble spots."

That drew a scathing glare-and-grin from Garak. "Oh, I'm sure the castellan will *love* that idea."

"Indubitably," Bacco said, mimicking his inflection. "Maybe we'd best stick to the offer of planets for support, then."

"I have to ask why the Federation is willing to pay so high a price for what seems like a comparatively small boon."

"We're not paying you for the service of your ships and their crews," Bacco said. "You aren't mercenaries. It's your public show of support that makes this worthwhile. Emphasis on the word 'public.' Do I make myself clear?"

He bowed his head without breaking eye contact with her. "Unmistakably clear, Madam President." He stood up and handed the padd back to Piñiero. "With your permission, I'll return to my embassy and relay your offer to the castellan."

"By all means, Your Excellency." Bacco stood, stepped around her desk, and offered her hand to Garak, who shook it. "Can you speculate as to when we might have her answer?"

His grip was firm and feverishly warm. "Soon," he said, releasing her hand. "Good day, Madam President." Nodding to the chief of staff, he added, "And to you, Ms. Piñiero." Both women nodded their farewell to him, and he turned and walked to the north door, escorted by Agent Kistler.

As the door closed behind Garak, Piñiero's shoulders slumped, and her whole body sagged as if she had just been partially deflated. "I don't trust him," she said.

"He's not the problem," Bacco said. "Ambassador Garak is a lot of things, but foolish isn't one of them. He knows a good offer when he hears it. The problem is going to be his castellan. If she turns us down, his hands will be tied."

Piñiero shook her head. "It's not his hands I'm worried about; it's our necks."

The combat operations center on the uppermost level of Starfleet Command was frantic with activity. Uniformed officers hurried past Seven of Nine and the other high-ranking Federation government visitors, who were gathered around a central strategy table with a handful of senior admirals.

"We're too damned spread out," insisted Admiral Nakamura. He gesticulated angrily at the two-dimensional starmap that currently dominated the table's surface. "If Picard's right, then we need to start redeploying everything we've got toward the Azure Nebula."

A chorus of shouting voices tried to respond and fell silent only when one succeeded in drowning them out. "We've given Picard everything we can," Admiral Jellico said. "But we still have to be ready for a dozen other scenarios. And if we learned anything from the Dominion War, it's not to leave the core systems undefended."

The conversation devolved into another round of side-by-side debates between admirals and undersecretaries from the Department of the Exterior. Bored with the round-robin argument, Seven considered walking away and returning to her regeneration alcove, just to see if anyone noticed.

All the admirals looked crisp and polished, while their subordinates had the frazzled, harried look of people who had been worn down by dodging a nonstop fusillade of enemy fire. Fearful looks haunted their faces.

The spacious, high-tech facility was rank with the odors of stale sweat and unwashed uniforms. Plastic cups, half full of cold coffee, littered every level surface. Against the backdrop of gleaming machines and towering display screens, the biological occupants of the facility looked soft, fragile, and slow to Seven's unforgiving eye.

Her patience expired, and she timed her declaration to fill an anticipated conversational lull. "Captain Picard's plan is fatally flawed," she said in a raised voice, silencing the admirals and the politicians alike.

"Finally, we agree on something," Jellico grumbled.

Admiral Nechayev cocked an eyebrow and adopted a defensive tone and posture toward Seven. "Would you care to explain that assertion, Miss Hansen?"

She ignored Nechayev's dismissive use of her former appellation. "Captain Picard—and by extension, this admiralty—proceeds from a false assumption. Your expeditionary force will not be sufficient to repel a full-scale Borg invasion."

Admiral Hastur—an olive-skinned, red-eyed, white-haired Rigellian flag officer with a reputation for strategic prowess—protested, "President Bacco is recruiting more allies for the task force right now. When we're ready, we'll have enough firepower to hold the line."

"No, Admiral, you won't."

Flustered, Hastur replied, "It's not as if we're trying to invade Unimatrix 01! All we have to do is hold one choke point until we can seal the breach in our defenses."

"Irrelevant," Seven said. "If your task force fails to find the Borg staging area before they begin their final invasion, your preparations will be for naught. And if they do locate the staging area, they will be forced to engage hundreds of Borg cubes. Your recent losses should make it clear that you are ill-equipped to fight even *one* Borg cube at a time."

"Aren't you forgetting something?" asked Nakamura, who looked far too smug for his own good. "We have the transphasic torpedo. One shot, one kill."

She directed her stern gaze at Nakamura, and for a moment she almost felt pity for him. "The Borg will adapt to your new weapon, Admiral. The only question is how long it will take. To survive a full-scale counteroffensive, your fleet will be forced to expend hundreds of transphasic warheads in a matter of minutes. The Borg will sacrifice as many cubes as necessary to devise a defense."

Seven paced slowly behind the admirals and civilian security advisers, all of whom tensed as she walked by. "There is no way that you can destroy the entire Borg Collective quickly enough to prevent them from adapting." She dropped her voice and spoke into Nakamura's ear as she passed him. "They will learn to defend themselves from your weapon." To Hastur, she said, "Then they will assimilate it." She continued past Nechayev, the only one of the admirals who had been sensible enough to demand moderation in the use of the transphasic warheads, and told Jellico, "And then they will turn it against you, and destroy you."

He bristled at her prediction. "So what do you suggest we do? Retreat?"

Without humor, she replied, "Yes."

Jellico lifted his arms and looked around in feigned confusion. "To where?"

"Anywhere you can," Seven said. "Some of the subspace tunnels the *Enterprise* discovered might lead to other galaxies. If you can isolate such a passage and collapse the others before the Borg have a chance to invade, you could organize a mass evacuation of the Federation."

Seven's governmental superior, security adviser Jas Abrik, looked horrified. "Are you insane?" the Trill man bellowed. "You want us to abandon the Milky Way galaxy to the Borg?"

Jellico, who was standing next to Abrik, rolled his eyes away from Seven, shook his head in disgust, and said, "This is why we don't let civilians write the battle plans." Snorts and chortles of dismissive laughter spread like a virus through the room, all of it at Seven's expense. Then Jellico turned his back on her and said to the others, "Let's keep working."

Seven had no conscious plan or moment of premeditation. In a snap of action, she locked her right arm around Admiral Jellico's throat. She pulled him backward, off balance. Borg assimilation tubules extended from the steely implant still grafted to her left hand as she pressed her fingertips against his jugular. The tubules hovered above his skin but did not penetrate it—yet.

Around her and the admiral, the combat operations center became deathly quiet.

"If you do not escape beyond the Borg's reach, you will never be safe," she said, all but hissing the words into the trembling man's ear. "They know where you are, and they are now committed to your annihilation. Even if you collapse the subspace tunnels, they can still reach you by normal warp travel. It may take them decades. Perhaps even a century. But they *will* come. And when they do, your civilization will be eradicated. All that you have built, all that you have labored to preserve, will be erased from history. You cannot stop them, ever. As long as they exist, you will never be free."

The terror in Jellico's eyes was the same one she saw in her own when she awoke from nightmarish hallucinations during her regeneration cycles.

It was her only real fear: *I will never be free.*

Behind her back, the rising whine of charging phaser rifles cut through the silence. A security officer said in a carefully mannered voice, "Professor Hansen, let the admiral go. Now." She looked over her shoulder at the man, who met her gaze with his own unblinking stare. "Please release the admiral, Miss Hansen."

They will not listen to reason, Seven decided. *So be it.* She retracted her assimilation tubules and removed her arm from Jellico's throat. "I trust I made my point clearly, Admiral?"

"Get out of here before I have you shot," Jellico said, massaging his bruised windpipe.

The security guards advanced to within a few meters of Seven and kept their weapons aimed at her. One of them said, "Please proceed to turbolift four, Miss Hansen."

She met Jellico's furious stare. "You are only postponing the inevitable," she said. "When the Borg have the Federation by the throat, they will not release it—they will destroy it."

Jellico scowled. "Over our dead bodies."

"Precisely," Seven said.

Ambassador Derro was an old-fashioned Ferengi. He liked his profits large, his females naked, and his lobes stroked every night before bed.

All those pleasures had been in short supply during the reign of Grand Nagus Rom, however. Rom had granted Ferengi females the privilege to walk about in all manner of garb, and they had been invested with the right to work and earn profit. With those opportunities they had gained a new independence, and Derro's harem of solicitous females had evaporated all but overnight. Worst of all, he had spent the past few years cut off from the vast profits of the arms trade, as a consequence of being relegated to the pacifistic, economically backward world known as Earth.

He searched his memory for any clue as to what he might have done to anger Grand Nagus Rom. A grudge was the only explanation he could think of for his exile on this rock without profit. Rom, of course, had saddled Derro with the diplomatic posting as if it were a gift. As the Grand Nagus had smiled and waxed ecstatic about how much he expected Derro to learn about humanity and the Federation, Derro had brooded that Rom was either the most diabolically clever charlatan ever to occupy the nagal residence, or he was the most dangerous simpleton ever to stumble lobes-backward into power.

Derro's shuttlepod pilot, a Bolian woman named Doss, snapped him back from his bitter reverie by asking, "Is everything all right, Mister Ambassador?"

"Yes, Doss, I'm fine." He watched the rain slash against the shuttlepod's cockpit windshield. "This weather just makes me think of home, is all."

A male comm voice squawked from the overhead speaker, *"Ferenginar Transport, you're cleared to land on pad three."*

Doss activated the reply channel. "Acknowledged, Palais Control. Down in T minus ten. Ferenginar Transport out."

Outside the cockpit window, Derro saw nothing except a gray curtain of fog and rain. Then the façade of the Palais de la Concorde emerged like a phantom that quickly became solid, and Doss guided their two-seat transport pod inside the Palais's lower-level docking area. Ground crews with lit batons waved the transport to an air-soft landing.

The side hatch unlocked and opened with a loud pneumatic hiss and a hydraulic whine. Derro unfastened his safety restraint and got up. "Keep the engine running," he said. "I won't be long." He slipped between their seats and made his way out of the pod and down the ramp, to a waiting detail of four Federation plainclothes security personnel.

One of them, the leader, was a tall human female who had pale skin and a tightly wrapped bun of chalk-white hair. She hid her eyes with a black, wraparound sunshade, and her lean physique was concealed by the kind of dark suit that served as a uniform for President Bacco's protection agents. "Your Excellency," she said. "The president's expecting you. Please follow me to the transporter station." Without waiting for his reply, she turned and began walking in long strides toward the core of the Palais.

Derro followed her, and he heard the other three agents—all men: a Vulcan, an Andorian, and a Trill— fall into step around him. He was uncertain whether their presence was intended to make him feel protected or intimidated. In a peculiar way, it managed to do both at the same time.

They reached an internal transporter node, the kind that was used for secure site-to-site beaming inside a protected environment such as the Palais, which was surrounded by a scattering field to prevent unauthorized transports in or out. The albino female ushered Derro onto the platform. As soon as he'd found his place on the energizer pad, he turned back and saw the Vulcan initiate the dematerialization sequence. *Good,* he thought. *I hate long good-byes.*

A white haze erased the transport level from his sight and replaced it in a slow fade with the luxurious confines of the lobby on the uppermost level of the Palais. As the shimmer of the transporter beam faded and its confinement field released him, he found himself being greeted by a beefy, dark-haired human male who wore a familiar style of dark suit. "Welcome, Ambassador," the man said, motioning Derro toward the nearby door to President Bacco's office. "We apologize for the short notice." At the door, they stopped. "Just a moment, sir."

On the far side of the lobby, the other door to Bacco's office opened, and Zogozin, the Gorn ambassador, was escorted out by a man whom Derro recognized as Bacco's senior bodyguard, Agent Wexler. Zogozin halted, turned, and looked directly at Derro, who reacted with a nervous smile. The archosaur returned the gesture with a broad grin of bared fangs.

Then a transporter effect began dissolving Zogozin, and the door in front of Derro opened.

Derro stepped inside, followed by the agent. President Bacco crossed the room to meet Derro. She pressed her wrists together, palms up, fingers curled inward. "My house is my house," she said, offering a traditional Ferengi salutation.

"As are its contents," Derro replied, imitating her gesture of greeting. He was secretly impressed that Bacco had made the effort to learn this peculiar domestic ritual of his people. In keeping with tradition, he reached inside his jacket pocket, removed a strip of latinum, and handed it to Bacco as the price of admission for a private audience in her official sanctum.

"Thank you for coming, Your Excellency," she said, pocketing the strip. She walked back to her desk. "Come, sit."

He followed her and settled into one of her guest chairs. "The Grand Nagus has ordered all armed Ferengi ships to your aid," he said. "Though he regrets their numbers are so few."

"I'm grateful to the Grand Nagus for all his efforts," Bacco said. Despite the fact that she was swathed in clothes, and that her tiny lobes were mostly concealed by her close-cut, paper-white hair, she radiated authority. "However, I've asked you here to discuss a more urgent and . . . *sensitive* matter."

She waved over a young Trill female and an Orion man who had been lingering on the far side of the room. The pair approached carrying trays that were loaded with foodstuffs. Only when they had reached the president's desk and set down the trays did Derro realize he had been presented with a smorgasbord of Ferengi delicacies: jellied gree-worms, live tube-grubs, soft-shelled Kytherian crabs, and an ice-cold Slug-O-Cola.

"Now I know you want something big," he said, flashing a snaggle-toothed grin and plucking a crab from the plate.

"Correct," she said, as the aides withdrew and left the room. "I've persuaded Ambassador Zogozin to remind Imperator Sozzerozs that the Gorn Hegemony stood with the Federation against the Dominion, and benefited from that decision. Zogozin believes that Sozzerozs will choose to side with us again."

Derro's teeth had pierced the crab's tender shell just before Bacco began her revelation about the Gorn. Now the feisty crustacean writhed in his jaw as he sat paralyzed by the news that she had completely reversed Zogozin's position. He withdrew his bite from the pincered delicacy in his hand. "How, may I ask, did you *persuade* Ambassador Zogozin of this?"

"The specifics aren't important right now," she said. "What matters is that we have our coalition for the expeditionary force. However, there's another matter for which the Federation needs the help of the Ferengi Alliance, and we'll be *extremely* grateful if you and the Grand Nagus can assist us."

He took a solid chomp out of the crab. Masticating the crunchy treat into paste, he asked, "What do you need? A loan?"

"Not at the moment. What we need you to do is cut the Tholians off at the knees, and quickly."

His throat tensed as he tried to swallow, and he struggled to force the mouthful of food down so he could speak again. "Excuse me, Madam President? I'm afraid I don't understand."

Bacco got up and walked around to his side of the desk. "We've made our deal with the Cardassians, and I expect to have Gorn ships in the Azure Nebula the day after tomorrow." She sat back against the edge of the desk. "But I know the Tholians, Your Excellency. They've been waiting for a chance to stab us in the back, and now is probably the best chance they've had in decades. The only way to stop them is to isolate them—contain them on all fronts, without angering the other local powers."

He washed the dry, sour taste of fear from his mouth with a sugary, slimy swig of Slug-O-Cola. "What does that have to do with Ferenginar, Madam President?"

"I'm glad you asked," she said. "The best chance the Tholians have of undermining us is to ally with the Breen and harass our border. But that won't happen if the Breen have already committed the bulk of their forces to another battle."

Every time she spoke, the situation seemed to get

worse. "I'm still not following, Madam President. Are you suggesting the Ferengi Alliance start a war with the Breen Confederacy?"

"Of course not," Bacco said. "I'm saying you have so few ships at your disposal that you need the Breen's help to press the fight against the Borg." She reached over and pinched a fingerful of tube grubs from the bowl on the tray. "The Federation Council would never let me hire Breen mercenaries for the expeditionary force. But the Grand Nagus can take whatever steps he deems necessary to protect his people."

Derro was flabbergasted. "Striking bargains with the Breen is risky business, Madam President."

"The riskier the road, the greater the profit, Your Excellency." Before he could compliment her invocation of the Sixty-second Rule of Acquisition, she continued, "If the Grand Nagus's foresight—and yours—leads to the continued safety and survival of the Federation . . . the Ferengi Alliance would prove itself to be a steady and trusted ally. Naturally, allies rank ahead of neutral powers when the Federation Council determines which states receive most-favored trade status." She popped the grubs into her mouth.

He took another healthy bite out of his crab, savored it, and swallowed. "So . . . what you're saying is, you'd like us to subcontract your war and leave the Tholians with no friends."

"Exactly."

"Sounds profitable." He sleeved the greasy bits of shell from his mouth. "What about that loan? I can guarantee very good terms, and I have a few ideas about modernizing the Federation's economy that I'd love to share with you."

"Maybe next time," Bacco said.

"Suit yourself," he said with a shrug. He got up. "If you'll excuse me, Madam President, I have to go make a business proposition to Ambassador Gren."

She pressed her wrists together to bid him farewell. "Don't let him try to charge you extra for torpedoes."

"Give my lobes more credit than that," Derro said, returning the valedictory gesture. "When I get done with Gren, the Breen will be buying their torpedoes from *me*."

Less than two hours after Ambassador Derro had left her office, Nanietta Bacco's attention to a report from Starfleet was broken by the sharp buzzing of the intercom.

It was followed by the voice of her assistant, Sivak. *"Madam President, Tholian Ambassador Tezrene is here to see you. She appears to be in a rare state of heightened dudgeon."*

On the other side of Bacco's desk, Piñiero looked up with a droll countenance. "That didn't take long," she said.

"Send her in, Sivak," Bacco said.

The intercom switched off, the southern door opened, and Ambassador Tezrene swept into the room, her scorpion-like body wrapped in a golden shroud of silk that was taut from the high-pressure, searing-hot gases it contained.

Agents Wexler and Kistler followed close behind her, and two more protection agents, Lovak and de Maurnier, entered through the office's other door. All of them kept their eyes on the agitated Tholian diplomat, who was following a direct path toward Bacco. The president stood and held her ground.

"You'll regret this," Tezrene said through her vocoder, which barely muffled the metallic shrieks it was translating.

Bacco replied with transparently insincere concern, "Is something wrong, Your Excellency?"

First came a string of angry scrapes and clicks the vocoder couldn't parse, then Tezrene said, "Your backroom deals with the Gorn and the Cardassians were expected. But sending the Ferengi to do your dirty work—you disgust us."

"Forgive me, Madam Ambassador," Bacco said. "I don't know what you're talking about. There was nothing secretive about my meetings with Ambassadors Zogozin and Garak. As for the Ferengi, they're a sovereign power who can do as they wish."

A flurry of furious clicks and scrapes telegraphed Tezrene's ire. "Using them to marginalize us, contain us . . . you have overstepped your bounds."

Piñiero leaned forward to join in the conversation. "Excuse me, Madam President. I think the ambassador might be referring to the Ferengi's recruitment of Breen and Orion mercenaries to serve as their proxies on the expeditionary force."

"Oh, I see," said Bacco, feigning sudden understanding. Then she changed tack. "No, I don't see, actually. Why would the Tholian Assembly take offense at that, Madam Ambassador? You weren't planning to use those same mercenary forces to launch proxy attacks on *our* territory, were you?"

"Our concern was merely for the defense of our borders from the Borg," Tezrene said. "You've deprived us of our allies when we need them most."

It took real effort for Bacco not to laugh with contempt. "Do you really think the Breen would hold the line for you against the Borg?" she asked. "If the Collective comes for you, who do you plan on asking for help? The Orions? The Tzenkethi? Do either of them have a history of benign foreign intervention that I've just never heard of?"

A threatening twitch jerked Tezrene's stinger-tipped tail to and fro, lending her seething a mesmerizing quality. "The Tholian Assembly does not need the Federation's help."

"Maybe not," Bacco said. "But you should know that Starfleet won't sit by and let the Borg attack Tholian worlds. If your people send distress signals, we will answer."

"Your gestures change nothing," Tezrene said. "Hollow promises do not erase the sins of the past. We remember the crimes of the Taurus Reach."

Bacco turned her palms upward and spread her arms, hoping that the gesture would not be misunderstood or ignored by the Tholian diplomat. "Madam Ambassador, history is offering us a unique opportunity. We're faced with a common enemy, a shared need. This is a chance to put aside old hatreds."

"Not for us," Tezrene said.

Without another word, the Tholian ambassador turned and stalked away, flanked by all four of the presidential security agents. Bacco and Piñiero watched Tezrene exit. The last agent out of the room was Wexler, who nodded to Bacco as he shut the door behind him.

"Well," Piñiero said. "That went better than I expected it to. Now all we have to do is keep the ships of two warring Romulan factions from shooting at each other, find a way to reimburse the Ferengi Alliance for all the privateers they hired, and figure out how to make the Klingons give back eight systems they took from the Gorn over a century ago."

Bacco relaxed into her chair. "Let Safranski squeeze concessions from the Klingons," she said. "As for paying the Ferengi, get Offenhouse up here. It's about time he started earning his keep as secretary of commerce." She picked up her black, sweet coffee and enjoyed a long sip.

Piñiero asked, "What about the rival Romulan fleets meeting at the Azure Nebula?"

"That's Picard's problem, now," Bacco said. "He asked for everyone, and he's got 'em. The next move is his."

1574

12

—◆—

A lifetime of night surrendered to the day. The icy sterility of the starry reaches of space faded from view as the city of Axion descended into the pale corona of a planet's upper atmosphere.

Veronica Fletcher stood at the edge of the city and peeked over its rocky rim, at the lush green orb flattening beneath her. Fiery wisps danced past the city-ship's invisible sphere of protection, and a great roar, like that of an engine, chased away all the stray thoughts that had been lingering in the forgotten tenements of her mind.

Next to her, Erika Hernandez perched on the corner of the precipice and watched the Caeliar's new world rising to meet them. Fletcher recalled how different she and Hernandez had looked in their youth— Fletcher had been pale and golden-haired, in contrast to Hernandez's black hair and olive complexion. Now they looked all but identical: pale, snow-maned, withered, and ravaged by time and gravity. Their stooped, fragile bodies were both clothed in silvery-gray wraps that reminded her of both togas and saris. Even their shoes had been replaced by flexible, synthetic-fiber slippers made by their captors.

She had never forgotten. Not even now, watching mountains of clouds race past into a blue sky, did she forget where she was, how she'd come to be there, and who was responsible. All the beauties of creation wouldn't have been enough to make her forget that she was a prisoner, a dying bird in a gilded cage.

The city broke through the bottom layer of cloud cover, and the details of a majestic landscape were revealed below them. Rugged, reddish-brown cliffs flanked abyssal canyons, and in the distance lay a range of charcoal-hued mountains topped with sun-splashed snowcaps. In the middle distance, a verdant landscape of rolling hills and broad plains was cut by wide rivers.

Hernandez sounded awed. "Amazing, isn't it?"

"It's everything I'd hoped it would be," Fletcher replied in her ancient rasp of a voice.

A knifing jab of pain pushed between her ribs, and she fought for breath as a fierce pressure clamped around her heart. *Not here,* she commanded her failing body. *Not yet. I won't die in this damned city.* Slowly, the pain faded.

The horizon became all but level as the city-ship of Axion settled into a stable, hovering position above the planet's surface. Then there was a subtle change in the air around them. A soft hush of moving atmosphere. The natural perfumes of flowers and green plants and living things. Thousands of tiny olfactory details came to Fletcher, like whispers half heard.

She became aware of warmth on her skin, and she looked up at the yellowish-orange sun high overhead.

It was the first time she had felt natural solar radiation in more than fifty years. "The Caeliar must have turned off the shields," she said.

On the surface, a herd of graceful-looking animals gamboled across the open plains and stopped every few paces to graze on grass and flowers.

Hernandez stretched her arms over her head and smiled. "It's like paradise," she said.

An electric tingle on the back of Fletcher's neck served as a herald of Inyx's arrival. She turned, regarded him sourly, and said, "Yes, it's paradise. Complete with an apple salesman."

Inyx, who looked exactly as he had when Fletcher and the *Columbia*'s landing party had first come to this city decades earlier, ignored her comment and bowed to Hernandez. "We have completed the transit," he said as he straightened. "Thanks in no small part to your efforts, Erika."

"You're quite welcome," Hernandez said. "But it was only possible because of everything you've taught me."

Watching her captain curry favor with the enemy made Fletcher feel ill. Or homicidal. Sometimes both simultaneously. "I hate to break up your mutual admiration society," she said, "but can Erika and I make a visit to the surface? Now?"

The looming Caeliar scientist extended his arm, waved the three cilia at its end, and conjured a large-diameter, razor-thin, levitating disk of quicksilver. He stepped up onto it and gestured for Fletcher and Hernandez to join him. "It would be my pleasure to bring you there."

"Thanks," Fletcher said, forcing her arthritic knees to bend and propel her aching body up the short step onto the disk. Beside her, Hernandez was having almost as much difficulty mounting the transportation platform. It took several seconds, but they soon were safely in its center.

Hernandez nodded. "Let's go."

The forward motion was slower and gentler than it once had been. Fletcher presumed that Inyx must have realized how frail his passengers were and adjusted his control of the disk to a more appropriate velocity. They drifted away from the city in a slow turn, taking in the panorama of pristine wilderness that surrounded them. In a pleasant change from past rides on the circular platforms, gentle winds teased Fletcher's face, tossed her hair above and behind her head, and fluttered her clothes. It felt good, like a memory of freedom.

She pointed toward a low rise in the smooth plain, a knoll graced by a stand of three thick-trunked trees topped by proud green crowns of leaves. "There," she said. "Set us down on top of that hill, will you?"

"As you wish," Inyx said, altering the disk's path.

Less than a minute later, the disk touched down without any vibration of contact on the grassy hilltop and dissolved like a mirage. Fletcher felt the pliant sensation of grass bending under her feet, the cool touch of a gentle breeze scented with flowers and warm earth. She reached over and took Hernandez's hand. "Come with me," she said, leading Hernandez forward. Looking back at Inyx, she added, "You stay here."

He responded with an obedient nod.

Fletcher and Hernandez moved away from him in small, careful steps. Their slow progress gave Fletcher time to savor all the small details of this serene spot. The lilting of birdsong in the boughs above. A bright rhythm of sawing insect noise. The rustling of leaves, whose gentle dance in the wind dappled the sunlight falling between the three mighty trees.

When they reached the point at the center of the trees' irregular, triangular formation, Fletcher stopped. She breathed in the air, nodded in confirmation to herself, and permitted herself a bittersweet smile. "This'll do," she said.

"For what?" asked Hernandez.

"My grave," Fletcher said. "When I die, this is where I want to be buried."

Back in the embrace of a planet, it became easier for Hernandez to measure time. Sunrises and sunsets were novelties again. Each new dawn was another mark on Hernandez's calendar, and she noted the passage of weeks, and then months.

The Caeliar had wasted no time admiring the scenery. Instead, they'd set to work acclimating to their new home. Soil and plant seeds had been harvested from the planet's surface, to restore the landscaped sections of Axion that had been destroyed in its hasty flight from Erigol. Trees, shrubbery, and flowers were transplanted; water was taken from the rivers to replenish the city's many fountains and artificial waterfalls.

Edrin, the quiet and modest chief architect of the Caeliar, had supervised the design and construction of a residence for Hernandez and Fletcher. It was a spacious home of cedar-like wood and rough-hewn gray stone, with an open floor plan. Broad windows on its walls and strategically placed slanted skylights set in its sloped roof filled its common areas with large amounts of natural illumination throughout the day.

In the evenings, voice-activated lights concealed in the walls lent a warm glow to the two women's shared living space. Though neither of them had seen any sign of plumbing while the house was being constructed, it nonetheless featured clean hot-and-cold running water from a variety of locations, including both of their bathrooms and the kitchen.

Because neither of them had much interest in or energy for cooking, Edrin had provided them with a food synthesizer. As Hernandez had come to expect living in Axion, its entire menu consisted of vegetables and nondairy vegetarian dishes. Only after many experimental mishaps had Hernandez been able to help the Caeliar devise a leavening agent for bread that didn't contain eggs or anything patterned on them. The result was less than successful, but it was at least recognizable as bread, and it had opened the door to making noodles and other pasta, providing a much-needed respite from the Caeliar's endless variations of ratatouille.

In the back of the house there was a brick patio and a wading pool. Though their home had been built on a hill with a commanding view of the surrounding landscape, the vista from the back of the house, facing west, was the only one not obstructed by the looming mass of Axion close overhead. That one fact made the western view Fletcher's favorite. Hernandez found it harder to enjoy, however, because it looked out on the adjacent hilltop, where three trees stood their silent vigil over Fletcher's self-selected grave site. It was a daily reminder for Hernandez of an inevitable truth she didn't want to face.

Put it from your mind, she told herself. *Focus on each day as it comes.* Hernandez regretted not having been able to find a hobby during her long decades on Axion, because now that the Caeliar had settled upon this world as New Erigol, she no longer had a job to perform in the observatory. As dark and as imposing as the Star Chamber had seemed to her, now that it was in her past, there was a hole in her life.

It was about an hour past dawn. Hernandez set two plates of toast with jam and fresh fruit on the patio dining table, across from each other. Moving in slow, measured steps, she made her way back to the kitchen and retrieved a tray on which sat a pot of tea, a dish of sugar, and two delicate cups. As she carried it past Fletcher's bedroom door on her way out to the patio, she called out in a brittle voice she still couldn't believe was really hers, "Breakfast is ready."

A few minutes later, after she'd spread the jam on her toast and stirred a spoonful of sugar into her tea, she looked up and wondered what was keeping Fletcher.

Nagging concern impelled her from her seat and back into the house. *Let me be worrying over nothing,* she prayed to no one. *Let her just be sleeping in, or deaf under a hot shower.*

She pushed open the door to Fletcher's bedroom suite. In a timid voice, she called out, "Ronnie?"

Fletcher lay supine in her bed, one arm dangling half off the side. She lolled her head and stared blankly in Hernandez's direction. Though her mouth moved, no sound issued from her throat, only hollow gasps.

Hernandez wanted to run to her friend, but panic rooted her feet to the floor. It took all her strength to draw a breath and make a desperate cry for help: "Inyx!"

Fletcher's end was close, closer than Hernandez had thought only a few minutes earlier. Sprawled on a quicksilver disk, cradling her friend in her lap, it was all Hernandez could do to stay focused on the details of the moment. The cool kiss of the wind. The fragile, parchmentlike quality of Fletcher's skin, and the golden radiance of the morning shining on this hideous moment.

"We're almost there," Inyx said, looking back and down at them. "Just a few seconds more."

Looking around in confusion, Hernandez saw that Axion was far behind them, and slipping farther into the distance with each moment the disk spent in flight. Nodding toward the city-ship, Hernandez shouted, "Inyx, we're going the wrong way!"

"No," he said. "We're not."

Then she looked past him, ahead of the disk, and saw the three trees on the hill directly ahead. "Inyx," she demanded as they passed under the trees' branches, "what are you doing?"

"Exactly what Veronica asked me to do," he said. The disk touched down with preternatural grace and seemed to soak into the dark, rich earth. Beside the two women was a freshly excavated grave with near-perfect corners and a neatly piled mound of dirt waiting to be returned whence it came.

Hernandez shook her head, denying what was right in front of her. "No, Inyx. You can't just let her die! There has to be something you can do!"

"There are many things we can do," Inyx said. "But it's Veronica's wish that we do nothing."

With a weak grip, Fletcher clasped Hernandez's hand. "It's okay, Erika," she said. "It's what I want."

"How can you say that?" She clutched Fletcher's hand with both of hers. "The Caeliar could give you medicines we've never dreamed of, synthetic organs, gene therapy—"

Fletcher cut her off with a derisive laugh that became a hacking cough. A moment later she steadied herself and replied, "Gene therapy? Like in the Eugenics Wars? No, thank you."

"All right, forget I said that," Hernandez said. "But try the medicine, at least, or a synthet—"

"No, Erika," Fletcher said, more gravely. "This is my choice. It's my time. Accept it, and say good-bye."

"Veronica, as your captain, I'm *ordering* you to let the Caeliar try to help you."

A sardonic grin lit up Fletcher's wrinkled visage. "Pulling rank, eh? Go ahead—court-martial me, Skipper."

Hernandez let go of Fletcher's hand and twisted so she could glower up at Inyx. "She's being irrational," she insisted. "She needs help, but she won't admit it."

Inyx shrugged by raising and lowering his gangly forearms. "She seems perfectly lucid to me," he said. "And the refusal of medical treatment is an entirely valid decision."

"You can't be serious," Hernandez said. "After all your speeches about the sanctity of life and not letting it come to harm, you'll just stand by and watch her die?"

The Caeliar lowered himself into a deep squatting stance, putting his bulbous head and stretched face on the same level with the seated Hernandez. "Everything dies, Erika," he said. "Sometimes, death can be resisted and kept at bay. At other times it's natural and logical, and should not be resisted with too much vigor. Veronica has chosen to accept the natural lifespan of her biology."

"But you can fix that, can't you? Extend it?"

"Just because we can do a thing, it does not follow that we should do a thing. Veronica made her wishes clear long ago. For us to defy her stated desires and impose our cures upon her would be a violation of her personal sovereignty, and an act of unforgivable violence."

Tears of rage fell from Hernandez's eyes and were warm against her cheekbones. "You 'violated' Valerian, didn't you?"

"Only with your permission," he said. "As her guardian, you assumed the right and responsibility for making that decision. But Veronica is capable of making her own choice, and she has."

Fletcher's faint whisper, like a breath across dried leaves, commanded Hernandez's attention. "Don't fight it, Erika. Let me go. . . . I beg you."

Hernandez's thoughts were trapped in a storm of chaotic emotions—remorse and denial, rage and guilt. She picked up Fletcher's hand again and held it more tightly than before. Her sorrow was a tourniquet around her throat, and her voice quavered as she choked out the words, "I don't want you to go."

"Promise . . ." Fletcher's voice faded as she ran out of breath. She wheezed as she inhaled and continued, "Don't be seduced, Erika. Refuse their gifts. Don't take their medicine. *Please.*"

It wasn't the last request she had expected. "Why not?"

"Because the price . . . is too high."

A spasm jerked Fletcher's body into grotesque poses and blocked her airway. Her eyes squeezed shut as her face tensed, and her hands clenched like spiders shriveled in a flame.

All that Hernandez could do was weep and wail as Fletcher twitched in her death throes. Then the seizure stopped, and the tension left Fletcher's body. A soft gasp escaped her mouth, and she looked up at Hernandez with a beatific smile.

"It's okay," she said. "I'm free."

From that moment to the next nothing seemed to change, but Hernandez felt the difference, and she knew that everything had. Fletcher's eyes were still open, but they no longer saw. The warmth was still in her hand, but it would soon fade. Life had become death cradled in Hernandez's arms.

Inyx reached out and caressed Fletcher's brow with the delicate cilia that the Caeliar used as fingers. "I'm sorry, Erika," he said. His visage was as stern as ever, but the tilt of his head and the timbre of his voice emoted sympathy. "Would you like to say something before I inter her remains?"

She let go of Fletcher's hand, closed her friend's eyelids with a gentle pass of her fingertips, and lowered the body to the ground. As she stood on trembling legs, Inyx straightened to his full height beside her. Hernandez looked again at the dark pit in the ground that was waiting to receive her friend.

"I have nothing left to say," she declared, and then she turned and walked away from the three trees, and down the hill.

He called out, "Can I take you back to your house?"

She didn't answer him. There were no words.

No place felt like home for Hernandez.

The house on New Erigol was too big for her to live in alone. Though she and Fletcher had resided there for less than half a year, it had been built for the both of them. It was theirs, and with Fletcher gone, its open spaces had taken on a conspicuously empty quality. Hernandez's footsteps echoed when she crossed its hardwood floors; the pattering of rain resounded on the roof, reminding her that what had been meant to serve as a home was now just another hollow cage.

Worst of all, no matter where in the house Hernandez went, her eyes were drawn to the world outside her windows, and it seemed as if every view was of the three trees on the hill, where Fletcher lay buried. She tried to shut it out, ignore it, look away, pretend she didn't see it, and go on with her life. But it was always there, the defining element of the landscape.

After six days sequestered in her house, Hernandez stood in her kitchen and called out in a loud voice, "Inyx!"

It took him a minute to answer her summons. She'd expected another of his trademark light-show entrances. Instead, she heard a knock at the front door. Doddering steps carried her there. She opened the door to see Inyx standing with his head atilt. "Is everything all right?"

"No," Hernandez said. "I want to come back to Axion."

He pulled back and sounded confused. "Are you certain?"

"Yes." She turned and felt overcome with melancholy as she looked at the barren confines of her house. "I can't stay here."

Inyx stepped back from the door, onto the edge of a travel disk. "I will do as you ask," he said. "But I would like to know why you've chosen to abandon your home."

"It's not a home," she said. "It's just a house." She stepped outside, intending to leave without a look back, but she couldn't help herself. As she turned to take a final gander at the house, she said, "I always knew that, barring some event that killed us both, either I or Veronica would die before the other. I used to tell her I didn't want to die first, because I refused to let her have the last word. But the truth is, I didn't want her to die first, either—because I just don't want to go on without her."

She offered a silent valediction to her short-lived house in the country and stepped onto the silvery disk with Inyx.

He asked, "Is there anything I can do to help?"

"Yes," she said, looking at the house. "Raze it."

Night in Axion was never silent. The Caeliar didn't sleep, and their labors respected not the hours.

Large crystalline pods had departed the city-ship weeks earlier and fanned out across the star system, to begin the Herculean labor of preparing the next phase of the Caeliar's all-consuming Great Work. Inyx had kept the details of their task from Hernandez at first, but when she saw the thin dark line being traced across the dome of the sky, she began to suspect the nature of their new project. "Are you building a planetary ring?" she'd asked, full of renewed hope and wonder, eager to witness the creation of such a marvel.

Then Inyx had dashed her optimistic fantasies by telling her the truth. "No," he said. "We're building a shell."

"Around the entire planet?" she'd protested.

"And its star," Inyx said. "Privacy is essential now."

In the weeks that had passed since that conversation, on those rare occasions when she was able to sleep, she'd been plagued by nightmares of being sealed in a brick wall, buried alive, or trapped in a covered well. The smothering terror of being confined alone in the darkness had roused her again this evening. Driven by lingering fear and adrenaline, she rose from bed and drifted like a shadow through her compact quarters.

Her body felt lighter than air, insubstantial. She'd lost the will to eat days earlier, and the gnawing feeling in her stomach had abated quickly. Since then, her senses had taken on a dreamlike surreality; her vision felt softened at the edges, and sounds were muffled, as if underwater. Air smelled sweeter, and she was convinced it was because part of her essence had begun to transcend the mundane limits of sensation.

Walking the boulevards of Axion, surrounded by the milling packs of Caeliar, Hernandez felt as if her own passage had become as effortless and graceful as theirs. She let herself stare freely at all of them; wide-eyed and slack-jawed, she displayed all the bewilderment they'd provoked in her since her first day in their city.

Not one of them looked at her.

She realized that to most of them, she was a nonentity. Except for Inyx, and occasionally Edrin, none of the Caeliar regarded her as anything more than a nuisance and a burden—a pet they had been duped into adopting, and whom they either resented or ignored, depending on whether she misbehaved.

A crowd of them gathered in an open amphitheater, hovering in tiered rank and file, listening to a mournful musical performance that resonated from beneath a perfectly engineered acoustic half shell. There was only one performer on the stage far below, but she sounded like a quartet.

It had been so long since Hernandez had seen the city at its best that she'd forgotten the wonders it contained. The Caeliar, with their staggering gifts of art and science . . . their casually dynamic habit of coming and going in flurries of light, or just floating away, like soap bubbles on a warm summer breeze . . . their unaging bodies and unfathomable machines . . . they were power personified.

Standing alone among them, Hernandez saw herself as she really was: tiny, weak, old, and fragile.

She looked up at the stars, which once again flickered on the other side of an atmosphere, and her eyes were drawn to the empty patch of black sky where the view of the starfield had been obstructed by the Caeliar's shell-in-progress. *A bigger and better prison,* she brooded. *They'll even take the sky from me.*

Eyeing the towers that loomed overhead, she thought of Johanna Metzger's fatal leap. Then she pictured Sidra Valerian, reduced to a screaming puddle of burning flesh. Desperate to exorcise that horrible memory, she forced herself to remember Veronica Fletcher's dignified, quiet exit, but it brought her no solace. Envisioning her friends in happier times yielded no comfort, either.

Hernandez had only the most tenuous grasp of her present moment as she wandered and explored the empty avenues and plazas of the darkened city. Her mind cast itself back to her life-that-was: the *Columbia* NX-02, her crew, the people she'd left behind on Earth . . . Jonathan. They were all hundreds of years in the future, and from her perspective they were all long gone.

She stood at the top of a steep staircase of white granite, high above a circular plaza. In the plaza's center was an inverted fountain, a circular cavity into which water poured from a surrounding ring. A geyser of spray shot up from the hole's center, dozens of meters into the balmy night air. The falling mist caught the pale starlight while it still could.

Holding out her arms as level with her shoulders as she could, Hernandez felt for a fleeting instant as if she could fly. Vertigo twisted her thoughts even as it seemed to lift her bare feet from the cold ground. She gave a push with her toes, shifted her weight incrementally forward, and hoped she was strong enough to do what she should have done so long ago.

Gravity made her its slave and tugged her into a tumbling plunge down the staircase. Delirious and feather-light with hunger and dehydration, she barely felt the easy snaps of her brittle old body breaking with every rolling impact, with every hammering collision against the corner of a step. The pummeling was unrelenting and overwhelming, and it pushed her to the brink of euphoria. Then she slammed to a halt on the plaza and lay very still, her body throbbing with the tactile memory of violence. She focused on the icy caress of the stone under her twisted body and imagined it bleeding away her last ounce of heat and life, snuffing her out with a cold and gentle embrace.

As she lay on the ground waiting for death, an amber shimmering of light formed on the periphery of her vision. At first she hoped it was her final hallucination before expiring.

Then the light began to assume a familiar shape.

Please let him be too late, she prayed, as she let go of awareness and sank into what she could only hope was oblivion.

"Are you in any pain?"

Inyx's question awakened Hernandez. She opened her eyes and was partly blinded by the flood of white light that was focused on her. It took her a moment to realize that she could see only with her left eye. She thought about his query, took stock of herself, and said, "No, I don't feel anything at all."

He leaned forward, blocking some of the light. She was relieved to have a respite from the glare. Staring up at his enormous, silhouetted head, she asked, "Where am I?"

"A sterile facility," he said. "I was concerned about a risk of infection by organisms from the planet's atmosphere."

A wave of his hand conjured a rectangular sheet of reflective liquid metal above and parallel with Hernandez's supine body. At first it showed only her reflection—broken, bruised, and bloody—but as Inyx spoke, the image on the sheet rippled and shifted to reveal scans of her internal organs, deep tissues, and endoskeleton.

"Your fall caused great damage, Erika," he said. "You've suffered compound fractures in both femurs, as well as simple fractures in your left tibia, right fibula, right humerus, the left ulna and radius, and the pelvis. In addition, you've cracked the parietal and occipital bones of your skull, concussed your brain, detached your right retina, and ruptured your liver and spleen. You'd also collapsed your lungs, but I took the liberty of repairing them and blocking your pain receptors so that I could discuss your options with you."

Lolling her head away from him, she muttered, "What's there to discuss? I'm dying, Inyx."

With another gentle sweep of his arm, he dispelled the reflective liquid screen as if it were nothing more than smoke. Gradually, the bright lights dimmed. When he spoke again, his voice was quiet and close to her ear. "You will die today if I don't treat your injuries," he said. "Is that what you want?"

Part of her wanted so badly to cry, but she felt emptied out, desiccated. "I don't know what I want," she said. "But I feel like I can't go on. Not alone."

Inyx stepped behind her head and walked around to the other side of the metal surface on which she lay. He passed out of her field of vision for just a moment. When he reappeared, she saw him completing the final details of his physical transformation into the likeness of Veronica Fletcher, as she had been in her youth. The sight of him wearing her friend's appearance like a cloak filled her with fury. "Don't do that," she snapped at him.

"I'm sorry," he said in Fletcher's voice. In a blink he altered himself into the semblance of Fletcher as she had been only weeks before her death. "Is this—"

"Stop it! I don't want your imitations, or your illusions."

Fletcher's face and form expanded and changed color and texture until Inyx stood beside her again. "Forgive me," he said. "I only meant to offer some comfort."

"Well, it didn't help," she said.

He pivoted away from her for a few seconds, apparently feeling chastened. Then he turned back and said, "You have not answered my question. Do you want medical treatment?"

"What good would it do? It's not like I have long to live."

"That might not be true," Inyx said.

She harrumphed. "Of course it's true. Look at me, Inyx, I'm an old woman. How long do you think I've got?"

"As long as you want," he said. "If you let me help you."

"The way you helped Sidra? No, thanks."

He squatted beside her and dropped his voice to a whisper. "After the incident with Sidra, Ordemo and the Quorum ordered me to cease my research into your species' physiology and genetic structure. I acknowledged their order. And I disobeyed it."

The intensity of his words alarmed her. "Why?" she asked.

"Because I had to know the truth about what happened to Sidra," he said. "I needed to know if she died because of my error, my negligence. But I found no evidence to support that." His tone brightened. "As a result of my investigation, however, I learned a great deal about your species and how to treat its myriad diseases—including what you call 'natural' death."

Hernandez rolled her good eye. "Death isn't something you cure, Inyx. Death is a constant, not just another illness."

"In your species, natural death is the end result of unchecked cellular senescence," Inyx replied, with profound earnestness. "Most of the problem is related to the shortening of your cells' telomeres, which are sacrificed, bit by bit, to prevent the loss of your working DNA during cell division and replication. But these losses lead to your aging process, and, eventually, you run out of telomeres. That triggers your cells' preprogrammed senescence—cell death. Then your organs fail."

"That's a long way of saying humans get old and die."

"What I'm saying is that I believe I can correct that flaw in your genetic program. Aging and death are a disease, Erika. Don't you want the cure?"

She considered the implications of what he was saying. Beyond mending her shattered bones and ruptured organs, he was offering her something that humanity had searched for and dreamt of for eons: eternal youth and near immortality. A bite of the fruit of the Tree of Life itself.

"No," she said. "It's too much. I can't."

He lowered his head and sounded despondent as he said, "I wish you would reconsider."

Fletcher's defiant warnings echoed in Hernandez's thoughts, and she gave them voice. "Inyx, if I accept that kind of gift from you, it would be the same as sanctioning my captivity and that of my crew. I'd be dishonoring all their sacrifices."

A note of desperation crept into his voice as he replied, "Erika, your crew and your friends are gone. Only you remain. And no matter what they might have wanted or believed, you should make the choice that's best for you, here and now."

"I think I am," she said, feeling her strength ebb.

He reached out and transformed his waggling cilia into more human-looking fingers and a thumb, and took Hernandez's hand. "I've seen how much death frightened you in the past," he said. "But I don't want to appeal to your fear, and I won't ask you to set aside your resentment of me and my people for having imprisoned you. I'd like you to consider an entirely different rationale for accepting my help."

Hernandez's curiosity overcame her guilt. "Which is . . . ?"

"By your reckoning, I've lived for tens of thousands of years," Inyx said. "In all that time, I have encountered very few sentient life-forms from outside of my society. But of all the beings I have met, you are one of the most . . . vital."

She tried to swallow the saliva pooling in her mouth, but her tongue and throat felt like poorly lubricated gears grinding to no avail in a dusty machine. "Ironic of you to say so," she said in a hoarse croak of a voice.

"Even in your present state, you're more vibrant than any of the millions of Caeliar in Axion. And though our association has so far been—from my perspective—incredibly brief, I have come to think of you as my friend. And so . . . for purely selfish reasons : . . I want you to survive, and enjoy living, and help me continue the Great Work." His words were heavy with sorrow as he added, "I don't want you to die, Erika. So I'm begging you to let me help you. Please don't make me stand aside and watch you die. If I cannot give you your freedom . . . at least let me give you back your life."

His heartfelt plea would have brought her to tears had her eyes not been as red and dry as the Martian desert. "All right," she said, flashing a sad smile. "But only because you're doing it for selfish reasons." Noting his confused silence, she explained, "It makes you seem a little more human."

"I'll try to take that as a compliment," he said.

Hernandez was only partially conscious as Inyx levitated the metal slab on which she lay and guided it telekinetically through the vaulted, cathedral-like spaces of Axion.

As they passed a long line of massive, narrow open archways that looked out on the landscape of New Erigol, she caught the sweet, heavy scent of a gathering storm. She turned her head and saw the hills and trees strangely luminous with bright sunlight, beneath ominous clouds that were black and pregnant with rain.

Then she and Inyx turned down a dark, narrow passage that led to a dead end in a circular chamber. The ceiling spiraled open above her, and the walls rushed past as she and Inyx were lifted in silence to the top of one of the city's towers.

She asked, "Where are we going?"

"To my operating theater," he said, evoking heartbreaking memories of Valerian's ugly demise. Perhaps sensing Hernandez's unspoken reaction, he added apologetically, "It's the only facility equipped for the procedure."

Their ascent slowed.

"What will the Quorum say?"

"They'll forbid it," Inyx said. "Which is why I won't tell them until after it's done."

Hernandez chuckled softly at Inyx's insolence toward his superiors. "I knew there was a reason I liked you."

They arrived in a circular room much like the one at the start of their vertical journey, and Inyx guided her steel stretcher down another passage that was far shorter. At its end, a door slid open, admitting them to his laboratory.

Nothing had changed about the lab since her last visit, except that the carbon-black stain on the metal operating table had been expunged. The tall and narrow space was still packed tightly with machines throbbing with low-frequency sounds and pulsing with scarlet light. Overhead, a web of slack, silvery cables surrounded the room's periphery. The only gap in the tangled mess was directly above the operating table, where the long, irregular machine hovered without support beneath the closed, clamshell-shaped skylight.

Inyx guided the stretcher onto the operating table, and out of the corner of her eye, Hernandez saw the two metallic surfaces fuse into one.

Above her, the protruding implements of the surgical machine began to glow with crimson energies, and a surge of terror coursed through her.

"It's important you understand the procedure and the risks," Inyx said. "I want you to make an informed decision."

"So, inform me," Hernandez said, hiding behind bravado.

He gestured to the hovering contraption. "With this machine, I will introduce a limited quantity of catoms into your body. These nanomachines will effect repairs to your damaged bones and organs, and they'll modify your genetic code."

Hernandez swallowed her anxiety. "Sounds okay so far."

"Because of certain immutable limitations of organic cellular replication, the catoms will need to remain part of your body to monitor the Change's effects. Once incorporated into your body, the catoms will be sustained partly by your biology, but primarily by Axion's zero-point quantum field."

"You talk like you're selling me a used car," she said. "Skip ahead to the risks."

Her rebuke silenced Inyx for a moment. Then he continued, "My chief concern is that you will not be able to commune with the gestalt. Sidra died because her mind rejected contact with the Caeliar. The catoms in your body will not stabilize unless they can form a bond between your mind and the gestalt."

"Bond? Commune with the gestalt? What does that mean?"

A long huff of breath puffed the sacs that curled over Inyx's shoulders and dilated the ends of the tubules on his head. "It's difficult to explain, Erika. It's about becoming part of something greater than yourself and accepting your place in it. Reduced to its most basic level, you must surrender or perish."

Fletcher's warning came back to Hernandez: *They want our surrender.* "And if my subconscious mind resists . . . ?"

"Then what happened to Sidra will happen to you, as well."

New waves of anxiety christened her forehead with sweat. She glanced nervously at Inyx. "How hard is it to surrender?"

"That depends on you." He looked up at the machine, then back at her. "We don't have to do this. I can mend your immediate injuries and forgo the rest of the procedure."

She shook her head, feigning defiance and resolve. "No," she said. "If I back away from this now, I might never have the courage to come back. I'm ready now."

"Are you sure?" he asked, sounding doubtful.

"Yes," she said.

Inyx levitated up from the floor. "Very well," he said, and he began making his final adjustments to the machine.

DAVID MACK

A guilty voice inside Hernandez's head justified the rashness of her choice: *If it goes wrong, and I die like Sidra did, it'll be justice. I'll get what I deserved.* As the device looming directly above her face thrummed with power and glowed with light, she lost herself in its ruby glare. *No turning back now,* she told herself. *Whatever happens . . . happens.*

Inyx rested his cilia on her shoulder and spoke in a soothing baritone. "I'm going to use a low-power energy wave to guide your brain into an unconscious state. Most of the changes to your body will take place while you're sedated. When the catoms have completed their fusion with your genetic matrix, I'll bring you back to consciousness. Those first moments will be critical, Erika. As you awaken, you must open yourself to the gestalt and accept its embrace. Do you understand?"

She nodded. "Yes. And, Inyx . . . ? Thank you."

He gently nudged a few snowy-white hairs from her eyes. "Breathe deeply," he said to her. "We're about to begin." Then he withdrew, floating like a ghost to the master control panel behind the transparent wall to her right. She did as he asked, and slowly inhaled, filling her lungs. Then, as she let the air escape, her senses faded, and she knew that she was being sedated. When she opened her eyes again, it would be to face either a new life or an instant death.

Darkness fell for a moment that might have lasted forever. Then the distant glimmer of light and life beckoned her upward, out of an abyss of shadow.

She felt like flowing water, free and moving in the current of something greater than herself, a fluid with no boundaries, no beginning and no end, just momentum and union. For a moment, part of her mind cried out in alarm that she was drowning. Through an act of will, she silenced her fear and gave herself a new frame for the experience: *I'm in the womb.*

There were voices, millions of them, each distinct, none exalted over the others. Ideas and forms and concepts filled Hernandez's thoughts, every one of them hers for the taking if she wanted it, but if she averted her thoughts they fell away, forgotten. Images and sounds buoyed her. She was afloat in a sea of memories and daydreams, all equal in substance and value.

All of it was hers to enjoy, but none of it was hers. It wasn't anyone's, and it was everyone's. Information and power were all around her, as abundant as the air she breathed. She was immersed in it, was part of it, and gave it a focal point. Other loci were moving throughout the city, and one was beside her. They and she were like stars orbiting Axion.

Sound returned. "Open your eyes," Inyx said softly.

Her eyelids parted with reluctance. Above and around the operating table, Inyx's lab looked exactly as it had before the procedure, but Hernandez saw it with a new vision. She felt a reciprocal tug from the machines that surrounded her—a give and take that enabled her to sense their energy levels and, she presumed, direct their function by thought alone.

Rain slashed against the clamshell skylight directly above her, and the storm-blackened sky flashed with lightning. Half a second later, thunder rocked the city.

Inyx stood at her side, his cilia-fingers waggling together in front of him. "Your catoms are stable. How do you feel?"

"I don't know," she whispered. Then she looked down at her hands. Their skin was rosy and taut and their muscles toned, and all the scars she had acquired in her youth as a rock climber had been erased. At first, she sat up slowly, in the cautious manner to which age had made her accustomed. None of her old aches and pains were with her, so she pivoted and swung her legs off the side of the bed, appreciating all of a sudden how lean and firm they were beneath her delicate silver-white raiment.

As she leaned forward to stand up, her hair spilled in front of her face—in long, lustrous black coils. She touched her face and throat. Gone was her brittle and age-loosened skin. Her fingertips found only the soft, graceful lines of her jaw. In a moment of vanity, she wished for a mirror . . . and one took shape in front of her, coalesced from billions of motes of nanoscopic, programmable matter that lingered in the air.

"Did I do that?" she asked, staring in wonder at the free-floating oval mirror, which reflected back the sight of her as she might have been at the age of eighteen, had she worn her hair in an epic, wild mane that fell to her lower back.

"Yes," Inyx said. "You did. And you can do much more, if you want to. I can show you how."

Giddy with excitement, she tore her eyes from the lissome echo of her youth in the mirror and looked at Inyx. "Show me everything," she said.

"Look up," he said. She did as he asked. Above them was the skylight, rattling beneath the fury of the wind and rain. "Open it," he told her. "See it open in your mind."

The moment played in her imagination and became clear.

Then it became reality. The skylight opened.

Rain, warm and pure, surged through the open space and doused Hernandez and Inyx. She closed her eyes and reveled in the sensation of the droplets pelting her face and bosom.

He placed his arm against her back. "Rise with me."

Her feet lifted from the floor of the lab.

She and Inyx levitated together, ascending into the downpour. They passed through the frame of the open skylight, into open air. Until that moment, she'd thought Inyx alone had lifted her up. Then he removed his arm . . . and she soared.

Violent gales buffeted her with rain, and twists of blue lightning split the stygian shadows and cracked the heavens with thunderclaps. She cried out in a panic, "Inyx!"

He was nowhere to be seen, but she heard his calming counsel close by. "Don't be afraid . . . it can't hurt you now."

And she knew that it was true.

She opened herself to the power that radiated up from the city and unlocked the potential that now suffused her body. Gaining speed, she shot upward, slicing through the stormhead, fearless, baptized by the storm as she flew like a bullet.

She wept with joy; it felt like freedom incarnate.

Like an arrow piercing a target, she burst free of the tempest and exploded into blue sky and golden light. Spreading her arms wide to embrace it all, she turned in a slow spiral, feeling the wind and the sun warming her rain-drenched body, and her head lolled back to glory in her transformation.

Then came the gentlest tug of restraint.

It was subtle but undeniable, as if an invisible, silken cord had been tied around her ankles, anchoring her to Axion and rescuing her from her inner Icarus.

"Everything has a limit," explained Inyx's disembodied voice. "Our gifts are made possible by Axion's quantum field. Beyond a certain distance, our powers diminish greatly. Within and near the city, however, you'll have nothing to fear."

His words haunted her thoughts as she looked again at the sky and saw the dark scar of the planet's growing shell taking shape in high orbit. *This is what Veronica was warning me about,* she realized. *How could I have been so stupid?*

The Caeliar had granted her eternal youth and functional immortality—but only as long as she remained in Axion. It was nothing less than a life without end in captivity. She would never be freed, not even by death.

Her joyful tears turned bitter as she confessed the truth to herself: *I just made myself a prisoner forever.*

2381

13

"Aperture two-alpha, opening now," reported Lieutenant Sean Milner, the *Enterprise*'s gamma-shift operations manager. "Ship emerging. It's the *Aventine*. They're signaling all clear."

Picard nodded. "Noted, Lieutenant."

A demonic whispering stole the captain's attention for a moment: it was the voice of the Borg. He tried to see through the cerulean churning of the Azure Nebula on the main viewer. The susurration had no words, no message he could discern. After a few seconds he realized that the Collective wasn't speaking to him; it didn't even seem to be aware of his presence . . . yet. But he knew that it was nearby, somewhere on the other side of one of these shortcuts through space.

An electronic tone warbled from the operations console. Milner, a tall and square-jawed Londoner, checked his console and pivoted around to report, "It's Starfleet Command, sir."

"On-screen," said Picard, rising from his chair.

Admiral Nechayev's image appeared on the main viewer. *"Good news, Captain,"* she said. *"Reinforcements are on the way."*

"Glad to hear it, Admiral. Who's with us?"

She arched one eyebrow in apparent amusement. *"Everyone except the Tholians, apparently. The Ferengi even paid off the Breen to send a fleet. I don't know how President Bacco did it, but if we get through this, I might ask her to turn some water into wine."*

Picard feigned high spirits. "How long until our force assembles?"

Nechayev checked something off-screen before she replied, *"The Klingons and the Romulans will have several dozen ships at your position in less than thirty-six hours. Our forces start arriving in forty-eight. A Cardassian battle group will reach you in fifty-six hours, and the Talarians, Ferengi, Breen, and Gorn will be the last to arrive, in about four days."*

"Understood," Picard said. "We'll continue scouting the subspace tunnels and holding the line until they arrive."

"Good luck and godspeed, Captain," Nechayev said. *"Starfleet Command out."* The main viewer blinked back to the cloudy sprawl of the nebula.

Picard looked at Worf. "Commander. Status report."

Worf checked the display on the end of one of his chair's armrests. "Repairs complete," he said. Looking up, he added, "Lieutenant Elfiki is ready to open tunnel three-alpha."

"Very good," Picard said. To Milner, he added, "Put me on internal speakers, Lieutenant."

Milner keyed in the command. "Channel open, sir."

"Attention, all decks, this is the captain," Picard said. "The *Aventine* has just returned from its first jaunt. In a few minutes, we'll be making our own first trip through one of the subspace tunnels. Please report to your primary duty stations. Senior command officers, report to the bridge. Picard out."

As Picard settled back into his command chair, Worf said to tactical officer Abby Balidemaj, "Sound Yellow Alert. Raise shields, transphasic torpedoes to standby."

"Aye, sir," Balidemaj replied, executing the order.

Picard threw a questioning look at his first officer. "Feeling anxious about our first scouting run, Mister Worf?"

"No, sir," Worf said, with a ferocious gleam. "*Eager.*"

Drawing strength from Worf's confidence, Picard sat up a bit straighter in his chair and fixed his eyes on the main viewscreen. Far away, beyond a veil of shadows, the voice of the Collective still whispered . . . and he vowed that he would silence it—soon, and forever. No matter what the cost proved to be.

Miranda Kadohata looked up from the desktop monitor in her quarters as Captain Picard's voice echoed over the intraship comm. *"Attention, all decks, this is the captain,"* he said. *"The* Aventine *has just returned from its first jaunt. In a few minutes, we'll be making our own first trip through one of the subspace tunnels. Please report to your primary duty stations. Senior command officers, report to the bridge. Picard out."*

The comm clicked off, and Kadohata resumed staring at the blue-and-white Federation emblem on the screen in front of her. *Connect, dammit,* she fumed.

Can't wait much longer. An icon in the lower right corner of the screen changed, indicating that the real-time signal had been routed to its destination. *Pick up, Vicenzo! Hurry!*

An image blinked onto the screen: her husband, Vicenzo Farrenga, looking frazzled and standing in a sunlit corridor of Bacco University, on Cestus III. *"Miranda? They pulled me out of a lecture. Hope I didn't keep you waiting."*

"I have to make this quick, love," she said. "I can't explain, but this might be the last time . . . for a while . . . that I get to talk to you, and I need you to pay attention."

He reacted attentively to her urgent tone. *"I'm listening."*

Kadohata wanted to shout, *Run! Take the children and go, and don't look back!* But she knew that all communications were monitored at times like this, and Starfleet regulations forbade her from sharing what she knew of the rapidly worsening tactical threat against the Federation. Fomenting fear and panic about the imminent Borg invasion would only serve to destabilize the situation. To save her family, she'd have to be more discreet.

"Do you remember Judi and Adams?"

Vicenzo thought for a moment. *"You mean that nice couple who lived out on Dundee Ridge? Didn't they move?"*

"Yes," Kadohata said. "They started a farm on Kennovere."

"Right, Kennovere," he said, nodding in confirmation. *"That crazy, low-tech organic colony out past Typerias."*

"Organic, yes. Crazy, maybe not. That's a way of life I'd really like the kids to see."

He rolled his eyes and combed his fingers through his unruly dark hair. *"Okay,"* he said. *"I'm not sure I can fit that in during spring break. Maybe when the semester's over—"*

"They ought to see it as soon as possible," Kadohata said, more sharply than she'd meant to. "Before the growing season ends on Kennovere next month."

She recognized the look of slowly dawning understanding that was changing Vicenzo's face. *"It'll be tricky getting out there in time,"* he said, doing a poor job of pretending to be nonchalant. *"We'd probably have to hop a transport out first thing tomorrow to have a chance at seeing the harvest."*

"Trust me, love," she said, her eyes misting with tears as she fought to bury her fears. "It'll be worth it."

The overhead comm beeped twice and was followed by Commander Worf's irate baritone. *"Commander Kadohata, report to the bridge immediately."*

"On my way, sir," she answered. "Kadohata out." Then she looked back to her husband and touched her fingertips to his lips on the screen. "Duty calls, love. Safe travels."

He touched his screen and replied, *"You, too, sweetheart."*

The signal ended abruptly, and her monitor went black.

Kadohata stood, tied her hair back in a utilitarian knot, and smoothed her uniform while looking in the mirror.

It'll be all right, she assured herself. *He'll get the kids out of Federation space. Out of the war zone.*

As she left her quarters and hurried to the bridge, she kept telling herself that everything would be okay, but she knew that unless the Borg invasion was halted soon, having her family flee their home wouldn't be enough to save them. Because when the real invasion came, there would be nowhere left to run to.

Worf detested sitting still. All around him, the *Enterprise* felt as if it was shaking itself to pieces while making its transit of the subspace tunnel Elfiki had opened. At flight control, Joanna Faur fought to steady the *Sovereign*-class vessel's passage, and from ops Commander Kadohata called out over the rumbling of the engines and turbulence, "Shields weakening."

Defying his instincts, Worf looked at the captain and said, "Sir, I suggest we route phaser power to shields."

Picard assented without hesitation. "Make it so."

Worf delegated the order with a glance at Choudhury, who nodded and entered the command on the tactical console.

"Picking up speed," Faur reported, reacting quickly to the changing data at the conn. "Full impulse plus ten percent."

Lieutenant Elfiki looked up from the starboard science station to add, "We're reading an extreme-gravity environment ahead, past the tunnel's terminus. We should be able to compensate for it with a low-power subspace field."

"Bridge to engineering," Worf said.

La Forge answered. *"Go ahead, bridge."*

"Stand by to generate a low-power subspace field, on Commander Kadohata's signal."

"We're on it," La Forge said. *"Engineering out."*

Instead of the proverbial light at the end of the tunnel, Worf saw a circle of darkness growing larger and emptier with each passing moment. Then the *Enterprise* shot out of the subspatial anomaly, and it seemed to be bashed in three directions at once. The force of the impacts hurtled Worf out of his chair onto the deck. As he struggled up onto one knee, a mournful groaning of stressed duranium resonated through the hull. Over the deep, metallic howls, Worf bellowed to Kadohata, "Initiate subspace field!"

Kadohata was half on the deck, clinging with one arm to her station and manipulating its controls with her free hand. Seconds later, the banshee moans of the hull ceased. Everyone clambered back into their chairs. Once they were settled, the captain said with stern equanimity, "Report, Mister Worf."

"No damage, Captain," Worf said, checking the status screen beside his chair. "A few minor injuries in the cargo bay." He looked toward the conn officer. "Lieutenant Faur—position."

"Still calculating, sir," Faur replied. "I'm not reading any of the nav beacons." As she continued, Captain Picard got up from his chair and walked slowly toward the main viewscreen. "There's a lot of signal interference, too. Background radiation's off the scale."

Picard stood behind Kadohata and Faur and stared in silence at the image on the massive screen at the forward end of the bridge. Worf looked past the captain and realized why: There were practically no stars anywhere to be seen, just a few lonely dots of light separated by unimaginable reaches of icy void.

"Where are we?" Picard wondered aloud.

Worf stood and stepped forward to stand with his captain. "Perhaps we are in a region between galaxies," he said.

"Negative," said Elfiki. "The gravimetric disturbances we're reading are from massive numbers of black holes, including a few that are bigger than any ever seen before." She tapped commands into her station's controls. A false-spectrum image was superimposed over the emptiness on the screen, so that violet-hued rings of various sizes could represent the black holes. "In addition to the singularities, we've detected enough mass to suggest that there are billions of very old stars in this galaxy."

Kadohata gestured at the black screen. "So where are they?"

Elfiki layered another computer-generated image over the first, this time stippling the view with brilliant points of light. "All around us," said the science officer. "The reason we can't see them is that they've all been shrouded."

Picard turned aft to face her. "Elaborate."

"If the nearest star is any indication," she said, "the shells are some kind of neutronium composite. I'm sorry I can't be more specific. The one shell within sensor range is proving resistant to most of our detection methods."

The captain glanced at Worf, as if to confirm that he wasn't the only one hearing Elfiki's report. Then he asked the young lieutenant, "What about planets?"

She shook her head. "So far, we aren't reading any.

No nebulae or interstellar dust, either. It's like some-one vacuumed up all the loose matter in this galaxy—and probably from a few neighboring galaxies—to make those shells."

Dread and awe both showed in Picard's eyes. "What is the purpose of these shells, Lieutenant? Energy? Concealment?"

"Maybe both," Elfiki said. "But I can't imagine what anyone would need that much power for."

"Some acquire power for its own sake," Worf said.

Faur swiveled away from the conn. "I hope they didn't do it to impress the neighbors, because it's a long way to the next galaxy," she said. "It's hard to be certain, but this could have been one of the first proto-galactic clusters. It might date all the way back to first light."

"Remarkable," Picard said, his voice reverentially hushed. "One of the universe's first galaxies, completely harnessed." He looked back at Elfiki. "Can you determine which galaxy this is, Lieutenant?"

She shook her head. "I'd doubt it, sir. Our records of the early proto-galaxies are based on redshifted images that date back nearly thirteen billion years. Comparing those images to this shrouded galaxy would be like using a baby picture to try and identify an old man wearing a bag over his head."

"Lieutenant Choudhury," Picard said. "Transmit a standard greeting hail, on all frequencies, and in all directions."

"Aye, sir," replied Choudhury.

Worf tensed as the security chief carried out Picard's order. It was difficult for Worf to suppress the urge to tell Choudhury to belay the captain's command, but he knew it would be wiser to reserve such a blunt tactic for a moment when it was more critically needed. Instead, he stepped closer to Picard and lowered his voice. "Sir . . . discretion might be a more prudent choice, in this situation."

Emulating the XO's muted tone, Picard replied, "What's your objection, Mister Worf?"

Before he could answer, Choudhury cut in to report, "No reply to our hails, Captain. Shall I try again?"

Taking note of Worf's clenched jaw and intense stare, Picard responded with a small shake of his head. "No, Lieutenant." He met Worf's glare and said, "This might be one of the oldest civilizations in the universe, Mister Worf. And it is the mission of the *Enterprise*—in times of both war and peace—to seek out new life-forms and attempt peaceful first contact."

"Perhaps," Worf said. "But imagine what kind of a people would wield technology like this in such a brute manner. Then ask yourself: Is this the kind of civilization whose attention we want to attract?" While the captain pondered that, Worf added, "In any case, our mission is to seek out the staging area for the Borg invasion. This is not it. For the safety of the ship, and the sake of the mission, I suggest we reopen the subspace tunnel and return home as soon as possible."

The captain looked unhappy. "Very well," he said. "Have the astrometrics teams continue their research until it's time to head back. There's no telling when a Starfleet vessel will get another opportunity like this one."

"Aye, sir," Worf said.

Picard wore a grim expression as he walked toward his ready room. "You have the bridge, Number One."

After the ready room door closed behind the captain, Worf settled into the command chair. He had just started reviewing the results of the ship's last combat-readiness drill when Lieutenant Elfiki stepped beside his chair. "I wonder why there was no answer to our hail," she said.

"There are many possibilities," Worf said.

Elfiki tilted her head and crossed her arms. "Well, yes. Maybe they don't listen to the frequencies we transmit. Or maybe they're unable or unwilling to respond."

"Or perhaps they are extinct," Worf said.

The science officer looked taken aback. "Would that make you *less* anxious about being here, sir?"

He looked at the great swath of blackness and imagined a hundred billion stars held captive inside dark metal spheres.

"No," he said. "It would not."

14

———◆———

Deanna Troi had thought that having Erika Hernandez stand beside her while she addressed the Caeliar Quorum might be encouraging. Instead, as Troi had feared, Hernandez said nothing while Troi stood before the eerily hovering throng of the Quorum and faced off in a futile dialogue with the Caeliar's *tanwaseynorral,* the officious Ordemo Nordal.

"All of your suggested resolutions have been proposed here before," Ordemo said, his stately voice resounding in the vast, crystal-walled, and pyramidal space of the Quorum chamber. "Interdicting our sector by means of your laws will only inflame others' curiosity and draw the attention of precisely the sorts of visitors we most wish to avoid.

"Altering your logs and even your memories would seem to be a viable tactic," he continued, "until one considers that certain immutable laws of physics would inevitably give the lie to our ruse, and your subsequent investigation would, in all probability, lead you and your ship directly back to us."

The throng of Caeliar that surrounded Troi on three

sides murmured in low concurrence with Ordemo's statement.

Troi looked to Hernandez for some kind of cue as to how she ought to proceed, but Hernandez stood with her eyes averted, staring down at the fractal pattern that adorned the chamber's floor. Finding no help, Troi turned back toward Ordemo and waited for the Quorum's susurrus to abate. "Answer me this," she said to him. "If your people are so averse to contact with other species, why don't you just leave the Milky Way? There must be a few million galaxies quieter than this one."

"Indubitably," said Ordemo. "However, we have yet to find another that is blessed with the sheltering effects that this spiral formation takes for granted."

At a loss for understanding, Troi shrugged and raised her eyebrows. "Sheltering effects?"

Hernandez interjected, "He means the galactic barrier."

"Correct," Ordemo said. "We explored other galaxies as platforms from which we could continue the Great Work. However, all such efforts to establish ourselves met with resistance."

"By whom?" asked Troi. She couldn't name many species that would be capable of mounting significant resistance against a people as technologically advanced as the Caeliar.

Ordemo turned away to huddle with his colleagues. The teeming mass of Caeliar that was levitating several meters above the hall's floor filled the cavernous space with a muffled, low-frequency groaning and rapid clicking noises. Then the *tanwa-seynorral* rotated back to face Troi and said, "We think it would be best to tell you only that, beyond the confines of this galaxy, there are many powers of varying degrees of malevolence. The only sanctuary we've found from their malicious interferences has been here, within the protective embrace of the galactic barrier."

Troi fought to hold the reins of her temper. "So what you're saying is, since you can't leave, neither can we?"

"Well," Ordemo said, slightly recoiling from her, "that's a crude reduction of an extremely complicated situ—"

"Yes," Hernandez interrupted. "What he's trying to say is yes. Whether you should think of it as 'You're stuck on this planet with them' or as 'They're stuck in this galaxy with all of us,' is entirely up to you."

A new, acute twinge of pain inside Troi's abdomen made her wince just a bit, and she did her best to conceal it by putting on an exaggerated frown. "Thanks for the translation," she said.

"My pleasure," Hernandez said, with a ghost of a smirk.

Troi realized that Hernandez's mannerisms had become less stilted as she'd spent more time interacting with the members of *Titan*'s away team. *Maybe I'm looking for allies in the wrong places,* she speculated.

"Deanna," Ordemo said, "unless you have further proposals, we consider this discussion to be at an end."

"Fine," Troi said, concealing her irritation at being addressed with her given name by a being who had no right to affect such a degree of familiarity.

"Then, on behalf of this Quorum, I thank you for your input, and I hope that the rest of your residency in Axion, or on New Erigol, is pleasant and comfortable. You may go."

As Troi tensed in a prelude to a protest, Hernandez took Troi's shoulder in a gentle grip and steered her away from the Quorum and toward the circle in the chamber's center. "Trust me when I say they weren't giving you permission," she said. "They were giving you an order."

The two women stepped into the middle of the circle, which began its swift drop back to the entrance level of the pyramid. As the dark walls blurred past with just a hint of displaced air, Troi sighed. "You were right. They're very stubborn."

Troi's empathic senses felt Hernandez's aura of sympathy as she cracked a bittersweet grin and said, "I told you so."

Xin Ra-Havreii yawned. It had been twenty-four hours since Captain Riker had tasked him and Pazlar with finding a way to penetrate the Caeliar's cloak of secrecy; in that time, the chief engineer had stolen less than thirty minutes for a nap, sometime just after eating dinner.

He was certain that he was on the verge of a breakthrough. Somewhere in the flurry of subspace emissions and energy pulses, he knew there was a pattern. It was elusive, though. The harder he worked to pierce the clutter of noise to find the truth of the signal, the more chaotic everything seemed.

Worst of all, it was so close. *If only I could see it,* he brooded, rubbing the itch of exhaustion from his eyes. Then he scratched his bushy white eyebrows and massaged the dull ache from his temples.

A new bundle of data packets appeared on his lab's status display. It was a wealth of new sensor readings compiled and annotated with painstaking precision by Pazlar. *The answer's in this batch,* he told himself. *This time for sure.*

He had drained the last dregs of iced *raktajino* from his insulated mug and had started browsing through the new data when he was interrupted by the buzz of the door signal. "Come in," he said, too tired to mask his irritation.

The door opened, and Dr. Huilan waddled in. The diminutive S'ti'ach blinked his large, black eyes and presented himself as the very picture of innocence. "I hope I'm not interrupting."

"Actually, Counselor, I'm in the middle of working on a priority assignment for the captain," Ra-Havreii said.

Ambling closer, Huilan replied, "I'll be brief, then. I've come to talk to you about the holopresence system you built for Melora Pazlar."

Ra-Havreii turned away from Huilan, back toward his work, and asked in a dismissive tone, "What of it?"

"I'd like you to shut it off," Huilan said, sidling up behind the Efrosian. "Maybe even dismantle it."

A flash of temper spurred Ra-Havreii to pivot and loom angrily above his meter-tall visitor. "I'll do no such thing."

Huilan reacted defensively, raising the fearsome spikes that lined his blue-furred back. "There's no need to get upset, Commander," he said.

"Sorry," Ra-Havreii said, feeling self-conscious. He took a deep breath, smoothed his snowy, drooping mustache through the loop of his thumb and forefinger, and backed off half a step. "What's your objection to the holopresence module?"

The counselor's dorsal spines retracted gradually as he answered, "I'm concerned that it's serving as a new kind of crutch for her—and another crutch is the last thing she needs."

Shaking his head, Ra-Havreii said, "That's ridiculous. It's not a crutch at all. It's *freedom* from crutches."

"I see," Huilan said, easing forward, his large ears twitching with interest. "What was your reason for building it?"

The chief engineer recoiled from what he inferred was an impugning of his motives. "I designed it and created it to help Melora live more freely and more fully aboard *Titan*."

"I'm just curious, Commander. What part of interacting with holographic phantoms—or acting as one— is helping her live more fully? How is her life enriched by having her body weakened?"

Ra-Havreii held up his hands, palms facing Huilan. "Stop right there. What're you talking about?"

"Melora seems to think that your clever invention has absolved her of the need to brave the ship's one-gee spaces," Huilan said. "Instead, she's content to live and work in a centigee simulacrum of *Titan*. If she doesn't occasionally push herself to stay acclimatized, the physical abilities she worked so long to acquire will atrophy."

Getting angrier by the moment, Ra-Havreii shot back, "So what? When was the last time any of us one-gee natives tried to make ourselves function in a fifty-gee environment? Or even a ten-gee field? We can't adapt to that any more than she can adapt to our standard gravity, so why try?"

Huilan was quiet for a few seconds. "You may be right," he said. "But that still doesn't explain why you went to such absurd lengths to build a holopresence network inside *Titan*."

"I'm not seeing your point," Ra-Havreii said.

"There are easier ways to help Melora adapt to *Titan*'s environment," Huilan said. "All our shipboard gravity is artificial, so why not just program the graviton emitters to sense her combadge, or even her unique biosignature, and reduce the local gravity field wherever she goes?"

To keep from laughing, the chief engineer smiled. "That might seem like a good idea—until she and a regular-gravity crewmate step on the same deck plate at the same time, and the other person winds up embedded skull-first in the overhead. And may the spirits help her if the main computer gets overloaded or loses track of her—she'd be crushed under her own weight."

"All right," Huilan said. "I'm no engineer, but I'm sure you could equip Melora with a graviton-deflecting module for her uniform. You could make her immune to most of the ship's synthetic gravity without affecting anyone else. Right?"

As much as he wanted to dismiss Huilan's second idea, he had to think about it. Though it would be a tedious process to find exactly the right settings for such a device, it would be a fairly elegant solution to Pazlar's gravitational vulnerability. "That's not a bad idea," he admitted. "With the right adjustments, it might even let her move freely on a planet."

"Which brings me back to my earlier question,"

Huilan said. "Why did you build the holopresence system? I'll give you a hint: I don't think you really built it for her."

"Don't be absurd," Ra-Havreii replied. "Of course I did."

Huilan shrugged. "I don't doubt that you believe you did."

"If I didn't build it for Melora, then who is it for?"

"For yourself."

The chief engineer crossed his arms. "This I have to hear."

"I think the solution you concocted for her is just a proxy for your own issues," Huilan said. "I know that Efrosians are a very empathetic people—not in the telepathic sense, of course, but definitely in the emotional one. It makes you keenly aware of others' needs—but in this case, I think the need you're responding to is your own."

Ra-Havreii sighed. "Counselor, I have a lot of work to do, so if you're not going to get to the point—"

"Melora's vulnerability in the months after Tuvok assaulted her reminds you of your own emotional weak spots," Huilan said, his manner more aggressive than Ra-Havreii would have expected from such a small being. "So you tried to help her cope in much the same way that you do—by keeping personal interactions at a figurative distance, so they'll seem 'unreal.' You treat your emotional relationships like holograms—as purely superficial amusements—to shelter yourself from loss. To stay safe."

"You're half right about one detail," Ra-Havreii said. "I was trying to help Melora. Speaking of whom— when you came in, you said this was about her. So how did this conversation suddenly become about me?"

Huilan flashed an unnerving grin full of fangs. "Isn't everything all about you?"

"Well, yes—I can't fault your reasoning on that point," Ra-Havreii said, not too proud to accept the barbed compliment. "But tell me, do you counselors always try to make people feel bad about doing something good?"

"I'm just trying to help you understand your own motives," Huilan said. "You spent weeks building the holopresence system. Why did you go to so much effort for the benefit of one person? Why work so hard to reshape *Titan* just for her? What does it mean for you to make a gesture like that?"

Something about the question demanded a genuine answer and not just another flip remark. Ra-Havreii pondered it carefully, and then he said, "It makes this ship into something tangibly good that I've done for someone . . . instead of a reminder of a mistake I made that cost good people their lives."

"To be honest, Commander, I don't really fault you for what you've done here," Huilan said. "But I don't think you were trying to improve the ship—I think you were trying to improve yourself, and Melora's a big part of the reason why. All I want you to think about is whether, in the long run, the holopresence module is really the best thing for her—and whether you might both benefit from a life that's a little bit more . . . real."

Huilan walked away, leaving Ra-Havreii to mull over what the S'ti'ach had said.

Have I made an illusion of my life? Did I just pretend to care about the women I've known? The notion that his many and varied fleeting romances might all have been as emotionally sterile as a holodeck simulation troubled him—no, it *disgusted* him. And yet, he couldn't dispel it from his mind. In the passion of those moments, it all had seemed like harmless erotic fun, and he couldn't bring himself to regret any of it.

But if Huilan's right, he cautioned himself, *if I have been reducing romance to a superficial game to isolate myself, then Melora deserves better than that. She deserves something real.*

He began imagining all the ways he might express this revelation to Melora. Then his search for perfect words was interrupted as he stared blankly at a wall companel, across which raged the flood of data she had sent him.

In the moment he had stopped looking for it, he'd found a sudden flash of insight.

He saw the pattern.

"Ra-Havreii to Lieutenant Commander Pazlar," he said, putting aside his personal epiphany for a professional one. "Please report to my lab immediately. We have a breakthrough."

Most of *Titan*'s away team gathered around Christine Vale as they sat down in their common dining room to a late-morning breakfast, which had been provided to them by the Caeliar.

For the humanoid members of the team, the meal consisted of pancakes, fruits, nuts, and juice. Ensign Torvig's plate, however, was piled high with fresh greens, a variety of raw tubers, and a colorful assortment of wildflowers.

The one member of the team absent from breakfast

was Dr. Ree. He had been granted special permission by the Caeliar for a visit to the planet's surface. There he was being allowed to hunt prey animals for his sustenance, because his biology couldn't be sustained by the vegetarian diet that the Caeliar insisted upon within the confines of their city.

Chief Dennisar and Lieutenant Sortollo wolfed down their tall stacks of hotcakes with gusto. Vale arranged her two pancakes and wedges of sliced fruit into something that pleased her eye. She nudged Tuvok. "Pass the syrup."

He handed her a small ceramic pitcher. She poured a small reservoir of the amber fluid into an open space she'd left at the edge of her plate. Then she cut off a small wedge of pancake with her fork, speared it, dipped it in the viscous liquid, and tasted it. It was more like a clover honey than a maple syrup, but it was pleasant enough.

Across from her, Deanna Troi picked at her breakfast without actually eating much of it. Vale asked, "How did your meeting with the Quorum go?"

"They're not interested in negotiating, if that's what you're asking," Troi said. A small, pained grimace played across her face as she broke eye contact with Vale, who made a mental note to have Ree give Troi a medical exam when he returned.

Letting her die isn't worth it just for the right to say "I told you so," Vale mused.

"All right, we know they're listening to everything we say," Ranul Keru said. "And they're watching us every minute. So what's our game plan here?"

Vale swallowed another mouthful of syrup-drenched pancake. "Just like they taught us at the Academy," she said. "It's the Tanis scenario."

Keru shot her a look that made it clear he recognized the reference. The Tanis scenario was named for a plan that had used sabotage as a diversion to enable the theft or recovery of a vehicle for making a fast escape from hostile territory.

"Okay," he said. "Assume you're right. We're still stuck with a Pollux IV situation."

"True," Vale said, understanding that the security chief was talking about *Titan* being held by the Caeliar. "But Starfleet didn't gather laurel leaves then, and I don't think we ought to start now." *In other words, we're getting the hell out of here, no matter what it takes.*

Lieutenant Sortollo leaned forward, to look past Chief Dennisar at Vale. "Sir? Maybe we should hold off on making plans until we see if the captain has anything in the works."

"No," Vale said. "We have to assume we're on our own."

Ensign Torvig craned his long neck forward, mimicking Sortollo. "Erika Hernandez has lived with the Caeliar for a very long time," he said. "And we know she has some of their abilities. Maybe we should ask her for advice."

Tuvok replied, "That would be inadvisable. She seems to identify more readily with them than with us. For now, we should consider her an agent of the Caeliar."

"I disagree," Troi said firmly. "She's a prisoner like us, and I think we ought to reach out to her—for her sake, as well as our own."

Keru shook his head. "She may be a prisoner,

Counselor, but she's *definitely* not like us. I have to concur with Tuvok—she's been compromised, and she can't be trusted."

"Agreed," Vale said. To Troi she added, "Leave Hernandez out of the loop. Until further notice, we need to stay focused on the Tanis scenario."

Another tiny wince at the corner of Troi's left eye made Vale suspect that a profound discomfort was continuing to plague the counselor. Vale wondered if anyone else at the table was noticing it. Then Troi set down her utensils on her plate, stood, and said to Vale, "Can I speak to you in private?"

"Of course," Vale said, pushing away her own plate and rising from her chair. As soon as Vale was on her feet, Troi was already walking away, out of the dining room and across their residence's great room, toward the terrace.

As she stepped outside and followed Troi to the far end of the broad balcony, Vale squinted against the bright morning sun and took a deep breath of the crisp, cool air.

What a lovely day for an argument, she mused, stepping with a sardonic grin into Troi's harangue.

"You're being an idiot," Troi said. She had meant to take a more diplomatic tack with Vale, but the pain in her stomach had left her with a short fuse—which Vale had unwittingly ignited.

Vale continued smiling, but her narrowed eyes and furrowed brow belied her pleasant façade. "Care to re-phrase that?"

Troi leaned with one hand on the terrace's low barrier wall and rested her other hand as casually as she could over her aching abdomen. "You're making a mistake, Chris."

"I'm doing my job, Deanna. If you don't approve, I'm willing to hear your objections, but once I've made my decision, the discussion's *over*."

Irked by Vale's sudden display of authoritarian behavior, Troi couldn't help but frown. "You haven't spent any time with Hernandez, and neither have Tuvok or Keru. None of you know her, and none of you can sense her emotions the way I do. So why are you dismissing my opinion?"

"I can't speak for Keru or Tuvok," Vale said, "but I'm worried *your* judgment might be a bit impaired right now."

Pointing at her belly, Troi snapped, "Because of this?" Vale looked away, visibly discomfited. Troi pressed on. "If you think a few cramps are enough to wipe out twenty-six years of Starfleet experience and cloud my empathic senses, you're sorely mistaken, Commander."

"Cramps aren't the kind of pain that worry me, Deanna."

If there was a glib retort for that, Troi couldn't think of it. She paused, took a deep breath, and quelled her temper. "Let's not make this personal," she said. "We need to be careful what we do. The Caeliar's technology is extremely advanced. A mistake could have disastrous consequences for all of us. And it seems like a violation of Starfleet ethics to use force against a race of avowed pacifists."

Vale rolled her eyes. "They can call themselves pacifists if they like," she said. "But that doesn't change the fact that they're holding us, our ship, and Hernandez against our will. No matter how they try to excuse it, that's a hostile act, and one that merits a proportional response."

"The Caeliar make a compelling case for their right to protect their privacy and territory from outsiders," Troi said. "They believe they're acting in self-defense."

"So are we," Vale said, cutting off Troi's reply to add, "Not another word about this, Counselor. And don't talk to Hernandez or the Caeliar—that's an order."

A surge of resentment and anger left Troi feeling tense, as if her body wanted to defy her mind and lash out at Vale. She clenched her left hand into a fist behind her back. "Yes, sir."

The XO started to move back toward the residence, but then she turned around. "One more thing. If you're wondering whether I've noticed you're in pain, I have. As soon as Ree gets back from his morning hunt, you're getting a checkup."

Vale walked away as Troi protested, "I don't need one."

"It wasn't a request, Counselor."

Before Troi could reply, Vale went back inside.

Alone on the terrace, Troi watched sunlight shimmer across the titanium-white towers of Axion. The city was so beautiful but so cold—she couldn't imagine being confined to it for even one lifetime, never mind the hundreds of years that Hernandez had dwelled there. It would be enough to break anyone's spirit.

I don't care what the others say, Troi decided.

Erika's not the enemy. If we get a chance to escape, we have to at least try to bring her with us. She deserves a chance to go home, too.

Will Riker entered the Deck 1 conference room. His eyes were bleary and his hair was slightly tousled. He was met by Commander Ra-Havreii and the holographic avatar of Lieutenant Commander Pazlar.

"It's three minutes past 0400," Riker said. "Why doesn't this crew ever make any progress during alpha shift?"

The chief engineer shrugged. "I wish I knew, Captain." Nodding to Pazlar, who turned and activated the wall companel, Ra-Havreii added, "But I think you'll forgive us this time."

"We'll see about that," Riker said, settling into his chair at the head of the table. "What have you got?"

Pazlar called up a screen of complicated and very colorful diagrams and equations. "The energy pulses we detected from the Caeliar's planet are soliton waves that have been tightly focused and amplified to a degree we never thought possible."

Ra-Havreii interrupted, "The soliton pulses, as we're calling them, tunnel through subspace."

"Drilling might be a better metaphor," Pazlar cut in.

The Efrosian nodded. "Quite right. They bore through the fabric of subspace much like a wormhole punches through normal space-time." The door slid open and a young, male Bolian yeoman entered. He moved toward the replicator as Ra-Havreii continued. "We believe that each tunnel is held open by a subharmonic resonance between the frequencies of its apertures."

Over the musical *whoosh* of the replicator, Pazlar said, "The same resonance also compresses the distance between the apertures by folding them toward one another across a subspatial curvature." She paused as the yeoman handed Riker a mug of piping hot *raktajino*. "We thought you might like to have a quick jolt before we got too deep into this," Pazlar said.

"I'd prefer a peppermint tea," Riker said. With speed, agility, and silence, the yeoman spirited away the mug and returned to the replicator.

"Despite the astronomical energy levels we've been reading, the tunnels being generated by the Caeliar are minuscule in diameter," Ra-Havreii said.

The replicator hummed again with activity as Pazlar said, "The passages would be barely large enough for a person to move through, so we know they aren't being used by the Borg fleet."

Accepting his mug of mint-flavored tea from the yeoman, Riker asked the engineer, "Then what are they for?"

Ra-Havreii raised his white eyebrows. "They're just large enough to transmit a compressed data stream."

Riker set down his tea without taking a sip. "A subspace crystal ball," he muttered.

"Exactly," the Efrosian replied. "A perfect espionage tool. Point it anywhere in the galaxy and see anything you want, in real time—and be all but undetectable while doing it."

"All right, I'm impressed," Riker said. He got up and stepped between Pazlar and Ra-Havreii to study their schematics on the companel. "Is there some way we can tap into this, see whatever it is the Caeliar are spying on?"

An anxious look from Pazlar drew a frown from Ra-Havreii, who said, "Maybe, but it won't be easy."

"It never is," Riker said.

Pazlar pointed out some details on the screen. "Tapping into the soliton pulse will mean matching its frequencies and resonance harmonics."

Ra-Havreii interjected, "The hard part is putting that much power into the sensors without blowing them to pieces. They're just not made for that. We'd have to rebuild the grid to handle the stress."

"And rewrite the software," Pazlar added. "If we don't, one feedback surge could cripple the ship—or worse."

Riker had heard enough caveats. "Yes or no," he said to Ra-Havreii. "Can we do it?"

The chief engineer shrugged. "In theory, yes."

"Then it's time to put the theory into practice," Riker said. "I want those soliton pulses tapped in twenty-four hours."

Pazlar threw a wide-eyed glance at Ra-Havreii, who looked at Riker and asked, "Do you care whether we blow up *Titan*?"

"I'd prefer we didn't."

"Then I'll need at least forty-eight hours. Sir."

He gave Ra-Havreii an encouraging slap on the shoulder. "Clock's ticking," he said with a grin. "Get started."

Vale stood behind Dr. Ree as he examined Troi with a medical tricorder. The counselor sat on the edge of the bed in her private room, and Ree was crouched in front of her. Beneath the tricorder's high-pitched whine, Vale heard the reptilian physician's rumbling growl of dissatisfaction.

"Forgive me, Counselor," he said. "The news is not good." The tricorder went silent as he switched it to standby mode. "Your body has rejected the targeted sythetase inhibitor," he said. "As a result, your fetus has resumed growing. This new scan suggests that it will rupture your uterine wall in less than forty-eight hours."

Troi leaned forward and planted her face in her palms. It was painful for Vale to watch her friend crumple under the weight of such a tragedy. She wanted very much to say something comforting, something not trite, but she couldn't think of anything. *It's not fair,* she lamented. *After all Deanna and Will went through, why did this have to happen to them?*

Ree reached forward, and with what looked like a surprisingly delicate touch, took Troi's hand. "Deanna," he said, his voice a deep whisper, like a breath through an oboe. "We need to operate, soon."

The counselor lifted her head, and Vale saw tears streaming from Troi's eyes. "No," she said to Ree. "Not here. Not yet. I'm not ready. . . . *Please.*"

The doctor turned his long head so that one side faced Vale. "Operating here would not be my choice, either," he said, revealing chunks of fresh red animal tissue caught between his fangs. "Not unless the Caeliar have a sterile facility."

"I'm sure they can make one if we ask," Vale said.

"No," Troi said. She continued with uncharacteristic ferocity, "I want to be with my *Imzadi* when it's time. We're doing this on *Titan.*"

Vale folded her arms and said, "Our hosts might have other plans, Deanna. And if you're counting on me to get you back to the ship, you're not leaving me much time to do it."

"Call this an incentive to work more quickly," Troi said.

A derisive noise—like a cross between a laugh and a cough—issued from Vale's throat. "No pressure," she said. "What about not ticking off the Caeliar?"

"To hell with them," Troi said, grimacing as she pulled her hand away from Ree and stood up. "I'm not ending this without Will, and I don't want him coming down here and winding up a prisoner." She walked with halting steps to her bedroom window and glowered at the sunny, pristine cityscape outside. "Get me home, Chris. Before it's too late."

Vale stepped past Ree on her way to the door. "Let me know if her condition changes."

"I will," Ree said with a dip of his scaly snout.

She contemplated the task ahead of her as she went in search of the rest of the away team. *I've got less than two days to outsmart an enemy that sees everything we do and hears every word we say. Two days to outmaneuver a foe that can be anywhere, lurking in thin air.* She shook her head. *Why do I get all the fun jobs?*

1574—2095

15

———•———

Sleep was the first casualty of Hernandez's former life.

After her rejuvenation, she had returned with Inyx to Axion. He'd left her at her residence while he went alone to face the censure of the Quorum. Daylight had faded, night had fallen, and she had waited for a tide of fatigue and exhaustion that never came. Then the sun rose again, and the previous day bled into the next. As did every day that followed.

Days lost their meaning for her. Light and darkness were no more than ephemeral conditions in what she quickly began to perceive as a steady continuity of experience. Time flowed as it ever had, but she no longer felt caught up in its currents. The past seemed deeper. The present was sharper. The future was closer at hand than it had ever been.

The second casualty of her humanity was her appetite.

"Your catoms manufacture your body's needs now," Inyx had explained one evening, while watching the sunset with her. "They fuel your cells and stabilize your neurochemistry. You will never hunger again."

She stared directly at the descending sun and was amazed to find that it wasn't painful. The fiery orb looked as bright as it ever had, but its fire was no longer blinding. "You haven't told me everything about my transformation, have you, Inyx?" Turning her head toward him, she asked, "What else can I do?"

"A great deal," he said. "But it would be best if you learned it in stages."

Gazing back at the orange blaze on the horizon, she smiled. "In other words," she said, "you're not going to tell me."

"No," Inyx said. "I'm not. Not yet."

Hernandez didn't mind waiting. She had time.

As her routine became a rhythm, Hernandez expected she would eventually lose count of the number of sunrises and sunsets that she witnessed from the ramparts of Axion. Instead, she found that she could remember every one in exquisite detail. In fact, all her memories since the Change were clear and immediately at hand. She could compare them, contrast them, and replay them in her mind's theater without losing focus on the present moment.

On the occasion of her seven-hundred-eighty-first sunset since the Change, she emerged from a newly composed concert in the city's main amphitheater, looked to the horizon, and realized that the city was moving.

Reaching out with her thoughts, she located Inyx. He was on a widow's walk, on the edge of the city, facing in the direction of its movement. She summoned a quicksilver disk and sped over the boulevards and between the towers until she hovered above him. He glanced upward. "You're just in time," he said. "The sun's going down."

She lowered her disk to within a few meters of the widow's walk and stepped off. Envisioning herself as a feather, she drifted gently down to his side. The landscape blurred as it disappeared beneath the edge of the city, which raced westward in pursuit of the falling sun.

"We're on the move," she said. "Is there a reason?"

"I thought it was time," Inyx said.

The city gained altitude as it cruised toward a range of mountain peaks whose caps burned with the dying light of day.

Hernandez was silent while she admired the beauty of the passing moment. Then she asked, "Time for what?"

"For you to stop staring at the three-tree hill," he said.

Dusk smothered the shallow degrees of the sky. "A clean break, then," she said.

"A new horizon," Inyx said.

Darkness loomed over Axion and sparkled with stars—except for one widening strip of the sky, which was blank and black, as if someone had erased the heavens with malice aforethought. Hernandez sighed. "Fine," she said. "No more sunsets, then. From now on . . . all I want to see are sunrises."

"I think that sounds like an excellent idea," Inyx said.

The city roamed New Erigol like a nomad. Hernandez and Inyx continued to time their meetings to coincide with the sunrise, which dimmed by slow degrees as the decades passed.

Over lush jungles and glaciated alpine slopes, above the deep deserts or the fathomless seas, every new dawn made Hernandez feel as she had at the moment of her rebirth, breaking free of the storm into the blue sky and sunlight. It reminded her to focus on beginnings instead of endings.

"Clear your mind and listen," Inyx said.

Hernandez closed her eyes. "I'll try."

"Focus," he said, guiding her through an exercise they had practiced many thousands of times since her Change. It had become part of their daily ritual, a catechism meant to improve her control over the gifts granted to her by the Caeliar. "You should hear the voices of the Quorum, guiding the gestalt."

She shook her head. "I'm sorry, I don't hear anything."

Inyx seemed to deflate, as usual, at her reported failure. "Perhaps it will take more time," he said. "I don't understand how you could master so many of the catom-based powers so quickly, yet not have a conscious link to the gestalt."

"Maybe it's because of a difference in our brain anatomy," Hernandez said. "Or it could be linked to the fact that you and your people are almost entirely synthetic, while I'm still mostly organic."

The Caeliar scientist sounded perplexed. "I thought I had compensated for those differences," he said. "It's possible, I suppose, that when the catoms altered your genetic structure, they shielded you from the gestalt in response to your own subconscious desire for privacy."

"Who knows?" She shrugged. "We can try again to-morrow."

"Yes," Inyx said. "These things don't always work right away. We should give it a little time."

A smirk teased the corners of Hernandez's mouth. *A little time,* she mused. It had been 14,387 sunrises. Thirty-nine years, five months, and two days. *And he wants to give it more time.*

"Whatever you say," Hernandez replied. "You're back to the Great Work, now?"

Levitating from the widow's walk, Inyx replied, "Yes, it's time. Will you be continuing to work on your mural today?"

"As I do every day," Hernandez said.

"Until the next sunrise, then," Inyx said, conjuring a disk under his feet. It shot away, carrying him back toward the city.

Hernandez watched him go, and she kept her preternaturally keen eyes fixed on him until he vanished inside one of the platinum towers. Then she quieted her inner voice and opened her mind to the conversation that was all around her.

Brighter and clearer than the muddled rumble of the masses of Axion, the Quorum's debate was like a beacon. She picked out dozens of individual voices, including the *tanwa-seynorral* himself, Ordemo Nordal. It was a day of mundane details, as the tedium of the Great Work was engaged with unflagging attention and passion.

The numbers and details were difficult for her to follow; though she had learned the Caeliar's written language during her years working in the Star Chamber with Inyx, until the Change she had never had unfettered access to their native tongue. She suspected that she could translate it easily if she used her body's catoms to filter the discussion, but she worried that doing so would draw the attention of the gestalt.

She didn't know how long she could continue lying to Inyx, or how long she could keep this ability hidden from the gestalt at large or the Quorum in particular.

For the moment, however, it was her secret, and she intended to keep it that way.

No sooner had the sun crested the horizon than it was swallowed by the black edge of the planet's dome, which now encompassed more than fifty percent of New Erigol's sky.

"This is unacceptable," Hernandez said. "I won't live in the dark again, Inyx. I can't."

Her companion gazed to the horizon, arms folded in front of him. "You will not live in the dark, Erika. None of us will."

"How do you figure? Is that dome of yours going to turn invisible from the inside?"

"No," he said. "But we are taking steps to replicate the illumination and beneficial radiation effects of this planet's star, using a traveling artificial solar generator on the interior surface of the shell."

Hernandez grinned at him. "The sun will rotate around the planet. How Ptolemaic of you." Looking back at the masked sky, she said, "How long until it's finished?"

"Soon," Inyx said, without elaborating.

By her own estimations—including information she had gleaned by eavesdropping periodically on the Quorum—the shells around New Erigol and its star would be complete in less than another thirty years. The Caeliar had dismantled scores of worlds, harvested entire Oort clouds and asteroid belts, and even stolen superdense strange matter from distant neutron stars to construct these monstrous cocoons. Whenever she looked at the one above New Erigol, she thought of it as the lid of a coffin, slamming shut forever above her head.

Even as she contemplated the possibilities of eternal youth, she found that the wonders of an endless galaxy still held less appeal for her than the dream of her long-lost home.

In the deep watches of the night, perched alone like a bird of prey atop the city's highest spire, Hernandez often dreamed of infiltrating the apparatus that the Caeliar employed for their Great Work, and using it to send a desperate SOS to Earth. Then she would remember that her dreams of escape and rescue were ultimately futile: there was no one on Earth who could hear her cry for help. On the world of her birth, the current year, according to the Gregorian calendar, was only 1645.

John Milton's "L'Allegro" was being published. The English Civil War was tearing Britain to pieces. The Black Death was spreading out of control in Europe. The great Japanese swordsman Miyamoto Musashi was soon to die in his sleep. Humanity was still two centuries away from harnessing electricity and nearly five hundred years shy of inventing subspace communications.

There was nothing she could do but wait and learn. And she vowed that when the time came to act, she would be ready.

By day the sky was the same. The sun wasn't real and hadn't been for centuries, but its light was just as bright and its heat as genuine. Hernandez understood only the slightest fraction of the holographic manipulations that the Caeliar had created to preserve the illusion of a distant star, so that none of the planet's delicate ecosystems would be disturbed.

In fact, the surface of New Erigol was safer than it had ever been. It was protected now from such hazards as asteroid impacts or bursts of cosmic radiation. Phenomena that would extinguish all life on an ordinary Minshara-class world posed no danger to New Erigol.

At night, however, the illusion was revealed. New Erigol had never had a moon, and now its nights were starless. When the last rays of the ersatz sun faded away, the planet's surface disappeared into an absolute, unnatural darkness. Its purity made Hernandez ache for the light's return, and when the horizon betrayed so much as the slightest hint of indigo, she made her way to whichever peripheral platform faced the dawn.

Violet bands crept from the edge of the sea, beginning their slow climb to the midheaven. In the ascending twilight, Hernandez sensed Inyx taking form beside her.

"I heard part of your opus in rehearsal last night," Inyx said. "It sounded quite stirring."

Hernandez frowned. "It needs more work," she said. "Your people have a lot of.skill as musicians, but not much feeling. And my piece is all about evoking an emotional response."

"Are you trying to stir any emotions in particular?"

"Yes," she said. "Sorrow. And regret."

The sky brightened, and pastel colors bathed the misty streaks of cloud that raced past the city. Neither Inyx nor Hernandez had anything else to say that morning, and when the false orb of day breached the horizon, they parted ways.

She overheard enough conversations through the gestalt—after more than five centuries, she understood enough of the Caeliar's language to make sense of what she heard—to know that Inyx and his colleagues spent their time fine-tuning their new apparatus, which had been moved out of the city and ensconced in the protective shell high above the planet. Much of what she'd heard led her to believe that the machine was ready to resume the Great Work, yet the Caeliar seemed to be procrastinating. Hernandez wanted to ask Inyx why, but she knew there was no way she could pose the question without betraying her ability to eavesdrop on the Caeliar's communal dialogue.

Her own days since the Change had been spent in such artistic pursuits as painting murals, sculpting abstract stone forms, and composing instrumental music. Freed of the need for sleep or any sense of time's limitations, she learned through repetition or trial and error. She remained convinced that she possessed no natural talent for any of her hobbies, but she now had more than five hundred years of experience and skill, which masked her dearth of true inspiration.

Being able to shape molecules and tint pigments by thought alone also made it a bit easier to master the fundamentals of her visual endeavors.

Music, on the other hand—she couldn't force it or coax it into doing her bidding. Drawing the melodies from her mind was like hunting an elusive prey in the dark. It was the single most difficult thing she had ever tried to learn, and her obsession with it was a welcome distraction from her fixation on the slow machinations of the universe.

Centuries had passed while she was searching for the elegiac tune that she felt inside herself every time she closed her eyes. When she tried to hum it, her voice broke or veered off-key. Trying to produce it on a range of instruments created by the Caeliar had proved equally fruitless. The song was locked inside some vault she didn't know how to open.

Another in an endless string of daybreaks brought her back to a place she hadn't visited since before the Change. At the end of the long rectangular pool of jet-black water, the dead tree stood atop its dusty isle. Gnarled and blackened, it had a peculiar shine to it. Hernandez drew close to it and saw that its bark had the glossy sheen of stone. It had been petrified.

A dead relic, preserved forever, she brooded. *Just like me.*

With her hand pressed against cold stone where life had once flourished, she felt a deepening grief. The tree would stand here, unchanging but unfeeling, impenetrable but isolated, unbowed but alone. *Once I might have cried,* she realized. *Now I don't know if I remember how.*

The glassy bark felt like ice, and she recalled the fates of traitors in Dante's *Inferno*. Those found guilty of betrayal weren't condemned to an eternity of fire and brimstone; they were cast down to Hell's lowest level, the Ninth Circle, and sealed into Cocytus, a frozen lake where all human feelings and memory died. The few who cried went blind as their tears froze and sealed their eyes shut forever.

Hernandez wanted to weep, but she didn't dare. She had lost the way to her grief, and she was certain that the only way to find it again was to return home.

It would be another seventy-three years before she caught up to her own history. Then time's shape would no longer be in jeopardy, and she would feel free to plan whatever rebellion she could manage.

Seventy-three years. A few grains of sand through the neck of the glass. A blink in the stare of eternity.

She could wait.

She had time.

2381

16

———

Tuvok worked quickly, manipulating the tricorder's settings into a decidedly nonstandard configuration. There was little time to spare; Ensign Torvig was waiting for his signal, and it was imperative that they act before the Caeliar realized what was happening. He heard the shallow breathing of Lieutenant Sortollo and Chief Dennisar, who stood behind him keeping watch for any sign of the Caeliar or Erika Hernandez.

Keeping the plan a secret from the ever-attentive Caeliar had demanded a personal sacrifice on Tuvok's part. He had mind-melded with Commander Vale to devise the plan, and then with Lieutenant Commander Keru to refine its details.

Vale's mind had been a tumult of contradictory impulses. Despite her professional demeanor, Tuvok now understood that she was driven by powerful inner conflicts. Keru's psyche, on the other hand, was remarkably disciplined and focused. Tuvok was duly impressed at the Trill man's emotional equanimity, given the tragedies of his past.

Remain focused, Tuvok reminded himself. *Timing is critical.*

Their captors had confiscated the away team's weapons but allowed its members to retain their tricorders, on the condition that they not be used against the Caeliar. The *Titan* personnel were about to violate the letter and spirit of that agreement. Tuvok had made a detailed analysis of the structure and composition of a helically twisted tower of smoky glass and immaculate titanium, half a kilometer from his position, on the far side of an open and unoccupied plaza.

He evaluated the results of a rudimentary simulation he had just conducted, and he judged it adequate for his purpose. A tap of his thumb sent an encrypted signal to Keru's tricorder, several kilometers away. A moment later he received Keru's confirmation. The second team was in position and ready to proceed. From his tricorder, he transmitted a hypersonic oscillation that was calibrated specifically to induce a resonance wave inside the spiral-shaped tower, which would then amplify it by several orders of magnitude.

It would take a few seconds to build up to full power. While he waited, Tuvok appreciated a breath of warm, dry air and admired the powerful heat of the sun, high overhead. The city of Axion was cruising over a stretch of deep desert, and for a moment it made Tuvok nostalgic for the serenity of his home on Vulcan. Then a shiver traveled through the ground under his feet, and he heard a growing buzz of quaking metal and glass.

Watching the reflections of the cityscape quiver on the disturbed glass of the spiral tower, Tuvok tapped his combadge. "Tuvok to Ensign Torvig. Acknowledge, please."

"Torvig here, sir. Go ahead."

The buzzing became a bright, metallic ringing. Then it turned to thunder, and every pane of dark-gray crystal on the tower exploded outward, pelting its neighboring buildings and the plaza below with jagged shards of glassy shrapnel.

"Proceed," Tuvok said.

Torvig had known his part of the away team's escape plan for exactly sixty seconds. His friend, Lieutenant Commander Keru, had revealed it when he'd tapped Torvig's flank, offered him a tricorder, and said, "Hey, Vig. Take a look at this."

On the tricorder's screen was a miniaturized replica of the operations control panel of the shuttlecraft *Mance*. Somehow, Keru had reprogrammed the handheld device into a remote control for the shuttlecraft's command systems. The small vessel's one-person emergency transporter had been powered up and readied for a beam-up sequence, and it was targeted on Keru himself.

"Not until it's time," Keru said.

The young Choblik engineer clutched the tricorder in both bionic hands as he looked up at the burly Trill. "How will I know when it's time?"

"You'll know," said Keru.

They stood together atop a rampart at the city's edge, directly across the hundred meters of empty space separating them from the *Mance* and its platform, which were being towed on an invisible tether behind Axion. Dunes the color of nutmeg and cinnamon stretched across the landscape to the horizon in every direction. Torvig saw no vegetation or animals in the parched land; if not for the dull roar of hot, moving air, there would have been only the silence of a wasteland.

Then came a voice, tinny from being filtered through his combadge: *"Tuvok to Ensign Torvig. Acknowledge, please."*

"Torvig here, sir. Go ahead."

A distant *boom* echoed through the metallic canyons of Axion, and Torvig hoped that it was part of the plan and not a sign that something had just gone terribly wrong.

"Proceed," Tuvok said, and Keru nodded in confirmation.

Torvig initiated the transporter's dematerialization sequence. A mellifluous drone filled the air. Keru was enveloped in a cocoon of shimmering particles. In seconds, the Trill officer was gone from sight. According to the tricorder, he had rematerialized safely aboard the *Mance*.

Then all that Torvig could do was turn off the tricorder and wait to see what the next step of the plan was.

Keru had called it a stupid plan from the beginning, but it was the only real option available to them, and risking their lives on a desperate scheme had seemed preferable to surrendering.

As soon as the transporter's confinement beam released him, he bounded off the lone pad and sprinted to the cockpit. The air inside the shuttlecraft was stuffy from having been sealed off for more than two days. He planted himself in the commander's seat, next to the pilot's station, and powered up the craft's sensors and communications suite.

His first task was to verify their position, relative to the gap in the planet's shell through which they had entered. Then he checked to see if the passageway was still open. It wasn't. He began a sensor sweep of the observable surface of the shell, looking for another egress point. There were none.

So much for flying out, he grumped in silence. *Can't get a signal out, either. Time to explore tactical options.* He reached forward to raise the shuttlecraft's shields—and every console in the ship went dark. His shoulders slumped. *That's not good.*

A tingling sensation raised the fine hairs on the nape of his neck. The darkened companels reflected a magenta glow that was emanating from behind him. Keru swiveled his chair to see Inyx hunched over, his tall form awkwardly confined in the tight quarters of the *Mance.* "Fancy meeting you here," Keru quipped.

"I must confess, I'm impressed by the versatility of your equipment," Inyx said. "It's a vast improvement over that of your recent predecessors." He paused, apparently expecting a reply, which Keru didn't give him. "I have to take you back, Ranul." He opened the shuttlecraft's side hatch with a wave of his arm and motioned for Keru to step out.

Keru walked to the open hatchway and looked out at the silver disk waiting at the end of its extended ramp. "I feel like I'm walking the plank," he said. He looked at the doubled-over Caeliar, and said, "After you."

"Gladly," Inyx said, squeezing his gangly limbs through the exit. As soon as he was over the threshold, he straightened to his full height and seemed to be a great deal more relaxed. He walked onto the silver disk and beckoned Keru forward. "Your chariot awaits," he said.

Stepping down the ramp, Keru said with guarded interest, "Did Erika teach you that phrase?"

Inyx seemed immediately self-conscious. "Yes, she did," he replied. "Did I use it correctly?"

"Yup," Keru said, wondering just how close Hernandez's bond with Inyx really was. He boarded the disk and moved behind Inyx. "I suppose we're all facing some kind of punishment now."

"No," Inyx said. "A degree of rebellion is expected. In time, you will grow out of such behavior—as Erika did."

Troi felt as if a balloon filled with acid had just burst inside her stomach. Hot bile was being pushed up her throat, the pressure in her head was dizzying, and a rush of fever alternated with waves of chilling cold. Determined to hide her symptoms, she steadied herself with one hand on the terrace railing and funneled all her pain into a steely glare at Hernandez. "This is unacceptable, Erika."

"It's done," Hernandez said. "Inyx warned you not to use your scanners for hostile action, but you did anyway."

Another bloom of toxic pain stirred inside Troi's belly, and she turned her grimace of pain into a scowl. "We need those tricorders," she said, "and you disintegrated them."

"I did no such thing," Hernandez said.

"Fine," Troi replied. "The Caeliar destroyed them."

Hernandez nodded. "Yes, in self-defense."

"But they destroyed the medical tricorder," Troi said.

"If you require medical attention, the Caeliar are fully equipped to provide—"

"We don't want their help," Troi snapped. For a moment, her anger was stronger than her pain, and it felt good.

Her remark seemed to provoke a melancholy reaction from Hernandez, who looked away from Troi, out past the cityscape to the desolate beauty of a violet sunset over desert canyons. In a soft voice, she said, "I used to feel as you do. My first officer was especially vocal on the subject. She used to tell me that accepting the Caeliar's help was like sanctioning what they did to us. And maybe she was right. There have been times when I feel like I betrayed her by letting the Caeliar change me. But it's not as if the Caeliar forced any of this on anyone. No one made us visit their homeworlds. It's just bad luck we invaded their privacy, that's all." With a sad smile, she looked at Troi. "They're not evil, Deanna. They just want to help."

Troi felt the sincerity of Hernandez's words. She didn't have to ask if Hernandez believed what she said; it was obvious that she did. "You identify with them, don't you?"

That caught Hernandez off guard. "What? No, of course not."

"It's perfectly understandable, Erika," Troi said, affecting her most sympathetic tone. "In a situation such as yours, it's a normal defense response to seek an emotional connection with the most powerful figure, for protection. It's what infants do naturally."

Looking offended, Hernandez replied, "I'm not an infant."

"No, you're a prisoner," Troi said. "And you wouldn't be the first person to succumb to Stockholm syndrome. Is that why you gave up trying to escape, or to contact Earth?"

Hernandez turned sullen. "I gave up because there's no way out. You can't outsmart them. They're always a step ahead."

"Really? Even with your abilities?" Noting the apprehensive glance her question provoked, Troi continued, "I know you were at a disadvantage facing them alone, first without powers, and then without your ship. But we have a ship in orbit, and our technology's come a long way since your time."

Shaking her head, Hernandez mumbled, "It won't be enough."

"How do you know until you try?" She grabbed Hernandez's sleeve and made her turn to face her. "You've been slapped down so many times by the Caeliar that you've gotten used to defeat."

The look on the other woman's face became one of pity. "It'll happen to you, too. It's just a matter of time."

"Time is what we don't have, Erika. Earth is in grave danger, and so are hundreds of other worlds."

At the mention of Earth, Troi sensed a profound surge of emotion from Hernandez, who replied, "In danger? From what?"

"Something worse than I can describe. We came here because we thought it might help us save Earth.

Now we have to escape for exactly the same reason." Watching doubt and hope struggle against each other in Hernandez's eyes, Troi added, "If you won't take a risk to help us, take one to help Earth."

Conflicting emotions played across Hernandez's face, and for a moment Troi thought that she might have reignited some dormant spark of fighting spirit in the youthful-looking woman. Then Hernandez levitated up and over the terrace's railing. "I need to think," she said, drifting down and away.

"Earth needs you," Troi replied.

Hernandez was silent as she descended into the gathering darkness. As she vanished into the shadows, Christine Vale stepped out onto the terrace with Troi and peeked over the railing. "Nice try," she said to Troi. "But I don't think we can count on her."

"Maybe not," Troi said. "But I get the feeling we shouldn't count her out, either."

17

—•—

Dax watched the blurred rings of light on the main viewer as the *Aventine* neared the end of its tenth journey through a subspace tunnel in forty-eight hours.

After unlocking several subspatial apertures each, the crews of the *Aventine* and the *Enterprise* had detected patterns that helped accelerate the decoding process. At their current rate, Dax figured, they were less than half a day from finding the Borg's staging area and launching the allied counterattack.

From the conn, Ensign Erin Constantino called out, "Clearing aperture twenty-one alpha in three . . . two . . . one."

A slight lurch accompanied the ship's return to the Azure Nebula. As a flicker of electrical discharge lit up the roiling blue cloud, Dax saw the shadows of many starships, most of them holding position in tight formations. A few cruised in patrol patterns behind opaque swells of dense, semiliquid gases.

Bowers said, "Lieutenant Nak, report."

Gaff chim Nak, the beta-shift operations officer, reviewed a cascade of data on his console and replied,

"All systems nominal, sir." A signal beeped on the Tellarite's panel, and he silenced it with a tap. "*Enterprise* is hailing us."

"On-screen," Dax said.

Nak patched in the signal, and the image of the nebula was replaced by the aquiline visage of Captain Picard, on the bridge of the *Enterprise*. *"Welcome back,"* he said. *"Any luck?"*

"Negative," Dax said. "Passage twenty-one leads to the intergalactic void, roughly nine hundred eighty-two thousand light-years from NGC 5078." She smirked and added, "I see we have a few more friends than when I left."

"Yes," Picard said. *"Unfortunately, this group of vessels represents the last of Starfleet's battle forces in this sector. Everything else is being held back to defend the core systems."*

Dax frowned. "It'll have to do. How long until the Cardassian fleet arrives?"

"Twelve hours," Picard said.

"Time enough to run a few more sorties," Dax said.

Picard nodded. *"Perhaps more. If we go through together, our computers can share the work of unlocking the return aperture and reduce our round-trip time by a third."*

She signaled her approval with a smile. "Sounds like a plan, Captain." Pointing upward, she added in jest, "Will our reinforcements be able to hold the line with both of us gone?"

"There are only three hundred forty-two ships here, but I think they'll muddle through." His serious demeanor returned. *"In fact, I've ordered five pairs of ships to help us open and scout the remaining pas-*

sageways. We're also taking additional precautions: We've sent all our data about the subspace tunnels, and what we found on our scouting runs, to Starfleet Command and the Klingon High Command."

Her eyes widened with surprise. "The Klingon High Command?"

"President Bacco's orders," Picard said. *"We've also been directed to share all Borg-related tactical data with the Klingon Defense Force."*

"Understood," Dax said. She looked to Bowers, who nodded and moved off to delegate the necessary tasks. "We'll start transmitting our logs now. As soon as we're done, we'll be ready for the next jaunt."

Picard replied, *"We've already unlocked aperture twenty-two alpha. Enterprise is standing by to proceed, on your signal."*

"Acknowledged," Dax said. *"Aventine* out."

Nak cut the channel, restoring the nebula to the main viewer. Klingon and Romulan battle cruisers moved in and out of the turbulent sapphire mists, like predators of the deep circling before the kill.

Bowers returned to his chair and sat beside Dax. He muffled a quiet chortle and shook his head as he looked at his feet.

Dax had seen that reaction from him before, and she knew that it wasn't good. "Something wrong, Sam?"

"Twenty-one passages checked, six to go," he said. "It reminds me of a famous Earth game."

Eyebrows lifted with curiosity, she asked, "Hide-and-seek?"

"No," he replied. "Russian roulette."

The trip through subspace passage twenty-two was shorter than Captain Picard had expected, but only because its end came with no warning. Instead of the circle of darkness that he and his crew had seen on their previous jaunts, this time there was only light—followed by the deafening thunder of impact.

"Shields collapsing!" declared Choudhury, whose hands moved quickly over the security companel. "Hull temperature forty-two hundred Kelvin and rising fast!"

Kadohata raced to orient herself at ops. "We're caught in a plasma stream, between a binary pair!"

Picard shouted over the wail of the alert klaxon, "Helm! Full impulse! Move us clear!"

Lieutenant Faur answered, "Full impulse! Aye, sir!" The engines whined and groaned as the *Enterprise* struggled to break free of the stellar inferno. Explosions rocked the ship.

"Hull breaches, Decks Five through Eight and Twenty-one through Twenty-four," Kadohata called out as the overhead lights stuttered and failed. She cringed and ducked as the starboard auxiliary stations erupted and shot sparks across the bridge. "We're losing main power."

"Clearing the stream in six seconds," Faur reported.

Worf threw a look at Choudhury. "Position of the *Aventine*?"

"Bearing one-nine-seven mark twelve," the security chief replied. "Following us out at full impulse."

The white-hot blaze on the main viewer faded to yellow, then dimmed through shades of orange and red before yielding to the star-flecked blackness of space. As the ship made a slow turn, Picard saw the crimson glow of a red-giant star, from which a blazing river of coronal mass was being torn by its black-hole companion. "We're clear," Faur said, "but the conn's sluggish because of interference from the singularity."

"Weapons are offline," Choudhury said. "Overloads in the tactical power grid."

La Forge's voice crackled from the overhead comm. *"Engineering to bridge."*

"Go ahead," said Picard.

"Captain, we've got a lot of damage down here. I need to take warp power and the main impulse reactor offline, now."

Worf cut in, "For how long?"

"I don't know," La Forge said. *"But if we don't shut them down now, we'll have a containment failure in sixty seconds."*

"Do what you have to, Mister La Forge," Picard said. "Make a full report as soon as you can."

"Aye, Captain. Engineering out."

Faur swiveled her chair to face aft, toward Picard and Worf. "Position verified, Captain. We're on the outer rim of the Carina Arm, near the meridian of the Delta and Gamma Quadrants."

Kadohata turned her chair aft, as well. "No sign of Borg vessels within sensor range," she said.

"That could change," Picard said. He suspected she might be mistaken, because he heard the voice of the Collective, and it was getting louder and drawing closer with every moment. "We need to remain alert," he added, "given our present condition."

On the main viewer, he saw the scorched and scarred hull of the *Aventine,* and he wondered whether his own ship looked as distressed. "Commander Kadohata, hail the *Aventine*."

"Aye, sir," Kadohata said. She and Faur turned their chairs forward and resumed work. "I have Captain Dax for you, sir."

"On-screen," Picard said.

Dax and Bowers appeared on the main viewer, wreathed in gray smoke and backed by a bulkhead of smoldering, sparking companels. *"I think we took a wrong turn somewhere,"* Dax said.

"What's your status, Captain?"

"Shields are fried, main power's down, and we've got some major hull damage," she said. *"A dozen of my crew are seriously injured, but no fatalities."*

Worf handed Picard a padd showing the casualty report from sickbay. Picard blinked, and suddenly his vision was bathed in sickly green light and muddy black shadows.

The conversation between Worf and Ezri was continuing in front of him, but he could barely hear it. It was like trying to eavesdrop from underwater. His ears were filled with the roar of the Collective, and its sinister palette had tainted every facet of his perception, from the taste of tin on his lips to the sharp odor of chemical lubricants in his nose and the clammy sweat on the back of his neck.

Marshaling his senses into revolt was a single word.

Locutus.

He heard it being whispered beneath the raging tide of the Collective, and he knew the speaker's voice even by intimation. It was *her*—the Borg Queen. She was aware of his presence, he was certain of it. He concentrated on blocking her out. It took all his willpower to restore the sanctity of his thoughts.

Then Picard snapped back into the conversation with Captain Dax, and he became aware that Worf— and everyone else on the bridge of the *Enterprise*— was staring at him. Worf regarded Picard with an attentive gaze that made it clear Picard had been asked a question which deserved a response. Rather than ask for the query to be repeated, Picard volleyed the request to his XO in an interrogative tone. "Mister Worf?"

Worf said, "I concur with Captain Dax's recommendation, sir. Modifying the shields would be a prudent step."

"Very well," Picard said. "Make it so."

"Aye, sir," Worf replied, delegating the job with a look and a nod to Kadohata. To Dax, he added, "These repairs will take time. We should use it to start looking for the frequency to reopen the subspace tunnel."

"Already on it," Dax said with a grin. *"Tell Clipet and Elfiki they're free to jump in anytime."*

"Understood," Worf said. *"Enterprise* out." The screen switched back to the placid vista of stars.

Picard stood and nodded to Worf. "You have the bridge."

As he retired to his ready room, Picard was relieved to be able to seek some privacy while Worf managed the business of directing the ship's repairs. Alone with his thoughts, however, Picard fell to brooding. The Borg Queen's voice haunted him.

You should not have come looking for me, Locutus, she taunted with cold menace. *I'll be with you soon enough.*

He put on his bravest face and whispered with false courage, "I killed you once. I look forward to doing it again."

Bravado doesn't suit you, Locutus, she replied. *And you know as well as I do that the next time we meet, it won't be* my *neck that gets snapped.* She pulled her thoughts away from him. *Soon, Locutus, soon. Until then . . . dream of my embrace.*

Terrible events were in motion; Picard felt it.

A shadow had gathered. Its hour was at hand.

"Shields are fried, main power's down, and we've got some major hull damage," Captain Dax said. *"A dozen of my crew are seriously injured, but no fatalities."*

As Worf handed a padd to Captain Picard, he saw the captain blink and take on a blank, anxious stare. In a glance, Worf realized that Captain Picard had become mired in one of the dark fugues inflicted on him by the Borg.

Raising his voice to draw attention to himself, Worf said to Dax, "The *Enterprise* has sustained similar damage and casualties." He looked toward ops. "Commander, recommendations?"

Kadohata looked up and said, "We have to focus on repairing our shields—we can't get back without them."

Nodding, Dax said, *"My science officer suggests we modify our metaphasic shielding protocols, to compensate for the relativistic properties of the plasma jet."*

"Sounds reasonable," Kadohata said. She looked up at Picard. "With your permission, Captain?"

Worf froze as he waited to see if the captain would react. Kadohata's query had turned everyone's eyes to the captain, and if it became apparent that he had been distracted, it might undermine the crew's already damaged morale.

Picard blinked, and Worf noted a spark of alarmed recognition in the captain's eyes as he saw that he'd become the center of attention. As if reaching for a lifeline, the captain looked toward him and said, "Mister Worf?"

Instinctively covering the captain's momentary lapse, Worf replied, "I concur with Captain Dax's recommendation, sir. Modifying the shields would be a prudent step."

"Very well," Picard said. "Make it so."

Worf divided his focus between the continuing conversation with Captain Dax, directing the *Enterprise*'s bridge officers, and keeping a discreet watch on Captain Picard's reactions. As soon as Worf had concluded the conversation with Dax, Captain Picard stood, said, "You have the bridge," and excused himself to his ready room, leaving Worf in command.

Coordinating damage-control teams was a task Worf normally found tedious. Tonight he felt that a profound urgency was driving the *Enterprise* crew to speed its repairs for the return journey to the Azure Nebula. He knew the crew was talking about Picard. "If he's hearing the Borg, they must be close," he overheard contact specialist Lieutenant T'Ryssa Chen whisper to relief tactical officer Ensign Aneta Šmrhová.

The focus and intensity of the repair efforts felt almost like a battle to Worf, whose chief role was to set priorities for the various departments. The sciences division was devoting its time and resources to unlocking aperture twenty-two beta for the trip home. Engineering had been instructed to restore shields first, warp drive second, and weapons last. The medical group had been directed to send out roving teams of medics and nurses to perform first aid on personnel who were too busy—and too vital—to be sent to sickbay for minor injuries.

He was about to forward the latest status reports to Captain Picard in the ready room, when a silent communiqué appeared on the command panel next to his chair. It was a message from Lieutenant Choudhury at tactical, summoning him and Commander Kadohata to the tactical station, where Choudhury huddled with Ensign Šmrhová.

Kadohata looked up from her work at ops and glanced back at Worf, who stood and motioned with a subtle, sideways nod of his head for her to follow him to tactical. She got up and walked aft to join him, Choudhury, and Šmrhová.

Choudhury pointed at the tactical display. "Šmrhová picked up multiple signals on long-range sensors," she said. "They're on an intercept course, at warp nine-point-nine-seven."

Worf anticipated the worst. "Borg?"

Šmrhová replied with a mild Slavic accent, "No, sir. Hirogen." The pale, dark-haired woman tapped the screen and called up a dense page of data. "Based on the energy signatures, it's an unusually large hunting pack—ten ships."

"Pretty far from their home territory," Kadohata said.

"They could be renegades," Choudhury said. "Or they might just be more adventurous than other Hirogen."

Cutting off further speculation, Worf said, "The reason for their presence is not important. What matters is the danger they pose to us and the *Aventine*." He asked Choudhury, "What is the hunting pack's ETA?"

"One hour and fifty-three minutes," she said.

Nodding, Worf continued, "Then we have just less than that to complete our repairs and make the return jaunt. The Hirogen must not learn about the subspace tunnels."

Kadohata asked, "Won't the plasma jet from the binary pair mask our exit?"

Choudhury replied, "Yes, as long as the Hirogen aren't within weapons range. But if they get that close, their sensors could pierce the interference and detect our frequency for opening the tunnels. Then they'd have a free pass to bring their hunt to Federation space whenever they want."

"Not today," Worf said. "Commander Kadohata, tell Mister La Forge that his priorities have changed: shields first, weapons second, warp drive last. Ensign Šmrhová, begin combat drills as soon as we have weapons back online. Lieutenant Choudhury, tell your people to prepare to repel boarders. I'll notify the captain and alert the *Aventine*."

The three female officers acknowledged his orders with curt nods and stepped away to start preparing for battle. He returned to his chair and opened a comm to the ready room. "Captain Picard, please report to the bridge."

"On my way," the captain replied. *"Picard out."*

Worf had never fought the Hirogen, though he had read of their ferocity, prowess, and strength. As the first officer of the *Enterprise,* he hoped that his ship and the *Aventine* escaped before the battle was joined. But as a Klingon warrior, his heart swelled with anticipation.

The Borg were a plague, an infestation to be stamped out from a distance. A Hirogen hunter, on the other hand—that was a foe he had often tested himself against on the holodeck. Even there, they were formidable; in fact, he had yet to defeat one.

There is a first time for everything, he mused darkly.

18

———•———

An eerie silence pervaded Axion. It was sunset, and the city had halted its aimless wanderings of the sky. Hernandez felt the change in the air as the shield was raised, quelling the wind. From her favorite vantage point, clinging to a spire high above the towers of the Caeliar's last metropolis, she saw the city's denizens turn out en masse into the boulevards and amphitheaters.

Hernandez had never seen them do anything like this before. Opening her mind to the gestalt, she listened for its voice. It, too, was silent. Then she reached out with her senses and found Inyx among a throng gathered in a great plaza. She let go of the spire and floated down, hundreds of meters, guiding herself between the buildings, by what had come to feel like instinct.

Her feet touched the ground, bringing her to a stop at Inyx's side. He and the thousands of other Caeliar in the plaza gazed skyward, all looking in the same direction. There was something reverential about their united attention, and through the gestalt she felt an overwhelming collective sorrow.

All at once, the spell was broken, and the crowd began to disperse in seemingly random directions. Hernandez took Inyx's arm to prevent him from leaving. "What just happened?"

"We observed the moment of the Cataclysm," he said.

It took her a moment to grasp his meaning. "The destruction of Erigol?" she asked.

"Yes," Inyx said. "It just happened, moments ago."

After drifting like a ghost through centuries, fearful of causing the slightest disruption to the timeline, Hernandez was surprised to find herself feeling so rooted in the present moment. It was December 23, 2168. Erigol had just exploded. Her ship had just been destroyed. And her earlier self had just been flung six hundred fifty years into the past. Now she and Axion had come full circle, back to the present, and once again were forging ahead through time's uncharted waters. It was the end of history and the beginning of the future.

She let go of Inyx's arm and asked, "What happens now?"

"The Great Work goes on," he said. "As it always has."

He began rising from the ground, en route to one of his arcane tasks, whose details he rarely shared with Hernandez. Not content to let him escape from her so easily, she willed herself into the air alongside him, the catoms in her body and the air drawing power from Axion's quantum field to free her from the hold of mere gravity. "If we're past the Cataclysm, then we no longer pose a danger to the timeline, do we?"

"No," Inyx said. "All is as it was."

"Then there's no harm in letting me see what happened to Earth during the years I was out of contact."

Inyx's reply sounded both cautious and dubious. "Are you certain you want to know?"

"Why wouldn't I?" she asked, as they drifted toward the great dome that shielded the Apparatus.

He replied, "What is the boon of wisdom when it brings no solace to the wise, Erika?" He looked at her, and perhaps noting her confused expression, added, "If your people have suffered, you'll feel guilty that you didn't share their misfortunes. If they've thrived, you'll feel cheated out of your portion of their happiness. Would it not be better to make a clean break from the past and embrace the future you've chosen?"

She halted herself in midair and let him continue alone. Watching him grow smaller against the massive bulk of the dark crystal dome, she kept her bitter rumination to herself.

I didn't choose my future. It chose me.

It was like sensing heat or a chill—Hernandez knew the airborne catoms in her vicinity were dormant. There were no Caeliar minds lurking unseen in the shadows. Though she lacked their ability to transmit herself from one cluster of molecules to another, or pass unseen like a breath on the wind, she moved through the night as if it was natural to her.

The portal to Inyx's laboratory wasn't secured. None of the few doors in Axion ever were, it seemed. She coaxed it open with an impetus of thought, and it spiraled apart as she stepped through into the darkened research space.

Ahead of her was the metallic slab on which Valerian had died and Hernandez herself had been Changed. Droops of metallic cabling reached from corner to corner around the tall, narrow room. Beneath the skylight, hovering, was the principal machine of the lab, the one into which all the others fed power and particles and data. All the occult instruments of Inyx's private labors were dark and cold.

Hernandez closed the entrance behind her, then concentrated on awakening the lab, one component at a time. She needed no instruction to know which machine was which; the catoms that infused her body gave her a link to all these devices. If she wanted to know what one was, she merely thought of the question, and the object provided its own answer.

I know they've spied on Earth before, she reasoned. *They knew about us—they even spoke English when we got here. And they've probably been watching thousands of other worlds, too. I just have to figure out how they do it.*

She thought about looking far away, across space, for tiny details, and her mind took the measure of the various implements available to her. It was as if the objective in her mind was an unfinished puzzle. All she needed was the missing pieces.

One by one, they revealed themselves.

A soliton projector. A triquantum stabilizer.

A chroniton generator. A subspace transceiver.

A subspace signal amplifier.

She told the machines what she wanted, and they obeyed.

Hernandez shaped them, granted them energy from Axion itself, and focused them with her mind. Then she was surrounded by fleeting, holographic images and a flood of data. Had she still been merely organic, it would have been far too much to witness, never mind comprehend. But she felt the catoms in her brain accelerating her synaptic responses, to help her mind keep pace with the whirlwind of information she'd tapped.

Within seconds she was perusing Earth's current historical archives and learning the entire chronology of the Earth-Romulus War. It had started shortly after her ship's ambush by the Romulans, and it had lasted nearly five years. In the end, it had led to a bloody and bitter stalemate, and the creation of a no-man's-land between the Earth Alliance and the Romulan Empire—the Neutral Zone.

If only I could have warned them, she lamented. *Earth's early losses could have been prevented. We might have saved thousands of lives. We might even have won the war.*

But if Earth had been unable to claim victory, neither had it conceded defeat. And the alliances it had forged to repel the Romulans had led to something new: a coalition of many worlds, and soon after that, the establishment of the United Federation of Planets. Finally, in all that perilous darkness, Earth was no longer alone. Humanity had grown up and become part of something bigger than itself. *Maybe some good did come of the war,* she admitted to herself. But then she felt a wave of deep sadness at being so far away from such a wondrous time in human events. *Life goes on without me,* she realized.

A morbid pang of fear nagged at her from the dark corners of her memory, and she plumbed Earth's archives for information about her lost love, Jonathan

Archer. She hoped and prayed that he hadn't been a casualty of the war. . . .

Then his biography was at her fingertips, and she breathed a sigh of relief. His service during the war had earned him numerous commendations and a seat with the admiralty. He was still alive, and had just announced that he would retire his post as Starfleet chief of staff on the first day of the new year, to accept a diplomatic assignment as the Federation's newest ambassador to Andoria.

Jonathan's done all right for himself, Hernandez mused with a grin. Then she was gripped by a powerful temptation. *If he knew I was alive, he'd come for me. He'd never leave me here.*

She was tapped into Earth's planetary information network, which was utterly vulnerable to the Caeliar's superior technology. Finding Jonathan's personal contact information would be as easy as wishing for it. In a moment she could be speaking with him, seeing his face, his distinguished gray temples, those wistful smile lines. She could be hearing his voice, his laughter, the wonder and relief he'd feel at learning she was alive. . . . It was all a thought away.

Then all of it vanished, and Hernandez was alone in the dark surrounded by cold machines. The dream had been there in front of her, the lifeline had been in her hands. In the space of a breath, it all had been torn asunder. She had nothing.

A grave and booming voice came from nowhere and assaulted her senses as if it had come from everywhere. *"Erika,"* said Ordemo Nordal, the Caeliar's perpetually arbitrary first among equals. *"We are very disappointed in you."*

"That's a shame," she said, her eyes narrowed and her brow creased with naked contempt.

Ordemo continued, *"The Quorum wishes to speak with you and Inyx. Come to us at once."*

She rolled her eyes, uncertain if the entity behind the disembodied voice could even see her. "Aren't you going to send someone to collect me?"

"You know the way, Erika. Do not make us ask you again."

"Or else what?" she taunted him. "You'll ask me again?"

"Don't test our patience. Even our courtesy has limits."

She knew that the Caeliar's pacifistic ethos wouldn't permit them to harm her or kill her, but she reflected somberly that it hadn't stopped them from taking her prisoner and holding her for what might effectively be forever. *They won't kill me,* she thought, *but there are plenty of ways to punish someone without touching them*. Then she thought of Valerian, who went slowly mad and lived out her days inside an illusion.

Deflating with a sigh, she replied to the *tanwa-seynorral*, "I'll be there in a few minutes, Ordemo."

Inyx stood before the Quorum and waited for Hernandez to arrive. The ruling body radiated condemnation, and he expected little from them in the way of understanding.

As the Quorum members conferred through the gestalt, Inyx sensed their impatience at Hernandez's absence. He wanted to speak in her defense, remind the Quorum that she wasn't able to move her mind from one catom cluster to another. But acting as her apologist would do nothing to appease the *tanwaseynorral* or the Quorum at large. Instead, Inyx remained silent and watched the portals that had been prepared for Hernandez's arrival.

Then the Quorum looked up in surprise, and Inyx turned to face the cause of their alarm. It was Hernandez, hovering high above them, in an open frame of one of the pyramidal Quorum hall's walls. She had dissolved the triangular pane of crystal without making a sound. With her arms at her sides and her ankles crossed, she floated down toward the shocked mass of the Quorum and said with prideful insolence, "You called?"

Concealing his amusement from the gestalt, Inyx marveled at how intuitively Hernandez wielded the powers he had given her.

"Stand next to Inyx," said Ordemo Nordal.

Hernandez glared at Ordemo as she descended to the main floor of the hall. "As you wish," she said. She took her place with Inyx in the center of the fractal-pattern mosaic. "But only because I know how much you enjoy looking down on others."

A murmur of disapprobation coursed through the Quorum. Ordemo muted the protest with a calming wave of emotion through the gestalt. "Recent events have made it clear that we have been too permissive with both of you," he said aloud, his voice amplified and thunderous. "Inyx, you defied our wishes by Changing her, and you jeopardized our new homeworld by failing to impart the proper respect and self-control to your new disciple. From this time forward, we will hold you accountable for her actions. It is your responsibility to secure your lab from intrusion, and to see that Erika respects our laws."

Inyx wanted to protest, *Am I a mere watchman now? Shall I abandon my work and spend my every moment lording over her?* Instead, he made a small bow to the *tanwa-seynorral* and replied, "I understand, Ordemo." He felt Hernandez's hateful stare.

Directing his next verbal barrage at Hernandez, Ordemo continued, "As for you, Erika . . . it troubles us to see you abuse such powerful gifts. If it were possible to revoke them without harming you, we would do so. Unfortunately, your catoms are part of you now, and to forcibly remove them from you would be fatal. Because the Change cannot be undone, it is imperative that we ensure your compliance with our laws. Do you understand?"

"No," Hernandez said. "I don't." She threw an angry look at Inyx, then continued to Ordemo, "Why can't I learn about events on my homeworld? You spy on the galaxy. Why can't I?"

"Because you cannot be trusted not to try to contact your people," Ordemo said.

Hernandez pressed her palms against her forehead and pushed her fingers through her hair. "So what? The timeline's not at risk anymore. Would it be such a tragedy if I sent one message, one farewell to tell someone I'm okay?"

"You know our laws, Erika," Ordemo said. "Our privacy is of paramount importance to our work. Letting you send messages home risks exposing us to outside scrutiny. We can't allow that."

Nodding, Hernandez replied, "I see. It was never about the timeline. It's always the same thing with you people: fear."

"That's a simplistic—"

"Spare me, Ordemo," Hernandez interrupted. "Don't you understand that your obsessive need for privacy is completely incompatible with your Great Work?" Inyx turned to listen more closely as Hernandez made the argument he had long wished to espouse but had never had the courage to speak aloud.

"You say you're looking for civilizations equal to or more advanced than your own, but you act as if you live in fear of the less-developed cultures that are thriving all around you. Can't you see that your self-imposed isolation is making you narrow-minded and provincial? How can you devote yourselves to seeking out new worlds when you shrink and hide from the ones in your own backyard?"

She turned and scowled at Inyx. "And what about you? I know this is what you've been thinking all along, so why don't you speak up? Why don't you say something?"

Paralyzed by her accusation in front of the Quorum, Inyx hesitated, then said, "I wouldn't know where to begin, Erika."

"No," she said, looking away from him in disgust. "I suppose you wouldn't."

Ordemo hushed another susurrus of the scandalized Quorum. Then he fixed his gaze on Hernandez. "You are an outsider," he said, "and you've been with us only a short time. Perhaps in a few thousands of your years, you'll gain a deeper understanding of our motivations. For now, however, it is clear that we'll need to be more vigilant in policing your actions." He looked at Inyx. "See to it that this incident is not repeated, Inyx."

"Understood, Ordemo."

"Erika, you may go," said the *tanwa-seynorral*. Hernandez took immediate advantage of the dismissal and ascended in a swift arc, back through the open pane, which reappeared, solid and unblemished, as soon as she was outside the Quorum hall.

Alone before the Quorum once again, Inyx said, "Will that be all, Ordemo?"

"For now," Ordemo replied. "But if you cannot control her, Inyx, we will—in the only way open to us. Do you understand?"

Dread and resentment welled up within him; the Quorum was threatening to banish Hernandez to some distant galaxy, where she would be cut off from Axion's sustaining energies. She would weaken, grow old, and die alone on an uninhabited world. It was a sentence of lifetime solitary confinement and certain death.

He swallowed his fury. "I understand," he said.

Hernandez chafed at the notion of being leashed, and it wasn't long before she put Inyx's vigilance to the test.

She had thought she was being subtle. Her first challenge to the Quorum's edict was a message embedded in the matrix of one of their soliton pulses. It was a simple message, a basic SOS coupled with a Fibonacci sequence, to get the attention of whoever might receive it. Once decoupled from the soliton pulse, it would have propagated on several frequencies, both in subspace and on regular light-speed radio waves.

Inyx had appeared before Hernandez one morning to report the failure of her attempt. "It was elegantly simple," he'd said. "However, it was intercepted by the signal filters I've implemented for all outgoing energy pulses."

Years elapsed while she investigated the nature of Inyx's data filters, and eventually she concluded that she couldn't fool them. That left her only one reasonable course of action: She would have to bypass them by altering the configuration of the transmission hardware and software.

Unfortunately, almost all of the stations were permanently supervised by the Caeliar. By the time she had clandestinely followed the soliton generation network to an automated backup relay, decades had passed since her first attempt at subversion. During all those years, she had presented Inyx with a pleasant façade, to allay his suspicions. Pretending to trust him and treating him like a boon companion had secretly vexed her, but she reminded herself after every encounter, *Think long-term.*

With patience and effort, she had converted the backup relay into a primary transmitter, one with an unmoderated uplink to the soliton emitters. To evade detection of her transmission, she had been forced to wait until a scheduled emission surge in the service of the Great Work. By listening to the Caeliar's plans via the gestalt, pinpointing the time to act was easy.

On the night she'd chosen for her plan's fruition, however, she'd arrived at the backup relay to find it sealed off. Forcing her way through the seals, she'd received another rude surprise: a hollowed space. Not only had her modifications been undone, the auxiliary system itself had been removed.

She'd returned to her residence that evening to find Inyx waiting for her, with two of her rebuilt components, one in each hand. "Fine workmanship," he'd said, dropping them on the floor. "It was all that I've come to expect from you, and more."

"The backup relay was a lure," she'd replied.

"Yes. I wanted to see how far your skills had progressed."

"And are you satisfied?"

"Quite," he'd said, before vanishing in a flare of sparks.

Resentment had fueled her surreptitious efforts for several more decades. She had long used the Caeliar's technology without really understanding how it had been built. Even a grasp of its essential operating principles proved elusive, and she'd dedicated the better part of a century to probing them, molecule by molecule, to unlock the secrets of their construction. Then she'd undertaken her boldest stroke of defiance yet: crafting her own soliton emitter, one that would interface with the systems in New Erigol's shell without utilizing the Caeliar's data network. Each component had been painstakingly crafted from the subatomic level, shaped by Hernandez's obedient catoms.

One month before she'd heard of the approach of the *Starship Titan,* Hernandez had finished her machine and was ready to infuse it with power and bring it online. She had taken every imaginable precaution, and had dispelled the Caeliar's surveillance catoms from her vicinity whenever she'd traveled to her hidden, underground lab deep inside Axion's core. She'd built each part separately, never bringing any two of them together until all had been made and were ready to be assembled.

Then, as the last element had been fitted into place, Inyx had appeared from a smoky swirl in the darkness and with a wave of his arm disintegrated Hernandez's machine. A human lifetime's worth of labor was turned to dust in an instant.

"Why?" Hernandez had cried in anguished rage. "You said you were my friend! They've censured you, too—so why do you betray me? Why are you doing their dirty work?"

For the first time in the centuries that she'd known him, he had sounded afraid. "It's for your protection, Erika. If I don't enforce their laws, you'll be exiled, left to grow old and die in some remote corner of the universe." Sinking into his own despair, he had seemed to diminish before her. "I can't let them do that to you, Erika. I couldn't bear to lose you."

In that unguarded moment, she had realized how much Inyx cared about her, and she for him. Their threatened punishment had been sobering enough, but the realization of its potential impact on Inyx was what had swayed Hernandez. He had done so much for her, had taught her so many things, that she couldn't conscience inflicting such sorrow upon him. For the sake of her friend, she had surrendered. After more than eight centuries of low-intensity resistance to the authority of the Caeliar, Hernandez had buried the last ember of her fighting spirit.

But she'd learned something she hadn't known before: She could survive outside of New Erigol, despite the Change. *Grow old and die,* Inyx had warned. And she'd dreamt anew of escape.

Then *Titan* had come to New Erigol.

Inyx had arranged permission for their away team to visit the planet's surface. At his request, she had joined him and Edrin to greet them, and had appointed herself as their liaison.

Now, less than three days later, she stood under a starless night, beside the petrified tree and the deathly still black pool, and she asked herself what she had done.

For all the Caeliar's talk of her being a "guest with restrictions," despite the role she had played in helping them find this new world to call their home, regardless of the superhuman abilities bestowed upon her by the Change, looking at her reflection on the preternaturally still water, she saw herself as she was: a prisoner with a nigh-eternal sentence.

And, as the instrument selected to impose the Caeliar's rules on *Titan*'s crew, she had become a jailer, as well.

"All things considered, I think the op went fairly well," Vale said as she paced. "Right up to the point where it fell apart."

Tuvok stood in the main room of the away team's Axion residence, apart from the rest of the group, while Vale led the post-mission debriefing. Several hours had passed since Keru had been intercepted aboard the shuttlecraft *Mance.* Rather than meet immediately after their return to the residence, when the group was still agitated by its setback, Vale had suggested that everyone take some time alone to consider what had gone wrong, so that they could discuss the details later, in a calm and professional manner. Now it was later, and no one was calm.

"It was a total bungle," said Lieutenant Sortollo, who sat on a sofa with fellow security personnel Keru and Dennisar. "The Caeliar saw us coming a hundred klicks away."

Tuvok stepped forward and replied, "Not necessarily. If they had, it is unlikely they would have permitted us to beam Mister Keru onto the *Mance*. The fact that we did so would suggest that at least that much of our plan was a success."

Keru nodded. "I agree. That caught them looking. But once they knew where I was, it didn't take them long to shut us down. And now we've lost the element of surprise."

"More important," said Ree, who, with Torvig, flanked Troi's chair, "we've lost our tricorders. And the shuttlecraft."

Vale closed her eyes and pinched the bridge of her nose for a moment. Then she sighed and opened her eyes. "It could be worse," she said. "At least they didn't destroy it."

"So they say," Keru replied. "For all we know, they ditched it in the ocean. Or blew it to pieces."

Sortollo, Dennisar, Keru, and Vale overlapped one another with vitriolic remarks, but Tuvok ignored them. Something else drew his attention. A psionic pain shadow was lingering in the group's midst. It was a dull suffering, the kind of malaise produced by illness or deep discomfort. He quieted his thoughts and reached out with a gentle telepathic touch, seeking the source of the pain. Within moments, his mind focused on the source: Commander Troi.

As the discussion continued, he kept his psionic senses attuned to Troi's condition.

"All I'm saying," Dennisar snapped, "is that there's a lot of planet down there, and searching it for the shuttlecraft without tricorders or *Titan*'s sensors is going to take a *very* long time."

Sortollo rolled his eyes at his Orion colleague. "And what we're saying is, we'll need to use the Caeliar's technology to locate the *Mance*."

"And the only way to access that is to get Hernandez to help us," Keru added.

Torvig raised one mechanical hand. "Commander Vale? Did you not prohibit us from soliciting aid from Erika Hernandez?"

"Yes, I did," Vale replied, shooting a glower at Keru and Sortollo. "I considered her unreliable before the mission, and I haven't seen anything since then to change my mind."

"We're not saying it'll happen overnight," Keru argued. "If we want her help, we'll have to cultivate a relationship with her, win her over."

Dr. Ree signaled his disagreement with a rattling rasp. "You'll find that difficult with the Caeliar watching us every minute of the day," the reptilian physician said. "It stands to reason that if they consider us dangerous enough to merit constant surveillance, they must be doubly cautious of her."

Troi looked up. Her face was ashen and her voice hoarse. "Doctor Ree is correct. The Caeliar don't trust her much more than they trust us. Besides, I've tried reaching out to her, and she doesn't seem interested. Unless she comes to us, we shouldn't think of her as an ally."

The security personnel raised their voices in a clamor of protest, which Vale silenced by raising her hands and barking, "Enough!" She waited until the group fell silent. "Does anyone have any ideas about how we might apply what we've learned today? Or what we might do next?"

Keru mumbled, "We can start by building new tricorders."

"I'll take that as a 'no,'" Vale said. "Let's call it a night, then. But tomorrow at breakfast, I want to start hearing new ideas. We all know what the challenges are. Let's start coming up with solutions." With a nod, she added, "Dismissed."

Most of the away team members split up and plodded off toward their respective bedrooms. Tuvok watched as Dr. Ree hovered close behind Troi, shadowing her down the corridor to her quarters. Then the Vulcan tactical officer turned back and observed Commander Vale walking outside, onto the terrace. He made a discreet survey of the others' positions, and then he joined the first officer on the wide, open-air balcony.

She noted his approach but did not turn around. "Taking the air, Tuvok?"

He stood next to her and rested his palms on top of the broad railing. "Commander Troi is in serious physical distress," he said. "And she is masking her symptoms."

"I know," Vale said.

"Is her condition serious?"

"I'm not at liberty to say," Vale replied. "But Doctor

Ree is aware of the situation. Please keep this information private."

He nodded once. "Of course. If there's anything I—"

"That'll be all." She threw a guarded look at him. "Thank you."

"I could be of assistance to the doctor," Tuvok said. "Counselor Troi and I have compatible telepathic gifts. Perhaps I could help her to control her pain until such time as—"

"I said that'll be all, Tuvok. *Thank you.*"

He stiffened and took half a step back from the railing. "Understood, Commander. Good night." He turned and went back inside, concerned for Deanna Troi's safety but bound by the chain of command. It had been a long day for the away team, but by the time Tuvok reached his quarters, he had already decided he would not be sleeping tonight. If necessary, he could forgo sleep for several days or longer. Until he was convinced that Troi was no longer in danger, he would remain awake and monitor her unconscious telepathic emissions for any sign of distress.

And if Troi's condition demanded that the chain of command be broken, that was a decision Tuvok could live with.

Hernandez held herself aloft through will alone. Feet together, arms wide apart, head bowed in concentration, she levitated many kilometers above the Quorum hall and immersed her thoughts in the hubbub of the gestalt.

There were hundreds of voices vying to be heard, expressing themselves in images and feelings as often as in words, and when they did speak in concrete terms, it was in the ancient tongue of the Caeliar. Fortunately for Hernandez, her centuries of scholarship, aided by her catoms, made it easy to understand.

Much of the argument receded as Ordemo asked, "Why have we not known of these passages until now?"

"Because," Inyx replied, "until mere weeks ago, they had been dormant. Lying fallow in the ubiquitous realms of subspace, they were all but invisible to our sensors." He offered the members of the Quorum a visual representation of the tunnels through subspace; it reminded Hernandez of a wheel with uneven spokes, and Erigol's former position was the hub. One of the spokes shone much more brightly than the others. "This was the first of the passages to be accessed, and it has been the most frequently traveled. In the past few days, all but a few of the remaining passages have been exposed, as they were transited by one or more vessels."

Low drones and rumbles of anxiety coursed through the hovering ranks of the Quorum. Above the din, Ordemo replied, "Inyx, the primitive civilizations of the galaxy cannot be trusted to use those passages wisely. If they should destabilize one or more of them, the effects would be catastrophic. Entire star systems could be annihilated."

"I am aware of that, Ordemo," Inyx said. "Now that the passages' recent usage has enabled us to pinpoint all their locations, I have begun calculations for a series of soliton pulses that will safely collapse them at their point of common intersection, without posing any risk to the galaxy at large."

Ordemo sounded assuaged. "Will it take long to effect?"

"No," Inyx said. "We'll begin the process momentarily. It should be complete within a matter of hours."

"Very good," Ordemo said. "Well done, Inyx, thank you."

Before Inyx could erase his catom-animation of the passages and their hub, Hernandez followed its data stream back to its source. She found herself gazing through a narrow pinhole in subspace, spying on events nearly half a galaxy away.

Hundreds of ships moved through her gestalt-vision, vessels of many different designs. Several she recognized as having the familiar configurations of Starfleet spacecraft, with their saucers and nacelles. Klingon ships were equally distinctive, and there were many of them, too. In addition, there were scores of ships whose provenances were unknown to her. All of them seemed to move in concert, unified in purpose, rallied around the clustered apertures of the subspace passages.

This has something to do with the threat Deanna was telling me about, Hernandez intuited. *The passageways,* Titan, *the threat to Earth. It's all connected somehow. But how?*

A moment later, one of the passageways spiraled open inside the blue night of the distant nebula. Fear like a fist of cold steel seized her heart. And she had her answer.

Madre de Dios.

Deanna Troi awoke in a panic, a fugitive from a nightmare of knives and vipers. Gasping for breath and drenched in her own sweat, she lurched to a sitting position in her bed and was restrained by scaly talons locked around her arms.

"Easy, my dear counselor," said Ree through his maw of fangs. "Your symptoms are getting worse."

She struggled frantically in his grasp. "Let me go!"

"Counselor, please, you're in no—"

Troi spat in his left eye and tried to lift her foot to kick at him. "Take your hands off me!"

He let go, and she fell backward into bed. "As you wish."

Rubbing her abraded wrists, Troi sat up. Then a rush of nausea hit her, and she doubled over. Ree stepped back as Troi vomited a thin stream of watery stomach acid on the floor.

As a wave of dry heaves convulsed Troi's abdomen and left her dizzy, the Pahkwa-thanh physician inched toward her. "Counselor, without my tricorder, I can make only an educated guess as to your condition. But it is my belief that you are suffering from an internal hemorrhage."

She gulped a deep breath and pulled herself back onto her bed. The room felt as if it were spinning above her.

"Deanna," Ree continued, "we need to ask the Caeliar if they have medical facilities that we can use to treat you."

Pursing her lips, Troi lolled her head side to side. "No," she insisted. "Don't let them touch me."

"Counselor, we have no choice," Ree said, looming over her. "Your condition is deteriorating. It's time to let me operate."

His heartfelt-sounding plaints didn't fool her. She

saw the predatory gleam in his cold, serpentine eyes. "Liar!" she screamed. "Butcher! You want to kill my baby!"

"Counselor, please, you're delu—" Her foot struck his snout and shut him up. As he recoiled from the blow, she rolled out of bed and landed hard on the floor. Escape was all that mattered now. Crawling away from him toward the door of her room, she focused on pulling herself with her hands and pushing herself with her feet. Then the doctor's bony, three-taloned feet landed in front of her. He had leaped past her with ease and blocked her exit. Turning, he confronted her. "Your skin was very warm to the touch, Deanna. I believe you're running a fever, possibly as a side effect to your body's rejection of the synthetase inhibitor. And the fever is making you delusional."

Scuttling backward on her palms, she rasped, "Get away from me! Monster!"

"Counselor, I don't have time to argue with your mental infirmities. Your life is in jeopardy, and you're not acting rationally. If I have to, I'll relieve you of duty."

The door swung open behind him and rebounded off the wall. He turned and was confronted by Sortollo, Dennisar, and Keru.

"We heard shouting," Keru said.

Troi pointed at Ree. "He attacked me!"

"I did no such thing," Ree said to Keru. "Counselor Troi is feverish, and I believe she's suffering an internal hemorrhage."

"He wants to give me to the Caeliar!"

Ree spun and hissed at her. "I need their help so I can operate on you."

Cowering in a corner beside her bed, Troi kept an accusing finger leveled at Ree. "Keep him away from me."

Dennisar and Sortollo stepped into the room between Ree and Troi. Keru reached forward and took hold of Ree's shoulder. "Okay, Doc, let's all just take a step back and—"

"There's no time for this!" Ree growled. "Her pulse is thready, her blood pressure is dropping—"

Dennisar and Sortollo began herding Ree backward, toward the exit. Behind the doctor, Keru said in a cajoling manner, "Just step out for a few minutes, Doc, let her calm down."

"She could be bleeding out! I need to operate!"

"No!" Troi called out. "No surgery!"

Dennisar shrugged at Ree. "You heard her. No surgery."

The therapodian physician stopped retreating, lowered his head, and fixed his jeweled-iris glare upon Troi. "Fine."

He burst forward, trampling over Sortollo and Dennisar. Keru lumbered after the lunging Pahkwa-thanh, but the Trill seemed to be moving in slow motion and lagging meters behind. Troi, paralyzed with terror, could only cringe and stare in mute horror as Ree descended upon her, his long jaw of razor-sharp teeth wide open.

Vale, Tuvok, and Torvig appeared in the corridor outside the doorway and looked on with shock and dismay as Ree pinned Troi to the floor—and sank his fangs into her chest.

19

Captain Picard stepped out of his ready room and onto the bridge of the *Enterprise*. The electric crackling of high-energy tools mixed with the low buzz of comm chatter and muted conversation. His bridge was crowded with engineers, junior officers, and his senior command officers, all of whom were working with great focus and alacrity to finish the ship's repairs.

Kadohata interrupted her report to Worf, who was seated in the command chair, and nodded to Picard. Worf stood and handed Picard a padd. "Captain, calculations for opening aperture twenty-two beta are almost complete. However, shields are at less than fifty percent, and engineering is having difficulty adjusting the emitters for the new metaphasic frequencies."

"Not ready to enter the plasma jet, then," Picard said. He noted a silent exchange of anxious glances between Worf and Kadohata. "How much longer, Number One?"

"At least thirty minutes," Worf replied.

The note of regret in Worf's voice compelled Picard

to ask, "And what is the ETA of the Hirogen hunting pack?"

Worf looked at Kadohata, who folded her hands behind her back to affect a nonchalant pose. "Twenty minutes," she said.

"This is not the fight we came for," Picard said. He stepped past Kadohata and raised his voice to snare Choudhury's attention. "Hail the *Aventine,* Lieutenant."

The security chief tapped commands into her console and then looked up to respond, "Ready, sir."

"On-screen," Picard said.

The main viewer switched from an image of stars to the face of Captain Dax. *"You don't look like you're breaking good news, Captain,"* she said.

"I'm not," he replied. "The *Enterprise* won't be ready to reenter the plasma stream before the Hirogen arrive."

A worry line formed a single, wavy crease across Dax's brow. *"The metaphasic recalibration, right?"*

Picard nodded. "Has your crew finished the modifications? Can you extend your shields around the *Enterprise*?"

Dax shook her head. *"We'd have to be at full power to make it to the aperture and survive the jaunt back. Right now, we're at fifty-three percent."*

"We can't risk letting the Hirogen detect the frequency for controlling the apertures," Picard said. "If we can't make the return in the next fifteen minutes, we'll have no choice but to stand and fight."

"Agreed," Dax said. *"I suggest we spend the time we have left restoring our tactical systems and preparing coordinated attack-and-defense protocols."*

Resigned to the coming battle, Picard consented

with a grim nod. "Make it so. Good luck to you and your crew, Captain."

"And to yours, sir. Aventine *out."*

The channel closed, and the main viewer reverted to a backdrop of stars overlaid by a tactical display of information about the approaching Hirogen hunting pack. "Mister Worf," said Picard, "ready the ship for battle."

"Aye, sir." Worf turned toward Choudhury. "Hirogen use energy dampeners during boarding operations, to render phasers and internal security systems inoperable. Issue projectile rifles and bladed weapons to all security teams." To Kadohata he added, "Tell Mister La Forge to prioritize tactical repairs."

As the Red Alert klaxon wailed throughout the ship, Picard returned to his command chair, sat down, and steeled himself for the impending fray. A new degree of intensity drove the crew's efforts now, and it was almost enough to push all thought of the Borg from his thoughts.

Then Worf was at his side. "Permission to leave the bridge for five minutes, sir."

"Now? For what reason, Mister Worf?"

The Klingon averted his eyes from Picard's and frowned before he replied, "To retrieve my *bat'leth,* sir." Then he met Picard's gaze and added with stern surety, "As a precaution."

For once, Picard saw the logic of Worf's thinking. "Permission granted."

Captain Chakotay had been itching for a fight for a long time. It had been several months since Kathryn

Janeway had been taken by the Borg, and not a night had passed that he hadn't dreamt of vengeance. Payback. Blood for blood.

In the aftermath of the Borg's most recent, devastating sorties into Federation space, he'd persuaded Admiral Montgomery to petition Admiral Nechayev to reassign *Voyager* to combat duty on the homefront. When the call had gone out for a fleet to assemble in the Azure Nebula, to support the *Enterprise* in a daring counteroffensive against the Borg, he'd made certain that *Voyager* was the first ship assigned to the battle group.

We've faced the Borg more than anyone, Chakotay brooded as he stared out his ready room window. *It should be us leading the scouting runs.* He clenched his fists and set his jaw. *Patience. Soon, we'll all get to fight. Until then, we hold the line.*

It was precisely because of Chakotay's personal experience against the Borg, and *Voyager*'s reputation in Starfleet, that Captain Picard had placed them in command of the allied expeditionary force while the *Enterprise* and the *Aventine* were off to who knew where on a recon run. Watching the silhouettes of hundreds of starships massing for a battle royal, Chakotay felt his pulse quicken. A red hour was close at hand.

A door signal interrupted his ruminations. "Come in." He turned as the portal sighed open to admit his first officer, Lieutenant Commander Tom Paris. "Tom," Chakotay said. "How're you holding up?"

"I'm fine, sir," Paris replied, with the demeanor of a razor's edge. It had been four days since he had received a posthumous message from his father, Admiral Owen Paris, who had been killed during the Borg's attack on Starbase 234.

Had such news come at any other time, Chakotay would have suggested his XO take bereavement leave, but a declaration by the Federation Council three days earlier meant that the UFP was now in a state of open war against the Borg. Starfleet no longer had the luxury of time for its sorrows.

Paris continued, "Captain T'Vala says the *Athens* is ready to open aperture twenty-three alpha, and the captain of the *Mendeleev* estimates his crew will open twenty-four alpha in less than an hour."

Chakotay nodded. "What about apertures twenty-five through twenty-seven? Any progress there?"

"Some," Paris said. "The warbird *Tiamatra* and the *I.K.S. veScharg'a* are working on twenty-five and twenty-seven. We've been trying to help the Gorn cruiser *Lotan* break the lock on aperture twenty-six, but it's not responding at all."

Suspicion and concern hardened Chakotay's already stern expression. "Prioritize that," he said. "What about the *Enterprise* and the *Aventine*?"

"Three hours overdue," Paris said.

"That's long enough," Chakotay said. "We have the frequency for twenty-two alpha. Send the *T'Kumbra,* the *Templar,* and the *Saladin.* Make sure they treat it as a combat sortie, not—"

"Captain Chakotay and Commander Paris, please report to the bridge," Lieutenant Harry Kim interrupted via the comm.

Paris threw a look at Chakotay, and they both

moved at a quickstep out of the ready room, onto the bridge of *Voyager*. Paris centered himself behind the forward duty stations.

"Report," Chakotay said, dropping into his chair.

"Aperture twenty-six alpha's opening," Kim said. "But it's not us. Something's coming through."

Anticipation and dread entwined like snakes inside Chakotay's gut. "Red Alert," he said. "Battle stations. Alert the fleet, and get ready to target whatever comes out."

"Aye, sir," Kim said, arming weapons and raising shields as the alert klaxon whooped.

Let it be a Borg cube, Chakotay prayed. *Hell, let it be five. We've got enough firepower to pulverize* ten *of them.*

"Tare," Paris said to the conn officer, orchestrating the battle preparations, "bring us about, bearing one-three-one mark five. Lasren, tell the warbird *Loviatar* and the *I.K.S. Ya'Vang* to come about and guard our flanks."

Everyone reacted with quiet efficiency. Then all eyes turned toward the main viewer and the expanding circle of light that began to wash away the dreamlike cyan glow of the nebula.

A dark corner appeared in the blinding radiance, followed by another, and Chakotay prepared to sate his appetite for revenge. He was about to give the order to fire when the true scope of what he was seeing began to reveal itself. In that moment all his dreams of retribution left him.

"All ships, open fire!" Paris shouted, but it was too late.

Darkness fell upon *Voyager* like a hammer, and

then all that was left were the flames, the terror, and the screaming.

Ezri Dax felt every blast that rocked her ship. The ten Hirogen attack craft swarmed the *Aventine* and the *Enterprise* and harried the Starfleet vessels with powerful subnucleonic beams.

Over the bedlam of explosions, Dax hollered to her first officer, "Sam! Return fire!"

"Aft torpedoes, full spread!" Bowers shouted through the din. "Helm, roll forty degrees port! Phasers, sweep starboard!"

Every command was carried out with dispatch, and the searing orange glow of phaser beams sliced across the image on the main viewer. Flashes from detonating quantum torpedoes were coupled with violent tremors in the *Aventine*'s hull.

"One enemy ship destroyed," Kedair reported from tactical. "Acquiring new targets."

Bowers replied, "Keep firing, Lieutenant."

Another fusillade of Hirogen fire raked the *Aventine*. An auxiliary tactical station on the starboard side of the bridge exploded, hurling Ensign Rhys backward in a jet of sparks and shrapnel. His scorched, bloody body fell in an unnatural pose in the middle of the bridge.

A Vulcan paramedic stationed on the bridge rushed forward, with a tricorder open in her hand, to Rhys's side. More blasts pounded the ship as she looked up at Dax and shook her head. There was nothing she could do—the man was dead.

Thunderous impacts buffeted Dax's ship and caused

the overhead lights to dim. "Port shields failing," Kedair called from tactical. "Incoming!"

Bowers shot back, "Roll one-eighty to port! All power to starboard shields!"

It was too late. The Hirogen had spotted the weakness in the *Aventine*'s defenses and exploited it without hesitation. Dax held on to her chair's armrests as the bridge pitched sharply, knocking Bowers and the Vulcan medic off their feet. The ops console exploded, engulfing Oliana Mirren in superheated phosphors and shattered isolinear circuitry. When the flash faded, the reed-thin blonde went limp in her chair.

Casting off sentiment, Bowers shouted to the relief ops officer, Lieutenant Nak, "Reset science two for ops!"

"Aye, sir," replied the shaken young male Tellarite, who scrambled to reconfigure the bridge's backup science console.

The *Aventine*'s phasers shrieked as Kedair unleashed three barrages in rapid succession, and the torpedoes-away signal had never before sounded so sweet to Dax's ears. On the main viewer, another Hirogen ship was vaporized as it blundered into the *Aventine*'s tandem firing solution with the *Enterprise*.

"Eight Hirogen ships left," Kedair announced. "They're splitting up, four and four, on attack vectors."

"Tharp," Bowers said. "Hard about, let *Enterprise* cover our flank."

Phaser blasts slashed through two of the *Aventine*'s Hirogen attackers, but the last pair of enemy ships accelerated on an unswerving intercept course.

Kedair shouted, "Collision alarm!"

The two Hirogen ships made impact. A violent jolt shuddered through the deck and made Dax wince.

"Report," Bowers said.

From the new ops station, Lieutenant Nak replied, "Hull breach, Decks Seventeen and Eighteen, Sections Five through Nine. Force fields are up, damage-control teams responding."

"Intruder alert!" Kedair said. "Four Hirogen, moving in pairs on Deck Seventeen." She looked up at Bowers. "They're heading for crew quarters."

"Evacuate that deck," Bowers said. "And tell your people to shoot to kill. Hirogen don't take prisoners, so neither do we."

The bridge of the *Enterprise* was heavy with smoke and fumes. Sparks rained down from buckled overhead panels. Pressure-suited damage-control specialists jogged past behind Jean-Luc Picard, on their way to extinguish a fire in his ready room.

In front of him, off to starboard, a Kaferian medic was treating Lieutenant T'Ryssa Chen, whose right arm had been burned black when she'd pushed tactical officer Šmrhová clear of an overloading companel just before it exploded.

At the conn, a surge of electricity had stunned Lieutenant Faur, who had been taken to sickbay. Lieutenant Weinrib had taken over the ship's flight operations. In a pitched voice he declared, "Two Hirogen ships on ramming trajectories!"

Worf bellowed, "Evasive! Starboard!" He thumbed open the intraship comm. "All decks! Brace for impact!"

Two collisions in quick sequence pummeled the *Enterprise*. Choudhury held on to her console with one hand and worked its controls with the other. "Hull breach, Deck Ten! Ventral shields are down, and the last two ships are making another attack run."

Picard gripped his armrests so tightly that his knuckles turned white. "Helm, intercept course. On my mark, make a shallow, full-impulse dive across their path, then pull up."

"Aye, sir," Weinrib said.

"Divert phaser power to dorsal shields," Picard said to Choudhury. "Arm aft torpedoes, dispersal pattern Bravo."

"Weapons ready," Choudhury said.

Kadohata looked back from the ops console. "Dorsal shields are as strong as we can make them."

"Steady," Picard said, projecting unflinching confidence.

He watched the range and speed data on his chair's armrest tactical monitor. As he'd suspected, the Hirogen showed no sign of breaking off their attack or changing their course. They weren't going to surrender or relent.

So be it, Picard decided. "Now, Mister Weinrib."

The engines throbbed and whined as the *Enterprise* slipped below the Hirogen's glide plane at full impulse for just half a second. As the two enemy ships rolled to attack the *Enterprise* from above, it soared upward, ramming them from underneath. Bone-rattling concussions resounded through the hull as the massive starship slammed aside its smaller attackers. "Hard to port," Picard commanded over the hue and cry of explosions and damage reports. "Fire aft torpedoes!"

Bright feedback tones from Choudhury's console confirmed the release of the torpedo volley. Seconds later she reported, "Both Hirogen ships destroyed, Captain."

He threw a look at Worf. "Damage report."

"Hull breaches on Decks Two through Six, Sections Nineteen through Fifty-one," Worf replied. "Dorsal shields have failed."

It was no worse than Picard had expected. "Casualties?"

"Several," Worf said. "We also have nine crewmen missing from the breached compartments."

Picard watched the firefighting team shamble out of his smoky ready room. "Begin search-and-rescue operations, Mister Worf." He asked Choudhury, "What's the *Aventine*'s status?"

"They've been boarded," she said. Then her eyes opened wider as a signal shrilled on her console. "And they're not the only ones—we have four intruders on Deck Ten."

Lieutenant Randolph Giudice led his security team into position on Deck 10 of the *Enterprise*. He ducked into a shallow recess along the corridor, hugged his TR-116 rifle to his chest, and held up a fist to halt the rest of the squad. Across from him, Lieutenant Peter Davila backed into another nook in a bulkhead, his own TR-116 clutched tightly.

A few meters behind them, past a curve in the passageway, four more security officers crouched, awaiting the signal to advance. Lieutenant th'Chun, Lieutenant Harley de Lange, and Ensign Manfred Vogel all were armed with the same kind of rifles as Giudice. In addition, th'Chun and Vogel carried collapsible stun batons for hand-to-hand combat, and de Lange wore a Nausicaan sword in a sheath across his back. The melee weapon was not a standard armament, but the TR-116s and bladed weapons had been issued from the armory on the XO's orders.

At the rear of the group was Lieutenant Bryan Regnis, the team's sharpshooter. He carried a specially modified TR-116. At the end of its muzzle was an inertia-neutral microtransporter, which was linked to an exographic targeting sensor that covered his left eye like a translucent crystal patch.

The sensor let him peek through decks and bulkheads, and the microtransporter enabled him to shoot through them as if they weren't there. His rifle fired ten-millimeter monotanium projectiles at nine hundred twenty meters per second—and materialized them ten centimeters from his target, with their kinetic energy unchanged. In essence, he was able to target his foes from several decks away and inflict damage as if he had shot them at point-blank range.

Giudice looked back at Regnis, made a "V" with his first two fingers, and pointed at his own eyes. Then he made a jabbing forward motion with his whole hand. The lean, boyish-looking sniper nodded, unslung his rifle, and peered through the exographic sensor, seeking out the Hirogen boarding party.

After several seconds of adjustments, Regnis frowned, met Giudice's questioning stare, and waved his hand up and down in front of his eyes: Something was blocking the exographic sensor.

There's the dampening field, Giudice figured. *So*

much for doing this the easy way. He waved de Lange and Vogel forward.

The two men stayed low and skulked forward, rifles braced and level. Davila and Giudice kept their own weapons aimed past the duo, ready to lay down covering fire. Regnis and th'Chun hung back, behind cover.

At the far end of the corridor, beyond the next curve, the overhead lights began going out. The leading edge of darkness moved swiftly closer, blacking out companels and even emergency lighting where the bulkheads met the deck.

A dull, heavy *thump* was followed by the sound of something rolling. Giudice saw a glint of light reflecting off a small, metallic orb the size of a baseball. It ricocheted off the bulkhead several meters away and rolled toward him and his team. A wall of darkness preceded it.

An energy dampener. "Back!" he snapped.

Vogel halted and stared forward into the darkness as it overtook him. A meaty *thunk* of metal striking bone followed a moment later. Lieutenant de Lange had turned back and was in the midst of his first sprinting stride when he was knocked forward. He fell facedown, revealing a sunburst-shaped throwing blade buried between his neck vertebrae, just beneath his skull.

Giudice and Davila scrambled backward as they opened fire, lighting up the darkened passage with tracer rounds from their TR-116s. Bullets sparked as they were deflected by the two Hirogen hunters' armor. The height and bulk of the invaders shocked Giudice; he and Davila were big men, broad-shouldered and thickly muscled, but they were dwarfed by the Hirogen.

Stumbling in reverse around the curve in the passage, Giudice almost ran into th'Chun, who was dashing forward. He tried to grab the Andorian. "Neshaal, stop!" He lunged forward to follow th'Chun around the curve, leading with his rifle.

The *thaan* rolled across the deck and came up shooting in full automatic mode. In a blaze of crimson tracers, he peppered one of the Hirogen with high-explosive rounds, blasting him to a dead stop. A handful of shots struck the hunter in the unarmored areas of his face, and he collapsed.

Then an ovoid hunk of metal arced out of the shadows and bounced across the deck toward th'Chun.

Giudice turned and dived for cover. "Incoming!"

Regnis and Davila retreated ahead of him. Behind him, th'Chun fought to go from a kneeling crouch to a standing run. He didn't make it. The explosion threw the Andorian forward and slammed him into Giudice and the others. Searing-hot shrapnel pelted them as they rolled in a jumble.

Giudice shook off the worst of the blast and pulled Davila back to his feet. One look at th'Chun confirmed that he was dead. "Redcaps," Giudice said to Regnis and Davila, using the slang term for high-explosive ammunition. "Suppressing fire. Fall back to Section Nineteen."

The trio quickstepped backward to an intersection that was still lit. Davila and Regnis switched their weapons' ammunition clips on the move. They ducked around the corner into Section Nineteen, and Giudice gave the signal to halt. He tapped his combadge. "Giudice to bridge. One hostile down. Need backup."

Lieutenant Choudhury replied, *"Acknowledged. Be advised, we've confirmed the Hirogen are using energy dampeners."*

The three men swapped angry, exasperated glares. "Thanks, bridge," Giudice said. "Noted." He looked across the passageway to note the bulkhead numbers. "I need force fields at Section Ten-nineteen Echo."

"Negative," Choudhury said. *"The energy dampeners will just knock them out. Forget containment protocols. Shoot to kill."*

He pulled a clip of redcaps from his belt. "Acknowledged," he said. In a deft, practiced motion, he ejected his weapon's emptied magazine to the deck and slapped in the replacement. "Can you tell me if our blind spot's moving?"

"Affirmative," said Choudhury. *"It's flanking you. Center of the scrambled zone is Section Ten-twenty-one Delta."*

. The corridor to his right grew dark. "Copy that, bridge. Giudice out." He tapped Regnis's shoulder and motioned for the sniper to watch the dimming corridor. Then he gave a sideways nod to Davila to follow him to a panel that was marked as a storage space for emergency supplies.

Davila put his back to the wall and shifted his focus every few seconds, wary of an ambush from any direction. Giudice opened the bulkhead panel and retrieved a bundle of chemical emergency flares. He unrolled the bundle between himself and Davila. "Pop 'em, toss 'em, and make it quick," Giudice said.

The two men cracked the flares to life by the fistful

and flung them wildly down the corridors. Even as the corridor's overhead lights faded to black with the Hirogen's approach, the pale lime and cyan glows of the chemical flares remained bright and undimmed. Lit only by the flares, the passageway took on a surreal cast of harsh shadows and unnatural hues.

Giudice watched the corridor opposite the one guarded by Regnis, and Davila monitored the intersection from which they'd come less than a minute earlier. "Stay frosty," Giudice whispered. "Check your targets, controlled bursts."

Waiting in the dark, lying in ambush, Giudice felt as if the seconds were being stretched by the adrenaline coursing through him. His pulse slammed with a steady tempo in his head, and the beating of his heart shook his entire body. Fat beads of sweat rolled from his thinning hair to his heavy eyebrows.

He thought he heard Regnis start to say something. Over his shoulder, he said in a hushed voice, "Bry? Report."

No answer came. Giudice looked back and strained to pierce the shadows. Then he saw Regnis dangling several centimeters above the floor, flailing desperately at his blood-drenched throat. The sniper looked as if he was levitating—until Giudice caught a glimmer of light on the monofilament wire that had been lowered through a ventilation duct to garrote his comrade.

"Heads up!" Giudice unleashed a staccato series of short bursts at the overhead panels. The ceiling caved in.

Davila opened fire on the hulking forms of three Hirogen hunters, who let Regnis fall to the deck as they dropped into crouches, scythe-like blades in hand.

One hunter lunged at Davila, thrusting a dagger at the man's chest. Davila parried the blow with the stock of his rifle, only to get slashed across the chest by a curved blade in the Hirogen's other hand.

Giudice continued firing until his rifle clicked empty.

A hand locked on his throat, and cold steel bit into his gut and pierced his back. He'd been impaled on the sword of the Hirogen leader, the alpha. The alien, whose face was marked by broad stripes of bright war paint, yanked his blade free and tossed Giudice aside. The brawny security officer struck the bulkhead and fell bleeding to the deck.

A buzz-roar of weapons fire filled the corridor.

In the strobed light of tracer fire, the alpha convulsed as chunks of his armor were blasted from his body in a bloody spray. Giudice winced as he watched the stuttered-motion retreat of the other two Hirogen, one of whom hurled a fist-sized charge through an open escape pod hatch.

They ducked past the portal, and an ear-splitting blast vomited fire and debris into the corridor. Then everything was drowned out by a terrifying howl of escaping atmosphere.

Water vapor condensed into white plumes racing toward space, and the sudden plunge in air temperature stung Giudice's eyes. He forced them open long enough to see the two Hirogen, whose armor suits were equipped with breathing masks and visors for survival in the vacuum of space, clamber out through the ragged new gap in the *Enterprise*'s hull.

The rush of air slowed, and Giudice's head swam. *We're running out of air,* he realized. Struggling to concentrate through his pain and hypoxia, he deduced that the Hirogen's energy dampener was preventing the ship's force fields from sealing the breach and repressurizing the isolated sections.

Several meters down the passageway, his rescuers had collapsed, robbed of breath. Regnis and Davila were down.

Lying next to Giudice was the dead Alpha-Hirogen. And on his belt was a spherical device like the one that had rolled out of the darkness minutes earlier. With weak, trembling fingers, Giudice detached the sleek, silvery globe from the alpha's belt. Barely able to see, unable to hear, he crawled forward on his knees toward the rent in the hull. To his relief, he felt the artificial gravity fail beneath him, lightening his burden.

He chucked the globe through the gap, out into the zero-g emptiness. It spun as it vanished into the eternal night.

The corridor lights snapped on, a force field shimmered into place across the rip in the ship's skin, and a flood of sweet air rushed over Giudice, who collapsed into the restored artificial gravity.

Boots clattered as a security team ran to Giudice and his men. Leading the reinforcement squad was Lieutenant Rennan Konya, the ship's Betazoid deputy chief of security. "Medics up here, stat!" he shouted back down the corridor.

"Good to see you back on your feet," Giudice said. From his vantage point lying on the deck, he noted the chrome stripe on the bottom of the ammunition clip in Konya's rifle: bullets with pointed monofilament tips—the ultimate armor-piercing rounds. He grinned up at the Betazoid. "Silver bullets, eh?"

Konya smiled back. "When only the best will do." As a team of medics and nurses arrived to tend to Giudice and his wounded men, Konya eyed the damage in the escape-pod bay and tapped his combadge. "Konya to bridge: Hostiles have gone EVA."

Sam Bowers dodged through smoke and past a running engineer to join Lonnoc Kedair at the security console. "They're *where*?"

"Heading aft on the outside of the dorsal hull," Kedair replied. Her green, scaled hands moved with speed and grace over her dust-covered controls. "Four Hirogen wearing pressure-support gear. One of them has a pretty serious-looking piece of shoulder-fired artillery." An alert beeped and lit a pad high on her console. She silenced it with a quick tap. "Power failures are following them every step of the way."

Lieutenant Gaff chim Nak called across the bridge from the new ops station, "*Enterprise* also has two EVA hostiles."

"Our guests must be using magnetic boots," Captain Dax said, thinking aloud. "Can we electrify the hull? Maybe short out their armor?"

"It'd take about fifteen minutes to set up," interjected science officer Gruhn Helkara. "And with their energy-dampening field, there's no guarantee it would even reach them."

Kedair added, "We can't use phasers, either. Even if we target them manually, the beam would disperse before contact."

DAVID MACK

"What about the runabouts?" Dax asked the security chief.

She shook her head. "Same problem, sir. Phasers won't hit the targets, and even if their microtorpedoes explode on impact, shooting them at our own unshielded hull is a *bad* idea."

The captain heaved a frustrated sigh. "How soon can we send our own people out to engage?"

"Not soon enough," Bowers said, pointing at the enlarged image on the main viewscreen.

The Hirogen who carried the shoulder-fired weapon raised it, braced it, and aimed it at a central section of the *Aventine*'s secondary hull. His comrades moved behind him.

Dax tapped her combadge. "Bridge to engineering! Prep for hull breach!"

A fiery streak from the Hirogen's weapon left a trail of quickly dissipating expended chemical propellant. Then a flash on the main viewer coincided with a deep, angry rumbling in the hull. A port-side engineering status console became a chaotic scramble of symbols and static.

"Breach, Deck Twenty, Section Forty-one," Nak replied, before he covered his mouth and coughed painfully into his fist.

"They're heading for main engineering," Dax said. She snapped orders around the bridge. "Sam, get Leishman and her people out. Gaff, isolate all command systems on the bridge. Gruhn, lock down the engineering computer core. Lonnoc, we can't let the intruders control our warp core—get your people down there, and dead or alive, *get those bastards off my ship!*"

As the bridge officers scrambled to their stations to carry out their orders, Bowers saw Kedair summon relief tactical officer Talia Kandel to take over for her at security. Then the security chief walked briskly toward the turbolift.

Bowers intercepted her before she boarded the lift and snapped, "Lieutenant Kedair! Where are you going?"

"Main engineering, sir," Kedair said.

He folded his arms. "I don't recall you asking permission to leave your post, Lieutenant."

She bristled and then snapped to attention.

"Sir. Request permission to lead the counterattack and make our boarders sorry they ever set foot on Captain Dax's ship."

"Permission granted," Bowers said, stepping aside to let her enter the turbolift. "Give 'em hell, Lieutenant."

The doors hissed shut as Kedair replied with an evil smirk, "That's the plan, sir."

Ormoch had earned his place as an Alpha-Hirogen through daring and resilience. Sacrificing his ship in order to breach the defenses of this exotic alien vessel had cost him many fine relics, but he was certain that, once subdued, this ship's crew would yield many superb trophies.

Kezal, his beta hunter, returned from one of the access corridors that led to the main engine compartment, which the two of them had commandeered without facing any resistance. "Scramblers and countermeasures are in place," the beta said. The muffled thunder of a distant detonation reverberated through the abandoned corridors.

"That should keep our prey busy until we've bypassed their computer lockouts," Ormoch said. "Then we can use their own antipersonnel systems to neutralize their energy weapons and test their skills in personal combat."

Something large and dense clanged heavily to the deck beside the matter/antimatter reactor and replied, "Why wait?"

Kezal and Ormoch turned to see a massive, reptilian biped with leathery brown scales, clawed extremities with opposable digits, and a face dominated by an ivory beak. Its round eyes were a solid, glossy black and utterly inscrutable. Fabric in the style of what Ormoch had come to recognize as this ship's uniform was fitted snugly across the creature's barrel chest. It hunched and prowled forward with an ornate and fearsome curved-blade axe clutched in one hand.

"This," Ormoch said to Kezal with a gleam of anticipation, "looks like worthy prey indeed." The alpha drew his own long blade and squared off against the greenish behemoth. "Stay clear, Kezal. This one is mine."

The alien shifted his grip on his axe. "Don't be greedy, friend," he said. "I'm willing to kill you both at the same time." He clicked his beak at Kezal. "Bring it on."

"Mind your place, Kezal," warned Ormoch.

Ormoch lunged at the alien. It moved quickly despite its bulk. The alpha's first thrust and slash missed completely, and he barely dodged a scalping blow from his foe's axe. He ducked under another lateral cut and chopped away a wedge of flesh from above the creature's knee. Dark blood ran down its leg.

Circling the reptilian, Ormoch studied its movements to see whether it favored its wounded limb or made a greater effort to defend it from further injury. To the alpha's surprise, it did neither. Either the creature had tremendous self-discipline or its species possessed an unusually high pain threshold.

Best not to linger too long on this one, Ormoch decided. A feint and a lunge slipped him inside the creature's circle of defense, and a well-placed stroke of his monotanium blade cut a deep wound across the creature's throat. He thrust his sword up, through the reptilian's gut and into its chest. As the creature twitched in its death throes, it tried to bring its axe down on Ormoch's neck. The alpha reached up and swatted the weapon from his foe's hand. It clanged and bounced across the deck.

Then the reptilian's other hand struck Ormoch's face like a spiked hammer, tearing ragged wounds across his cheek and brow. Blood drizzled over the alpha's eyes as the creature's last breath rattled from its throat. Ormoch lowered his blade and let his prey's corpse slide off, into a heap on the deck.

He wiped his blood from his face, looked at Kezal, and laughed. "Not the best I've ever fought, but not bad," he said. "Look at that beak and those claws. They'll make fine relics."

A woman's voice added, "Don't forget this."

Again, Ormoch turned to find an unexpected visitor. She was tall for a humanoid, slim but muscular, and not unattractive, in his opinion. Though her olive-hued hide was scaly, it was much finer in texture than that of the creature he'd just fought. And she twirled the first creature's weapon with ease and grace.

"You think you know how to handle that axe?" taunted Kezal.

The woman spared him only the briefest glance. "It's not an axe, it's a Rigellian voulge." Her grin, Ormoch was certain, hid the subtle hint of a sneer. "And I wield it better than most."

She stalked around Ormoch in a wide circle. Her stride exhibited balance and confidence. Kezal fell into step directly opposite her, circling Ormoch.

"I'm sure you think yourself capable," Ormoch said to the woman. "But you're hardly what I'd call worthy prey."

"Are you sure?" She reached to the rear of her belt, detached two large pieces of metal, and tossed them at Ormoch's feet. He recognized them as Hirogen breathing masks. "Maybe you should ask Dossok and Saransk." Feigning forgetfulness, she added, "Oh, right, you can't. Because I killed them already, up at the engineering computer core—where *you* sent them, Ormoch."

She knows our names. The woman's detailed knowledge of him and his hunters lent credibility to her boasts. "Impressive," the alpha said. "And now you've come to fight me?"

That drew a snide chortle from her. "No." She pointed behind Ormoch, at Kezal. "I'm here to kill him."

Ormoch's temper flared. "I am the alpha!" he shouted, with such fury that it made his entire body tremble. "He is only the beta. Your life is *mine* to take, not his!"

The green woman stopped moving. "Not anymore.

In a few seconds, he'll be the alpha. Because you'll be dead."

Quaking with rage, Ormoch felt like a spring that had been coiled past its breaking point. "You think you can kill me?" He waved his sword erratically. "You're welcome to try!"

"I don't have to," the woman said. "My comrade, Lieutenant Simmerith, killed you ninety seconds ago." Her smile turned into a glare. "You have a few seconds left, so permit me to educate you. Simmerith was a Rigellian Chelon. In times of stress or combat, their skin secretes a deadly contact poison. And you got a faceful of it."

Ormoch was about to call her a liar when his knees buckled and dropped him in a quivering mass to the deck. Reduced to a helpless pile of flesh, he filled with shame.

Kezal wasted no time assuming his new status as the alpha. The young Hirogen hunter drew his sword and charged, leaping over Ormoch to attack the woman. The pair danced in and out of Ormoch's line of sight as he lay all but paralyzed on the deck. The engine compartment rang with the clashing of metal against metal, underscored by deep grunts of exertion. Then the duelists loomed back into sight almost on top of him, and Ormoch grinned as he saw the woman overextend herself into a fatal mistake. Kezal, to his credit, exploited it without mercy, driving his sword through the woman's chest.

Her voulge tumbled from her hands. She gurgled and gasped for air with a horrified expression as Kezal lifted her off the deck and admired his kill. When he raised his blade higher, her body went limp and slid down the blade until it came to a stop against the crossguard.

The new alpha breathed deep of the scent of his prey, committing it to memory. He brought her face level with his own and brushed her black hair from her shoulders, no doubt pondering where to begin her osteotomy for his newest trophy.

Then her eyes snapped open.

She plucked his short blades from the scabbards under his arms and lopped off his head with a scissoring cut.

His decapitated body fell limp at the green woman's feet. She discarded the two short blades and turned toward the fallen Ormoch, with the blade of Kezal's longsword still protruding from her back. Unsheathing it from her torso with a slow pull, she walked to Ormoch's side.

"Last lesson for today," she whispered in the former alpha's ear. "My species is called Takaran. We don't have vital organs, just a distributed physiology." She pulled open a rip in her uniform jacket and wiped the blood from her stab wound, which was no longer visible. "And, as you may have noticed, we're really good at healing."

He forced words past his dry, swollen tongue. "Your kind . . . are . . . worthy prey," he rasped.

The green woman wrapped her arms around Ormoch's head in an almost tender embrace. "Funny," she whispered. "That's how I feel about you." She torqued his jaw, and the last thing he heard was the crack of his spine snapping in two.

Worf's blood burned with anticipation, and he smelled the scents of the two Hirogen hunters who were climbing the port-side auxiliary turbolift shaft toward the bridge of the *Enterprise*.

"Power failures are moving up the shaft," Choudhury said, reading her tricorder. "Deck Six just went dark. Deck Five . . ."

"Here they come," said Captain Picard.

Kadohata herded the junior officers off the bridge and into the observation lounge. "Weinrib, Elfiki, Chen, let's go," she snapped, hustling them out of harm's way. Then she and tactical officer Šmrhová confronted the captain.

"You too, sir," Kadohata said.

"I belong here, Commander," Picard said with pride.

Choudhury called out in a steady voice, "Deck Four's dark."

"No time to argue," Kadohata said. She snapped her fingers at three of the ten security officers who had come to defend the bridge. "Mars, Braddock, Cruzen—front and center." The three security lieutenants stepped forward. "Give us your rifles, then fall back to the observation lounge and have the armory beam you three more." They traded confused looks, and Kadohata sharpened her tone. "That's an order, Lieutenants!"

Mars was the first to comply. The compact, gray-haired man handed his TR-116 and belt of spare clips to Captain Picard. Braddock, a trained sniper, reluctantly surrendered his weapon and rounds to Kadohata, and Cruzen seemed relieved as she passed her rifle and clips to Šmrhová.

"Right," Kadohata said. "Fall out." The three un-armed security officers exited the bridge. Kadohata looked at Picard and Šmrhová and nodded toward the mission-operations consoles to starboard. "Take cover there," she said. "Fire through the gaps in the console stands. Controlled bursts. I'll be close by."

Picard checked the settings on his weapon. "Very good," he said, and then he followed Šmrhová to cover.

Static filled the main viewer, which flickered and switched off, revealing the blank forward bulkhead. Consoles stuttered and went dark. The overhead lights failed, and the bridge's vast assortment of computers went silent.

Choudhury and Worf flanked the auxiliary turbolift doors. He kept his grip on his *bat'leth* firm but supple. She kept an equally lithe hold on her twin Gurkha kukri daggers. "Flares," Worf said to the security personnel who had taken cover around the bridge. Snap-cracks filled the deathly quiet, and then the bridge was aglow with pools of magenta- and lemon-hued light.

Fire and thunder tore through the doors of the aux-iliary turbolift. Jagged hunks of the shattered portal caromed off the bulkheads and dormant companels, and a few slammed into random security personnel, who cried out in pain.

Amid the patter of falling debris, Worf heard two bright plinks of small metallic disks striking the deck. Searing flashes of light turned the smoky shadows of the bridge as bright as the sun, and for a moment he had to avert his eyes. He tried to stay alert as two Hi-rogen battle roars echoed on the bridge, but all he could see were purple retinal afterimages.

Tracer rounds filled the darkness, all of them targeted into the turbolift shaft. The strobing light and deafening buzz of gunfire were overwhelming to Worf's finely attuned senses, especially since he was all but standing atop the target.

His eyes and ears had almost adjusted when the barrage stopped, leaving the bridge steeped in dim shadows, acrid smoke, and tense silence. Nothing stirred in the turbolift shaft.

Then came the first choked-off scream, followed by the sickly gurgle of a humanoid with a slashed throat. Worf couldn't tell where the sound had come from, but his instincts told him that the Hirogen had slipped past him and Choudhury, probably in the moment of the first blinding flashes.

"Blades!" he shouted to the security team, and he heard the soft scrapes of combat knives being pulled from sheaths.

He stalked away from the blasted-open turbolift portal and hewed close to the aft bulkhead. On the other side of the bridge, Choudhury followed his lead, moving at a quickstep in pursuit of foes who knew how to use the darkness.

Another wet crunch and muffled cry, from the portside consoles. Choudhury leaped toward it as a yelp of alarm from the starboard side was cut short. Worf sprinted, hurdled over the command chairs, and found Ensign Carr from security with his throat slashed open—and no sign of his attacker.

One soft breath behind his back was Worf's only warning.

He spun, his *bat'leth* held vertically, and blocked what had been meant to be a silent killing stroke.

Looking down at him was the grinning, scaled-and-painted face of a Hirogen.

The hunter snap-kicked Worf in the groin. Worf doubled over, sick with nausea, and the Hirogen kneed him in the jaw, knocking him through the air. The enraged Klingon landed hard and rolled quickly to his feet, ready to hit back.

Behind him, a battle cry preceded the agonized scream of Lieutenant ch'Kerrosoth, who tumbled wildly away from the second Hirogen hunter, into the middle of the bridge. The tall Andorian clutched at the stump of his left arm, which had just been severed a few centimeters above the elbow.

Pandemonium erupted on the bridge. Security officers broke cover and converged on the two exposed Hirogen, who cut them down with the smooth precision of butchers in a slaughterhouse.

Then the Alpha-Hirogen spotted Kadohata and Šmrhová trying to smuggle Captain Picard off the bridge to the observation lounge. He pointed at the captain. "Kill that one!"

Both Hirogen charged, knocking aside the security officers in their way. Worf sprinted to cut them off. Šmrhová and Kadohata closed ranks in front of the captain and fumbled as they tried to reload their TR-116s.

Choudhury buried one of her Gurkha knives in the charging Beta-Hirogen's unarmored knee joint. He spun and swung his own blade at her head. She ducked his slashing attack. He lunged forward, grasping at her throat. The limber security chief caught the beta's wrist, employed a move that was half judo and half *Mok'bara* to flip him onto his back, and used his own momentum to drive his dagger through his eye and into his brain.

Worf tackled the alpha, who jabbed an elbow backward, only to be blocked by Worf's *bat'leth*. The Hirogen rolled free of Worf's grip, and they came up facing each other. A feint by the hunter put Worf off balance. Next he felt the hot sting of a slash across his chin. He lunged and swung his *bat'leth* in a deadly downward stroke. It slammed impotently against the shoulder plate of the alpha's blue-black armor.

The alpha swatted the *bat'leth* from Worf's hands. Then he lunged and thrust his dagger forward and up, to stab Worf under his chin—exactly as Worf had hoped he would.

The rest happened in less than three seconds.

Worf pivoted away from the striking blade. He let himself flow like water, his limbs as free as the wind, and the dagger missed him. He ducked under the Hirogen's right arm, caught it by the wrist, and flipped the hunter over his shoulder.

The alpha struck the deck at Worf's feet, his wrist still caught in Worf's grip. Worf yanked the hunter's forearm taut and struck it with his knee. The elbow broke with a crack like a rifle shot. As the blade fell from the alpha's fingers, Worf landed a stomping kick on the alpha's neck. The fatal snap was muffled by the Hirogen's armor.

His dropped blade bounced across the deck and came to a stop as the Hirogen's body went limp.

"Turn off his energy dampener," Picard ordered, moving back toward his command chair.

Worf found the device on the alpha's belt and switched it off. Instantly, the overhead lights, companels, and main viewscreen became operational again. He noticed several of his crewmates recoil as the return of normal lighting revealed the copious amounts of blood that stained the deck around them.

Captain Picard, however, remained stoic and calm. "Hail the *Aventine*," he said. "Signal all-clear and confirm their status."

"Aye, sir," replied Kadohata, who stepped over the bodies of several dead security officers on the way to her post at ops.

Apprehensive looks and discomfited expressions marked the faces of the other bridge officers, who were led back in from the observation lounge. Elfiki lifted a hand to block the carnage from her sight as she hurried to the science station. Weinrib maintained a rigidly focused stare on the main viewer as he returned to his seat at the conn. T'Ryssa Chen looked as if she might become physically ill.

The main turbolift doors opened, and a team of medics emerged. As expected, they had come bearing a large number of blue body bags. The two who had actual medical equipment were led to the unconscious Lieutenant ch'Kerrosoth.

Kadohata glanced back at Worf and the captain. "*Aventine* confirms all-clear, sir."

"Splendid," Picard said, sounding enervated.

From the auxiliary science station, Lieutenant Chen stammered, "Um . . . sirs?"

Worf replied gruffly to the half-human, half-Vulcan contact specialist, "Report, Lieutenant."

"We have a new problem," she said, patching her sensor data onto the main viewer. "New readings from the subspace tunnel," she explained. "Long story short: It's becoming unstable. If we don't go back *right now,* we might never be able to."

Elfiki turned from her station, eyes wide with alarm. "Captain, without our shields at full power, we can't go back into the plasma stream."

"Bridge to engineering," Picard said.

"La Forge here."

"Geordi, we need full shields, immediately."

"After the beating we just took? Captain, we won't have full shields for at least six hours."

Everyone looked at Chen, who shook her head. "We don't even have *six minutes.*"

"Then we need a new solution," Kadohata said.

The normally shy Elfiki spoke up. "Mister Weinrib, how are your reflexes?"

The flight controller replied suspiciously, "Pretty good."

Elfiki threw a look at Kadohata. "And yours?"

"I've had no complaints," said the second officer.

"Well, you'd both better be fantastic if we want to get out of this." She shouldered aside Šmrhová from a tactical console and routed new information to the main viewer. "If we detonate two transphasic warheads—one *here* and the other *here*—we can create a six-second gap in the plasma stream. Which means we and the *Aventine* will have that long to emit the pulse that opens the aperture, navigate into it, and get both our ships inside the tunnel before the plasma stream catches up and slags us."

Chen added, "And we have about five minutes to do it."

Picard gave a fast nod. "Make it so."

The crew snapped into action. Worf settled into his

chair and sleeved a smear of blood from his chin. He looked left and caught the captain's eye. In a sub rosa voice, he said, "A pity she did not devise her plan *before* the Hirogen attack."

The captain lifted his eyebrows and sighed. "Starship command is like comedy, Number One. Timing is everything."

Dax stood in the center of the *Aventine*'s broken, smoldering bridge and felt precious seconds slip away. Her crew was racing to prepare the ship for its return journey while she stared at the main viewer and watched a raging flow of stellar plasma be siphoned from a red giant into its black-hole companion.

Bowers bounded from the science console to Dax's side. "We're ready," he said, wiping his soot-stained hand down the side of his grimy uniform jacket.

"Kandel, hail the *Enterprise*," Dax said. "Start the countdown. Nak, charge up the main deflector." Looking past Bowers to the ship's senior science officer, she added, "Get ready to pick that lock, Gruhn."

The svelte Zakdorn kept his eyes on his just-repaired companel as he palmed a sheen of sweat from his broad, high forehead. "Give the word and we're in, Captain."

Bowers confided to Dax, "Let's just hope the deflector's strong enough to shield the entire ship from the radiation inside the tunnel."

"If it's not, we'll know in about fifteen seconds," Dax said, watching the synchronized countdown on the main viewer.

A series of chirping tones sounded on the tactical console. Lieutenant Talia Kandel reviewed the incoming data. "*Enterprise* is arming torpedoes and targeting the plasma stream," she said.

"Tharp," Bowers said to the Bolian conn officer, "full impulse, on my mark. Gruhn, open the subspace aperture on the same mark."

Kandel called out, "Torpedoes away in three . . . two . . . one . . ."

"Mark," Bowers said, as a pair of blue flashes sped from the bow of the *Enterprise* toward the plasma stream.

The vibration of full-impulse thrust resonated under Dax's feet as the *Aventine* accelerated instantly to one-quarter light speed, following the transphasic warheads toward a river of fire hanging in space. Six hundred meters to port, the *Enterprise* was pacing the *Aventine* in their race toward the subspace tunnel.

Electric blue flashes whited-out the main viewer. Then the image returned, and the first step of the plan had worked: The transphasic warheads had blasted a lacuna into the black hole's relativistic jet stream of superheated coronal mass.

Ahead of the two starships, the subspace aperture spiraled open as if rent from the fabric of reality itself. As it loomed larger on the *Aventine*'s main viewer, however, so did the tide of burning stellar plasma advancing from behind it.

"This is the fun part," Dax said, then inhaled sharply.

The blue-white rings of the subspace passage pulsed beyond its aperture's edges into the golden blaze of the plasma stream.

Then the *Aventine* was inside the passageway, shaking and pitching as strange energy currents hammered its hull. "Nak!" Dax hollered over the steady roar of turbulence. "Report!"

"Shields holding," the Tellarite shouted over the noise. "Hyperphasic radiation leaks on Decks Twenty-five and Twenty-six, Sections Thirty to Thirty-three."

Dax nodded. Nak had predicted leaks in those areas when he'd configured the deflector dish as a backup shield emitter, and they had been evacuated before the plan had been engaged.

A brutal tremor rocked the ship. Consoles stuttered light and dark, and white-hot phosphors rained down around Dax and Bowers as another EPS capacitor overloaded above them.

Bowers staggered across the heaving deck toward Helkara, and then a violent jolt of acceleration sprawled the first officer roughly against the science console. Through gritted teeth, he said, "Gruhn, what's going on out there?"

"The tunnel's imploding!" said Helkara, raising his voice so that Dax could hear his report, as well.

"What's causing it?" she demanded, falling awkwardly into her chair.

Helkara waved a drift of smoke away from his console. "Someone's bombarding it with high-energy soliton pulses," he said. "It's disrupting the tunnel's topology."

"Helm, all ahead full!" Dax yelled to Tharp.

"Almost there," the Bolian replied, even as he patched in every ounce of reserve power, including the ship's spacedock thrusters. "Clearing the passage in five . . . four . . ."

Ahead of them, the once-circular aperture of the tunnel had become deformed and irregular, like an amoeba. Its contours rippled, undulated, and began retracting and fusing together.

"I think it's trying to eat us," Nak blurted out in horror.

The melting edges of the aperture reached precariously close as the *Aventine* breached the subspace tunnel's threshold—and then the chaotic blue-and-white kaleidoscope was behind them, and the ship's main viewer was once more awash in the radiant, deep-blue serenity of the Azure Nebula.

"*Enterprise* is clear," Kandel reported over the relieved collective sigh of the other bridge officers. Then she gasped.

Dax glanced back at the Deltan woman to see what was wrong, only to see the shocked tactical officer raise her terrified stare toward the main viewer.

As she turned forward, Dax realized that all her officers were gazing at the viewscreen, looking transfixed and stunned.

Then she saw why.

The cerulean clouds and swirls of the nebula were aflame and littered with the wreckage of countless vessels.

Where she had expected to find the allied expeditionary force, all Dax saw was a smoldering starship graveyard.

Jean-Luc Picard didn't need sensor readings to know what had wrought the vast swath of carnage he saw on the *Enterprise*'s main viewer. The voice of the Collective was no longer distant; it was ubiquitous and deafening.

We warned you, Locutus, the Borg Queen declared. *We offered you perfection, and you refused us. Now you, Earth, and your Federation will suffer the consequences.*

"We're reading Borg weapon signatures everywhere," said Choudhury, whose console was only partly functional because of recent battle damage. "Massive subspace signal interference, too. I'll try to compensate for it."

Kadohata coaxed intermittent bursts of data from the ops panel. "I don't see any ships intact," she said. "Hang on—I'm picking up a Mayday on the emergency channel." Working quickly at her uncooperative controls, she added, "We have a visual."

Picard forced the Collective's voice from his mind and struggled to remain stoic as he faced the maelstrom of destruction that surrounded his ship and the *Aventine.*

Then the image was magnified, and he saw the shadow of an *Intrepid*-class starship. One of its warp nacelles had been sheared away. Ragged chunks had been torn from its elliptical saucer, and sparking trails of half-ignited plasma streamed from its fractured secondary hull. It was trapped in a slow, random tumble, at the mercy of the nebula's currents.

With grim reverence, Kadohata said, "It's *Voyager,* sir."

He stood and tugged his uniform jacket taut. "Hail them."

The image on the main viewer sputtered in and out. Random signal noise hashed diagonally across the screen, and harsh static punctuated the high-frequency wail that tainted the audio. Even without the interference, however, Picard would barely have recognized the face of *Voyager*'s commanding officer.

Captain Chakotay's nose was broken, and the lower half of his face was caked with blood, some of it fresh and bright red, some dried and brown. All the hair had been scorched from the left side of his head, revealing burned, blackened skin. He was slumped at an awkward angle in his command chair, with his left arm pinned underneath him. A pink froth of bloodied saliva bubbled over his lip as he mumbled, *"Picard . . . ?"*

"Captain Chakotay," Picard replied. "Stand by to receive rescue teams from the *Enterprise* and the *Aventine.*"

"The Borg," Chakotay spluttered.

Nodding, Picard tried to calm him. "Yes, Captain. We—"

"Rammed us," Chakotay continued, mumbling in a monotone born of severe shock. *"Smashed the whole fleet . . ."*

Picard nodded to Kadohata and Choudhury, who understood his unspoken intention and began discreetly directing the deployment of medics and engineers to *Voyager.*

"Weapons did nothing," Chakotay went on, no longer looking at Picard but at some distant point in his imagination. *"Couldn't stop them. Too many."*

"How many?" Picard asked, not sure he wanted to know.

Chakotay didn't answer. He started shaking his head, and then kept on shaking it, as if denying the truth with enough vigor would make it go away.

Worf stepped forward beside Picard and said, "You need to see this, sir." The XO nodded to tactical officer Šmrhová, who split the main viewer image to present a sensor readout on the right-hand side. It was a long-range tactical scan. And the widening circular formation of red icons around the Azure Nebula stabbed an icy blade of fear through Picard's brave façade, down to his very core. "This is confirmed?"

"Aye, sir," Worf said. "At least seven thousand Borg ships have deployed into Federation, Klingon, and Romulan territory."

"Thousands," Picard mumbled, his voice barely a whisper. "Enough to send one to every inhabited world in known space."

Choudhury added, "With enough left over to target every starbase, outpost, and shipyard within a thousand light-years."

Under his breath, Picard said, "It's begun."

It was the day he had dreaded for sixteen years, since his first encounter with the Borg, in System J-25, during his command of the *Enterprise*-D. His inaugural experience with the Collective had spurred the Borg to step up their efforts to move against the Federation. But as horrific as the battles of Wolf 359 and Sector 001 had been, Picard had long suspected that they were little more than tests of the Federation's strengths and weaknesses—preludes for the true invasion that would bring Earth and its allies to ruin.

Now his greatest fear was made manifest, and there was nothing he could do to stop its deadly advance.

Kadohata tapped silent a comm signal on her panel. "The *Aventine* is hailing us," she said.

"On-screen," Picard said.

Dax appeared on the main viewer. She looked shell-shocked. *"Good news,"* she said. *"Helkara says all the subspace tunnels have collapsed, so there's no more back door to the Federation."*

Worf grunted. "Unfortunately, they have closed too late to make a difference."

"Well, I guess making a difference is our job now," Dax replied. *"We're setting course for Earth."*

"To what end?" asked Picard, openly skeptical of Dax's proposed plan of action.

The headstrong young Trill woman shrugged. *"I'm playing it by ear. Maybe we can find the Borg Queen and take her out."*

Her naïveté inflamed Picard's temper. "It won't make any difference if you do," he told her. "They'll just raise another queen, and another."

"Then we'll do something else," Dax said, her own ire coming to the fore. *"But I won't just sit back and do nothing."*

He stepped forward, hoping to make a stronger connection with Dax through virtual proximity. "Be rational, Captain," he urged her. "The Borg fleet numbers in the thousands, and it's moving away at speeds we can't match."

"Maybe your ship can't," Dax said. *"Mine has a prototype slipstream drive, and this seems like a damned good time to fire it up."* She nodded to someone off-screen. *"There's a war on, Picard, and I plan on being part of it. Keep up if you can.* Aventine out."

The screen snapped back to the nebula full of broken starships and burning debris. The *Aventine* cruised past and then accelerated away, vanishing into the midnight-blue mists.

"*Aventine* is leaving the nebula at full impulse," Choudhury said, checking her console. "She's on course for Earth and powering up her warp drive."

Worf threw a sharp look at Picard. "Orders, sir?"

Picard knew that the logical response was to let the *Aventine* go on its quixotic tilt, keep the *Enterprise* hidden in the nebula, render aid to any survivors, and contact Starfleet Command for new orders.

He turned from the main viewer, walked back to his chair, and sat down. "Helm . . . go after them."

The news hit President Bacco like a gut punch.

"I need to sit down," she said, easing herself into the chair behind her desk. Outside the massive, curved window that served as a wall of her office in the Palais de la Concorde, Paris was resplendent beneath a blue sky and a golden sun, but Bacco felt as if someone had just turned out all the lights. "It's an entire fleet of Borg ships?"

Standing on the other side of Bacco's desk was Seven of Nine, who cocked her head and replied, "It would be more appropriate to call it an armada."

Flanking the ex-Borg security adviser were Bacco's defense secretary Raisa Shostakova, whose squat frame looked stouter than usual by comparison with Seven's trim, lanky physique; and Bacco's trusted chief of staff, Esperanza Piñiero, whose olive complexion and dark hair made Seven's fair skin and blond hair look almost albino pale.

Shostakova placed a padd on the desk in front of Bacco. "Long-range sensors have detected as many as seven thousand, four hundred sixty-one Borg vessels moving through our space, as well as in Klingon and Romulan territory."

Bacco read the intelligence estimate with growing dismay. "And the expeditionary force . . . ?"

"Wiped out," Piñiero said. "Their final transmissions were Maydays from *Voyager,* the *I.K.S. Chorbog,* and the *Antietam.*"

Pushing another padd across the desk to Bacco, Shostakova added, "The Borg have already started exterminating populations on Beta Thoridor, Adelphous IV, and Devnar IV. We project they'll launch attacks on Japori II and Gamma Hromi II in four hours, and H'Atoria within six hours."

A crushing despair settled on Bacco's shoulders. She looked to Seven. "How do we stop them?"

"You can't," Seven replied, her absolute certainty cold and unforgiving. "Without the subspace tunnels, there is nowhere you can go that the Borg will not find you."

The brutal truth and utter finality of Seven's words left Bacco with her head in her hands, pondering the possibility that she might have to preside over the end of the Federation.

"I need the room, everyone," she said, looking up.

Piñiero and Shostakova volleyed bemused glances before the chief of staff replied, "Ma'am . . . ?"

"Just for a few minutes, Esperanza. Please."

"Of course, ma'am," Piñiero said. Protection agents Wexler and Kistler appeared, as stealthy as shadows, behind the three women, and escorted them out of the president's office. Wexler was the last person out. He nodded to Bacco and shut the door.

Bacco was too keyed up to remain seated. She stood and paced along the panoramic window-wall, taking in what she belatedly realized might be Earth's final day.

As the elected leader of the Federation, there were so many events whose outcomes she could affect or direct that it made her dizzy sometimes to try and think of them all. Trillions of beings depended on her judgment. Countless technological marvels were at her command, tools she could use to shape the present and the future, to change the path of galactic destiny.

Not one of them was of any use against the Borg.

She stopped at her desk and pressed her palms flat upon its brilliantly lacquered surface. The true weight of her presidency settled upon her, an Atlas's burden, and she bowed her head as her late father's advice echoed in her memory: *Everything we do today defines us—because tomorrow might never come.*

Brushing a tear from her cheek, she whispered through a fearful grimace, "You didn't know how right you were, Dad."

20

———

William Riker hurried out of the turbolift onto the bridge of *Titan,* to find Pazlar and Ra-Havreii waiting for him at the engineering console. "What have we got?" asked Riker, walking quickly to join the exhausted, frazzled-looking duo.

"Just what you asked for," said Ra-Havreii, pointing at the upper display screen. "We tapped into the Caeliar's soliton pulses about an hour ago."

Pazlar lifted her arm to gesture at a different screen, and Riker noticed only then that the science officer was once again outfitted in her powered, musculature-assistance armature. "It's taken us since then to decode their signal patterns," Pazlar said. "We'll get the descrambled feed in a few seconds."

Ra-Havreii smoothed the top of his frost-white mustache with his thumb and forefinger. "Do you want to join their feed in real time or see it from where we first tapped in?"

"From the beginning," Riker said. The chief engineer nodded, and then he and Pazlar both keyed in commands as Riker added, "Excellent work, both of you."

They accepted the compliment with polite nods, and Pazlar said, "Here it comes." Garbled blurs and a stutter of sounds resolved quickly into a sharp and chilling spectacle.

A massive wave of Borg cubes was emerging from an anomaly that resembled a wormhole. The steady stream of black starships coursed like poison into an indigo nebula and rammed through a fleet of hundreds of ships; many of them were Starfleet and Klingon vessels, but there were also dozens of Romulan and Cardassian ships. The Borg crushed them all like children's toys beneath the boots of angry giants.

Even after the fleet had been pulverized and scattered into the blue storm, the anomaly continued to hemorrhage Borg ships.

Riker swallowed and pushed down the sick feeling that was rising from his gut. "Do we have a fix on those coordinates?"

"Aye, sir," Pazlar said. "It's the Azure Nebula."

He had seen enough of the slaughter. "Switch to real time," he said to Ra-Havreii.

A single tap by Ra-Havreii changed the image to one of quiet desolation. Broken hulls and fragments from a variety of ships drifted into random collisions, driven by the nebula's chaotic currents.

"Where's the anomaly?" asked Riker.

Radiant warmth filled the bridge behind him, and he noticed an overpowering smell of ozone. "It was a subspace tunnel," answered a female voice. "And it's gone."

He turned and saw an attractive young woman, ostensibly human and barely out of her teens. Her long, wild mane of black hair was out of proportion to her

slender figure, which was garbed in silvery-white
drapes of diaphanous fabric that were one trick of the
light away from being scandalous. There was a steely
quality to her eyes that belied her youthful mien.

Ensign Rriarr leveled his small sidearm phaser at
the woman. "Don't move," he said.

She glanced at the Caitian security officer, and the
weapon in his hand turned to dust as she strode forward to meet Riker. "There isn't much time, Captain,
so please listen to me. My name is Erika Hernandez. I
used to be the captain of the Earth starship *Columbia*.
And I've been a prisoner of the Caeliar for more than
eight hundred years." She waved away his unvoiced
question. "I'll explain later. Right now, answer me
this." Nodding at the science monitor that showed the
Azure Nebula, she asked, "Do you want to take your
ship there?"

Riker looked at Ra-Havreii and Pazlar, whose be-
fuddled expressions offered him no guidance. He
turned back to Hernandez. "Yes," he said.

"I can get you there," Hernandez said, "using the
same device that helped me get here—but only if we
leave *right now*."

Lieutenant Sariel Rager swiveled her chair toward
the conversation and interjected, "Sir, the away
team—"

Silencing his ops officer with a raised hand, Riker
asked Hernandez, "What about my people on the surface?"

Hernandez shook her head. "They're all being
watched," she said. "There's no way to free them without alerting the Caeliar." She glanced anxiously at the
image of the nebula. "They've already shut down the

subspace tunnels. Any second now they'll terminate this surveillance wormhole, and once they do there won't be any way out of here, for any of us—*ever.*"

Torn by indecision, Riker clenched his fists. "You don't understand," he said. "My wife is down there."

"She's not going anywhere," Hernandez replied. "You can always come back to join her." She looked away, as if listening to something. When she turned back, there was fear in her eyes. "They know I'm missing. It's now or never, Captain. Call it."

Riker stared at the image of the nebula, wrenched between his desire to save his away team and his responsibility to save his ship; between his love for his wife and his oath to the Federation, which was about to face the darkest hour of its history. Acting for the good of the many was his sworn duty, but now it meant abandoning Deanna when she needed him most. No matter what he did, a sacred promise would have to be broken.

But a decision had to be made.

"Take us home," he said.

END OF BOOK II

Star Trek Destiny
will conclude in
BOOK III
Lost Souls

APPENDIX I
2156

Featured Crew Members

Columbia NX-02

Captain Erika Hernandez
(human female) commanding officer

Commander Veronica Fletcher
(human female) executive officer

Lieutenant Commander Kalil el-Rashad
(human male), second officer/science officer

Lieutenant Karl Graylock
(human male) chief engineer

Lieutenant Johanna Metzger
(human female) chief medical officer

Lieutenant Kiona Thayer
(human female) senior weapons officer

Ensign Sidra Valerian
(human female) communications officer

Major Stephen Foyle
(human male) MACO commander

Lieutenant Vincenzo Yacavino
(human male) MACO second-in-command

Sergeant Gage Pembleton
(human male) MACO first sergeant

APPENDIX II
STARDATE 58100
(early February 2381)

Featured Crew Members

U.S.S. Enterprise NCC-1701-E

Captain Jean-Luc Picard
(human male) commanding officer

Commander Worf
(Klingon male) executive officer

Commander Miranda Kadohata
(human female) second officer/operations officer

Commander Geordi La Forge
(human male) chief engineer

Commander Beverly Crusher
(human female) chief medical officer

Lieutenant Hegol Den
(Bajoran male) senior counselor

Lieutenant Jasminder Choudhury
(human female) chief of security

Lieutenant Dina Elfiki
(human female) senior science officer

Lieutenant T'Ryssa Chen
(Vulcan-human female) contact specialist

APPENDIX II

U.S.S. TITAN NCC-80102

Captain William T. Riker
(human male) commanding officer

Commander Christine Vale
(human female) executive officer

Commander Tuvok
(Vulcan male) second officer/tactical officer

Commander Deanna Troi
(Betazoid-human female) diplomatic officer/senior
counselor

Commander Xin Ra-Havreii
(Efrosian male) chief engineer

Lieutenant Commander Shenti Yisec Eres Ree
(Pahkwa-thanh male) chief medical officer

Lieutenant Commander Ranul Keru
(Trill male) chief of security

Lieutenant Commander Melora Pazlar
(Elaysian female) senior science officer

Lieutenant Pral glasch Haaj
(Tellarite male) counselor

Lieutenant Huilan Sen'kara
(Sti'ach male) counselor

Ensign Torvig Bu-kar-nguv
(Choblik male) engineer

APPENDIX II

U.S.S. AVENTINE NCC-82602

Captain Ezri Dax
(Trill female) commanding officer

Commander Samaritan Bowers
(human male) executive officer

Lieutenant Commander Gruhn Helkara
(Zakdorn male) second officer/senior science officer

Lieutenant Lonnoc Kedair
(Takaran female) chief of security

Lieutenant Simon Tarses
(human-Romulan male) chief medical officer

Lieutenant Mikaela Leishman
(human female) chief engineer

Lieutenant Oliana Mirren
(human female) senior operations officer

ACKNOWLEDGMENTS

For reasons most people don't understand, my wonderful wife Kara tolerates my dark moods and reclusive habits while I am at work on a new book. At this point, she has been putting up with this crazy behavior of mine for the better part of a year. There's no end in sight, either, and yet she hasn't abandoned me. For that alone, she ought to be considered for sainthood.

I remain grateful to my editors, Marco Palmieri and Margaret Clark, for their guidance during editing and rewrites on this and the other volumes of the *Star Trek Destiny* trilogy, and for the faith they showed in my abilities by entrusting this project to my hands.

My work on the trilogy in general, and on this book in particular, has been improved by the sage advice and literary contributions of many of my fellow *Star Trek* authors, in particular, Christopher L. Bennett, Keith R.A. DeCandido, Michael A. Martin, Andy Mangels, Kirsten Beyer, and Geoffrey Thorne. My heartfelt thanks go out to all of them.

And, if I'm being honest, I ought to thank google.com; dictionary.com; thesaurus.com; Memory Alpha and Memory Beta (the Star Trek wiki reference sites); and WikiPedia.

How did people write novels without the Internet?

ABOUT THE AUTHOR

David Mack is currently walking the Earth and getting into adventures. Read all about them on his blog: http://infinitydog.livejournal.com/.